D0957953

After thirty-five years as a nurse, **Patricia Davids** hung up her stethoscope to become a full-time writer. She enjoys spending her free time visiting her grandchildren, doing some long-overdue yard work and traveling to research her story locations. She resides in Wichita, Kansas. Pat always enjoys hearing from her readers. You can visit her online at patriciadavids.com.

Dana R. Lynn grew up in Illinois. She met a man at a wedding, then told her parents she had met her future husband. Nineteen months later, they were married. Today they live in rural Pennsylvania with their three children, two dogs, one cat, one rabbit, one horse and six chickens. In addition to writing, she works as an educational interpreter for the deaf and is active in several ministries in her church.

USA TODAY Bestselling Author

PATRICIA DAVIDS

His Amish Teacher

&

DANA R. LYNN

Plain Target

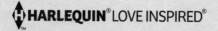

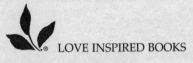

LOVE INSPIRED BOOKS

Recycling programs for this product may not exist in your area.

ISBN-13: 978-1-335-14691-5

His Amish Teacher and Plain Target

Copyright © 2018 by Harlequin Books S.A.

The publisher acknowledges the copyright holders of the individual works as follows:

His Amish Teacher
Copyright © 2017 by Patricia MacDonald

Plain Target
Copyright © 2017 by Dana Roae

www.Harlequin.com

Printed in U.S.A.

CONTENTS

HIS AMISH TEACHER

Patricia Davids

This book is dedicated to the memory
of Joan Stroda. Heaven gained a dear and wonderful
angel when she left this earth. Miss you, Mom.
Love you still.

Bear ye one another's burdens,
and so fulfill the law of Christ.
—*Galatians* 6:2

Chapter One

"We all know Teacher Lillian is a terrible cook, don't we, children?"

Lillian Keim's students erupted into giggles and some outright laughter. She crossed her arms and pressed her lips together to hold back a smile.

Timothy Bowman winked at her to take any sting out of his comment, but she wasn't offended. They had been friends for ages and were members of the same Amish community in Bowmans Crossing, Ohio. She knew he enjoyed a good joke as well as the next fellow, but he was deadly serious about his job today and so was she. The lessons they were presenting might one day prevent a tragedy.

He stood in front of her class on the infield of the softball diamond behind the one-room Amish schoolhouse where she taught all eight grades. Dressed in full fireman's turnout gear, Timothy made an impressive figure. The coat and pants added bulk to his slender frame, but he carried the additional weight with ease. His curly brown hair was hidden under a yellow helmet instead of his usual straw hat, but his hazel eyes sparkled with mirth. A smile lifted one side of his mouth and deepened the dimples in his tanned cheeks. Timothy smiled a lot. It was one reason she liked him.

His bulky fire coat and pants with bright fluorescent yellow banding weren't Plain clothing, but their Amish church district approved their use because the church elders and the bishop recognized the need for Amish volunteers to help fill the ranks of the local non-Amish fire company. The county fire marshal understood the necessity of special education in the Amish community where open flames and gas lanterns were used regularly. The Amish didn't allow electricity in their homes. Biannual fire-safety classes were held at all the local Amish schools. This was Timothy's first time giving the class. With Lillian's permission, he was deviating from the normal script with a demonstration outside. Timothy wanted to make an impression on the children. She admired that.

It was another unusually warm day for the last week of September. It had been a dry, hotter than usual summer. Timothy had chosen the bare dirt of the infield with an eye to safety rather than setting up on the brown grass of the lawn that could catch fire. The children were seated on the ground in a semicircle facing him. Only two of her older students, cousins Abe and Gabriel Mast, weren't paying attention. Abe was elbowing his cousin and the two were snickering and whispering behind their hands.

A red car sped past the school, and the driver laid on the horn. Abe jumped to his feet and waved wildly. The car didn't slow down.

Lillian did a double take. Was that her brother Jeremiah in the front passenger seat? Surely not. The vehicle rounded the sharp bend in the road and was gone from sight before she could be certain.

Abe grinned from ear to ear and kept jumping. "That's Davey's new ride. He's gonna teach me to drive, too. I want to go fast, fast, fast!"

Davey Mast was Abe's eldest brother. Davey had chosen to leave the Amish faith after his baptism and had been shunned for his decision. He had taken a job with a local *Englisch* farmer instead of leaving the area as most young people did when they didn't remain Amish. Lillian hoped her brother hadn't been in the car. If he had been, Jeremiah ran the risk of being shunned, too.

Abe ran toward the road. She called him back. "Abe, come sit down."

He ignored her.

"You need to pay attention. This is important." Timothy spoke sharply and leveled a stern look at Abe. The boy sheepishly returned to the group and sat down. Lillian wished she could use *the look* with the same effectiveness.

Timothy turned to a long table he had fashioned from wooden planks on a pair of sawhorses. A propane cook stove in the center held two pans that were both smoking hot. Various household items were arranged along the table, and a large pail of water sat on the ground in front of the table along with a red fire extinguisher.

He carefully carried one pan to the end of the table. Using a long-handled lighter, he clicked it once and the pan burst into flames. He looked at the children. "Let's pretend Teacher Lillian is frying chicken and a pan full of hot grease catches fire when no one else is around. What should you do?"

"Throw water on it," little Carl Mast shouted. The second grader was Abe's youngest brother.

"Carl says water will put out the fire. Let's see if that works." Timothy picked up a glass and filled it with water from a bucket beside the table. He flipped down the face shield of his helmet and tossed the liquid onto the skillet.

With a wild hiss and roar, the fire shot skyward in a flaming mushroom eight feet high. All the children drew back with wide frightened eyes. Lillian jumped, too. She wasn't expecting such a fireball. Puddles of burning grease dotted the ground.

Timothy lifted his face shield and looked at Carl. "Water isn't the right thing for putting out a grease fire, is it?"

Carl slowly shook his head, his eyes still wide.

Timothy used the extinguisher to put out the fires; then he lit the second pan ablaze with his lighter. "What is a safe way to put out a grease fire like this? Gabriel, Abe? What would you do? Quick. What's in the kitchen that will help?"

"I'd run outside and watch the whole thing go up in smoke," Abe said with a smirk, and elbowed his cousin. Gabriel nodded.

Timothy's eyes narrowed. "Not a very good answer, Abe. This isn't a joking matter."

"I'd get the fire extinguisher," Gabriel said quickly.

Timothy pointed to him. "*Goot*. Where is it kept in your home?"

A puzzled expression replaced Gabriel's grin. "I'm not sure."

Lillian calmly walked to the table. "A fine bunch of

firefighters you are if you can't put out a simple grease fire without help."

She picked up a dish towel, soaked it with water and gently draped it over the pan. The fire was instantly smothered. The children cheered.

Timothy nodded in appreciation. "I see Teacher Lillian has had lots of practice putting out her burning chicken. She did it the correct way. She smothered it. How else could she have smothered a grease fire?"

The children began calling out suggestions. He acknowledged each answer with a nod and a comment if it was a good suggestion. If it wasn't, he explained why. As he spoke, Lillian noticed he held the attention of all the children now. He had a knack for engaging them.

Timothy laid aside his lighter. "Now let's imagine that Teacher is burning leaves in the fall and she sees her *boo-friend* driving past." Again, the children giggled.

Lillian scowled at him, not amused this time. Timothy continued speaking. "She is so busy waving at him that she doesn't notice the hem of her dress has caught fire."

Sending him a sour look, she said, "I don't have a boyfriend, but I would certainly wave if one of my scholars were to pass by my home."

He wiped the grin off his face. "All right, one of your students has distracted you and now your hem is on fire."

She raised her arms in mock horror and shouted, "This is terrible! Help!"

"What should she do?" Timothy cupped one hand to his ear and leaned toward the children.

"Stop, drop and roll," the group yelled.

Lillian covered her face with both hands, dropped to the ground and rolled back and forth. She lifted her hand from her face and squinted at Timothy. "Did I do that right?"

He looked at the children. "Scholars, did Teacher Lillian do it correctly?"

"Ja!" they shouted in unison.

He held out his hand to help her up, his eyes sparkling. "Exactly right, Teacher."

She took his offered hand. His firm grip sent an unexpected rush of pleasure spiraling through her. As soon as she was on her feet, she pulled her hand from his and brushed at her dusty dress. "Next time you can do the stop, drop and roll while I ask the questions."

He grinned. "But you did it so well. You were far more graceful than I could ever be."

Turning to the children, she said, "Let's all thank Timothy for taking the time to teach us about fire safety."

"Thank you, Timothy," they said in unison.

Hannah added, *"Danki, Onkel* Timothy." Hannah was the stepdaughter of Timothy's brother, Joshua. Lillian tried hard not to have favorites, but she couldn't help it where Hannah was concerned.

"We only speak English at school, Hannah," Lillian reminded her.

Hannah ducked her head. "Sorry, Teacher. I forgot. Thank you, Uncle Timothy."

Lillian softened her tone. "It's all right. Sometimes I forget, too. Now, let's review some of the points Timothy made. Susan, can you tell us how often to change the batteries in our smoke detectors?"

"Twice a year, and the detectors should be replaced if they are more than seven years old," the eighth-grade girl said quickly, proving she had been listening. Susan

Yoder was one of Lillian's best students. The girl hoped to become a teacher someday.

Lillian gestured to Timothy's niece in the front row. "Hannah, what are some ways to prevent fires?"

Hannah wasn't a bit shy. She shot to her feet. "Don't ever play with matches. I don't, but Carl does."

Seated beside Hannah, the young boy leaned away from her and scowled. "Not anymore."

"I'm glad to hear that," Timothy said, a smile twitching at the corner of his lips.

Lillian raised her hand. "How many of you have practiced a fire escape plan with your family at home?" Nearly all the students raised their hands. Abe didn't and neither did his little brother Carl.

"All right, I want you to go inside, take out a piece of paper and draw a diagram of your home. I want you to show at least two ways to escape from the house in the event of a fire and mark where your meeting place is outside. Siblings may work together on the project."

The children rose and filed toward the school. Lillian stopped Susan. The girl served as Lillian's much-needed teacher's aide. "Will you help Hannah with this project? She doesn't have older siblings."

"Sure." Susan smiled and followed the others.

Abe shoved past Hannah, almost knocking her down when they reached the steps at the same time.

"Sorry," he said quickly, but he didn't sound remorseful in the least. He caught Gabriel's eye and whispered something to him. They both laughed as they went in.

Timothy moved to stand beside Lillian. "I noticed the son of our school board president is a bit of a trouble-maker."

"Abe is, but I don't treat him differently because of his father."

Silas Mast, the school board president, had brushed aside her concerns about Abe's behavior when she tried to speak to him about it. His lack of support was making it more difficult to handle the boy.

Lillian watched until the last student entered the building; then she whirled to face Timothy with her hands on her hips. "What possessed you to suggest in front of my students that I have a boyfriend?"

He looked taken aback. "I didn't mean anything by it. I was making a point that you were distracted."

"You should have chosen better."

"Are you upset with me?"

She crossed her arms over her chest. "*Ja*, Timothy Bowman, I'm upset with you."

He relaxed. "*Nee*, you aren't. I can tell by the look in your eyes."

"How do my eyes look when I'm upset?" she demanded.

"Frosty."

Did he really know her so well? "And how do they look now?"

"Like you're trying to be serious, but you're smiling inside."

He was right, but she wasn't about to admit it.

He leaned one hip against the table. "How did I do for my first time giving a program?"

"Very well. You clearly have a knack for teaching."

"*Danki*. I tried to think about what I would say to my own children."

"Do you have a mother in mind for them?" she asked with false sweetness, knowing he was a single fellow.

She had heard a bit of gossip about him and wondered if it was true. Courting relationships were often closely guarded secrets in the Amish community.

He shook a finger at her. "Lillian Keim, you're prying."

She spread her hands wide. "You brought up the subject of children."

"I want a wife and children *someday*. I pray I will have sons to work beside me in our business as I have worked beside my father. I hope I may teach all my children to be good and faithful members of our church." His voice had grown soft. Lillian realized he was sharing something important with her.

"I hope God answers your prayers." A family of her own was something she would never have.

He tipped his head to the side as he regarded her. "What about you? How many children do you want?"

She gave a laugh but knew it sounded forced. "I have forty-one children to care for. That's more than enough. There will be forty-four next month because we have a new family transferring to our school. I hope the school board approves the hiring of a second teacher when they meet next Friday. I'm not sure I can manage that many."

"Still, you must want children of your own someday."

That wasn't possible. Only her parents knew about the surgery that had saved her life but left her barren. She'd never told anyone else. She didn't want pity. God had chosen this path for her. It wasn't an easy one, but she would do her best to live as He willed.

She drew a steadying breath and raised her chin. "Every morning I wake up and think about these children waiting for me and I can't wait to get here. I thank God every day and night for leading me to this work.

I love it. Are you shocked that I want a career instead of a family?"

"*Nee*, I'm not. Luke mentioned as much to me."

"You and your brother were talking about me?"

"It was last Christmas. Luke thought the reason I was helping with the school program was that I wanted to court you. He decided to become my unofficial go-between and have Emma find out if you would be interested in dating me. Emma told him you were devoted to teaching and not looking to marry. He relayed that to me."

"And was that the reason behind your offer to help at the school?"

Timothy shook his head. "You and the *kinder* needed help. Friends help friends."

A touch of disappointment pricked her, but she quickly suppressed it. She valued his friendship. Any sign of romantic attachment from either of them would make their friendship awkward and could bring censure down on her. As a teacher, she was expected to be a model of proper behavior. "Your help made the program extra special. *Danki.*"

He shrugged off her praise. "I didn't do much."

Now it was her turn to tease him. Checking to make sure they wouldn't be overheard, she leaned closer. "I understand you are Nellie Martin's come-calling friend. Is it serious?"

His eyebrows shot up. "What? Who told you that?"

"You were seen driving together last Sunday evening."

"I passed Nellie walking along the road after visiting her sister and I gave her a lift home because I was going the same way. That's all. I'm not her come-calling friend or anyone else's, for that matter."

"See how easily rumors get started?" She was glad he wasn't seeing anyone. When he did find the right woman, Lillian knew their friendship would change.

A gleam sparkled in the depths of his eyes. He leaned toward her. "Would you be jealous if I were going out with her, Teacher?"

Trust him to turn the tables on her. "Of course not, but rumors will soon circulate that I have a new *boo-friend*."

"Why?"

"Because these forty-one students will go home and repeat what they learned today. Some of them will fail to mention you were teasing about my boyfriend. By Sunday after the prayer meeting I'll be answering carefully worded questions from many curious mothers as they try to figure out who he might be."

A frown line appeared on his forehead. "Do you really think so? I didn't mean to make trouble."

"I know small children and the way they can mix up the simplest things. When people start asking, I'm going to tell everyone it's you."

He pressed his hands over his heart. "Teacher, don't get my hopes up unless you mean it."

It was her turn to frown. "What is that supposed to mean?"

"I would be your *boo-friend* in a heartbeat. May I come courting?"

Chapter Two

Timothy watched an array of fleeting expressions cross Lillian's delicate face. Surprise, dismay and finally skepticism narrowed her green eyes. He would cheerfully snatch back his words if he could. She had to know he was joking, didn't she? Had he gone too far this time?

Her eyes narrowed. "Where is that bucket of water? You need to soak your head."

"Is that any way to talk to the man you're dating?"

She jabbed her finger into his chest. "I'm too smart to go out with you, and it's nothing to joke about."

"You are right. Courting and marriage are not joking matters." Relieved that he hadn't truly upset her, he turned the conversation in a safer direction. "What did you think of the book I lent you?"

Her tense shoulders relaxed at his change of subject. "I haven't had time to sit down with it yet."

"Teacher hasn't finished her homework. Shame on you."

"I do have papers to grade and lessons to prepare."

"I will accept that excuse today, but I'm dying to

know if you find the story as funny as I did. The main character reminded me of you."

"I thought you said it was about a dog."

"It is. A lovable, devoted dog who believes she knows what's best for every creature in the barnyard. Truly, it's a great book with an excellent message."

"So I'm like a bossy dog, is that what you are saying?"

She rolled her eyes, and he chuckled. He enjoyed teasing Lillian. They had been close friends when they were younger, drawn together by a love of books and reading. He cherished the hours they had spent discussing the works of Dickens, Henry David Thoreau and the stories of their persecuted Amish ancestors in *The Martyr's Mirror*. His love of reading was something his brothers never understood.

Lillian and her family had moved away the summer he turned eighteen. He'd lost touch with her for a few years, but he never forgot the way she made him feel. The Amish valued hard work. Book learning had its place, but few people understood his desire to read and learn more about the world the way Lillian did.

When she returned to the area after six years away, he had been delighted but his first efforts to rekindle their friendship had been rebuffed. Lillian had changed while she was away. She had become remote and reserved. It had taken a great deal of patience on his part to repair the bond between them.

Besides helping with the Christmas program, he had done what handiwork was needed at the school without being asked. He sometimes bought books for the school library and occasionally suggested a new novel he thought she might like. His diligence over the course of the winter had slowly thawed her reserve. Now that they were enjoying an easy comradery again, he would do his best to keep it that way.

"Looks like you have a visitor," he said, gesturing to the road where a white car was pulling up to a stop on the narrow road in front of the school.

Lillian shaded her eyes as she gazed that way. A young woman got out of the car. She went to the back and opened the trunk.

"Do you know her?" Timothy asked.

"I had a letter from the public health department telling me Miss Debra Merrick would be here to do health screenings on the children today."

The woman closed the trunk of her car and picked up two large black cases.

"I'd better go help her with those bags. They look heavy."

He judged Debra to be near his age, somewhere in her midtwenties. She was dressed modern in a simple blue skirt and a white blouse with lace at her throat. Her black shoes were low-heeled and sensible, but they sported shiny buckles that wouldn't be acceptable in his Plain community. Her blond hair was cut short and floated in curls around her face.

He glanced at Lillian. Amish women never cut their hair. They kept it covered beneath a white prayer *kapp* like the one Lillian wore. The white ribbons of her bonnet fluttered softly in the breeze and drew his gaze to the slender curve of her neck. What would her hair look like if she wore it down? He could imagine it spilling in rich brown waves down her back. Would it reach the floor? He jerked his gaze away. It wasn't proper to think such thoughts about a friend. He focused on the woman beside the car.

"Can I give you a hand with those?" he asked as he and Lillian drew near.

"Thank you. That's very kind." She put the cases down and smiled sweetly as she tucked a curl behind her ear.

Lillian held out her hand. "I'm Lillian Keim, the teacher here. This is Timothy Bowman."

"I'm Debra Merrick." The woman shook hands with both of them.

"I was expecting you early this morning," Lillian said.

Debra flushed a rosy shade of pink. "I'm afraid I got lost on these winding rural roads. Twice."

Timothy began undoing his coat. "It happens. We aren't exactly in the middle of nowhere, but you can see it from here."

Debra's gaze carried a hint of gratitude for his understanding. She gestured toward the smoking pans on the table. "Has there been a fire?"

He chuckled as he pulled his helmet off and combed his fingers through his damp curls. "Only a fire safety demonstration. I'll bring your cases up to the school once I shed this gear."

He stepped over to his wagon, undid the heavy coat and tossed it along with his helmet on the wooden bench seat. He picked up his straw hat and settled it on his head.

Turning around, he saw Miss Merrick watching him with a look of surprise on her face. "You're Amish? I didn't know the Amish could be firemen."

He laughed heartily. "Then I reckon there's a lot you don't know about us Amish folk."

She gave him a sheepish smile. "I'm afraid that's true. My family has some Amish ancestry, but this is my first visit to Amish country and my first Amish school to visit."

"We are more than farmers and quilters. You'll find we're a lot like everyone else if you take the time to get to know us," he added.

"I'm always willing to learn new things, and I like getting to know new people."

He nodded once. *"Goot."*

Debra tipped her head to the side. "What does that mean?"

"It means good. It's Pennsylvania *Deitsch*. You might have heard it called Pennsylvania Dutch, although it's not Dutch at all. It's an old German dialect."

Her smile widened. *"Goot.* I'll remember that. Thank you for teaching me something new today, Mr. Bowman."

She seemed like a sweet woman. "Call me Timothy."

"All right, Timothy."

Lillian stepped between them and shot him a stern, frosty look before she turned to Debra. "Come up to the school and meet the children, Miss Merrick. They've been waiting for you."

Timothy stared after Lillian in puzzlement. What was *that* look for?

Lillian resisted the urge to grab Timothy by the collar and shake him. Didn't he realize the woman was boldly flirting with him and that he was encouraging her? Outsiders were to be dealt with cautiously. Timothy's behavior bordered on prideful. Being forward or asserting oneself in any way was contrary to their church's teachings and he knew that.

Once they were inside the school, she directed Debra

to a table at the back of the room to set up her equipment. Timothy placed the cases next to it. Lillian welcomed the health screening and other educational health programs presented by the local public health department. Each year her students received dental and eye exams as well as hearing screenings and classes on the hazards of tobacco use and smoking, all free of charge.

Debra looked over the room and spoke softly to Lillian. "I'm afraid I'm not going to get all the children done today. I don't want to keep them after school. Would it be all right if I return tomorrow?"

"That won't be a problem. School starts at eight o'clock."

Debra let out a sigh of relief. "That will be great. Now that I know the way, I should be here on time. On a personal note, I was hoping to purchase some authentic Amish-made gifts for my friends back home. Can you suggest somewhere to shop locally?"

"My mother runs a gift shop just over the river," Timothy said. "You passed it before you came through the covered bridge. You'll find everything there is reasonably priced and all handmade. If you'd like to see some Amish-made furniture, I'd be happy to show you around my father's woodworking shop."

"I'd like that very much. I'll stop by after I finish here tomorrow."

"Great. I'll see you then."

"Maybe you can teach me a few more Amish words." She gave him a sly smile and a wink.

"I've recently been told I have a knack for teaching."

He looked so smug that Lillian was tempted to kick his shin. She forced herself to remain polite. "We should let Miss Merrick get to work, Timothy. I'll help you clean up outside."

"It was nice meeting you, Debra." He nodded to her and went out the door. Lillian followed him to the make-shift table and checked the pans to see if they were cool enough to handle.

"Are you going to tell me what's wrong?" he asked.

"Nothing's wrong." Was it her place to correct his behavior? Her father would say it was.

"You've been giving me your *frosty* stare ever since Miss Merrick arrived."

"If you want to make puppy eyes at the *Englisch* lady, I'm sure it's none of my business."

He frowned as he snatched up the water pail. "I wasn't making puppy eyes at her."

"Ha! If you had a tail, it would have been wagging a mile a minute the second she smiled at you."

"How can you say that?"

"I say it because it's true."

"I was being *nice*. She seems like a very pleasant lady. Which is more than I can say for you at the moment." He threw the water out, picked up the fire extinguisher and headed for his wagon.

Lillian nibbled on the corner of her lip as she watched him stomp away. He was right. She wasn't being pleasant, and she had no right to chastise him. He hadn't broken any church rules. Friendliness with outsiders wasn't forbidden, just discouraged. She wasn't sure why it upset her to see him so at ease with the woman.

Timothy came back and carried a pair of sawhorses past her without comment. He set them in the back of the wagon. It was clear he was upset with her and that wasn't like Timothy.

"I'm sorry if I offended you," she said.

"You have." He brushed past her to pick up the last of the boards and carried them to the wagon, too. He threw them in and they clattered loudly. The horses shifted uneasily at the noise but quickly settled at a low word from him.

Lillian took a step closer. "I'm only looking out for your best interests. Your behavior could be seen as forward and unacceptable. I'm sorry if pointing that out makes you angry."

He leaned a hip against the wagon and folded his arms over his chest as he fixed his gaze on her face. "That you judge my behavior to be forward and unacceptable is what makes me angry. I thought you knew me well enough to know I wouldn't flirt with any woman, let alone someone who didn't share our faith."

She clutched her arms tight across her chest. "I do know that."

"Then why accuse me of it?"

She stared at her feet and tried to put her feelings into words. "You smiled at her."

"I smile at everyone."

"I know, but she smiled back. I saw that look in her eyes."

"What are you talking about? What look?"

Lillian glanced at his handsome face. "The look that said she was interested in getting to know you better. A lot better."

He shook his head in disbelief. "I'm not responsible for the way someone looks at me."

"I saw the attraction between the two of you. Such feelings can lead you down a forbidden path."

He threw his hands in the air. "I can't believe I'm

hearing this. I had no idea you thought I was so weak-minded."

"I don't." The last thing she wanted was for him to be angry with her.

"Your words say otherwise, Lillian."

He climbed in his wagon. With a slap of the reins, he headed his horses down the road, leaving her to watch his rapidly retreating figure and regret her ill-advised comments. They'd never had a disagreement, let alone an argument like this.

Had she damaged their friendship beyond repair?

Chapter Three

$\sim$

Drawing a deep calming breath, Lillian returned to the schoolroom determined to be pleasant to Miss Merrick. She would apologize to Timothy soon. Perhaps she could think of an excuse to visit the Bowman household after school tonight and find a way to speak to Timothy alone. And then again, maybe she was being foolish. Their friendship was surely strong enough to weather one disagreement. Wasn't it? She didn't need to run after him and beg his forgiveness.

Inside the school, she helped Debra set up the eye charts. Together, they taped off the correct distance on the floor where the children were to stand. Suddenly, the outside door burst open, and Lillian's little sister Amanda raced in.

Spying Lillian, the four-year-old dashed across the room and threw her arms around Lillian's legs. "*Shveshtah*, I *koom* to visit you at *schule*. Teach me something?"

Tiny for her age, Amanda had been born with dwarfism. Her arms and legs were short, but her body was near normal in size. Her blond hair was fine and straight as wheat straw with wisps of it peeking from beneath her white *kapp*.

Lillian scooped the child up in her arms and settled her at her hip. "The first thing my scholars learn is to be quiet in the classroom. No shouting. No running."

Amanda's smile faded. "I was bad, wasn't I?"

Lillian nodded. "A little."

The outside door opened again and Lillian's father, Eldon Keim, came in, his face set in stern lines. Something must be wrong.

Miss Merrick gave Amanda a bright smile. "Is this your daughter?"

"Amanda is my sister." Lillian introduced her father to Miss Merrick.

"I'm very pleased to meet you, Mr. Keim, and you, Amanda." Debra held out her hand to the child.

Amanda shyly shook it.

Debra's smile widened. "I have a brother who is a little person. His name is Brandon. He has cartilage-hair hypoplasia."

A rush of empathy caused Lillian to look kindly at Debra. Here was someone who understood the challenging life her little sister faced. "That is exactly what Amanda has."

"I mentioned my family has Amish ancestors. I'm sure you know CCH is one of the more common types of dwarfism among the Amish. I wish Brandon could meet Amanda. He loves children, especially little-people children. He and his wife have adopted two children with dwarfism. He's a professor of agriculture at Ohio Central University. I know that sounds like a stuffy job, but he's not a bit stuffy."

Her father spoke quietly in Pennsylvania Dutch. "I'm

going into town. Your mother said you needed something."

"*Ja*, I have two library books that are due back today. Can you drop them off for me?" It would save her a long walk this evening. Bless her mother for thinking of it.

"Fetch them quickly."

She put Amanda down, hurried to her desk and returned with both volumes. *"Danki."*

He scanned the titles and frowned. "Are these proper reading for an Amish woman?"

Lillian was glad he'd kept the conversation in Pennsylvania *Deitsch*. It stung that he didn't trust her judgment, but as a minister of the church, he had to make sure his family obeyed the *Ordnung*, the rules of the church. The books were teaching guides for elementary science, a subject she struggled to understand and teach. "They were recommended to me at the last teachers' conference I attended. What's wrong, *Daed*?"

He tucked the books under his arm. "I received a letter today from my sister in Wisconsin. My *onkel* Albert is gravely ill and wishes to see me. We are leaving tonight. I must speak with the bishop and let him know I won't be preaching with him on Sunday."

"I'm so sorry. Is Amanda going with you?"

"*Nee*, your mother and I think it best she stay at home with you and Jeremiah. Can she spend the rest of the afternoon with you today?"

Lillian winked at Amanda. "She isn't old enough to start school."

"If it is a problem, she can come with me to the bishop's home," he said.

Amanda's eyes widened, and she shook her head. The bishop was a kindly man, but his stern countenance and booming voice had frightened the child once and she remained leery of him.

Planting her hands on her hips, Lillian pretended to consider the situation, then finally nodded and smiled. "*Ja*, she can stay with me."

After her father left, Debra took a tentative step closer. "Is something wrong?"

Realizing Debra hadn't understood their exchange, Lillian explained. "My father has been called to his uncle's deathbed in Wisconsin. He and my mother must make arrangements to travel there as soon as possible."

"They can't go that far by horse and buggy, can they?"

"They will hire a driver to take them. We are not allowed to own cars, but we are not forbidden to ride in them. Many local people earn extra money by driving their Amish neighbors when there is a need."

"I see. I'm sorry your father's uncle is so ill." Debra laid a hand on Lillian's shoulder. Lillian was surprised by the sincere sympathy in her eyes.

"He has lived a long full life." Lillian recalled with fondness her great-uncle's gnarled hands and his toothless grin. He kept a tall glass jar by his chair and he always had a licorice twist to share with her and his many grandchildren and great-grandchildren. It was sad to think of his passing, but she knew he was ready to go home.

Debra stepped back. "I should get to work. Will the children have trouble understanding me? I know you speak a different language."

"Only the youngest will have trouble. Start with the upper grades today. They have all had eye exams before."

Lillian settled Amanda on a seat by her desk and gave

her several picture books to look at while she finished grading the spelling tests from the day before. Debra was only halfway through the eye exams when it was time to dismiss for the day.

Lillian looked out over the classroom. "Put your books away and quietly get your coats."

Abe and Gabriel rushed to the cloakroom and then dashed out the door before she could stop them. She couldn't very well chase after them. She would have to deal with their disrespectful attitude tomorrow. This couldn't continue.

She walked to the door and held it open. "Children, you are dismissed."

The rest of the children filed outside in an orderly manner that lasted only until they reached the final step on the porch. After that, they bolted like young colts being let out to pasture. Childish laughter and shouts filled the air as they said goodbye to each other and to her. For Lillian, there was always a sense of relief followed by a small letdown when they were gone from her sight. They were hers for seven hours each day, but none of them belonged to her.

Thankfully, she had Amanda. Her baby sister was as close as Lillian would ever come to having a child of her own. She looked toward her desk and saw Amanda was sharing her picture book with Debra.

"What is this?" Debra asked, pointing to the page. She had taken a seat on the floor by the child's chair.

Amanda said, *"Dess ist ein gaul."*

"Gaul. That must mean horse. Am I right?" Debra looked to Lillian for confirmation. She nodded.

"And this?" Debra pointed to the page again.

"Hund."

"So dog is *hund*."

Amanda grinned and turned the page. She pointed and said, *"Hohna."*

"Chicken is *hohna*." Debra giggled as she stumbled over the unfamiliar word.

"Hohna means rooster." Lillian sat in her chair and scooted closer to Amanda so she could see the pictures, too.

Amanda pointed to the drawing of a hen sitting on a nest of straw. *"Glukk."*

"That has got to mean chicken." Debra glanced at Lillian.

"Not exactly. It means a sitting hen, one who lays eggs."

"Goot, glukk, hohna, hund, gaul. Good, sitting hen, rooster, dog, horse. I've learned a pocketful of new words today. Thank you, Amanda. I shall thoroughly impress Mr. Bowman with my new vocabulary when I see him tomorrow."

Lillian's smile faded. She spoke quietly in *Deitsch* to her sister. "Put your things away. You may go outside and play on the swings until I'm ready to go home."

The child got up without further prompting. She put her colors and book away, and headed out the door.

"She's very sweet," Debra said.

"She is a great blessing to me and to my entire family."

"I'm glad to hear you say that. Children with special needs aren't always seen as a blessing." Debra's tone held a touch of bitterness that surprised Lillian.

"The Amish believe handicapped children are extraordinary gifts from God. A family with such a child faces difficulties, yes, but they know God has smiled upon them in a very special way."

"I wish my family held such a belief. My father saw my brother as a burden and wondered what he had done wrong to be cursed with a deformed son."

"I'm sorry for your father. I pray he comes to see the error in his way of thinking."

"He passed away a few years ago. I think in the end he came to accept Brandon as a gift, but growing up, my brother faced prejudices from inside and outside of our home. I'm amazed he has turned out as normal and happy as he seems to be."

"We have a proverb about our children. *The more a child is valued, the better his values will be.*"

"You are making me sorry my great-great-grandfather left the Amish. May I ask you something personal?"

Lillian thought their conversation was already personal, but she nodded.

"I had the feeling that you were upset after my arrival today. Did I do something wrong? I don't want to alienate you or others in this community. If I did do something unacceptable, please tell me. I won't be offended. I plan to begin teaching adult education classes in this area on health and food safety later this fall, and I know I need to learn more about your Amish ways if I'm to be effective."

Lillian looked down at her hands. "I was upset, and I beg your forgiveness for that. It wasn't your behavior, so much as the behavior of Timothy Bowman that upset me."

"His behavior? I found him incredibly friendly and very sweet. What did he do that upset you? He's a bit of a flirt, but that's harmless. Oh, unless you two are dating or something? That would put a totally different spin on it."

"Timothy and I are simply friends," she said quickly. Maybe too quickly. A hint of speculation widened Debra's eyes.

"He's a nice-looking fellow. Is he married?"

"Timothy is single."

"I notice you aren't wearing a wedding band. I take it you're single, too?"

"Amish women do not wear jewelry, even wedding rings, but I am single and I shall remain so. If I were to marry I would have to give up teaching."

"Really? That's very old-fashioned."

"We are an old-fashioned people. Becoming a wife and a mother is a sacred duty that must come before all else. Very few married Amish women work outside the home."

As an outsider, Lillian wasn't sure Debra would understand, but if she was going to be working in their community, she had to become informed about what was and was not acceptable. "You may have seen Timothy's behavior as harmless, but our church would take a very different view. We are to be meek before God and man, never drawing attention to ourselves or putting ourselves above others. We call it *demut*, humbleness."

"I think I see. I wouldn't consider Timothy's behavior humble, but it wasn't offensive."

"Timothy has a sweet nature, but his outgoing personality draws attention and that is frowned upon."

"I was told the Amish were cold and unwelcoming. I'm happy to say I have not found that to be true. Thank you for explaining this to me. I'll ignore Timothy's winsome ways and practice being modest and humble."

Debra leaned toward Lillian and grinned. "I'm afraid *that* will be a hard task for me to master."

Lillian decided she liked this outsider. "We have another proverb that may help. *You can tell when you're on the right track because it's usually uphill.*"

"Care to share with us, *bruder* Timothy?"

Timothy looked up from contemplating the coffee in his white mug to find his brother Luke staring at him. He glanced around and found his little brother Noah, his mother and his father all staring at him as if waiting for him to speak. He had no idea what they had been discussing. Lillian's accusation had been the only thing on his mind since he left the school yesterday afternoon. Why had she accused him of flirting with the English lady? Her lack of trust chafed at his mind.

Knowing only she could answer his questions, he forced his attention back to his family. "I'm sorry. What were you talking about?"

Luke chuckled. "Who put a knot in your tail?"

Timothy knew better than to ignore Luke's teasing. It would only get worse if he did. "No one has put a knot in my tail. I was thinking about my fire safety class and how I could improve things." It wasn't the whole truth, but he hoped it would satisfy his sharp-eyed brother.

"I asked you how it went." His mother refilled his coffee cup from the pot sitting on a hot pad near her elbow and offered him the last cinnamon roll in the pan. Ana Bowman was happiest when she was feeding someone. He was surprised that they weren't all as plump as bullfrogs.

He nodded his thanks for the refill but passed on the roll. "I think it went well. For the most part, the children paid close attention. They sure are a bright bunch. No wonder Lillian enjoys teaching them."

Ana put the pan aside. "You impressed Hannah. She told me all about it when she came home yesterday. I'm dying to know who Lillian's boyfriend is. Do you know?"

Timothy cringed. He would be in hot water with Lillian now for sure. "She isn't seeing anyone. I made up a story about her having a boyfriend to show how she might become distracted, and…never mind. I can't believe Hannah repeated that. Lillian doesn't have a beau."

"Told you she didn't." Luke stuffed his last bite of cinnamon roll in his mouth and reached for the pan. "If Lillian was seeing someone, Emma would know."

"But would Emma tell you?" *Mamm* asked.

Their father pushed away from the table. "If we are done gossiping about our neighbors, perhaps we can get some work done today."

His sons heeded the annoyance in his tone and quickly finished their coffee. They followed him out the door and across the graveled yard to the woodworking shop. The sun was just peeking over the horizon. It promised to be another warm day. One of the horses whinnied at them from the corral. The cattle and horses in the big red barn had been fed well before the men sat down to breakfast.

In the large workshop, they were joined by several other carpenters. Timothy's oldest brother, Samuel, moved to stand beside their father with a clipboard in his hand. Everyone gathered around him awaiting instructions for the day.

Samuel flipped through the sheets of paper on his

board. "We've received a new order for sixteen beds with carved headboards and footboards."

"Must be an order from an Amish family if they need sixteen beds," Noah said under his breath to Luke and Timothy.

Timothy choked on a laugh. Luke nudged their little brother with his elbow. "The Amish aren't the only ones with big families."

Noah elbowed him back. "Tell that to *Mamm*. She expects us to give her a dozen grandchildren each. Or more."

A grin twitched at the corner of Samuel's mouth. "I'm doing my part."

He and his wife had welcomed a baby boy in May to the delight of everyone, especially Ana Bowman.

"This order comes from an inn being built in upstate New York," *Daed* said, clearly struggling to keep from laughing. They all knew Noah spoke the truth.

Timothy thought of his conversation with Lillian about children. He did want a big family. He wanted a devout wife to be his helpmate, to share his burdens and his joys. A woman who was bright and quick-thinking. Someone who loved bringing out the best in others the way Lillian did. While there were a few nice women he could date, none of them ignited the spark he expected to feel when the right woman came along.

"We are blessed to have the quality of our work recognized by someone so far away." Samuel pointed to Timothy. "You and Luke select the wood to be used. They want oak and walnut with pine as a secondary wood. You know the kind of lumber we need."

"Straight with no knots in it." Timothy was already thinking of the boards that were stacked beneath tarps behind the shop. The last delivery of locally cut walnut had been above average quality.

Samuel nodded. "Exactly. Joshua and Noah, I want you to work on creating sixteen different but coordinated designs for the headboards. Each one has to represent an animal native to the northern woods. We have a list. Deer, moose, bobcat, bear, ducks, geese, raccoon, you get the idea." He handed the paper to Joshua.

"How about a skunk?" Noah suggested.

Samuel shook his head. "Are you ever serious?"

"Rarely."

Timothy spoke up. "I'm sure we can come up with sixteen that will satisfy the customer. How much time do we have to complete the order?"

Samuel flipped a paper over. "Ten weeks."

"Finally, an *Englisch* customer who isn't in a flat-out rush," Noah said.

His comment reminded Timothy that he had promised to show Debra around the shop after she was done at the school today. He had been happy to extend the invitation yesterday, but now he wished he hadn't. Lillian was sure to be upset if he spent more time with the pretty *Englisch* nurse.

Samuel handed Timothy a sheet of paper with the dimensions for the beds. He and Luke headed for the back door of the shop. A low beep made Luke stop and pull his fire department pager from his waistband. "Is it your turn to be on call or should I give it to Noah?"

"It's my turn. Does it need to be charged?" The family had a diesel generator to run the electric equipment in their business. A single outlet in their father's office was the only place the brothers could charge their pagers when the generators were running.

"*Ja*, it does. Wouldn't want you to miss a call. How many times have we gone out this month?"

"Eight." Twice as many as usual. Mostly rubbish fires that had gotten out of hand, but one had been a large hay fire that threatened a house and barn. Fortunately, no one had been injured and the blaze had been contained.

Luke glanced out the door. "This warm weather and lack of rain has left the land as dry as tinder. I pray it rains soon."

"Amen to that." Timothy followed him outside and around the back of the building where a covered shed housed their lumber.

Once they were outside, Luke faced Timothy and planted his hands on his hips. "Now that no one else in the family is listening, what's really bothering you?"

So he hadn't fooled his eagle-eyed brother. "If you must know, Lillian accused me of flirting with the visiting nurse who came to the school yesterday. I wasn't flirting. I was being nice to the woman."

"Was this nurse a pretty woman?"

"I guess you could say that."

"And Lillian became upset because you were being nice to a pretty woman."

"*Ja.*"

"Well, that explains a lot."

Timothy scowled at Luke. "Not to me, it doesn't. What do you know that I don't?"

"She's jealous."

"Lillian? You can't be serious. *Nee*, that isn't it."

"You and she are friends. Close friends. Right?"

"Since we were in third grade. Everyone knows that. So?"

"She has had your undivided devotion for years.

Maybe she saw for the first time that she might not always be the center of your life. You two aren't children anymore."

Timothy mulled over his brother's words. Was Luke right? If he was, what did that mean for the relationship Timothy cherished?

Chapter Four

Early the next morning, Lillian rounded the sharp bend in the road and was surprised to see Debra sitting on the school steps. The sun was barely up in the east. A thin mist hugged the river and low places. Lillian knew it would burn off quickly when the sun rose in the sky.

The sight of the young woman brought back the memory of Lillian's quarrel with Timothy. Her family's hurried departure as well as her false pride had kept her from seeking him out yesterday. He deserved an apology. After school, she would make a point to seek him out. She cherished his friendship and didn't want to lose it.

"Good morning," Deborah called out cheerfully as she waved.

"Good morning. You certainly arrived early enough."

"I was determined to be on time this morning. I parked my car beside that empty shed over there. I hope that's okay."

"It's fine. In poor weather I drive my buggy and park inside, but as you can see, I walked today."

"How far away do you live?"

"Not far. Two and a half miles."

"I wouldn't like to hike that far for my job. I spent some time doing research last night that I should have done before coming here. I'm afraid I discovered more questions than answers. Is it true that Amish children don't go to school beyond the eighth grade?"

Lillian climbed the steps and held the door open for Debra. "It is true."

"Even you, a teacher?"

"You must find that shocking. We believe that beyond elementary school, vocational training is sufficient for Amish youth. Some cases of higher education are permitted. I earned my GED and took some college courses by correspondence before I was baptized into the faith. Admittedly, I'm something of an exception. Amish teachers rarely have more education than their students, but I knew I was preparing for a lifetime vocation."

"I can certainly understand that. What is the curriculum like here?"

"I teach the basics of reading, writing and arithmetic just as the majority of public schools did over a century ago. In addition, I teach German." Lillian laid her books and papers on her desk.

"I'm aware that in the case of Wisconsin versus Yoder in 1972, the United States Supreme Court ruled that Amish children could end their formal schooling at the age of fourteen. But getting a good education is so important in this day and age. I'm not sure I see how your children can prosper without it."

Picking up an eraser, Lillian began to wipe away her class assignments from the day before. "Education must prepare our children to be productive members of our community, not productive members of the greater world. I teach English because it is the language of our neighbors and of our commerce. A man cannot sell milk or goods if he doesn't understand what his customer is saying. I teach German because we use the Bible written in that language just as our ancestors did in our church services. My students also learn about health and basic science, although not all Amish schools are as progressive as we are. Each school board decides what is important and what is to be taught. In some areas of education, you may find us lacking, but we do what is best for our children and our way of life."

"I certainly didn't learn a new language in grade school."

Lillian realized how puffed up she must sound and turned to face Debra. "And I am guilty of pride. Please forgive me for lecturing you."

"As I have said before, I enjoy learning new things. Thank you for the lesson and you are forgiven if you will forgive my ignorance and not take offense at my many questions."

"That is a deal. We Amish are free to read and study ways to improve our lives as long as they do not go against the teaching of our church. We believe higher education puts our children at risk of exposure to worldly behaviors that we do not condone."

"But what about doctors and nurses? Don't the Amish want their own people in such professions?"

"There is a need for doctors and nurses, we don't deny that. We are grateful for the men and women who seek to serve mankind in such a fashion, but the core of our faith is that we must be separate from the world. In it, but not a part of it. We must forsake all self-interest and humbly submit to the authority of the church. To us, this is the only way to be righteous in the sight of God.

Any display of pride is a sin. If we take pride in being Amish, that, too, is a sin."

"I respect your right to believe as you wish, but I can't say that I understand it."

Lillian smiled. "I won't hold that against you."

She had never met anyone as forthright as Debra. The two previous health workers who had come to the school had been all business and not talkative in the least.

The sound of childish chatter outside signaled the arrival of her first students. Most were able to walk to the school, but a few were delivered to her doorstep in buggies driven by their parents or older siblings.

Debra glanced at the clock on the wall. It was five minutes until eight. "I need a quiet place for the hearing tests later today. Where do you suggest?"

"The cloakroom, or we have a basement if you'd like to see it."

"I think the cloakroom will work."

Lillian helped Debra move an unused desk and chair into the room. Outside, the sounds of children at play grew louder. The swings and the merry-go-round were favorite places for the students to play before school started.

Debra moved to the window. "They were so quiet yesterday, but they sound loud and rambunctious now. Maybe I should use the basement."

"Noise won't be a problem." Lillian went to the front steps.

Hannah ran up to her. "Teacher, *Mamm* brought me to school in our new pony cart. Isn't it pretty? That's our new pony. His name is Hank."

Lillian looked toward the road. Mary Bowman waved from the seat of a small two-wheeled wooden cart painted sky blue. A small black pony with a snip of white on his nose tossed his thick black mane. Lillian returned Mary's wave and turned to Hannah. "It's a very nice cart, and he looks like a fine pony."

"I made these for you." Hannah thrust a shoe box toward Lillian.

"How kind. What can it be?" Lillian's heart expanded with joy as she lifted the box to her ear and shook it. The rattle and aroma of gingersnaps gave her a hint. She peeked inside the lid. "Did you make these all by yourself? They look scrumptious."

"*Grossmammi* Ana helped me."

Lillian laid the box aside. "Please thank your grandmother Ana for me."

"We have something for you, too." Karen and Carla Beachy, third-grade twins, came up beside Hannah. They had each drawn a picture of their favorite cow named Willow. Lillian took the pictures and admired them. "These are lovely. I shall put them on the wall for everyone to enjoy."

"*Guder mariye*, Teacher." Carl Mast rushed up with a big grin.

"It is a beautiful morning." This was truly her favorite part of the day. More of her children greeted her and shared the news from home and she realized once again how truly blessed she was.

She rang the bell. Her students who were still playing outside immediately stopped what they were doing and filed quietly into the schoolhouse. They came in, put away their lunches and took their seats. Even Abe and Gabriel were quiet this morning.

Lillian stood in front of her desk. "Good morning, scholars."

"Good morning, Teacher," they said in unison.

"As you can see, Nurse Merrick has returned to finish your health screenings. You are to go with her when it is your turn."

Lillian moved to the blackboard that covered the front wall of the school and wrote out the date and the arithmetic assignments for each of the classes. When she finished, she picked up her Bible. Each day she chose a passage to read from the Old or the New Testament. This morning she chose 2 Corinthians 6. After the reading, her students rose, clasped their hands together and repeated the Lord's Prayer in unison.

Lillian picked up her copy of *Unpartheyisches Gesang-Buch*, their German songbook, from the corner of her desk. Singing was a normal part of each school day. Without being told, the children filed to the front of the room and lined up in their assigned places. She chose two English songs out of respect to their guest and one German hymn. Gabriel, the best singer in the school, began the hymn. The other children's voices rose together in unison as they sang without musical accompaniment. When the songs were finished, they all returned to their seats.

Susan Yoder began handing out readers to the three lower grades. The older students took out their arithmetic workbooks. All the children knew what was expected of them, and they did it without instructions. After Susan finished handing out the readers, she went with Debra to translate for the youngest ones being tested.

By ten o'clock, it was time for recess. Debra emerged from the cloakroom as the children surged around her to hurry outside. She came to the open door, where Lillian stood watching her charges. "I have to say that I'm amazed by how well behaved your students are. I hope every school I visit will be this cooperative."

Lillian smiled at her. "Every Amish school will be."

By early afternoon, the day had become hot enough that Lillian opened a window near her desk. A gust of breeze blew in and carried the arid smell of smoke into the schoolroom. Lillian looked up from the paper she was grading and glanced outside. A large cornfield stood across the road from the school. The tall pale tan stalks hadn't yet been harvested and their dry leaves crackled in the brisk wind. She saw a thin column of smoke rising from the far end of the field near the river.

Frowning, she rose from her chair and moved toward the front door. Had Mr. Hanson decided to burn his trash today? The country was under an open burning ban because of the drought, but not everyone complied with the rule.

On the porch, Lillian shaded her eyes and looked south. Mr. Hanson's cornfield curved around the building on three sides like a wide horseshoe. A swirl of wind picked up fallen leaves from beneath the trees by the road and added them to the large pile that had accumulated beside the porch. Unease crept up Lillian's spine.

The school, situated on a small hillock, was backed by a taller rise with a thick stand of woods that ended in a sheer bluff above the river. To the north, a high wooded ridge separated the school from the collection of farms beyond that were also located inside the bend of the river. The road in front of the school made a loop through the area that was mainly Amish farms. The covered bridge at Bowmans Crossing was the only way in and out.

Susan came outside and stood beside Lillian. "Do you smell smoke?"

"It's coming from Mr. Hanson's farmstead."

"Surely he can see the wind is too strong and in the wrong direction for burning today."

A huge explosion rocked the quiet afternoon, startling Lillian and making Susan shriek. Flames and black smoke shot skyward from the Hansons' farm. Lillian watched in shock as flaming debris flew high into the air.

Susan gripped Lillian's arm. "What was that?"

"I'm not sure. Perhaps a gasoline tank." The noise of excited children's voices rose inside the school.

"Should I run to the phone shack and call 9-1-1?" Susan asked, poised to dash away. The community telephone booth was a hundred yards down the road. A car went speeding past the school. Lillian recognized it as the one that belonged to Davey Mast. Was he headed for the phone booth to call for help? She had no way of knowing.

"Miss Merrick has a cell phone. We'll use that."

Lillian hurried Susan back inside. "Remain in your seats, children. There has been an explosion at the Hanson Farm across the way. Miss Merrick, would you be kind enough to notify 9-1-1? I want to make sure help is on the way."

"Of course." She pulled out her cell phone.

A gust of wind-driven smoke billowed in through the open window. Several children started coughing. Lillian motioned to Gabriel. "Shut the window, please."

Debra Merrick came over with the phone in her hand. "The local fire department has been alerted."

Was Timothy on call today? Even if he wasn't, he was sure to be among the people who would rush to help the Hansons.

Abe and Gabriel were at the windows looking out. Gabriel turned to her. "Should we go see if we can help?"

It wasn't a bad suggestion. Lillian chewed her lower lip. Perhaps she should send several of the older boys.

"Teacher. The fire is coming this way." The fear in Abe's voice drew her quickly to the window.

A wall of flames spewing dense smoke was spreading into the cornfield. The broad tongues of fire bent low and surged forward with each gust of the wind. Behind it, she could see the fire had spread into the trees along the river near the bridge. The only thing between the school and the flames was a narrow road. Would the fire be able to jump it? There wasn't much fuel for the blaze in their short lawn, but the building itself was wooden. There was plenty of fuel in the woods behind the school. Would they be safe here? Even as the question crossed her mind, a burning leaf of corn spiraled down from the sky and landed in the center of the road.

No. They weren't safe. The wind was too strong.

"We could go through the woods behind the school and down to the river," Gabriel suggested.

Lillian assessed the possible escape routes. The hill was steep and densely wooded terrain. Getting up and over it and down to the river would take time. "The fire is already spreading through the woods along the river. With so much wind, it could get in front of us. I don't think we should chance it. The young ones won't be able to move fast enough."

Debra moved to stand beside Lillian. "I can take some of the children in my car and drive out of here."

Lillian considered the idea. The sun was almost blotted out by the dense billowing clouds of smoke, but it was easy to see the wall of flames growing closer. Even with the windows closed, the smell of smoke was over-whelming.

"The only way out of this area is back across the bridge. The road only leads to other farms and it curves back and forth in the woods as it goes over the ridge. You might become trapped. *Nee*, I will keep all the children here. You are free to go if you wish."

"I'm staying with you and the kids."

"Danki."

Lillian turned to the class and spoke in Pennsylvania *Deitsch* so they could all understand her. "Children, you must listen to me very carefully and do what I say without question. There is a fire heading this way. I want you seventh- and eighth-grade boys to wet your hand-kerchiefs from the water can. Use them to cover your noses and mouths. If you don't have one, borrow one. Get whatever you can find that will hold water and start throwing it on the school building outside. Use the water from the horse tank and make a bucket brigade from the pump. Wet the roof as well as you can. Soak the area around our propane tank, too. Be quick and come back inside when I ring the bell. Each of you choose a part-ner and don't get separated from that person. Gabriel, you're in charge. Go."

Eight boys scrambled to her desk for water and were soon out the door. She turned to the remaining children and prayed she was making the right decision. "I want the rest of you to file down quietly into the basement. Each student in the older grades will take the hand of one younger child and lead everyone downstairs. Susan, take them all into the coal cellar and check to see that you can open the outside doors. They haven't been used in years."

The school board had taken out the coal stove and installed a new propane furnace four years earlier, but the coal storage area remained. The cavelike structure jutted out from the side of the basement, so the building wasn't directly over it. It had a thick wooden door they could close off to the basement. The curved walls and roof of the cellar were hand-hewn stone and covered with earth. It was fireproof. They could escape through the outside chute doors if the school building caught fire.

Lillian turned to Debra. "Go with Susan. You'll be safe underground. Use your phone to tell the fire department what we're doing first, then help Susan keep the children calm."

"Are you sure this is wise?" Debra stared at her with wide fear-filled eyes.

"The firefighters will make getting here a priority," she said with absolute confidence. The closest fire station was across the river about a mile from Bowmans Crossing. One covered wooden bridge stood between them. Had the fire reached it already? Were they cut off? Only God knew, but Timothy and the Bowman family would move heaven and earth to save the children even if they had to swim the river. Of that she was certain. "Go downstairs, Debra. You'll be safe there."

"I hope you're right about this." Debra sprinted for the staircase leading to the basement.

Lillian untied her apron as she hurried to her desk. After wetting the material, she tied it around her face. At the front door, she paused and closed her eyes. "Dear Lord, let this be the right decision. Save these children and protect the men coming to help us."

Protect Timothy. Why did I let him leave in anger yesterday? Forgive me, Timothy.

Taking a deep breath, she pulled open the door and went out to ring the bell. She made sure she had all the boys as they raced inside. When they were safe, she said, "Get down to the basement."

Susan came up the steps just as Lillian reached it. "Teacher, I can't get the outside doors open."

"I'll go around to the back and see if something is blocking it." Gabriel started for the door.

Lillian grabbed his arm. "*Nee*, get downstairs with the others. I'll go."

When he did as she told him, Lillian pulled her wet apron over her face again and stepped out into the dense smoke.

Chapter Five

The sound of an explosion had pulled Timothy, his brothers and the rest of the men working in the Bowman furniture shop outside. Timothy stared toward the bridge and saw dense smoke billowing above the trees on the north side of the river. It was impossible to tell how far away the explosion had been, but he thought it had to have been from the Hanson Farm.

Timothy's mother came out of the house and stood on the steps, her eyes wide with fright. "What was that? Is anyone hurt?"

"It wasn't here," Isaac, Timothy's father, yelled across to his wife. "It came from over the river."

Timothy's pager started beeping. Noah's pager went off next.

"What do you think that was? Should we head over there?" Noah asked as he silenced his pager.

"Nee," Isaac said. "You should go with your fire crew. They will be here soon. Everyone else, come with me. Grab shovels, anything that you can use to beat out the flames. We must protect the bridge. Samuel, go to the house and have your mother give us all the towels

and blankets she can spare. If we soak them, we can use them to beat out the flames. Luke, bring every fire extinguisher from the shop." The men all ran to accomplish their tasks and were soon headed toward the footbridge.

Timothy and Noah ran up the lane toward the highway. As soon as they reached the road, a black pickup driven by their English neighbor and fireman, Walter Osborne, skidded to a halt on the pavement. Part of Walter's job was to collect the Amish volunteers and get them to the fire station as quickly as possible. He rolled down the window and shouted, "Get in. Hurry."

"What was it?" Timothy asked as he and Noah climbed into the backseat.

"We aren't sure. The call came from a woman at the school. Some kind of public health worker. All she knew was that the explosion came from the Hanson Farm. The field across from the school is on fire, and the flames are heading toward them."

Walter stepped on the gas. "I've got one more to pick up."

"Who?" Noah asked.

"John Miller." The burly local blacksmith and farrier lived a little more than a mile away.

"Did they evacuate the school?" Timothy asked, meeting Noah's worried gaze.

Walter sent the truck rocketing down the road. "No, the fire has them cut off. The teacher decided it was safer to put the kids in a cold room. You two went to that school. What kind of cold room does it have?"

Perplexed, Timothy glanced again at Noah. His brother shrugged. Suddenly, Timothy realized what the caller might have meant. "Not a cold room, the coal room. It's a cavelike area off to the north side of the school basement. The teacher there, Lillian Keim, is one of the smartest women I know. If anyone can keep the children safe, she can."

He prayed for all the children in peril and for her. He'd been foolish to let a misunderstanding jeopardize their friendship. He wasn't sure he could face himself knowing his last words to her were the ones he'd spoken in anger.

John was standing by his mailbox at the end of his lane. He still wore his big leather apron over his clothes. He didn't bother opening the door of the truck, but vaulted into the bed and pounded on the roof to let Walter know he was on board.

Walter hit the gas again. In a few minutes, they reached a white steel building that sat by itself on a plot of land just off the highway. The wail of a siren blared from a speaker on the roof as one of the two metal garage doors rose. The main fire engine pulled out just as a second pickup loaded with volunteers turned into the parking lot. The men, all Amish farmers and their non-Amish driver, piled out, grabbed their gear and quickly jumped onto the engine. There was none of the usual chatter today. Many of the men had children or grandchildren at the school.

As the others pulled away, Timothy and Noah entered the building and donned their fire gear. The coats, pants and hats were heavy, but if they had to enter a burning building, their fireproof gear would be needed along with their air packs.

The men quickly settled themselves in the station's smaller fire truck and pulled out of the building with Walter in the driver's seat. As they sped down the road toward the river, Timothy saw dozens of men and boys, some in wagons and some on foot and horseback, heading in the same direction.

The first fire truck had been stopped just past the covered bridge by a wall of flames. A burning tree blocked the road, and the woods on either side were heavily involved. Through the dense smoke, Timothy could make out the farmhouse with flames licking out from under the roof. This was a bad one.

Timothy's radio crackled and he heard the fire chief's voice. "Truck Two, get your hoses on that tree. We've got to get it out of our way."

Noah and Timothy leaped off the vehicle to comply. As they unreeled a line, Timothy found himself working side by side with men in fire gear and men in straw hats and suspenders. Every fire call he'd been involved with was the same. Neighbors rushed in to help each other.

With the line stretched, Timothy braced for the pressure surge as the water filled the hose. More men grabbed on behind him, and within a few moments he had a wide spray of water soaking the roadblock. The blaze was quickly extinguished. Timothy dialed back the pressure and kept a light spray covering the two men who rushed forward with chain saws. Someone produced a log chain. The downed tree was hooked to the main fire truck and quickly pulled aside.

The fire commander came up calling orders. "Truck One, get your crew up to the farmhouse. We have injuries there. Truck Two, get to the school. We have a tanker coming from Berlin, but they're twenty minutes out. This road is the only way in and there are ten farms past this point. I've called for aircraft support and we have a chopper coming."

"In this wind?" Walter asked in amazement.

"They know we have a school full of children out there, and the crew is willing to risk it. Let's pray they can get a dump on the school before it's too late."

They couldn't be too late. Timothy had to believe that Lillian and the children were safe.

He jumped back on board the engine. Their smaller vehicle held only five hundred gallons of water. The larger truck held a thousand gallons. Without fire hydrants to hook up to in rural areas, the only water available was what the trucks carried. Timothy looked at the blaze leaping from treetop to treetop and roaring through the cornfield in front of them. They were definitely going to need more water.

Thick smoke made Lillian's eyes water so badly she could barely see the heavy-gauge wire wrapped around the coal chute door handles. The stiff wire had been turned tightly and it refused to unwind. A burning corn leaf swirled in and landed on her arm, scorching her sleeve. She beat out the ember with her palm, but it left a charred hole in her dress.

The roar and crackle of the approaching fire was so loud she wanted to put her hands over her ears and hide. How could this be happening?

She glanced up into the roiling ember-filled smoke sweeping over everything. The firestorm would soon be past, but that didn't mean the building would be spared. The children were safe where they were, but they had to have an escape route if the school caught fire and they couldn't get out that way.

She bent with renewed determination and finally freed the wire, throwing it aside. She noticed blood on her hands, but she didn't take time to look for her injury.

Another blazing ember landed on her arm. She shook it off, stomping it out with her shoe as it started to spread through the grass at her feet. Looking around, she saw several other small fires in the grass. It was then she noticed the barn roof was already on fire. Flames were licking at the front of Debra's car from a cedar bush beside it.

Lillian grabbed the handle of one iron door. She needed to get under cover and out of the smoke. Although the wire was off the handles, the door wouldn't budge. She tried the other one without success. The smoke was choking her even through the cloth over her face. She grew light-headed. Fear and frustration tore a cry of anguish from her throat as she looked to the heavens. "Please, Lord, give me strength."

Walter drove into the dense smoke as quickly as he dared. Noah kept an eye on the right edge of the road while Timothy kept an eye on the left side and they were able to help guide him along. Once they passed out of the woods, the going was easier. The corn, while providing plenty of fuel for the fire, had burned off quickly, leaving only charred smoldering stubble in the field. Embers danced around them in the air. As they drew close to the school, Timothy could see a wall of flames in front of them being pushed by the wind.

"We've got to get in front of this," Walter said through gritted teeth.

Timothy tried to judge how far they were from the school, but he couldn't make out the building through the smoke. "The fire's speed may work in our favor."

"How?" Noah asked.

Walter swung the truck away from a blazing cedar at the edge of the road. "The fire can go around the school so quickly that the structure may not catch fire. A lot of buildings are lost to smoldering embers that ignite after the main fire has passed."

A gust of wind opened a break in the smoke. Timothy caught sight of the school. It was still standing. But for how long?

Please, Lord, keep them safe. Have mercy on the children. On Lillian.

Walter maneuvered the fire truck onto the front lawn of the school. The far end of the front porch was already burning. Noah, Timothy and John were out of the vehicle a second later and pulling the hose into position to soak the main building. Timothy saw that the small stable behind the school was already engulfed in flames. A blazing car sat beside it, but there was nothing they could do. They didn't have enough water. The heavy smoke made visibility almost nil as the wind whipped burning embers all around them.

Once they had a steady stream of water pouring onto the front of the school, Walter tapped Timothy on the shoulder. "Check inside. We don't have much water left."

Sprinting up the steps, he raced inside. The room was empty as he had expected, but he shouted for Lillian at the top of his lungs. He didn't get a reply. The stairs to the basement were at the rear of the building. The wooden steps were old and steep. In the pitch-black cellar, he turned on his lantern and shouted again. This time, he heard voices answering him.

He pulled open the coal room door. "Is everyone okay?"

Several dozen frightened faces stared back at him from the gloom. Lillian wasn't among them. His heart dropped like a rock. "Where's your teacher? Where's Lillian?"

Chapter Six

Timothy moved into the group of children and saw Susan Yoder sitting beside Debra on the floor. She pointed to the back of the room. "Lillian is outside trying to open the doors."

Timothy waded through the rest of the children to reach the back of the coal cellar. His torch illuminated the rungs of an iron ladder set into the stone wall. Overhead, a pair of rusty iron doors remained closed, but he could see light coming in around them. "Lillian, are you there?"

"I'm here." Her muffled voice came from above. "There was a piece of wire around the handles. I got it off, but I still can't lift the door. I think the hinges are rusted shut." A coughing fit followed her words.

He pushed against the door, but it wouldn't budge. Smoke swirled in through the opening. The crackle of the fire outside grew steadily louder.

He grabbed his radio mike. "Can someone get around back and help Lillian pry open the cellar doors on the north side of the building?"

"No can do at the moment," Walter's breathless voice

crackled over the radio. "The porch is on fire and we're out of water. Stay put if you and the kids are safe. Captain says the chopper is on its way."

Without water, all the men had to smother the fire with was the dirt they could dig and shovel on it. He glanced at the children gathered around him. "We're okay. Get Lillian to safety if it gets too close."

Timothy stepped up and wedged his shoulder against the door. If the school went up in flames, this would be the only way out. He shoved and it creaked open a bare inch. Abe and Gabriel came in with a couple of chairs, stood on them and reaching up added their strength to the task. It wasn't enough.

Then suddenly, the old door gave a groan and swung upward. Timothy saw Lillian looking down at him, and his heart started beating again. She was covered in soot but unharmed. He'd never been so glad to see anyone. Beside her stood John Miller. Timothy knew he had the blacksmith's strength to thank for getting the door open.

"Lillian, are you okay?" Timothy asked.

"*Ja*, I'm fine." She started down the ladder.

He climbed down and waited until she reached the floor beside him. Then he pulled her into his arms and hugged her tight. She was safe and it felt so right to hold her in his arms. "I didn't know what to think when I didn't see you with the children."

His radio crackled to life. "We have to pull back. The chopper is here. Prepare for a water dump," Walter shouted.

John shut the doors, plunging them into darkness. Timothy reluctantly let go of Lillian, fighting the urge to gather her into his arms and hold her close again. This wasn't the time or the place.

She took a step back, but her fingers caressed his cheek before she crossed her arms and dropped her gaze to the floor. Something was different between them. He forced his mind back to the crisis at hand. "Are all the children here?"

"*Ja*, they are all here."

He faced her students. "A helicopter is coming to dump a big bucket of water over the school. It's going to make a lot of noise, but we are safe in here. Your teacher picked the best possible place for you."

Lillian gave him a weak smile. He clicked on his radio. "Go ahead."

As soon as he spoke, the sound of the rotor blades roared in overhead. The building trembled in the force of the downdraft, sending dust drifting down from the basement ceiling. A loud swoosh was followed by the sound of water hammering onto the roof. Some gushed in through the old coal chute, soaking the stones at the back of the cave. Less than a minute later, the sound of the helicopter faded into the distance.

Noah came down the basement stairs, his helmet lantern casting a bright arc of light before him. "Is everyone all right?"

Timothy stepped out of the cave and slapped a hand on his brother's shoulder. "We're fine."

Susan stood up. "We have one injury. Debra twisted her ankle coming down the stairs."

"It's not serious. Take care of the children," Debra said from her place on the floor.

"Where's Hannah?" Noah looked over the crowd of children pressing close.

"I'm right here, *Onkel* Noah."

"They are all present and accounted for," Lillian assured him.

Noah's worried face relaxed. "The captain will let a convoy of vehicles in to collect the *kinder* as soon as the tanker from Berlin can put out any spot fires between us and the bridge. *Daed* told him everyone is welcome to go to our house."

"Is it safe for us to stay here?" Lillian asked.

"I think so," Noah said. "The fire has moved on."

"Then I'm staying here with the children until their parents come to collect them or it is safe to let them go home."

Walter came to the top of the stairs. "We have to go, guys. The tanker has set up the portable pond just up the road. We need to refill and get up to the ridge."

As much as Timothy wanted to stay with Lillian and the children, he still had a job to do. There were people, homes, livestock and crops still in danger. He knelt beside Debra. "Can you walk?"

"No, I don't think so."

Noah stepped up beside her. "Let's get you out of this dark cellar so we can take a proper look at your ankle." He lifted her in his arms.

The movement brought tears to her eyes. "How am I going to drive my car like this?"

Noah hesitated, but said, "The fire got your car."

She looked up with wide shocked eyes. "Are you serious?"

He nodded. "I'm afraid so."

"What am I going to do?"

Lillian patted her shoulder. "You're welcome to stay with me until you can sort it out. I'm sure we can find a driver to take you home if you don't have someone who can come and get you."

Timothy knew Lillian well enough to hear the slight hesitation in her voice. Her family wasn't as open to outsiders as his was. Plus, her family's farm was in the path of the fire on the other side of the ridge. She might not have a home to go to tonight. He followed as Noah carried Debra up the stairs, taking care not to jostle her more than necessary. Once he reached the schoolroom, Lillian stepped around him and pulled her chair away from the desk. He placed Debra gently in it.

Lillian turned over the wastebasket, pulled a sweater from the bottom drawer of her desk and folded it for Debra to elevate her foot on.

"*Danki*, Lillian." Noah gently raised Debra's leg. The ankle was swollen and turning dark. He gave her a half-hearted smile. "Nurse, what is your professional opinion? Do you need a doctor? I can call for an ambulance, but it may take a while."

She gently felt the sides and top of her foot. "I think it's just a bad sprain. Ice it, wrap it snugly and keep it elevated would be my professional advice. Leave the ambulance free for someone who truly needs it."

"As you wish. I know Lillian will take good care of you." Noah rose to his feet and headed for the door.

Lillian caught Timothy by the arm. "God go with you and be careful not to make His job more difficult."

He covered her hand with his own, willing her to understand how much her words meant to him. "I'll be careful, and I'm sorry. I hope you know that."

* * *

Lillian smiled tenderly. "Not as sorry as I am. Are we friends again?"

"Always," he whispered. His eyes darkened as he gazed into hers. His grip on her hand tightened, sending her pulse soaring.

Her racing heart was surely due to her close call with the fire and not to the simple touch of his hand. She stared into his eyes and saw deep affection in their depths. Was it only friendship, or something more? She looked away first.

They had both suffered a fright. It was only natural that it made her more attuned to him. She tried to get her jumbled emotions under control and put their relationship back on the proper path. Pulling her hand away, she took a step back. "*Goot*. Now go. Others need you."

"Keep an eye out for any hot spots that might flare up around the building."

"We will."

He nodded once and then hurried out the door. She listened to the sound of his fire engine as it faded in the distance, and swallowed back her tears. Their friendship was mended and he was in God's hands. She couldn't ask for more. She turned her attention to the children gathered at the windows looking out at the charred field and the towering smoke.

Susan looked at Lillian with tears in her eyes. "I can see Mr. Hanson's house is burning. I hope everyone is okay."

"We can pray for them."

"We should do something more. Can we take up a collection for them?" Susan asked hopefully. The Hansons were not members of their Amish community, but they were neighbors in need.

"Of course. When we come back to school on Monday, we will put together a gift basket for them." Lillian knew they might not hold classes on Monday, but she wanted to reassure the children that things would return to normal as soon as possible.

Debra adjusted her foot with a grimace. "I'm sorry to be so much trouble."

"You're not trouble. I need help getting the word out that the children are safe. You have a phone."

Lillian opened the top drawer of her desk. She took out a sheet of paper and handed it to Debra. "Here are some emergency contact phone numbers. They are our local telephone booths, some English neighbors of the children and several local businesses. Leave a message and your number if you get an answering machine."

"It's the least I can do." Debra took the paper from her.

Lillian went to the front of the school and looked out at the porch. The steps and railing were charred, but most of the damage looked superficial. Her barn and Debra's car beside it were little more than smoldering heaps of junk. Shading her eyes, she tried to pick Timothy out from among the firemen strung across the field and woods, but she couldn't tell one from the other.

Three fire engines were parked along the road. One, a tanker truck, was dumping water into a large square yellow holding tank. When the tanker was empty, it made a U-turn and headed back toward the river. A smaller engine crew dropped a fat hose into the tank. A few minutes later, the men pulled it out, jumped back on board their truck and sped toward the fire. A white

SUV with the sheriff's logo on the door stopped on the road. She recognized the officer who got out as Sheriff Nick Bradley. "Is Hannah okay?"

Hannah's mother was Sheriff Bradley's adopted daughter. The little girl ran out onto the porch steps and waved. "I'm fine, Papa Nick."

"Stay with your teacher until your mother gets here," he shouted, and got back into his vehicle. A second later, he took off toward the blaze.

A column of dense black smoke boiled into the sky as tongues of orange flames leaped along the base that stretched the width of the field. It was moving away from the school toward a heavily wooded ridge with frightening speed. Beyond the ridge were ten more farms, Amish and English, including her home. She prayed for the safety of her brother and sister and for the men risking their lives to stop the wildfire.

As she turned to go back inside, she noticed a wisp of smoke rising from beneath the lowest step of the porch. Timothy had told her to watch out for hot spots. She went back into the building. "Abe, bring the fire extinguishers and come with me. I want the first, second and third grades to stay inside with Susan until someone from your family arrives. The rest of you come outside and help me put out any smoldering spots."

The next hour was busy for Lillian. The Bowman women from across the river were the first ones to arrive. Ana Bowman, Rebecca, Samuel's wife, and Hannah's mother, Mary, climbed down from their buggy. Mary scooped Hannah into a fierce hug. Ana watched them with her hands pressed to her chest. "We give praise to the Lord this day. He has kept all our children safe."

Rebecca carried a large quilted bag slung over her shoulder. She placed her free arm around Lillian's shoulders. "I'm so glad you are unharmed. One of the firemen told us your visiting nurse was injured. Where is she?"

Before her marriage to Samuel Bowman, Rebecca had been a lay nurse in the community. She had plenty of experience treating sprains, burns, assorted injuries and illnesses. Lillian pointed toward the school. "She is inside. Her name is Debra Merrick."

"I'll see what I can do for her. It appears they may have the fire under control."

Lillian turned to look north. While there was still smoke rising, it wasn't as dense, and it didn't seem to be moving. She noticed only a few flickering patches of orange flames at the far end of the charred field. "God be praised."

Ana and Mary took Hannah home in the buggy while Rebecca remained with Lillian. By ones and twos, more mothers made their way to the school to collect their children. A half hour later, Lillian saw one of the fire trucks was making its way slowly back. It stopped in front of the school. Silas Mast, the school board president, climbed down along with Joshua and Timothy. Lillian's heart skipped a beat at the sight of Timothy's soot-covered face. He gave her a brief nod before walking around the back of the school. The truck drove on. Carl ran out to meet his father. Abe followed more slowly.

Silas knelt to put his arms around his youngest. "Are you boys all right?"

"It was a mighty exciting day at school, *Daed*," Carl said with a big grin. "Was it fun to ride on the fire truck? I want to do that someday."

"It wasn't as much fun as you might think." Silas rose and spoke to Lillian. "I will take them home now, for I know their mother is worried. Do you need any help here?"

"Not at the moment. We have some smoke damage inside, but I see no reason why we can't reopen the school after things are cleaned. It shouldn't take more than half a day. Joshua, Hannah has already gone home with Mary."

The tension eased on Joshua's sweat- and smoke-stained face. "My wife is a *goot* mother. You have my thanks for keeping the *kinder* safe."

"And my thanks, as well," Silas said. "I will come tomorrow and inspect the building to see what repairs are needed." Taking his boys by the hand, he began walking toward his farm on the far side of the ridge.

Timothy came around to the front of the building. "I don't see any problem spots."

Lillian resisted the urge to gently wipe the grime from his tired face. "My students have been diligently putting out any smoldering places."

Timothy nodded. "I think the danger of flare-ups here has passed, but someone should keep an eye on that car until we can get some flame-retardant spray on it."

Lillian scanned the charred field. "I can't believe you got the blaze stopped before it reached the forest on the ridge."

Timothy rubbed his eyes with his knuckles. "The water drops by the helicopter helped, but we wouldn't have been able to stop it if Davey Mast hadn't had the presence of mind and the courage to cut a firebreak between the burning field and the woods. He saw what was happening and raced to get a tractor and plow from his employer's farm."

"He may have saved every farm beyond the ridge, including his father's," Joshua said.

"I saw his car go past shortly after the explosion, and I wondered why he was driving so fast. Many will be grateful for his quick thinking. Perhaps this will lead to a reconciliation of their family." Lillian was surprised that Silas hadn't mentioned his oldest son's deed to her or the boys.

"I pray you are right, but Silas wouldn't speak to him today," Timothy said.

Silas wasn't forbidden to speak to his son by the rules of shunning. Baptized members of the Amish church couldn't eat at the same table with him, do business with him, accept anything from his hand or ride in his car. Thanking the boy for his quick thinking and courage was certainly permitted.

"Is Rebecca here?" Joshua asked.

"She is inside with the visiting nurse."

"Two nurses, that's great. We have several fellows with minor burns, including my reckless brother. I'll send them here."

She turned to Timothy in alarm. "Are you hurt?"

He shook his head. "I'm the cautious one. Noah is the fellow who rushes in where wiser men fear to go, and this time he paid a small price. Hopefully, it will teach him a lesson."

Lillian pressed a hand to her suddenly tight chest. Drawing a deep breath, she waited until the painful hammering of her heart slowed. She was being foolish. Timothy wasn't hurt. She could see that with her own eyes. "Bring anyone injured here. I will let Rebecca and Debra know they are coming. I have first aid supplies on hand, and I know Rebecca will have brought some with her."

He nodded. "We'll let them know." The two men headed back across the burned field. A short time later, she saw Timothy driving a wagon toward the school. Noah and two other men sat in the bed of the wagon. After pulling to a stop beside her, the men got out and went into the school building all under their own power. Noah was the only one limping heavily.

Lillian stood beside the wagon gazing up at Timothy. "You look worn out."

A half smile lifted the corner of his mouth. "Add hot and dirty to that description, and you'll have me in a nutshell. I may jump in the river on my way home."

At least he could joke about it. "Was it as bad as it looked from here?"

"It was. Do you need anything?"

"We're fine. Most of the children have been picked up already. Was anyone hurt at the Hanson Farm?"

"I heard Mr. Hanson suffered some serious injuries in the explosion. His wife passed out from the smoke in the house, but one of the firemen was able to get her out in time. They have both been taken to the hospital. I'm afraid their home is a total loss."

"How sad. Has anyone notified the family?"

"Sheriff Bradley said they notified a son who lives in Berlin."

"Have you heard how the fire started?"

"I haven't, but the men are saying it looks suspicious. I'm sure our fire chief will get to the bottom of it as soon as he can." Timothy licked his chapped lips and grimaced.

"Let me get you some water. You must be thirsty."

"I am, but I can get my own drink." He jumped down from the wagon and stumbled slightly. She put out a hand against his chest to steady him. A jolt of awareness surged up her arm and sent heat rising into her cheeks. She'd never had this reaction to Timothy before. What was wrong with her today?

Chapter Seven

Timothy looked down at Lillian's small hand pressed against his chest. The delicate hand of a capable woman. He covered her fingers with his own and wondered at the rush of emotion clogging his throat. He was a blessed man to have such a dear friend.

She pulled away from him. "You look ready to fall over, and Rebecca doesn't need another patient. Wait here, and I'll get you some water."

"Bossy, bossy, bossy. Just like the dog in the book." He winked, and she gave him a timid smile.

"It comes from being a teacher. I tell children what to do and I expect them to do it."

He leaned against the wagon wheel and sighed. He was bone-tired. "I shall be a good pupil and do as the teacher says."

"That kind of attitude will move you to the head of the class."

"I'm not at the head of your class already?"

"*Nee*, you are not. I consider you more of a problem child. You have plenty of room for improvement."

He laughed out loud. "I pity the fellows who come

looking to court you. I can imagine you handing out grade cards on their performance as suitors."

Her chin came up. "None have risen above a C-plus. Alas, now you know why I'm still unwed."

It was good to be teased by her and to respond in kind. This was the way their friendship had been for ages. He began to see how rare and special their relationship was, and he cherished it even more. "I'm glad none have made a better grade in your eyes."

She tipped her head to the side. A strange look entered her eyes. "Are you? Why?"

He almost blurted out that he was glad she didn't find anyone else attractive enough to court, because he wished to court her.

Where had that thought come from? The idea was as frightening as the fire had been.

He managed to say, "For the children's sake. You are a fine teacher, and they need you."

For a moment, he thought she looked disappointed, but she quickly smiled. "I do love my job. I can't imagine meeting someone who could make me want to give it up. I'll be right back with that drink. Should I send water out to the other men, too?"

"That would be great." As she walked away, he let out a breath he hadn't realized he was holding.

Courting Lillian was a ridiculous idea, wasn't it? They were friends and had been for years. Yet something had changed today. After fearing for her life and then holding her safe in his arms, he realized his feelings for her had gone beyond those of a friend.

What, if anything, should he do about it?

If he did ask her to walk out with him, what would she say? She was likely to tell him no. And then what?

How could they return to a simple friendship after that? And what if she said yes? Where would that lead?

Lillian returned with a large pail of water, a ladle and several plastic cups. "This is the best I could do."

"It's fine."

Her warm smile and her bright eyes gazing at him made it hard to think straight. He needed to put some distance between them before he said or did something stupid. Like kiss her. She had the most kissable-looking lips. Why hadn't he noticed that before?

He was definitely suffering from some kind of shock.

Taking the water and supplies from her, he put them in the back of the wagon. Then he climbed onto the seat, picked up the reins and put the horses in motion. He glanced over his shoulder to see her watching him with a worried expression on her face. He was overwhelmed with the need to go back and comfort her, but he didn't give in to that desire. Instead, he pushed the horses to a faster trot until they rounded the bend in the road and left the school behind.

If only his mixed up emotions were as easy to out-distance.

Lillian frowned as she watched Timothy drive away. Something about his abrupt departure didn't feel right. It was as if he were running away from her.

Sighing, she dismissed the notion. He needed to get back to his fellow firefighters, and she was reading too much into his behavior. It had been a trying day for everyone. Over the next half hour, she saw many of the volunteers returning home. A few of the men stopped to pick up their children. She kept watching the activity on the road, but she didn't see the Bowman brothers leave.

A short time later, she saw her brother coming across the field toward the school. She wasn't surprised to see him. He would've seen the smoke and come to investigate. He was riding bareback on Goldie, the little Haflinger mare who normally pulled their pony cart. He hadn't wasted time harnessing her.

Lillian waited until he drew close. "I am well, *bruder.*"

"I'm right pleased to see that. Looks like it might have been a near thing."

She glanced around at the blackened grass, burned-out barn and heavily damaged porch. "It was. We were truly blessed that it wasn't any worse."

"Whose car is that?" he asked, staring at the charred wreck that was still smoking.

"It belongs to the visiting nurse."

"I hope she wasn't in it."

"*Nee.* She was inside with us, but she is stranded here until tomorrow. Where is Amanda?"

"I left her with Granny Weaver." The elderly woman wasn't related to Lillian's family, but everyone in the area called her Granny. She lived with her son, and daughter-in-law on a farm a half mile down the road from Lillian's house.

Jeremiah waved a hand toward the charred cornfield. "Old man Hanson should have let me harvest his crop last week. I offered to do it for a fair price and he practically threw me off the place. Shouted at me like I was some kind of thief. Now he's left with nothing, and it serves him right."

"We must not take delight in another man's misfortune. He and his wife were injured."

His eyes filled with remorse. "I didn't know that. Were they badly hurt?"

"Timothy said they were both taken to the hospital. Have you seen him out there?"

"I saw all the Bowman brothers and Isaac, too. Why?"

"Most of the men have left, but I haven't seen Timothy leave yet."

"I'm sure some of the firemen will be watching for flare-ups for the next few hours. Have all the *kinder* gone home?"

"Sophie Hochstetler is still here. She is inside with the nurse. Once her father comes, I will be free to go."

"I saw Wayne helping roll up the hoses with the firemen. He should be along soon."

"There is something more I must tell you. I have invited Debra to stay the night with us."

"Who would that be? One of the children?"

"The owner of that burned-out car."

A quick frown creased his brow. "An *Englischer*? You should not have done that. You know our *daed* would object. We should not mix with outsiders."

"She is a person in need. I could not turn my back on her. Besides, you are hardly in a position to lecture me, *bruder*. I saw you riding in a car with Davey Mast, and he is shunned. What would *Daed* say to that?"

Jeremiah's lips pressed into a tight thin line, but he made no further comment. Lillian didn't expect that he would. "Debra has a badly turned ankle. Her brother will be here first thing tomorrow to take her home. Come and meet her."

"If I must." Jeremiah slid off his horse and followed Lillian to the school. Inside, she introduced him to

Debra. The poor woman looked deathly pale, and she had dark circles of pain under her eyes.

Sophie, one of Lillian's first-grade students, was seated at her desk nearby. The petite blonde girl looked up shyly and spoke in *Deitsch*. "Can I go now? I don't like this lady."

Sophie rarely liked anyone other than her father, but she tolerated her teacher. Lillian nodded. "Your father will be here soon. You can wait for him outside."

The child scampered out the door. Debra gave Jeremiah a weak smile. "Your sister was kind enough to offer to put me up for the night. I hope that's all right. I can surely find somewhere else to stay if it's an imposition."

"Its fine," Jeremiah managed to say in spite of his clenched jaw. "Can you ride a horse bareback?"

Debra's smile vanished and her eyes widened. "I've never been on a horse. I'm not sure today is the best day for my first lesson."

Lillian patted Debra's hand. "Goldie is not a big horse, and she is as tame as they come."

Debra still looked uncertain. "I'm always saying I like to learn new things. I guess I'd better prove it."

"That's the spirit." Lillian slipped her arm around Debra and helped her to her feet. Between Lillian and Jeremiah, they managed to get her outside and onto the docile mare. Wayne Hochstetler arrived to take Sophie with him, so Lillian was able to leave with Debra and Jeremiah. As she walked beside Debra to steady her on the horse, she couldn't keep her gaze away from the firemen still working in the distance. Timothy was out there somewhere.

Now that the rush of emotions and fear had passed,

she had time to examine her feelings more closely. Something had changed today. She had changed.

In her heart, she knew she would never forget how it felt to be held in Timothy's arms. And he must never know that.

Chapter Eight

The following morning, Timothy groaned when he realized he'd made another wrong cut in the board on the bench in front of him. It was his third mistake of the day, and it wasn't even nine o'clock. He wanted to blame his carelessness on being tired after firefighting the previous day, but he knew that wasn't his problem. His problem was Lillian. The way she had touched his cheek had almost been a caress. What did it mean?

"What's the matter?" Joshua asked when he finished drilling a hole in the block of wood he was working on.

"Nothing. Everything. Someone else needs to run this table saw, or we'll be out of good wood by noon." Timothy tossed aside the ruined piece.

"I can take over for you. It's not like you to make mistakes. Don't you feel well?"

Timothy glanced around the shop to see who else might overhear him. None of his other brothers were nearby. "You're married, Joshua. Can I ask you something?"

"Sure, but now you've really got me worried."

"When did you know you wanted to court Mary?

Were you worried she might not want to go out with you?"

"If I said I knew I wanted to court her the minute I laid eyes on her, I'd be lying. And of course, I was afraid she'd turn me down. Her father is the sheriff and I was fresh out of prison, remember?"

"For a crime you didn't commit," Timothy added quickly. Joshua had been wrongly imprisoned after he and Luke were picked up in a drug raid. Joshua had followed Luke to the city to try and convince their brother to give up drugs and return home. He'd spent six months in prison for being in the wrong place at the wrong time. It had been a difficult time for all the family, but in the end, God had shown them mercy. Luke was a reformed man and Joshua had married the love of his life.

Joshua folded his arms over his chest. "Are you planning to court someone?"

Timothy brushed the sawdust from the table. "I'm thinking about it."

"What's holding you back?"

"I'm afraid asking her out will ruin our friendship." It felt good to admit as much to Joshua. If he could talk about his feelings, maybe he could figure out what to do about them.

"Ah, you mean Lillian."

Timothy sent his brother a sidelong glance. "I reckon I shouldn't be surprised that her name sprang to mind."

Joshua laughed. "The two of you have been friends for ages. We all thought you would court her eventually. I'm surprised that you've waited this long. It's easy to see that she cares about you, so what's the problem?"

"She cares for me as a friend."

"Friendship is a fine place to start a courtship. It is a blessed man who calls his best friend his wife."

"It isn't that simple. If I ask her out and she says no, I'm afraid it will make things awkward between us. I don't want to lose Lillian's friendship. If I say nothing, we can stay friends."

"I understand your dilemma, but…can you remain her friend if you say nothing? Love is a hard emotion to hide. Do you love her?"

Timothy pondered his answer before he spoke. "I don't know. Maybe. I want to spend time with her. We have so much in common. I like to make her smile. I like the way I feel when she is near me. Is that love?"

"If you have to ask me that, then you aren't in love. Yet. What you have can grow into true love if that is God's will for the two of you, but many times a young man is simply infatuated with a woman. In love with the idea of being in love. Do you know what I mean?"

"How did *you* know when it was love?"

"I just did. I couldn't bear to be away from her. Look, why don't you ask Emma or Mary to broach the subject with Lillian? Lillian doesn't have to know the inquiry is coming from you."

But she would know. Timothy shook his head. "Forget I said anything. I'm happy being Lillian's friend, and I don't want to ruin that. It's foolish of me to think she might see me as anything else. I'm going to get another board."

"It doesn't sound to me like you're being completely honest with yourself. I still say send another woman to speak to her and see how she feels. Rebecca would do it."

"My wife will do what?" Samuel asked as he carried in a hand-carved headboard ready for sanding and propped it against the wall.

Timothy wasn't ready to share his feelings with his older brother. Joshua had no such reservations. "He wants to court Lillian, but he's afraid she'll say no and then they won't be friends anymore."

"And you want my wife to be your go-between? I don't see why not. It's a good idea."

"What is a good idea?" Noah asked from the open doorway of the workshop. Luke stood beside him.

Timothy stifled a groan. The last thing he wanted was to have all his brothers involved in this conversation.

Samuel slipped his thumbs under his suspenders. "Timothy is going to ask Rebecca to be his go-between with Lillian."

"I wondered when you two bookworms would get together," Luke said with a wink.

"We're not getting together in that way. I was considering the idea, but I'm sorry I brought it up. It wouldn't work. She loves teaching. She has often said she'll never give it up."

Samuel said, "She might feel that way now, but most women want families of their own eventually."

Was Samuel right? Timothy turned the idea over in his mind. Maybe all he needed to do was wait until she was ready to give up teaching. Then he wouldn't be asking her to choose between him and the job she loved. He could be patient.

But what if some other fellow caught her eye before he got up the nerve to ask her out? "Lillian isn't most women. Honestly, can we just forget I said anything?"

"Sure." Joshua exchanged a pointed look with Samuel. Timothy knew his brothers well enough to know they wouldn't let the subject rest. He shouldn't have said anything. He had been shaken up after fearing he'd lost her yesterday. A few days away from her would put everything back into perspective.

The sound of a car pulling to a stop in front of the workshop drew everyone's attention. "Who is it?" Samuel asked.

"It's our fire chief and the sheriff," Noah said from the doorway. "I think the state fire marshal is with them."

Timothy moved to look over Noah's shoulder. "That's him. I met him once at a training exercise."

Their father came out of the house and stood talking to the visitors beside their vehicle. After a few minutes, he turned to his sons and gestured for them to join him. When they reached his side, he spoke in *Deitsch*. "These men are investigating the fire at the Hanson Farm yesterday. They have evidence it was deliberately set. They would like to interview Lillian, her brother and the *Englisch* nurse. The sheriff would like one of us to go along."

"Why talk to Jeremiah? He wasn't at the school." Noah spoke quietly in *Deitsch*, too.

Isaac tipped his head toward the men. "They won't say."

Timothy exchanged a puzzled look with Noah, then spoke in English. "I'll go with you. Lillian's family won't readily speak to outsiders. They may be more comfortable talking to me."

Isaac nodded. "I will send your mother over, too. She is making up some things for the nurse."

As Timothy got in the car with the men, he realized he was thankful for any excuse to see Lillian again, even this one.

* * *

Lillian helped Debra hobble to the blue sofa in the living room. "Would you like a pillow to put your leg up on?"

"That would be great."

Lillian turned to Amanda. "Fetch the pillows from my bed and bring them here."

Amanda nodded and hurried away.

Debra sat down with a sigh. "You've taken wonderful care of me. I don't know how I can ever repay you."

"Repayment isn't necessary. We must do what we can for those in need."

"I'm grateful, I hope you know that. My brother should be here soon. He called when he left our apartment. I noticed that your brother wasn't at breakfast. Was that because of me?"

Amanda returned with a pillow, gave it to Lillian and rushed to the window. "There's a car coming."

"Perhaps that is your brother now." Lillian placed the pillows on the sofa and helped Debra get her foot settled comfortably, but she didn't answer Debra's question. Lillian didn't know where her brother was. He had been gone before she got up.

Amanda rushed to the screen door, eager to greet their visitors. "It's Timothy, sister. He is riding in an *Englisch* car."

"Then I had better go see what he wants. Amanda, stay with Debra, please."

Lillian struggled to hide the happy leap of her heart as Timothy approached the house. She schooled her features into what she hoped looked like mild curiosity. There were three men with him. She recognized his fire chief and Sheriff Bradley but not the other man.

"What brings you out this way, Timothy?" she asked, hoping her voice sounded normal.

He stopped at the front steps. "I came to check on you. You had quite a fright yesterday. Are you all right?"

She chuckled. "We all had quite a fright. I'm fine."

He nodded. "I should have known it would take more than a little smoke to rattle you."

"Don't let my calm teacher face fool you. I was scared out of my wits."

"I have to disagree. You kept your wits about you."

It pleased her that he thought well of her. "I'm sure you didn't come here to heap praise on my head. What can I do for you?"

His smile faded. He turned to the men who stood behind him. "Lillian, this is my fire chief, Eric Swanson. You know Sheriff Bradley, and this gentleman is Rodney George. Rodney is the state fire marshal. He'd like to speak to you. The fire yesterday wasn't an accident. It was deliberately set."

She stared at Mr. George in shock. "Who would do such a thing?"

Tall with a touch of gray at his temples, Rodney George seemed to be a man used to commanding others. "That is what I hope to find out. Is Miss Merrick still here?"

"*Ja*, Debra is inside."

"I'd like to ask the two of you some questions about yesterday?"

"I don't know what help we can be, but do come in." Lillian was curious to hear more details.

After everyone was seated in the living room, Mr. George took a notebook and pen from his pocket. "Did you see anything unusual yesterday? Anything you thought was out of the ordinary?"

Debra held her hands wide. "I was doing hearing assessments all morning. I didn't see anything."

Lillian folded her hands in her lap. "I was inside the school most of the morning. I stepped outside briefly at morning recess to watch the children and again when I smelled smoke. The children didn't mention seeing anything unusual. I certainly didn't."

But she had. She'd seen a car speeding past. Davey Mast's car. Should she mention that? She didn't want to get anyone in trouble.

"What about the car you saw?" Timothy asked, taking away her option to stay silent.

"When I smelled smoke and went outside, I could see smoke rising from the Hanson farmstead. I heard the explosion and saw flames shooting into the sky. It couldn't have been more than a minute later that I saw Davey Mast drive past."

Sheriff Bradley leaned forward with his elbows propped on his knees. "Are you positive the driver was Davey Mast?"

"I can't say for certain that Davey was driving, but I'm pretty sure it was his car. We saw it the day before. Abe Mast is one of my scholars, one of my students. He said the car belonged to his brother Davey. Has anyone talked to Davey? Perhaps he saw something."

"I have plans to interview him later today." Mr. George tapped his pen against the side of his notebook. "You said we. Who else was with you when you saw Davey's car?"

"All of my students and Timothy the first time I saw it."

"I was giving a fire safety talk at the school," Timothy explained.

Mr. George's sharp gaze came back to Lillian. "And the day of the fire?"

"Susan Yoder was with me. She may have seen the car."

Mr. George nodded, took a few notes and then looked up. "Do you know anyone with a grudge against Mr. Hanson?"

Lillian shook her head. "He isn't a friendly fellow. He and his wife keep to themselves. It's said they don't care much for the Amish."

Mr. George leaned back in his chair. "Why is that?"

Lillian looked at Timothy. "I don't know. Do you?"

"My father said it was something about a land dispute years ago. That's all I know."

"His wife mentioned that he had an argument with an Amish fellow a few days ago. Any idea who that might have been?" the sheriff asked.

Surely he didn't mean her brother. Lillian tried to remember exactly what Jeremiah had said about his conversation with Mr. Hanson. She was certain he hadn't mentioned having an argument, but he did say the man yelled at him. Even if her brother had been arguing with Mr. Hanson, Jeremiah would never retaliate in such a manner. It was unthinkable.

She raised her chin as she met Mr. George's steady gaze. "We Amish go to great lengths to avoid confrontations of any kind. We forgive whoever did this and pray for his soul."

"It's my job to ask questions. I meant no disrespect. Is your brother about?"

"I'm not sure where he is right now. Our parents are

away, and Jeremiah is taking care of my father's business."

"Have you noticed any strangers in the area? Anyone acting suspiciously?" the sheriff asked.

Lillian looked toward her guest. "Miss Merrick is the only stranger I've seen recently."

"There are very few people stranger than I am," Debra said glibly.

Mr. George's face remained stern. "Did you set fire to Mr. Hanson's tractor shed?"

Debra's grin faded. "No. I don't even know the man. My cooking has set off the smoke alarm in my apartment a few times, but that's as close as I've come to being a firebug."

Captain Swanson's cell phone rang. As he answered it, Sheriff Bradley's rang, too. Both men had short, terse conversations and hung up. The captain rose to his feet. "Mr. George, we need to get back to the station house. We have another fire."

Chapter Nine

Timothy shot to his feet when he realized he might be needed with his crew. "Luke has the pager today, but I can come with you."

His captain shook his head. "That won't be necessary. It's a hayfield. No structures involved. One crew should be able to handle it. Thankfully, we don't have the wind today that we had yesterday. I'll drop you off at your place on my way back to the station."

"There's no need. I can walk from here. Whose hayfield is it?"

"Bishop Beachy's." The captain was already moving toward the door.

"Was it deliberately set?" Lillian asked, but he was out the door and didn't answer her.

The fire marshal pulled a business card from his shirt pocket and gave it to Lillian. "Thank you for your time, Miss Keim. If you think of anything else, please get in touch with Captain Swanson. He will know how to contact me. I will get to the bottom of this, I promise. It doesn't matter to me if the arsonist is Amish or not."

Lillian followed them out the door. Timothy joined

her on the porch. As the men drove away, she turned to him with a deeply worried expression on her face. "Your captain doesn't think the fire was started by one of us, does he?"

"By an Amish? *Nee*, I don't think so, but I understand why he has to be sure. Mrs. Hanson is telling people an Amish fellow started it."

"She must be mistaken. I don't know anyone who would endanger the *kinder* so callously."

"I agree. From what I learned on the way over here, the fire was started inside the shed where Mr. Hanson kept his farm equipment. It could be someone wanted to destroy his new tractor. They didn't know or didn't care that he kept extra fuel in there, as well. The resulting explosion along with the high winds allowed the fire to get out of hand quickly."

"I pray whoever started the blaze will see how foolish he was, and I pray he turns to God for forgiveness."

"As do I." He wanted to put his arm around her and pull her close. He wanted to erase the worry he saw in her eyes.

She smiled at him. "Would you like some coffee? There is still some on the stove."

"Not this morning. I have to get back to work. I came along so that you wouldn't feel uncomfortable talking to outsiders."

"I appreciate that you were here."

"That's what friends do," he said softly.

Lillian managed a small smile at Timothy words. "*Ja*, that is what friends do."

Why was it that she suddenly wished they were more than friends? Would he ever see her in any other light?

A red low-slung sports car turned off the highway and drove slowly into the yard. It stopped next to the gate, and a young man rolled down his window. "I'm not sure I'm at the right house. Is Debra Merrick here?"

Lillian was glad of the interruption. "She is, and you must be her brother. I'm Lillian and this is my neighbor Timothy Bowman. Do come in. Debra is inside."

"I'm glad I have the right place. Thanks for taking care of my sister, Miss Keim. I will certainly pay you for your trouble." He opened the car door. It was then Lillian saw how short he was. He needed a thick pad to raise him high enough in the seat to see over the steering wheel.

Timothy moved closer to inspect the vehicle. "Nice car. Electric?"

"Hybrid."

"I see you've made some modifications."

Brandon slipped out of his seat and climbed down. "The foot pedals are the only thing that didn't come standard. They are detachable if my sister or someone of regular height needs to drive."

"No kidding? How do they hook on?" Timothy squatted next to the open door to peer in.

Brandon was soon showing him how to disassemble the pedals. Lillian knew Timothy's curious nature would have him checking under the hood before long. He always wanted to know how things worked. "I'm going to tell Debra you're here."

"We will be right in," Brandon said.

"I won't hold my breath," she answered with a chuckle and walked away.

"What did she mean by that?" Brandon asked.

Timothy grinned. "It means that she knows me pretty

well. Well enough to know I could spend the rest of the morning looking over your vehicle to see how it works."

"Perhaps we should save this for another day. I would hate for my sister to think I'm ignoring her in her hour of need."

"That would be wise."

The small man walked with a rapid rolling gait toward the house, and Timothy followed him. Before they reached the porch, Timothy heard the clip-clop of horses' hooves. A buggy turned off the highway into the lane and came to a stop in front of the house. Timothy's mother stepped down from the driver's seat. Mary and Hannah got out on the other side. Emma and Rebecca got out of the backseat. All of them carried large baskets.

Timothy made the introductions and took his mother's burden from her. He caught a whiff of cinnamon and baked apples. "What have we here?"

"Just a little something for Debra so she doesn't have to cook until her ankle is better."

"She should stay off her foot for at least a week," Rebecca added.

Hannah peeked around her mother's skirt at Brandon. "Are you a little person like Amanda?"

"I am," he said with a smile.

"Aren't you going to get any taller?"

"Nope, God made me exactly tall enough. Do you know how I can tell?"

Hannah shook her head. He grinned and pointed down. "Because my feet reach all the way to the ground."

Hannah looked up at her mother. "He's silly."

"Not as silly as you. I see Amanda at the window. Take her some of the cookies you helped me bake."

Timothy held the screen door open for Hannah and for the women to go inside ahead of him. Rebecca, the last one in line, stopped and whispered in his ear, "I will see which way the wind blows for you. Samuel warned me to be discreet."

Timothy stifled a moan. "Don't say anything. Please. I'm begging you."

She patted his arm. "Your secret is safe with me."

When a hole didn't open up in the floor to swallow him, he reluctantly followed Rebecca inside.

Brandon quickly crossed the room to hug Debra. "You and your adventures. What will you be up to next, sis?"

She returned his embrace. "There's no telling, but as long as I have you to race to my rescue, I'm just going to keep on having them. Thank you for coming so quickly." She sat up a little straighter, wincing as she moved her foot. He took a seat in the wingback chair opposite her.

"I'm just sorry I couldn't get here yesterday. I drove past the school and took some pictures of your car so you can file an insurance claim. I'm sure an adjuster will need to come out and verify the VIN before they pay up. In the meantime, I've arranged to get you a loaner car so you aren't stranded at the apartment."

"Thanks. You're a good brother."

"That's because you're my favorite sister."

"Ha! I'm your only sister."

"Thankfully. Growing up with you around stunted my growth. I'd never have survived another sister."

"You would have ended up two foot four instead of four foot two." They shared a grin that told Timothy it was a long-standing family joke.

Perched on a chair in the corner where he could see into the kitchen, Timothy watched his mother, Mary,

Emma and Rebecca as they took over Lillian's kitchen with practiced ease. Lillian and Rebecca were working side by side. He couldn't tell if Rebecca was posing the question to Lillian or not. He hoped she wouldn't find the opportunity, but knowing Rebecca, that was a slim hope at best.

The women soon had coffee cake dished up on plates and glasses filled with iced tea. Lillian carried them into the room and began to pass them out as she introduced everyone. Hannah and Amanda sat quietly at the table, but Timothy could see the girl's interest in Debra's brother.

Brandon accepted a plate and looked at Timothy. "I hope the owner of the cornfield across from the school has crop insurance."

"I'm not sure if he does or not. The Amish do not carry insurance, but Mr. Hanson isn't Amish."

"It's a shame if he didn't have it. I wonder if he would be interested in leasing that acreage to my university. I'm developing a new corn variety and I'm looking for test plots. His field location is excellent. With it burned off, I won't have to deal with any harmful insects, weeds or disease that could be left over in the crop residue. It would make planting there more cost-effective for me. I'd even be willing to put in a cover crop to improve the soil until next spring."

"What kind of cover crop?" Timothy asked.

"I'm a fan of daikon radishes. Their thick roots really improve soil compaction."

Timothy glanced at Lillian and they both started laughing. She held her nose. "I do not want that awful smell surrounding my school for the entire winter."

Brandon blushed bright red. "I'm sorry. I didn't consider that. The smell can be overpowering."

Timothy chuckled. "Our fire station was called out twice this past winter for a suspected natural gas pipeline leak. It turned out to be the oil radishes in a field across the river from here."

Lillian's chin came up as she leveled a stern look at him. "I had never smelled them before. I had no way of knowing it wasn't a gas leak. I was being civic-minded. There is a pipeline over there."

It was fun to stir that spark of indignation in her eyes. Timothy couldn't help grinning. "True. It was better to be safe than sorry. Why not plant Austrian winter peas as a cover, Brandon?"

"A good choice. I see you have kept up on the advances in no-till farming and soil conservation."

"We read the farm journals," Timothy admitted, trying not to sound offended. Why did people automatically assume that because they used horses they were backward farmers? When a man could only farm so much ground, he had to get the most out of each acre.

"If Mr. Hanson would be willing to lease his ground, I'd write up a lease agreement and get him a check by the end of next week."

Rebecca took a seat beside Debra. "Mr. Hanson is still in the hospital. I'm not sure how you would get hold of Mrs. Hanson. I heard she was staying with one of her sons."

"I'll ask Nick to find out where she is staying," Mary said as she handed Timothy a plate. "Nick Bradley is the sheriff. He and his wife are my adoptive parents," she explained for Debra and Brandon's benefit.

Brandon pulled a business card from his pocket and

handed it to her. "My cell phone number is on this. Tell Sheriff Bradley he can call me anytime. Day or night."

"What type of corn are you developing?" Timothy asked.

Debra laughed and held up her hand. "Don't get him started. He will talk about kernel size, drought tolerance and disease resistance all day. This is wonderful coffee cake. I must have the recipe. Which one of you made it?"

"That would be me," his mother said, blushing. "I have put the recipe in the thank-you basket I fixed for you. We know you won't be able to be up and around cooking for a few days, so we put together a few things for you. Consider them a small token of our thanks for helping take care of our *kinder*."

Debra pressed a hand to her chest. "I don't know what to say. Thank you. Lillian did so much more than I did. You should give them to her. I can't accept them."

"But my ankle is fine," Lillian said.

Brandon shook his fork at Debra. "I've seen the inside of your kitchen. I don't want you living on frozen pizza for a week or better. Be thankful and be silent."

In spite of Debra's warning, Timothy wanted to hear more about Brandon's work. "What traits are you trying to produce in your new variety? Is it hard to get the results you want?"

"I warned you." Debra gave her empty plate to Lillian. "Go ahead, Brandon. It's not often you find someone who actually wants to hear about your work."

"You're not in a hurry to get home, are you?" he asked hopefully.

"No, I have enjoyed wearing these same smoky-smelling clothes for two days."

"Okay. Come out to my car, Timothy. I have some of

my research data on my laptop. Producing hybrid seed corn isn't difficult, but it is labor-intensive. It requires an understanding of basic genetics, a lot of planning and attention to details, but you don't have to be a genetic engineer to grow your own hybrid seed. To do it yourself, you only need to copy what the seed companies do anyway. Select parent plants with the qualities you want, properly isolate the field to avoid pollen contamination from other sources, manage the seed fields and finally, you have to carefully harvest and store the seed produced."

Timothy couldn't decide if Brandon didn't hear the sarcasm in his sister's voice or if he simply decided to ignore it. "Perhaps another time. I know my father would be interested in your research. We raise a lot of corn for animal feed, but we also sell small amounts of seed corn to other farmers in the area. However, your sister has been through an ordeal and needs your attention today."

"Yes, I would like to go home, brother," Debra said, giving Brandon a no-more-nonsense-from-you look.

Brandon shot his sister a wry smile. "Sorry, you know how I get."

"I do, but I love you anyway."

He rose to his feet. "Timothy, I would like to take a look at your farming operation. Is it all by horse-drawn equipment?"

"For the most part, but we do use some gas-powered machinery we have adapted to be pulled by our horses. You are welcome to stop by anytime. I know your sister was interested in seeing our furniture shop and she wanted to take a look around my mother's gift shop, too, when her foot has healed."

Brandon looked impressed. "Seed corn, furniture, gift shop. It sounds as if your family has diversified past the simple farming I've always associated with the Amish."

"I have four brothers. Two are married and have started families of their own. One more will marry in November. There is only so much land to farm. Not nearly enough to support all of us. My parents were wise enough to seek other ways to provide for their family now and in the future."

"If you think they are only farmers and quilters, you don't know the Amish," Debra said with a wink for Timothy. She sobered and glanced at Lillian. "That was too forward, wasn't it? I told you I wasn't good at meek and humble."

"You are trying, and that is the first step to overcoming any problem," Lillian said gently, holding back a smile.

Debra held out her hand to her brother. "I think I have imposed on this family long enough. Lillian, I'll be back to finish the hearing tests at your school as soon as I am able."

Debra struggled to her feet with his help. Mary and Rebecca were beside her in an instant to help her out to her brother's car. Timothy hung back with his mother, Emma and Lillian.

Brandon looked into the kitchen, where Amanda and Hannah were still sitting. He spoke quietly to Lillian. "My wife and I have adopted two children, both little people, and my daughter looks to be about your sister's age. I would love to meet her."

Had her father been at home, Timothy doubted that

he would have permitted it, but Lillian surprised him when she said, "Of course."

She gestured to Amanda. "*Koom* here, *shveshtah*."

Amanda slipped down from her chair and came slowly into the room. She hid her face in Lillian's skirt. Lillian patted her on the head and looked at Brandon. "My sister doesn't speak English yet. I will translate for you."

"Tell your sister I'm delighted to meet another little person. She is a very pretty little girl."

Lillian relayed the message. Amanda gave him a shy smile, but whispered something to Lillian, making her chuckle. "*Ja,* you are."

"What did she say?" Brandon asked.

"She said she is plain, isn't she? I assured her that she is."

He looked troubled. "I don't understand."

Emma said, "We do not place value on beauty, only on faithfulness to God, commitment to each other and hard work. To tell a girl she is pretty can lead to *gross feelich*, a big feeling. Another way of saying pride."

"I see. Then please ask her if she is an obedient child and minds her sister."

Lillian smiled and translated his question.

Amanda nodded vigorously.

He grinned. "Good. And now I must go and mind my sister or she'll read me the riot act all the way home. Thank you again for taking care of her, Lillian. It was nice meeting all of you. Timothy, I look forward to visiting your farm."

As his mother and Emma went outside with Brandon, Lillian leaned close and whispered in Timothy's ear, "I need to talk to you."

His heart missed a beat. Had Rebecca spoken even after he begged her not to? "Okay. What's up?"

"Later, when we can be alone. Meet me down by the school after supper." She waved goodbye to Brandon and Debra and then went back inside.

He couldn't tell from her tone or her expression if this meeting was going to be a good thing or not.

Chapter Ten

Lillian sat on one of the chairs she had placed on the school porch and waited nervously for Timothy to arrive. Amanda was happily playing on the swings with two of her dolls. Lillian had hoped Jeremiah would watch their sister this evening, but he hadn't come home. She was starting to worry about him.

Silas had made good on his promise to see about repairs to the school. He and several other men had been finishing the inspection when she and Amanda arrived. It was his feeling that the essential repairs could all be done on Monday, and she agreed.

The sun was hanging low in the sky, turning the bellies of the few clouds gold and red. A light breeze had replaced yesterday's wild wind. It stirred the ashes in the field and carried the smoky smell to her. She marveled once again how merciful God had been toward her and all the children in her charge.

Timothy came walking along the road with long, easy strides. He had his straw hat pulled low on his brow and his hands in his pockets.

"You look deep in thought," she called out.

He paused and looked up, seemingly surprised to see her. He gave her a sheepish grin. "I was."

"Care to share?"

"Not really. What did you need to see me about?" He approached the school and took a seat beside her.

She checked to make sure Amanda couldn't overhear them, and then clasped her hands around her knees. "I'm not sure how to say this, but my brother may have been the Amish man who had an argument with Mr. Hanson. I didn't want to say anything in front of the fire marshal or sheriff, but I had to tell someone."

Her family had always been law-abiding, but distrust of *Englisch* public officials was deeply ingrained and had often been reinforced by her father. Everyone knew that Timothy's brother Joshua had been wrongly imprisoned by the *Englisch* law. It could happen to anyone. The Amish were pacifists and did not resist persecution by outsiders.

Timothy leaned close. "I understand your feelings and I'm glad you know you can talk to me."

"Jeremiah would never try to destroy someone's property. Never. I know he wouldn't. You believe that, don't you?"

"Of course I do. Have you asked him about it?"

She rubbed her palms against each other and wound her fingers tightly together. "He hasn't been home since yesterday. He was upset about Debra staying with us. He said I shouldn't have offered, that Father wouldn't have allowed it. I don't know how to ask him about the argument without sounding as if I'm accusing him of something. Have you learned anything else about the fire?"

He shook his head. "Not about the Hanson fire, but

the fire in Bishop Beachy's hayfield was also deliberately set. The field was a total loss."

"Oh, my! How awful for the bishop, and how awful to think there is an arsonist among us." She wrapped her arms around herself. She wanted to lean against Timothy and draw comfort from his presence, but she knew that wouldn't be modest behavior. "Do the *Englisch* officials have any suspects?"

"Not that they are saying, but I know they recovered some evidence. Luke found a small propane torch that had been left beside a haystack. Luke said it was the same kind Emma sells in her hardware store."

"That doesn't mean it was left by an Amish fellow. Anyone can buy a canister of propane. The *Englisch* use propane, too."

"Burning the bishop's crop makes it seem like someone has a grudge against him. He has very little contact with outsiders. On the other hand, there have been several people shunned by him in the past year."

"Shunned by all of us, not just the bishop. I don't want to believe anyone I know would do such a thing deliberately. It may sound awful, but I hope it turns out to be some *Englisch* vagrant, or wild teenagers, someone I don't know."

"I know what you mean. I feel the same way."

"I'm sure a collection is being taken up to cover the cost of Bishop Beachy's loss."

"*Daed* and *Onkel* Vincent are seeing to it."

The way church members rallied around one of their own in times of trouble was one more wonderful thing about being Amish.

"Was that all you wanted to talk to me about?" Timothy asked, giving her an odd look and then quickly looking away.

If he were one of her students, she would suspect he had done something that he shouldn't. "Were you expecting me to ask about something else?"

"*Nee*, I wasn't. What did you think of Debra's brother today?"

His question seemed forced, as if he were trying deliberately to change the subject. "Brandon seems like a nice fellow. He certainly likes to talk about corn."

Timothy chuckled. "That he does, but he caught my interest. I would like to learn more about producing a hybrid seed. The seed companies charge a premium for hybrid corn. It might be worthwhile to study the technique that Brandon uses so we could produce our own improved varieties."

"He presents it as a practical science, and I'm sure many farmers would be interested in hearing what he has to say." She leaned back against the riser behind her.

"And learning what he has to teach."

"Wouldn't it be wonderful if people like Brandon could present classes to our children?"

He drew back. "You mean invite outsiders into your classroom?"

"*Nee*, but you know what I'm trying to say. Have those people with special knowledge to pass on come in and teach. I sometimes struggle with teaching the older children science and arithmetic. Sometimes I am afraid I'm cheating my students by not giving them a proper education."

"You are a fine teacher. You should not doubt yourself. You have a God-given talent."

"For teaching reading and writing to the little children, but I know I lack the ability to hold the attention of the older ones."

"Just because Abe Mast is a class cutup doesn't mean you are a poor teacher."

"Just inadequate to that challenge."

Timothy slipped his arm around her shoulders and gave her a shake. "Enough with feeling sorry for yourself. I know you, and if there is a way to do something better, you will find it. You haven't been teaching that long. Experience counts."

She managed a smile. "You're right. I will find a better way even if it takes me years. Thanks for your confidence in my ability."

"That's what friends are for."

She gave in and leaned her head against him. "Thank you for being my friend."

She wouldn't allow her feelings for him to get out of hand. Friendship was enough even if there were times when she wished she could offer him more. It wouldn't be fair to him. She wasn't meant to be a wife and a mother.

Timothy breathed in the scent of Lillian. She smelled clean, like spring, like the flowers in his mother's garden early in the morning. It could be the shampoo she used or the soap she washed her clothes with, but whatever it was, he liked it. He wanted to go on holding her, but she soon moved away and he had to let her go. He clasped his hands together to keep from reaching for her again. After having assured her he was a friend, he couldn't start acting like a courting fellow.

He needed to turn his mind to other things. Looking down the south side of the building at the charred and smoke-stained wooden siding that had taken the brunt of the fire's heat, he gestured toward it. "The school needs a coat or two of paint yet."

"It does. We will also need a horse barn and corral before the weather turns cold. The children and I will clean up the school Monday morning and paint this porch if the weather is nice."

"I'll supply the paint and brushes and a ladder or two."

"As always, your help is appreciated." She smiled at him, and his heart missed a beat. If he moved a fraction closer, he could kiss her. Would she let him?

The sound of a car slowing down made them glance toward the road. Davey Mast's red car rolled to a stop beside the school. He stepped out and gave a low whistle. "You sure dodged a bullet, Teacher Lillian."

Dressed in blue jeans and a plaid shirt and wearing a tan cowboy hat over his blond hair, Davey could have passed for an *Englisch* man until he spoke. His Pennsylvania *Deitsch* accent was still strong. Lillian rose to her feet. "It was a near thing. God was good to spare us."

"Jeremiah told me you had a lot to do with saving the school by having the kids wet down the building. Quick thinking."

"You have spoken to Jeremiah today?" she asked.

"In passing. I saw him at the hardware store about an hour ago. No need to threaten him with shunning for spending time with a man under the *bann*."

"You would be welcomed back into our church if you gave up your car and repented breaking your vows to live Amish," Timothy said, still sitting on the steps. "Your own quick thinking spared many homes and farms and we are grateful."

"Not everyone was grateful."

From his sour tone, Timothy guessed Davey was referring to his father. "Many people saw what you did and knew it took courage."

"I had a hot time to be sure. That scorching wind almost turned me into toast. I didn't factor the fire's speed into my equation when I got on that tractor. I might have thought twice about doing it and let the rest of the valley go up in smoke."

"I am glad you didn't. It shows you have a good heart," Lillian said quietly.

He touched the brim of his hat. "That's me. Good-hearted Davey. I'll let you two lovebirds get back to making out on the school steps. Better be careful, Teacher. I happen to know the school board president would take a dim view of such behavior."

"Oh, we weren't…we aren't…" Lillian sputtered to a stop as Davey gave a loud hoot of laughter.

Timothy caught her hand. "Don't mind him. He likes to stir up trouble. He always has."

"Tell your brother Luke I sure miss partying with him. He knew how to have a good time. It's a shame he's been brainwashed back into the fold. You might mention there's a barn party over at Abram Coblentz's farm tonight and he's welcome. I'll have the good stuff there." With that parting shot, Davey got back in his car and roared away.

Lillian crossed her arms over her chest. "Just when I was starting to feel sorry for him. Do you think he will tell his father about us?"

Timothy laid a hand on her shoulder. "*Nee*, it was an empty threat, and I doubt Silas would believe such a thing of you. But it is getting late and we should both be getting home."

"You're right. What is your family doing tomorrow?"

It was an off Sunday, the Sunday without the biweekly church meeting. Most families used the day to go visiting or have family over, and his was no exception. "We are going to visit my mother's brother over by Longford. Everyone except Samuel and Rebecca. She has asked John Miller and his mother over. They were her in-laws before she married Samuel, and they remain close."

"I remember her first husband. He was a *goot* man. It was a shame he died so young, but God had a plan for the wife he left behind."

"He did, and my brother Samuel is grateful he was part of that plan. What about you?"

"We have been invited to visit our aunt and uncle in Hope Springs. Father had arranged for a driver to take us before he and *Mamm* had to leave to be with father's uncle. I almost decided to cancel the trip after the fire, but I think Amanda needs to be with her cousins. Two of them are little people, and she has so much fun when they get together."

"It will be good for you to get away, too. Have you heard from your parents?"

"Not yet. I expect a letter by Monday letting me know how things stand. I pray they were able to make it before my great-uncle passed. When we first moved to Wisconsin, it was so my father could work with my uncle in his construction business. They had a falling-out several years later, and that was the reason we moved back here. I pray they were able to make amends. I know my father deeply regretted the split."

"Will you be traveling there for the funeral?"

"*Nee*, it is too far, and I would not want to miss that much school. I would fall even further behind in my homework. I have not had a chance to open the book you gave me. Would you like it back?"

"Keep it as a token of my friendship and read it when you have the chance. I know you'll enjoy it. What time should I show up with the paint?"

"First thing Monday morning."

"Until then." He tipped his hat and started walking away. She watched him until he reached the bend in the road. He turned round and lifted a hand in a brief wave. She resisted the urge to call him back, to spend a little more time in his company. Instead, she waved, too. When he was out of sight, she went to get Amanda and together they started for home.

When she reached the house, she saw Jeremiah sitting on the bench on the front porch. His horse and buggy waited at the gate. He rose to his feet. "Where have you been?"

"I went to the school to check on the repairs that were done today. Where have you been?"

"Visiting a friend."

His brusque reply annoyed her. "Amanda, go in and start getting ready for bed." When her sister went into the house, Lillian rounded on Jeremiah. "Does this friend have a name?"

He strode past her. "I'm going out. Don't wait up for me."

"The driver taking us to Hope Springs will be here tomorrow at eight o'clock."

"I won't be going with you." He climbed into his buggy.

She followed him and put a hand on the buggy door. "Jeremiah, what is going on?"

"I'm sick of work, work, work. I'm going to go have a little fun."

"With Davey Mast? I saw him tonight and he told me there is going to be a barn party at Abram Coblentz's farm."

"You're welcome to come along. You might enjoy letting your hair down for once in your life."

"I had my *rumspringa*, and I took my vows. I hold to them. You have been baptized, too. You should put your running around years behind you before you find yourself in serious trouble."

"In serious trouble with who? Our stuffy old bishop? He won't be spying on anyone tonight," he said with a chuckle.

"What's that supposed to mean?"

"Didn't you hear? There was a fire in his hayfield."

"I did hear. The sheriff and the fire marshal were here today asking questions about the fire at the Hanson Farm when they got the call."

Her brother's grin disappeared, replaced by a deep scowl. "What kind of questions?"

"Mrs. Hanson told the sheriff an Amish man had an argument with her husband the day before the fire. They asked if I knew who that Amish man might be."

"What did you tell them?"

"Nothing. Even if you were the one Mr. Hanson had an argument with, I know you had nothing to do with the fire."

"I appreciate your blind loyalty, sister."

"It isn't blind. I know you as well as I know myself."

"I have to get going. I don't want to miss my ride."

"I wish you wouldn't go."

"I have to. It's a goodbye party for Davey Mast. He's moving away."

"Where is he going?"

"Philadelphia. Who knows when I'll see him again? Give Aunt Sarah and Uncle Howard my love and tell Cousin Ben he still owes me ten dollars." He snapped the reins to set the horse in motion and Lillian was forced to move aside.

She was more troubled than she cared to admit. She spent a long time on her knees praying for her brother that night and for Davey Mast. When she finally slipped beneath the pink-and-white-stitched quilt, her thoughts turned to Timothy. Alone in her room she faced her growing feelings for him and wrestled with what to do about them.

Her common sense said she needed to spend less time in his company and put some emotional distance between them. Her heart said otherwise. The memory of being held in his arms sent a pulse of warmth across her skin.

She pressed her hands over her eyes. This was completely ridiculous. They were friends and they would stay friends. She would recover from this emotional upheaval caused by her fright during the fire in a week or two. Until then, she would make sure she wasn't alone with him again. She would keep her guard up when he was near.

Turning over on her side, she pulled the quilt to her chin, determined to fall asleep. She did, only to dream of Timothy's bright smile and easy laughter. She woke with a vague feeling of happiness but quickly came to her senses.

Throwing the quilt back, she got out of bed determined not to see Timothy or dream about him again.

Chapter Eleven

Early Monday morning, a gallon of white paint in one hand and a stepladder balanced on his shoulder, Timothy headed across the covered bridge toward the school. Behind him came Joshua and Mary with Emma and Luke. Hannah skipped along ahead of them. The adults all carried supplies to help clean and paint the schoolhouse. While Timothy had enjoyed visiting with his relatives the day before, he was eager to see Lillian again. It was a little frightening how much he had missed her.

"What's the rush, *bruder*?" Luke called out.

Timothy realized he was several long strides ahead of the group. He stopped and waited for them to catch up. "I'm not in a rush. You just like to dawdle, Luke. The sooner we get started, the sooner we will be finished."

"And the sooner you can spend more time with that certain someone." Luke winked as he walked past.

Timothy turned his face to the sky, closed his eyes and shook his head. He never should have mentioned anything about Lillian to his irreverent brother.

"Don't tease him, Luke," Emma warned, giving her fiancé a stern look.

Timothy sent her a grateful look. At least he had someone on his side. "*Danki*, Emma."

"You won't let me have any fun," Luke said with an exaggerated pout.

She took his hand. "If you don't behave yourself, you will be walking home alone. Is that what you want?"

"I'll behave. I promise." Luke pressed her hand to his lips.

"Not much chance of that," Joshua called out. "*Mamm* will tell you Luke hasn't behaved since he was two years old."

"That's not so. I was a good kid. I got blamed for a lot of things you and Timothy did."

"Like what?" Timothy asked.

Luke stopped in front of Joshua. "Like the time the milk cows broke through the fence and scattered all over creation because someone threw firecrackers under their feet. Remember that, little *bruder*?"

Joshua stabbed his finger into Luke's chest. "Who gave me the firecrackers, lit them for me and told me where to toss them? You were older, and you should have known better."

Timothy laughed. "I believe those were *Daed*'s exact words when he settled on your punishment, Luke."

He grimaced. "And I still hate okra to this day. I had to harvest the biggest patch *Mamm* ever planted. Okra has little spines all over the leaves and stems. They stuck in my skin and itched for days."

"You are supposed to wear gloves and heavy long sleeves," Mary said.

"*Mamm* told me that, but I was in a hurry to get done and get to a softball game. Big mistake."

Hannah had stopped up the road waiting for them. "Hurry up. I don't want to be late to school."

"Go ahead without us, *liebchen*," her father said.

She took off at a run. Timothy knew exactly how she felt. He wanted to run ahead, too.

The school was already a beehive of activity by the time they arrived. Three men on ladders were scraping away the damaged paint on the south side. Lillian was standing on a smaller stepladder between two of them washing a window. Just seeing her made Timothy's morning brighter.

Emma and Mary went inside with their cleaning supplies. Luke and Joshua headed to check out the burned-out car that still sat beside what was left of the horse barn.

Timothy approached Lillian and stopped beside her. "*Guder mariye*. Timothy Bowman reporting for his assignment, Teacher Lillian."

"Good morning." She wiped her brow on her sleeve. She didn't smile the way she always smiled at him. She didn't even look at him.

She returned to scrubbing the glass without even a glance in his direction. "Silas is in charge of the men. Check with him. I believe he's by the old barn."

"Are you okay?" he asked. Something didn't feel right.

"I'm fine. Just busy." She kept scrubbing at a spot near the top of the window.

"Okay, I'll get to work." He walked away but glanced back once. She didn't look his way. What had happened to upset her between the time they parted on Saturday and this morning?

"Timothy, why don't you and your brothers start painting the porch?" Silas said, gesturing in the direction.

Timothy nodded and joined Luke and Joshua. As they set up two ladders, he opened the paint can and handed out the brushes. His brothers took them and dipped them in the pail. Timothy stared at the step where he'd put his arm around Lillian. It had been more than a friendly gesture on his part. Did she realize that? Was that what upset her? Or was something wrong at home? She'd been worried about her brother lately.

Timothy glanced toward Silas. Perhaps Davey had made good on his threat and reported what he thought he saw to his father. Had Silas berated her for unseemly behavior?

"What's the matter?" Luke asked.

Timothy wished his brother wasn't quite so observant. "I'm not sure, but I think Lillian is giving me the cold shoulder."

"What did you do?"

Timothy shook his head. "I don't know. She wasn't upset with me when I saw her last."

"Then maybe it isn't you and she simply has other things on her mind."

"You're probably right." He was making a big deal out of nothing. She wanted to get the school opened for the children again as soon as possible. And now he was the one dawdling. He dipped his brush in the paint and set to work.

By noon, the school had been cleaned inside and out. The windows shone brightly. The siding and the new porch gleamed with the still wet paint. A half dozen more buggies arrived along with several pony carts filled with older women, including his mother. Colorful quilts

were spread under the trees that had been spared by
the blaze at the back of the property, and families were
soon gathered around picnic hampers. Happy chatter and
shrieks of childish laughter filled the air, as children who
had been painting, scrubbing the floor and raking debris were free to play on the swings and teeter-totter. A
few boys and young men had gotten up a softball game.

Timothy was about to join them when he noticed a
wagon coming in loaded with lumber. Jeremiah Keim
was at the reins. He stopped by the burned-out barn.
Silas Mast spoke briefly with him, and then motioned
for Timothy to join them.

"Jeremiah has donated the lumber for the new horse
barn. Will you help him unload it?"

"Sure. Jeremiah, have you eaten?" Timothy asked.

"Not yet." Jeremiah's gaze was fixed on his sister.
She was busy cleaning white paint off Amanda's hands
and hadn't noticed him.

"Come over and join us. My mother always brings
way too much food."

"I will unless Lillian has something for me." He
started to get down from the wagon.

"Tell her that she and Amanda are welcome to join
us, too." Timothy walked away without waiting to see
what Lillian's response was. Lillian had made a point of
avoiding him all morning. He figured if she was truly
upset with him, and he had no idea why she would be,
then she wouldn't join them. If they were still friends,
she would take the invitation at face value and come
enjoy the company of his family.

He passed up the ball game and went to sit on his
mother's quilt. He was pleased a few minutes later when
Amanda came over to sit beside Hannah. Lillian and

Jeremiah soon followed. Lillian began setting out the ham and bread she had brought for sandwiches. She still wouldn't look at him. As he knew his mother would, she produced a mountain of food in plastic bowls and jars. Along with paper plates and utensils, she placed everything in the center of the blanket. The fried chicken, German potato salad, pickles, pickled beets, a stack of brownies and two jugs of fresh lemonade left little room for people to sit.

She made sure everyone had a heaping plate of food on their lap before she sat down with a sigh and leaned back against the tree trunk. She gazed out over the families gathered together. "It does this old heart good to see so many people willing to help."

"Not as many as usual," Mary said. "I've noticed everyone scanning the horizons looking for signs of smoke. I know I have been. I think every family has left at least one member home to keep an eye on their place."

Emma took a piece of ham and put it on her plate. "People are watching strangers closely. I've even been uneasy when someone I don't know stops at our store."

The threat was why there were fewer people helping today. Timothy's father and Noah had remained at home, since Noah was carrying the fire pager and had wanted to stay near the highway in case he was called out.

Emma passed around a tray of deviled eggs. "I'm sure many folks have gone to deliver hay to Bishop Beachy and take donations to his family. His buggy horse was in the pen closest to the blaze. It bolted in panic, tried to jump the fence and broke a leg. The vet couldn't save it and the poor thing had to be put down."

"How awful." Lillian's eyes glistened with tears. She

cared almost as much about animals as she did about the children in her care.

"To buy a well-trained horse broke to harness can cost over a thousand dollars. It's no small expense. The bishop doesn't have deep pockets." Luke handed the tray of eggs back to Emma minus the three he'd added to his plate.

Timothy's mother poured herself a glass of lemonade. "Isaac has lent him one of our horses until he is able to purchase another. Our congregation will give what they can to make up for his loss just as they are giving to repair this school. Did you boys know your great-great-grandfather donated this land and helped to build this school?"

Timothy nodded. "I heard the story a long time ago when Grandfather was still alive."

"I don't think I've heard it," Luke said.

"*Ja*, you did," Joshua and Timothy said together.

"Well, I don't remember it."

Timothy flicked Luke's hair. "Because you weren't paying attention. As usual."

Their mother smiled. "Grandfather Bowman wanted his children to have a better education than he had. In his time, there weren't so many Amish in this area. He went to public school, but he was teased and bullied there. It was during the First World War and many *Englisch* resented the fact that the Amish wouldn't serve in the military. So he built a school for his own children, all fourteen of them, and hired an Amish teacher."

"We are grateful for his generous deed," Lillian said. "Many Amish children have benefited because of it."

Joshua gestured toward Jeremiah's wagon. "That load

of lumber is a substantial donation from your family, Jeremiah."

"We can afford it." Jeremiah reached for another chicken leg, adding it to his plate.

Timothy caught the sharp glance Lillian shot her brother but she didn't say anything. Timothy knew her father's construction business along with her teaching salary was barely enough to support the family. While Amish families were expected to help one another, they weren't compelled to give more than they could afford. If there were more fires in their Amish community, it would put a strain on everyone.

"Who do you think is behind these fires?" Mary asked the question many of them were thinking.

"Someone with a grudge against the two men, maybe. Mrs. Hanson said her husband had an argument with an Amish fellow. She didn't know his name. The fire marshal hopes when Mr. Hanson is able to speak, he can name the man." Timothy pinned his gaze on Jeremiah, waiting to see his reaction. In his heart, he didn't believe Jeremiah was an arsonist. Timothy's faith required him to see good in every man, but he had heard Lillian's concerns and wanted to ease her fears.

Jeremiah looked at his sister. She bit her lower lip. He put his plate down and met Timothy's gaze. "I had a quarrel with Mr. Hanson the day before the fire, if you can call it that. All the shouting was done by him. I offered to harvest his corn for a fair price. I heard that he'd fired the crew he hired last month."

Luke leaned toward Jeremiah. "Then there were others who might have a grudge against him. Do you know who they were?"

Jeremiah's gaze shifted away. "I will not cast even the shadow of blame on another man."

"I don't see how a harvest crew could have a grudge against Bishop Beachy," Joshua said.

Timothy's mother heaved a deep sigh. "We may never know who has done these things. We must pray for them. We must ask God to open their eyes and hearts and allow them to see the error of their ways. Only God knows what is in the heart of a man. He is the ultimate judge."

They all nodded in agreement. The rest of the meal passed in silence. When everyone was through eating, the women were soon deep in conversation discussing plans for Luke and Emma's upcoming wedding as they gathered up the plates and flatware. Lillian smiled and added a few comments, but Timothy could see she was still distracted. Something was troubling her. Something more than her brother's argument with Mr. Hanson. Timothy wanted to find out what was wrong, but he couldn't do that in front of everyone.

He rose to his feet. "I think I need to walk off some of *Mamm*'s good fried chicken before I get back to work. Anyone care to join me?" He stared directly at Lillian.

For a second, Lillian looked as if she would, but then a shadow came into her eyes. She shook her head and looked away. "I must get back inside. I have paperwork to catch up on."

His spirits plummeted. For whatever reason, she was determined to avoid him. He racked his brain for the cause and came up with only one answer. He had overstepped the bounds of friendship by putting his arm around her.

* * *

Seeing Timothy's crestfallen expression tore at Lillian's heart. Her determination to avoid being alone with him was hurting him as much as it was hurting her. That was never her intention.

Joshua stood up. "I'll take a walk with you, Timothy. I'd like to take a better look at the Hanson Farm and see if there is anything our family can do to help."

"The old man doesn't want help from the Amish," Jeremiah said, an edge of bitterness in his tone.

The Bowman men looked shocked. Timothy said, "He may not want our help, but that doesn't mean we should ignore him."

"The *Englisch* have insurance that pays them well for their losses. They don't need our help." Jeremiah stomped away from the group.

Lillian shot to her feet. "Jeremiah didn't mean that. I've changed my mind about that walk, Timothy. I will come with you. I would like to see the damage, too. If there *is* something we can do, the family doesn't need to know the help came from us."

"Why is your brother so bitter toward the *Englisch*?" Mary asked.

Lillian sighed. Her family had never shared the story of their experiences, but perhaps it was time they did. "When our family moved to Wisconsin, Jeremiah and our father went to work for our father's uncle. Uncle Albert ran a construction business. It was a very successful business. Amish and *Englisch* alike appreciated the quality of work they produced. After a few years, Uncle Albert put my father in charge at the building sites and stayed in his office. He was getting on in years. Father was almost finished framing a fancy house for a rich

Englisch fellow when the man decided the work wasn't up to his standards. He refused to pay for the materials and time my father put in."

"How awful. That wasn't right," Mary said.

"A few days later, the home caught fire in the night and burned to the ground. The man blamed Father. He said the Amish didn't know how to work around electricity and that they had caused a short in the wiring. He refused to pay for the building materials and tools that were lost. He sued Uncle Albert and won. It was a huge blow to the business. Uncle Albert felt Father was partly to blame. It caused a split in the family. We found out later the homeowner had collected a tidy sum of insurance. He didn't need the money he got from the lawsuit to cover his losses. He ended up building a much bigger house."

"Not all *Englisch* are greedy," Ana said. "We have many *Englisch* friends who live upright lives and are faithful to God."

"I know that. I try to live my faith." Lillian had harbored bitterness for a time, but she was able to forgive the man when she realized her bitterness was only hurting her, not him.

"Was the cause of the fire ever determined?" Timothy asked.

Something in his tone made her look closely at him. She had tried to forget that stressful time and put it all behind her. "I'm not sure. Why?"

Timothy smiled at her. "Just wondering, that's all. I am a fireman, even if only a volunteer."

"Timothy is the curious one, Lillian," Luke said. "You should know that about him."

"Jeremiah may know." She caught the glance the Bowman brothers shared and wondered at it.

"I think I'll ask him about it," Luke said, and walked away to where Jeremiah was unloading the wagon.

Ana had Mary help her to her feet. "Let's get the quilts folded up and get home. I have a mountain of mending to do."

"I'll help," Lillian said.

Ana shooed her away with the wave of a hand. "*Nee*, take your walk. You have done enough this morning. I can manage."

"All right." Lillian glanced over her shoulder to where Luke stood talking to Jeremiah. The glare Jeremiah cast in her direction told her he wasn't happy that she had shared their family's story. He unhitched his horse from the wagon, got on the mare and rode away.

A fire there and now fires here. There couldn't possibly be a connection, could there?

Chapter Twelve

Timothy noticed Lillian's unease as she stared after her brother. She was clenching and unclenching her fingers tightly together. Something was wrong between them. He hoped and prayed her brother wasn't involved in these fires.

Joshua held out his hand to his wife. "Let's take that walk, shall we? I saw a car pull into the Hansons' lane a few minutes ago."

Mary smiled at him. "I need to get something from your mother's buggy first."

Timothy followed them. Lillian made sure Amanda knew where she was going and left her under the watchful eyes of Susan Yoder, and then Lillian joined Timothy, Mary and Joshua.

Mary pulled out another heavy-looking basket from the back of the buggy. Joshua took in from her and settled it in the crook of his arm.

"I need to get something from the school, too," Lillian said, and hurried away.

She rejoined them with a smaller basket over her arm. Timothy took it from her and the couples began walking side by side down the road. Timothy let his brother get a little way in front of them and looked at Lillian. "Are you okay?"

"A little tired."

"You worked like a beaver this morning."

"I feel responsible for getting everything done."

He wanted her to share what was troubling her even if it didn't reflect well on him. "I thought maybe something had happened that upset you."

She gave him a shy smile. "Is that your way of telling me that I've been cranky?"

"Don't go putting words in my mouth." At least she was beginning to sound like her old self.

"I'm sorry. I was out of sorts this morning."

"It's understandable. Many disturbing things have happened. But look on the bright side. You got the school painted two years ahead of time, and you are getting a new barn. I know you had complained to Silas that the old one had a leaky roof. Now I won't have to fix it."

"The school does look nice. Once the charred grass grows back, it will look like nothing has ever happened. I hope it entices one of our young women to step forward and take the new teacher position."

"I thought the school board hadn't decided if they were going to hire another teacher."

"I overheard some of the board members talking, and they are in favor of giving me the extra help."

"That's *goot*."

"For me and for my scholars." They had reached the lane that ran up to the Hanson farmstead. A man was posting a large No Trespassing sign on the fence.

Joshua stepped forward. "Can you tell us how Mr. and Mrs. Hanson are doing?"

The man folded his arms with the hammer still in his hand. "My grandparents have lost their home. How do you think they are?"

His tone and stance told Timothy he wasn't willing to be friendly. "You're Billy. I remember going fishing with you when we were little. You caught five nice catfish, and I didn't catch a thing."

The man's face softened. "Timmy, right? I remember you."

Lillian took the basket from Timothy and handed it to the man. "I'm Lillian Keim, the teacher at the school up the road. We are all sorry about what happened and the children wanted to help. They have put together a few things for your grandparents. Could you see that they get them?"

He hesitated and then took the basket from her. "Sure."

"We have something for them, too." Mary took her basket from Joshua and held it out. Billy laid his hammer on the post behind grasp the handles. "That's good of you folks. I'll admit it's unexpected. Granddad didn't care much for the Amish. I thought the feeling was mutual."

"We believe in helping our neighbors," Mary said shyly, and stepped back.

"If you really want to help, find out which one of your people did this. Don't just forgive them and let them get away with it." Billy's voice quivered with some strong emotion.

Mary laid a hand on his arm. "My father is Sheriff Bradley. He's a just man. He will uncover the truth. He doesn't play favorites."

"I can attest to that," Joshua said with a smile for his wife. "Nick threw me in jail not long after we met."

"And he let you out when he discovered you were innocent," Mary added.

Billy cleared his throat. "It's good to know the sheriff doesn't believe the Amish are above reproach. Thanks for this stuff. I'll see that Grandma gets it. Granddad is still in the hospital, but he should get out in a few days."

"We are praying for his speedy recovery," Lillian said gently.

"Thanks. Were any of the kids at the school hurt?"

"They were frightened, but the children are fine," Lillian assured him.

"Good." Billy turned away, but turned back after a few steps. "It takes a sick man to destroy someone's home and livelihood for no reason. My grandparents are getting too old to start over."

Lillian took a quick step forward. "Sir, do you think your grandfather would be interested in leasing his cornfield to Ohio Central University? Professor Brandon Merrick is seeking land to lease for a new hybrid corn test plot. He says they pay well and quickly."

"Ohio Central? I'll talk to Granddad about it. He's worried about money. They had insurance on the house, but not on the crops."

"This might be a way to help them," Timothy said.

Billy walked away with his head down and his shoulders bowed.

Timothy sent up a prayer for him and for his family.

Joshua took Mary's hand. "Let's go home, since we are almost there. I don't want to leave *Daed* with all the work that needs to be done in the shop today."

"I'll tell Hannah where you've gone and make sure she gets home," Timothy said.

Mary smiled and nodded. *"Danki."*

The pair left and continued walking toward the river hand in hand.

"Those two make me want to get married," Timothy said softly, looking into Lillian's eyes.

Lillian avoided Timothy's intense gaze. "They seem like a happily married couple. God has blessed them."

"God has blessed three of my brothers with pearls beyond price."

"If it is His will, you will be blessed as well in God's own time. We should get back to the school. I am hoping to hold classes this afternoon. The children need to know things are back to normal."

Timothy gestured toward the blackened field where a few charred pieces of corn stubble stood as a mute reminder of that frightening day. "It isn't exactly normal. They all have to walk past this reminder morning and night."

Lillian started walking. "Are you simply curious about the cause of the fire in Wisconsin, or are you looking for a connection to these fires?"

"I was curious, but you have to admit it is odd that your brother had angry words with both men involved."

"He has never had angry words with Bishop Beachy."

"That we know about."

"You can't suspect him, Timothy. He wouldn't do this."

"I don't believe he did, but I think you have some suspicions, as well."

She stopped and turned to face him. "I do and I am so ashamed of that. He is my brother."

"I know how you feel. When we first learned that Luke was using and selling drugs, none of us believed it. We were wrong."

"You weren't wrong to believe in him. He repented and became a stalwart member of our faith. Your belief in him was justified."

"I pray that your faith in Jeremiah is justified, as well. I really don't want to think that one of us is behind this. It goes against everything I cherish. Is that the only thing troubling you, or is there something else? I hope you know you can tell me anything. I'm your friend. If my behavior the other evening has upset you, just tell me."

Lillian glanced at him from the corner of her eye. He had his hands in his pockets. His shoulders were slumped and his hat rode low on his forehead. Having seen the same expression on some of her students when they knew they were in trouble, she couldn't help smiling. "We have always been at ease with each other. Perhaps too much so."

"You are upset with me. I thought as much."

"I know you were only trying to comfort me, but not everyone would view it that way. I can't afford to lose my job. The more I thought about Davey's comment, the more convinced I became that our relationship could be viewed in the wrong context."

"It was less complicated being friends when we were young. All I had to worry about then was being teased by my brothers for hanging out with a girl."

"Many things were easier when we were young."

"I value your friendship, Lillian. I would never do

anything to hurt you. The next time you need some comfort, I'll send Hannah to give you a hug."

"And I will send back a hug to you in the same fashion."

"*Goot*. Now that we have that out in the open and settled, can you smile at me once in a while?"

She couldn't hold back a grin. "If you insist."

"*Danki*, I feel much better now."

So did Lillian. She wouldn't have to avoid Timothy. He understood that their friendship was open to scrutiny and had to remain circumspect. She was the one who needed to remind herself of that fact. Because being alone with Timothy was like wading in the river. She never knew when she might step into a hole and find the water was over her head without warning.

A long day of soaking rain on Wednesday put an end to the dry spell and decreased the fire danger in the community. When there hadn't been another incident by the time Sunday services rolled around, Lillian and many others began to relax.

She helped Amanda into the family's black buggy, cleaned and washed for the occasion. Jeremiah drove his open-topped courting buggy, a sign he hoped to take one of the local girls home later that day. Lillian didn't think there was anyone special in her brother's life, but she didn't know for sure. Jeremiah had grown tight-lipped in the past few months. Maybe there was a girl.

The service was being held at the home of Isaac and Ana Bowman. Members of the community took turns hosting the bimonthly preaching service but never more than once a year to prevent it becoming a burden on any one family. Hosting the service required a great deal of preparation. Family members and friends gathered several days before to clean the house inside and out. Pies and cakes were baked to be served at the luncheon where nearly one hundred people would gather after the service. Cookies, brownies, punch and other treats were prepared for the young people who would stay until late in the evening to socialize and enjoy a singing.

Inside the Bowman home, the walls between the lower rooms had been opened up to make room for rows of backless benches. The early-morning sunshine poured in through spotless windows and cast low rectangles across the polished wooden floor. Women sat together on one side while the men sat across the aisle. Since the married women normally sat together, Lillian and Amanda sat behind them with the single women and young girls.

A visiting bishop arrived to help with the preaching, since Lillian's father had not yet returned. He turned out to have a great gift for speaking and everyone present felt his words were guided by the Holy Spirit. Following the three-hour service, the visitor gave a plea for help with one of his parishioner's medical bills. Their teenage son had been diagnosed with leukemia and his medical expenses were mounting. Donations were collected for that family, and then the minister passed the collection plate for Bishop Beachy. Lillian gave what she could but knew it was a pitifully small amount. Bishop Beachy then announced the banns of marriage for two young couples from the congregation. Neither of them was a big surprise.

Afterward, Lillian sent Amanda to play with several other young children under the watchful eyes of their mothers and then joined the women helping serve the light luncheon inside. The backless benches had been stacked together to make a half dozen narrow tables. The congregation ate in shifts with deference being given to the elders first. The teenagers and young children would eat last. The arrangement suited them, as it gave them more time to spend with their friends.

Lillian took her place washing dishes at the sink. Rebecca was helping her dry them. Ana came in and handed Lillian a tray of glasses. "I see your parents have not yet returned. Have you had word from them?"

"I had a letter on Friday. *Onkel* has rallied, and Father wishes to remain for the time being. They dearly miss Amanda. Mother regrets not taking her with them, but they never expected to be gone so long."

"Are you and your brother coping without them?" Rebecca asked.

"We are, although I think Jeremiah prefers Mother's cooking over mine."

Rebecca laughed. "Samuel never complains, but I know he prefers Ana's cooking."

"He has never said such a thing to me," Ana declared. "He says you are a *goot* cook."

"He eats two helpings of your meat loaf and he'll only take one of mine."

"I will write out my recipe for you, if you like," Ana offered.

Rebecca set her hands on her hips and stretched backward, making her rounded belly stick out even farther. "I would rather come over and eat yours. It's easier. I've been too tired to do much cooking lately."

Ana patted Rebecca's tummy. "I will make up some meals for you this week. You need your rest. This baby will be here in no time, and then rest will be out of the question."

Ana went back to gather more dishes. Rebecca frowned and pressed a hand to her ribs as she stretched sideways. "I wish he would find a new place to kick me. I must be black and blue on the inside on this rib."

"You look happy in spite of that." Lillian refused to dwell on the fact that she would never be a mother, but sometimes, like now, a stab of jealousy hit her hard. She willed it away.

Rebecca laced her fingers together over her stomach. "I am happy and yet I'm also afraid of that happiness. I know how easily it can be taken away."

"To worry is to doubt God," Lillian said, quoting one of the many Amish proverbs she'd heard all her life.

"You're right. God is good. I will trust the kindness of the Lord, for He has given me many blessings. Do you ever think about getting married, Lillian? I know you love teaching and you do a wonderful job with the *kinder*, but what if someone was interested in courting you? Would you be open to the idea?"

"Are you talking about someone specific or in general terms?" Lillian handed her friend another plate to dry, wondering if Timothy had put Rebecca up to this.

Rebecca rubbed the saucer slowly with her towel. "I'm speaking in general terms."

Which meant Rebecca would become more specific if Lillian admitted to being open to the idea. "In general terms, I love my job and I have no wish to give it up."

"Even for the love of a husband and children of your own?"

Lillian didn't normally have a problem denying her desire for love and marriage, but today the words stuck in her throat. If things were different. If she could give Timothy the family he wanted—but she couldn't. "I love the children I teach, and that is enough for me. Someday the right man may come along. No one can know God's plan. Until then, teaching holds sway over my heart."

She could almost imagine marrying a widower who needed help raising a half dozen children, but even then it would be a poor bargain for the man because her heart belonged to Timothy.

She kept her head down and vigorously scrubbed a sticky pan, hoping no one noticed the tear that slipped down her cheek before she could blink it back.

Chapter Thirteen

Lillian was delighted to see Debra and Brandon when they stopped by just as she was leaving the school on Tuesday afternoon. Debra, balancing on crutches, came around the front of her brother's car wearing a cast on her foot.

Lillian pressed a hand to her chest. "Don't tell me your foot was broken. You poor thing."

Debra extended her cast. "One small bone is all. This monstrosity makes it look worse than it is."

"I'm so sorry."

"It wasn't your fault, Lillian. It was my own clumsiness. How are you? How are all the children? Are any of you having difficulties with PTS?"

Lillian tipped her head. "With what?"

"Post-traumatic stress. Nightmares, excessive worrying, trouble concentrating, things that can happen to people after a frightening experience."

"Several of the *kinder* have told me they were scared to come back to school at first, but they seem okay now. Are you having such troubles?"

Debra shrugged. "A few nightmares, but they're getting better."

"I'm glad."

Debra moved toward the school. "I'm amazed. The building doesn't look like it just came through a fire. If it wasn't for the charred field across the way, I would think I was at the wrong school."

Lillian smiled broadly. "Our community comes together to help when there is trouble. We missed only one day of school. The paint, lumber and labor was all donated by the families of our children. The barn was rebuilt, too, but I'm afraid we couldn't do anything with your car."

"Hasn't my insurance company been here to tow it away?"

"Not yet."

Brandon folded his arms over his chest. "We can't get our insurance company to come pick up one car while in the same amount of time you folks have restored your school and built a barn. Something is wrong with that picture."

Debra hobbled toward the steps. "I'm telling you, Brandon, I'm going to become Amish. These people have the right idea about a lot of things."

Brandon laughed. "The only thing standing in your way is that you like driving, you love electricity, you couldn't live without your computer and you can't cook."

"Details, details. Lillian, I need my notes and to download the results from the machine I left behind. Are they still here?"

"I've kept your equipment and notes in the coatroom. I thought perhaps the health department would send someone to finish the tests, but I haven't heard from them."

"I'll be here Friday morning to complete them. I don't have to stand to do hearing screens, so my supervisor is letting me come back to work half days. I still can't drive, but Brandon has agreed to haul me out here and back."

"*Wunderbar* and so kind of him."

"Don't go assuming he is the kindly older brother. He has an ulterior motive."

Brandon gestured toward the burned cropland. "I spoke with Mr. Hanson, and he has leased his acreage to me for a test field. Thanks to you, I take it. Mr. Hanson's grandson told me you were the one who mentioned it."

"I was happy to do something that would benefit both of you."

"You'll be seeing a lot of me over the spring and summer months. I wanted to ask if you thought some of your students would be interested in earning extra money working for me next summer."

"Detasseling the corn? I'm sure they will."

Debra threw one hand in the air, almost dropping her crutch. "See how smart this woman is? I had no idea what detasseling was, and she knew right off the bat. What is it, anyway?"

Lillian suppressed a grin. "Detasseling is a form of pollination control. By removing the pollen-producing flowers, what we call the tassel, from the tops, the plant can't fertilize itself as corn normally does. Pollen is carried by the wind from adjacent plants of a different corn variety onto the silks of the forming ears. This produces a cross-breed or hybrid. They tend to be stronger and produce a better yield than either parent."

"An excellent explanation," Brandon said.

"I confess I have only recently read up on the subject," Lillian admitted. "Timothy lent me some of the farm journals he gets."

"I hope to get a cover crop planted in the next few weeks. Austrian winter peas, not daikon radishes."

Lillian tipped her head. "Thank you for that."

"I was also hoping to hire someone local to care for the field. By that, I mean plant the ground cover, cultivate, fertilize, monitor growth stages and that type of thing. Any suggestions?"

The project would be something Timothy would enjoy, but she wanted to offer the job to her brother first. They could use the extra income. "I'll ask around."

"Thank you. I considered running an ad in the local paper, but Debra told me it helps to have someone the Amish trust intercede for a non-Amish person like myself."

"She is right. Many Amish view outsiders with suspicion. Because we seldom involve the law in our troubles, outsiders have been known to take advantage of us."

"Speaking of the law, have they found out who set the fires?" Debra asked.

Lillian shook her head. "Not yet."

"I hope they catch him. I'd like to wring the hoodlum's neck for putting my sister and all your children in danger."

"We have forgiven him," Lillian said. "None of us bears him ill will. We pray that he repents, for God is the ultimate judge of a man's soul. Someday he will meet God face-to-face and answer for his sins."

Brandon shrugged. "That is gracious of you, but I'm

a man who likes to see justice done in this world as well as the next."

Debra began limping toward the school. "Don't let his bloodthirsty talk fool you. He may growl like a bear, but he's a kitten on the inside."

Brandon followed her. "I am not a kitten."

"Yes, you are," she called over her shoulder. "A spitting, fuzzy, fierce kitten."

"You got the fierce part right."

Lillian smiled at their banter. "Does your field manager have to be Amish? We have a few non-Amish farmers in the area who might be interested in working for you."

Brandon turned toward her with a sheepish grin on his face. "They wouldn't have to be Amish, but I wanted to see firsthand some of your Amish farming practices. Your friend Timothy got me to thinking about the advantages of horse drawn equipment. For one thing, soil compaction would be almost nil from the horses compared to tractors that can weigh in excess of a ton."

"That reminds me," Debra said. "I want to stop at that gift shop before we head home today. I have a friend expecting a new baby and one who just bought her first home. I wanted to get them something unique."

"Ana Bowman has some pretty baby quilts you might like. Timothy's brother Luke makes some interesting yard art. Did you notice the gourd bird feeders in the oak tree at the turn off?"

"I did. I also noticed the honor system payment box. Does it work? Do people put in the right amount or do gourds disappear without being paid for?"

"I have never heard Ana complain that she is being cheated."

Lillian followed the pair inside and waited until Debra had recovered the data she needed. As they left the building, Brandon popped open the trunk of his car. "I have a little gift for your sister."

He pulled out an aluminum folding step stool. "Is it all right if I give this to her? I don't want to break any rules. This has wheels under the suction cups on the legs. It makes it easy to move from room to room instead of having to carry a step stool and it's still safe."

Touched by his gesture, Lillian accepted on her sister's behalf. "This is a lovely, practical gift. I'm sure she will enjoy it. Now I can put her to work dusting the tall places she hadn't been able to reach."

"Little people must adapt to the world. The world rarely adapts to us. I get a newsletter from our national association. It often reviews new devices, offers tips and gives little people a place to tell their stories. It is free. I can sign you up to get a copy if you'd like."

"I will discuss it with my parents. If they don't object, that would be great. I'll let you know."

After waving goodbye to the friendly couple, Lillian walked the two miles to her home, stopping at their neighbor Granny Weaver's to pick up Amanda. As she suspected, Amanda was delighted with her gift. She rolled it from place to place in the kitchen and down the hall to the linen closet to get clean sheets for her bed.

Lillian decided to fix a quick supper of grilled cheese sandwiches and tomato soup. Jeremiah came in just as she was heating the skillet. Amanda pushed her stepladder over to him. "Look what I have. It has wheels, but when I step on it, it stops rolling."

Jeremiah watched as she demonstrated, then looked at Lillian. "Where did this come from?"

"From Brandon Merrick, the little person professor I told you about."

"Why is he giving our sister gifts?"

Lillian buttered the slice of bread in her hand and slipped the first sandwich in the hot skillet. "Because he is a nice fellow and he likes Amanda."

"The *Englisch* usually have a motive behind their gift giving. You'll see. He will want something from us."

She wished her brother wasn't so cynical. "He has leased Mr. Hanson's field for a test plot."

"What's he growing?"

"A new variety of corn. He's looking for someone to farm the ground and monitor the crop and he is hoping to hire an Amish fellow."

"Why one of us? So he can pay us pennies for our labor?"

"Not all *Englisch* are evil. There is good in every man. Brandon is interested in learning about Amish farming practices. Are you interested in the job or not? We could use the money."

"I'm not interested in entertaining some professor with our backward ways. We don't need money that badly."

She bit her lip to keep from arguing. Jeremiah wasn't open to reason on the subject of the *Englisch*. "Did you go through the mail today? I was hoping we'd get a letter from *Mamm*."

"I left it on the desk in the other room. *Mamm* says Uncle Albert wants *Daed* to work with him again."

She turned away from the stove. "Is he considering it?"

"He is."

"But that would mean moving the family back to Wisconsin."

"You and Amanda. I would stay here and keep running *Daed*'s business."

"I don't want to go back. I have a job. I'm needed here."

Amanda pushed her step stool up beside Lillian. "I don't want to go back, either. Granny Weaver makes me *wunderbar* cookies."

Jeremiah frowned at her. "You don't want to stay here without *Mamm* and *Daed*, do you?"

"Nee." Amanda's lower lip began to quiver. "I want them to come home."

Lillian hugged her. "They will. I'll read *Mamm*'s letter, but first let us have our supper."

After the meal, Lillian put Amanda to bed and sat down with her mother's letter. It was full of news about the community and about Uncle Albert's improving health. In the very last paragraph, she mentioned Uncle Albert's wish to have *Daed* working alongside him again and mentioned that they were considering it and praying about it.

Lillian folded the letter and slipped it back in the envelope. So her father really was considering moving the family back to Wisconsin. Would her parents allow her to remain with Jeremiah? Would she want to stay without Amanda?

Could she leave Timothy again? Her heart sank at the prospect.

On Wednesday, Hannah came home from school with a note for Timothy. Lillian wanted him to meet with Brandon Merrick on Friday after school. The note didn't say why.

Since he was on call for the fire department on Friday, he used the telephone in the community call box to let Walter know where he would be if they got called out, and then he walked to the school with jaunty steps. Any excuse to see Lillian was a good one.

Brandon and Debra were both sitting in students' desks at the front of the classroom facing Lillian's desk when he entered the building.

"Good afternoon," Timothy said, removing his hat. "You wanted to see me?"

Lillian gestured for him to join them. "Brandon has a proposal for you, and then I want your opinion about something else."

"I have plenty of opinions." He strolled to the front of the classroom, but chose not to try and fit into one the student desks. Instead, he pulled a folding chair from the rack in one corner of the room and sat down beside Brandon.

Brandon quickly explained his proposal, the type of information he would need collected and the fee he was authorized to pay. It seemed like a fair offer. Timothy had been dying to know what type of corn Brandon was developing. He would have taken the job for less.

"I accept." The two men shook hands.

Timothy looked at Lillian. "What proposal do you have for me, Lillian?"

"Not for you, for Brandon, but I want to know what you think of it."

Timothy marveled at the eagerness filling Lillian's eyes. She leaned forward and clasped her hands together. "Brandon, how would you feel about sharing your knowledge with my students? A guest speaker of sorts. The children could follow the progress of your crop, learn to compute the cost of fertilizer for each acre, identity weeds and insects and decide on the best treatments for each issue. We can do all this in a classroom setting, of course, but to have the hands-on experience in the field would be invaluable."

"Me, teaching Amish kids? Would that be allowed?" His expression showed his doubts.

Her gaze swung to Timothy. "What do you think? Would the school board approve a special guest lecturer? I think they will if I can show how much my scholars stand to gain by working with Mr. Merrick."

"He's talking about genetics, Lillian. Are you sure your church elders will allow that?" Debra voiced her doubts.

Lillian wasn't deterred. If anything, Timothy watched her grow more determined.

"We understand the benefits of good husbandry in our livestock. Leaning to raise a better corn crop is no different than learning to breed a better milk cow. Understanding the natural world and using that knowledge to our advantage isn't against the church's teachings. Timothy, what do you think?" She pinned her gaze on his again.

He hated to crush her eagerness. "I think the idea has merit, but I'm not a parent or a member of the school board. How I feel doesn't carry much weight. I can see one problem. Silas will be against it."

She sat back and crossed her arms. "I expect you are right about that."

Brandon glanced between the two of them. "Who is Silas?"

"The school board president. He doesn't care for outsiders."

"He's president for the rest of this year," Timothy added.

Lillian nodded. "That's true."

"His time on the board will be up in May. If he says no, you can wait until you have a new president and present your idea again." It wasn't much, but it was the best he could offer.

"Why don't you run for the office?" Debra suggested.

"I have no children. Only the fathers or grandfathers of our children are allowed to hold a school board office."

"Are you saying that women aren't allowed to be on the school board?" Debra looked at him, her eyes wide with disbelief.

"Don't get on your high horse, sis," Brandon cautioned. "We're visitors to this community."

She settled back and crossed her arms. "Scratch everything I ever said about wanting to be Amish."

Timothy met Debra's eyes. "More can be done behind the scenes at home than can be done at the meeting, at least according to my mother. My brother Joshua is on the board. I'll put your idea to him, Lillian. We'll see what he thinks of it. If he favors it, you have a chance."

"*Goot.* If I can get the board to agree, will you share your time and talent with us, Brandon?" Lillian asked with a sweet smile that would have made Timothy agree to almost anything.

Brandon nodded. "When is the next school board meeting?"

Lillian glanced at the clock on the wall. "In about two hours."

The pager on his hip started beeping. He read the message and looked up to find everyone staring at him. "It's not another fire," he said quickly. "It's a call for a medical emergency, but I have to go."

He put his chair back and headed out the door to wait at the roadside for his ride. Lillian came out and stood with him. "I wish you could be at the meeting. I'd feel better knowing there was one person who understands why I want to do this."

He wanted to pull her into his arms and kiss away her worry, but he knew he shouldn't. A friend would not act that way. "You'll make them see the value in your idea."

"I hope so."

"And if they say no, you can bring it up next year."

She crossed her arms tightly over her chest. "I may not be here next year."

His heart skipped a beat. "Why do you say that?"

"*Daed* is thinking of moving the family back to Wisconsin."

"You can't go back. You have a job here. The children need you."

"My family needs me, too."

He took her by the shoulders and turned her to face him, but she kept her gaze down. Crooking a finger beneath her chin, he gently forced her to look at him. "Lillian, I don't want you to go. Say you will stay."

He held his breath as he waited for her reply.

Chapter Fourteen

"I want to stay," Lillian said softly.

"You don't know how happy it makes me to hear you say that." Timothy's smile lit up his face.

His relief drove home how unfair the situation was. She could never be the woman he needed, yet she didn't want a life without him. She needed his friendship, his humor, his understanding. Perhaps she was being selfish, but she couldn't help it. She was lonely.

The arrival of Walter put an end to the conversation. Timothy took a step back. "I've got to go."

Lillian laid a hand on his arm. "Be careful."

He patted her hand. "I will. I'll be praying for the success of your proposal, since I can't be there in person." He smiled and took off at a run toward his friend's truck and they drove off.

Brandon and Debra came out of the school. Lillian walked to their car with them. "Thank you again for agreeing to speak to my students."

Brandon nodded. "I'll be interested in how this turns out. Expect me back a week from Saturday. I want to do some soil tests before Timothy starts planting."

After they drove away, Lillian found herself with some unwelcome time on her hands. She got out a broom and began to sweep the floor, but the mundane task didn't take her mind off Timothy. How much longer could she keep her growing feelings for him hidden? Each time they were together, it became harder to pretend what she felt was friendship and not love.

She stopped sweeping as the realization hit her. She was falling in love with Timothy Bowman and she had no idea what to do about it.

Maybe a move back to Wisconsin was the answer. Except she had told Timothy the truth. She wanted to stay in Bowmans Crossing. She wanted to teach school and watch all her wonderful children grow up and someday teach their children. And she wanted to be near Timothy. Perhaps if he married someday and she knew he was happy, then she would be able to leave.

When the board finally arrived, she noticed there were more parents in attendance than usual, but the meeting itself that was basically the same as every other school board meeting she had attended since she started teaching at Ryder Hill School. The main difference this time was that Silas Mast stood up and thanked everyone for the help in repairing the school. The meeting was nearing the end when he asked if she had any requests. The monthly school board meeting was when she received her salary. She had been hoping for a raise this year, but she knew it wasn't likely. What she really needed was another teacher to help carry the load. Forty-two students were a lot to manage.

Lillian took a deep breath. "We are in need of new writing textbooks for the third-grade class. Ours are falling apart. I don't know how many times I can continue to glue them back together. And I have a new program I would like the board's permission to implement."

"Go on," Silas said.

"Brandon Merrick is the brother of the *Englisch* nurse who did our health exams and who stayed with us the day of the fire. He's a professor of agriculture at Central University. His specialty is genetic research and development of seed corn. He has a great deal of information he is willing to share about the process of producing hybrid seed corn. He has been able to lease Mr. Hanson's farm ground for a test plot. It is his hope, and mine, that he be allowed to teach the older children how to produce a hybrid seed crop by having them help with the record-keeping, detasseling and harvesting of his field. He is willing to share his knowledge for free and will even pay the children for their labor."

Silas frowned. "It sounds as if this project would have you and the children spend an unseemly amount of time with an outsider. I don't believe we need the *Englisch* instructing our children on how to grow crops when their parents and grandparents have been doing it for generations. Does this man make his living farming?"

"*Nee*, he does not. He is a teacher and researcher."

"Then he can't know our way of doing things. I grow corn as my father taught me. Corn needs clover, and clover needs corn. That will be good enough for my sons."

"But why do we plant clover one year and corn the next? Because clover replenishes the nitrogen in the soil. This is science being applied to practical matters to improve our way of life, not to detract from it. Brandon will only be at the school a few times each month."

A murmur of dissatisfaction went through the crowd. Silas shook his head. "*Nee*, I have said all I wish to say on the subject. Now, for our last bit of business, that of hiring another teacher. We haven't found anyone willing to take on the job in this district. We will keep looking. I understand that you currently have more students than most teachers, but perhaps you can have some of the older children help you with the younger ones."

"I am already doing that." Lillian struggled not to let her disappointment come through in her voice.

"I have received a few complaints of discipline problems," the bishop said, casting an apologetic glance toward Lillian.

She felt the heat rising in her cheeks as she fastened her gaze to the floor. She could hardly stand here and tell everyone in attendance that the school board president's son was the problem. Most of them knew it anyway. Abe liked to pick on the younger children, and he liked to do it when Lillian wasn't watching. She needed eyes in the back of her head, or another teacher to take over the upper grades. Apparently, that wasn't going to happen any time soon.

Joshua Bowman raised his hand. "I know someone who would make an excellent teacher. I would like to put Timothy Bowman's name up for consideration."

"You did what?" Timothy stared at Joshua in stunned shock. The men were gathered in the Bowmans' living room on Saturday evening. The women had gone to a quilting bee, leaving the men on their own. The smell of popcorn still lingered in the air, as the two brothers faced each other over the chest board.

Joshua moved his knight. "You heard me. I submitted your name as a potential teacher. The school board is coming by tomorrow evening to interview you."

Timothy sat back in his chair. "Why would you do that? I don't know the first thing about being a teacher."

Noah was slumped on the sofa with a magazine open on his lap. "There isn't much to it. You go to the school-house every day, you give the *kinder* their assignments and then you grade those assignments. That's pretty much all there is to it."

Timothy rolled his eyes and shook his head. "That's what you think. I know for a fact that Lillian spends hours grading papers, assessing each child's learning potential and finding ways to help all of them reach that potential, to say nothing of the paperwork she has to keep up on."

Joshua stretched his palms out. "See, you already know a lot about being a teacher. Besides, I think you'll be good at it. And you'll get to see Lillian every day without having to make up excuses to go to school."

"I don't make up excuses. I simply think of things that other people don't."

"Look at it this way," Samuel said, "Monday through Friday, you'll have a chance to work beside Lillian. Imagine how grateful she will be that you're taking over some of her enormous workload. If you don't like the job, you don't have to do it next year."

"I can't be spared from the workshop until summer." Timothy looked to his father to support him.

Isaac stroked his beard with one hand. A sure sign he was carefully considering his words. "Actually, we will be able to spare you. I've had a letter from my brother Marvin. He wants his two oldest sons to ap-prentice with us."

Noah perked up. "Mark and Paul are coming to work here? Sweet!"

"I am considering it," Isaac said. "Your mother is in favor of it. With Joshua, Samuel and soon Luke out of the house, she's feeling down. She thinks having more young men in the house will cheer her up."

"Putting Mark, Paul and Noah together under one roof is a recipe for disaster." Samuel gave his little brother a hard stare.

"We got into a tiny spot of trouble once, but that was kid stuff." Noah dismissed his brother's worry with a wave of his hand.

"Joyriding and racing in a stolen buggy is hardly a tiny spot of trouble, and it happened last summer. If that buggy had belonged to anyone but Fannie Erb's father, you would have been in a *big* spot of trouble."

Noah held up both hands. "You are right. It was a foolish thing to do, but I've grown up a lot since then."

"Let us pray that Mark and Paul have, too," their father said.

Timothy paid scant attention to the rest of the conversation going on around him. The idea of working beside Lillian every day was both a good reason to take the job and the best reason to turn it down. The more time he spent with her, the harder it would be to maintain the guise of a friend when he wanted to be so much more. He looked at Joshua. "What does Lillian think of the idea?"

"She didn't say anything one way or the other. It's your move."

"But did she look pleased?"

"Surprised would be a better description."

That wasn't exactly encouraging. "What did the board say about letting Brandon Merrick teach a few classes?"

"Silas wouldn't hear of it. He doesn't want the children exposed to an outsider on a regular basis. A lot of the parents feel the same. Especially since these fires. Most people think they are the work of *Englisch* teenage mischief-makers. I hope they are right. I don't like thinking one of our own would do such a thing."

Timothy rose and headed for the door.

"Where are you going?" Joshua asked.

"To see Lillian. I'm not going to consider the teaching position unless she is completely in favor of it. The last thing I want to do is make her job harder."

Timothy left the house and walked down to the barn. He selected a young mare named Snickers, led her out of her stall and harnessed her to an open cart. A short time later, he crossed the river through the covered bridge and urged the mare to a fast trot up the road.

He passed the school without stopping. At the edge of the woods that marked the start of the ridge, he slowed the horse and allowed her to climb the winding road at her own pace. The thick woods were ablaze with fall colors. Crimson, gold and brown leaves that had already fallen made a lush and colorful carpet along the edge of the road. He was grateful that Davey Mast had stopped the blaze before it destroyed the beauty of the woodlands.

At the top of the rise, he noticed a black car parked a little way back from the road. A natural clearing on the top of the ridge was a spot favored by English and Amish teenagers alike. The view of the farmland below presented a pretty picture. When the trees were leafed out in the spring, it also provided a secluded spot for young couples looking to be alone.

Timothy didn't recognize the car, but the man beside it was Davey Mast. He appeared to be arguing with Jeremiah Keim. Jeremiah's horse and buggy stood on the far side of the car. Timothy caught only a few heated words the men exchanged before his horse took him over the rise and out of earshot. Whatever was going on, it was none of his business.

He forgot about the men when his mare reached the flat ground and picked up speed on her own. She was still fresh and happy to stretch her legs and he enjoyed the fast pace. He let her have her head until he reached Lillian's father's farm. Slowing the mare, he turned in the drive. Lillian was sitting on the front porch with Amanda on her lap. They held a children's book between them.

He pulled the horse to stop. *"Gutenowed."*

"Good evening, Timothy. What brings you here?" Lillian asked. "Would you like to come in?"

"It's too pretty an evening to spend inside. I'd rather go for an outing. Amanda, would you like to come for a ride with me?"

Amanda laughed as she pressed both hands to her mouth. Lillian whispered loudly enough for him to hear. "Timothy is asking you out on a date. Will you go?"

Amanda considered it and then looked up at Lillian. "If you come, too."

"I would be delighted to go for a drive with you. Fetch our shawls. The air will turn cool when the sun goes down."

Scrambling off her sister's lap, Amanda disappeared into the house briefly and came running back out with the shawls in her arms. Lillian fastened one around her sister's neck and then swung the other one over her own shoulders. Timothy got out of the cart to help them climb in. He started to pick up Amanda, but the child shook her head. *"Nee*, I can do it."

She went up the porch steps and grabbed a stepladder. She returned to Timothy's side, set the ladder in place and happily climbed up to the cart seat. "See, I can do it."

"Your little sister is getting an independent streak like her big sister." He spoke in English, knowing Amanda hadn't yet learned the language.

Lillian smiled. "Brandon gave her the stepladder. She drags it all over the house and farm. It's very lightweight and it has wheels. With it, she can reach the pump handle to fill a pail with water and even gather the eggs by herself. She is having a ball."

"Brandon is a special fellow."

"He and his sister both. I didn't know outsiders could be so kind."

As they spoke, a buggy came up the lane and stopped beside them. Jeremiah nodded to Timothy. "Good day."

"Timothy invited me on a date," Amanda declared happily.

Jeremiah gave Lillian a knowing smile. "Did he, now? I'm on my way to Merle Yoder's place to give him a bid on some concrete work. I heard his dog had puppies a few weeks ago, and I thought you might want to come along to see them."

Amanda's eyes lit up. "*Ja*, I want to see the puppies." She held out her arms for Timothy to help her down. He transferred her to Jeremiah's buggy.

"You two have a nice outing." Jeremiah grinned and winked at Timothy.

"Did you get the bid on the Troyers' new farrowing house?" Lillian asked.

Timothy had heard their neighbors to the north were expanding their hog production. Jeremiah's grin vanished. "They gave it to an *Englisch* crew from Berlin. I thought the Troyers were our friends, but money speaks loudly even to the Amish," he said bitterly. He turned his horse and drove away.

Lillian started to get out, but Timothy stopped her. "It's still a nice evening for a ride. My heart was set on taking Amanda, but I reckon you will do in a pinch. Will you come with me?"

He held his breath as he waited for her answer.

Chapter Fifteen

As Timothy had hoped, Lillian grinned at his teasing tone. Her chin came up. "As my *boo-friend* has not come by, I expect an outing with you is better than sitting home alone. And it is a pretty evening."

Timothy let out the breath he was holding and eagerly climbed up beside her. Time alone with her was exactly what he wanted. He slapped the reins to get the horse moving. When they reached the highway, he stopped. "Which way should we go?"

She pointed toward the ridge. "To the top."

"To the top it is." He headed the horse back the way he had come.

"Well?" Lillian asked after a few minutes.

"Well what?" He glanced at her out of the corner of his eye.

"Don't keep me in suspense a moment longer. Are you going to take the teaching job?"

"That depends." He kept his gaze straight ahead.

"On what?"

He turned to look her full in the face. "On you."

She looked away. "I think you would make a fine teacher."

"That's not what I'm asking. Do you want me to take the job? Will working with me make you uncomfortable?"

She gave him a bright smile. Perhaps too bright. "Why would I object to working with my best friend? I can teach the first four grades and you can teach the upper grades. My workload will be cut in half. If you behave yourself and don't flirt with strange women, we'll get along fine."

"I wasn't flirting and that's beside the point. Are you sure you are okay with the idea?"

"I am. When do you start?"

"I haven't been hired yet. The school board is coming to interview me tomorrow."

"They will take you. They're desperate."

"Now, just a minute. Desperation will have nothing to do with my being hired. They will examine my many fine qualities and beg me to accept."

She chuckled. "Your lack of *demut* might be your undoing."

"I am humble."

"That is not the word I would use to describe you."

"I have my faults like everyone else, but I'm teachable. Seriously, Lillian, are you okay with this?"

"Of course I am. So please stop asking unless you want a different answer. I do thank you for seeking my opinion. It didn't count for much with our school board when I put forth my proposal."

"I'm sorry they turned down the idea of having Brandon give a few lectures. I'm certainly interested in what he has to say. I think I could learn a lot from the man."

She twisted in her seat to face him. "Timothy, that's it. That's the perfect answer. You will learn all you can from Brandon while you are working for him and then pass that information on to your students. The board can't object if you are in charge of the project. Brandon doesn't have to speak to our students. You can."

"Our students. I like the sound of that. I never considered teaching as a vocation. I always thought of it as a woman's job."

"There aren't many men teachers in our Amish schools, but their numbers are growing. I've met several of them at our annual teachers' meetings. Parents and school boards have seen the benefits of having a teacher who remains for years instead of having young women who only teach a year or two before they quit to get married."

"I'm not sure I want to do it for years. I couldn't believe Joshua submitted my name in the first place. He should have asked me first."

"Perhaps the Lord prompted your brother to suggest you. The Lord moves in mysterious ways."

"His wonders to behold," he added softly, thinking she was a wondrous person, a true gift to her students and to her friends. He was glad to be counted among those.

As the horse climbed the hill again, she began listing the things the school board might ask about and gave him an impromptu interview.

Finally, she said, "I think you will do."

"What supplies will I need if they do want me?" He wasn't sure he would get the job, but he wanted to be ready if the board said yes.

She listed things he'd already thought about like pens,

markers and paper clips. A teacher was responsible for bringing his or her own supplies. At the top of the hill, Timothy turned into the now-empty clearing and stopped the buggy. The land spread out below was a colorful patchwork of fields and woodlands laid out like a giant crazy quilt.

Lillian sighed. "I love this spot."

"So do I. I saw Jeremiah up here with Davey Mast when I came by earlier."

A frown cut a deep crease between her brows. "Are you sure?"

"*Ja.* Why?"

"Because Jeremiah told me Davey had moved to Philadelphia."

"Maybe he's back to visit some of his family and friends. Or maybe he didn't like the city and has come back for good."

"It would be wonderful if he has returned to our faith."

"I don't think that is the case. The car I saw him with was new and he was dressed fancy, not plain." Should he tell her they had been arguing? He decided against it. He wasn't certain of what he had heard and seen.

"I pray for Davey because I know Jeremiah misses his friendship."

"Will Jeremiah move back to Wisconsin with your parents?"

"I don't know. He thinks *Daed* will let him take over the construction business here and run the farm."

"But Amanda will go with them. What will you do without her?" He knew how close she was to her sister.

"Cry a lot."

He laid his hand over hers and squeezed it gently. "I know it won't be the same, but you can visit her over the summer or she can stay with you when school is out."

Lillian drew comfort from his touch and laced her fingers with his. "You are always there for me, Timothy. You know what I'm thinking or feeling better than anyone. Better than my own family."

"Don't give me too much credit."

"I don't think I give you enough credit." She looked into his hazel eyes and saw understanding and compassion, the things she loved most about him.

There was no denying it. She was in love with him. Head over heels in love in spite of her best efforts to remain simply a friend. She wanted his touch, his kisses, she wanted to be held in his arms and be cherished by him.

His grip on her hand tightened. "You are a special person, Lillian. My life would be incomplete without you in it."

Lillian closed her eyes. She didn't want to look into the chasm his words had opened between them. His life would be incomplete *with her.* He deserved a loving wife who could give him children of his own. She wouldn't take that dream from him. She cared for him too much.

Pulling her hand from his, she brushed back a stray lock of hair at her temple. "Then it's a good thing we are going to be teaching together. Imagine the fun we will have. I know you are going to love the job as much as I do and you'll see why I won't ever give it up. It's getting chilly, isn't it? I think we should head back."

"Is something wrong?" he asked.

Lillian kept her gaze straight ahead. She didn't want

to see disappointment in his eyes. It was bad enough that she heard it in his voice.

She had her emotions under control, but it wouldn't take much to send her defenses crashing around her ears. "Nothing's wrong. I have enjoyed the evening, but I have work to do at home. It was nice of you to think of me and I'm very glad we will be teaching together. I promise to do everything in my power to help you."

It was a promise she intended to keep.

One week later, Timothy stood in front of the school and wondered what had possessed him to accept the job when the school board offered it. "I can't believe I'm going to do this. I'm no teacher."

"You did it for the money."

He spun around to see Lillian smiling at him. His spirits rose. "*Nee*, the salary won't make me a rich man, that's for sure, but this was a bad idea."

"So why did you accept?" She had her books clutched tightly to her chest.

"I knew you could use some help." It was true. He did want to lighten her load. More than that, he wanted to be near her. To see her smiling at him the way she was smiling now.

"I appreciate that, Timothy. Shall we go in?"

"Do I have to?"

"Well, you could stand out here the whole day. Or you could go home, but you wouldn't be much help to me either way." She started toward the door. Timothy took a deep breath and followed her.

Inside the building, he noticed someone had moved a scarred oak desk up beside hers. His desk. He really was going to go through with this. For one term. "Tell me everything I need to know before the children get here."

She started laughing. He scowled at her. "What's so funny?"

"I have been teaching for three years and I still don't know all I need to know. You will do fine."

Her belief in him bolstered his spirits enough to settle the butterflies in his stomach. "Can you at least give me some hints to get through the day?"

"Sure. Keep breathing."

"I can handle that."

"Relax. I don't plan to throw you to the wolves. I spent six weeks working with the last teacher before she left to marry. You are simply going to be helping me while you learn the ropes. Things haven't changed much since you and I sat in these desks. You already know the routine. What are some of your memories about school?"

He closed his eyes. "Getting here early enough to play ball for an inning before the bell rang. Putting my soup on the stove to stay warm until lunchtime. Copying the math assignment from the board. Saying the Lord's Prayer. Standing up front to sing poorly. I hated that. Slipping a note to Jenny Holms asking her if she would go to a singing with me when we are old enough and praying I wouldn't get caught doing it."

"You liked Jenny Holms? I never knew that. Did she ever go to a singing with you?"

"Sure."

"Who else did you walk out with?"

"Oh, I took a lot of girls home from singings in my time. During my *rumspringa*, I had a fancy open-topped buggy and a flashy fast horse. I even had a stereo installed under the dash of my ride. I rocked the whole country when I had it blaring."

"I'm shocked. Absolutely shocked. I thought you were the quiet one of the Bowman boys."

"I was. Our poor mother. You were in Wisconsin and missed all the fun here."

"So it would seem. What happened to the buggy?"

"I sold it."

"And the horse?"

"I still have her. She's not so fast these days, but she is gentle. Did you do much dating in Wisconsin?" He realized they had never talked about their years apart.

"I did my share."

"Were you ever serious about anyone?"

She sat down at her desk and propped her chin on her hand. "There was one boy. Arnold Weaver. He had red curly hair. We were in love for a few months."

"What happened?"

"I was in love with him, but it turned out that he was in love with Karen Coblentz. Happily, I realized Karen was a much better match for him. It wasn't true love for me, but it was for them. They married just before my family moved back here."

"And there was never anyone else?"

"Not to speak of. How about you? Did you ever come close to marriage?"

"I didn't. There are many fine Amish women in this community, but none of them made my heart beat faster. Maybe I'm too picky. That's what *Mamm* says. Maybe I should settle for nice and be happy."

"You shouldn't settle."

"No?"

"No. Find the one who makes your heart beat faster. She's out there."

He gazed into her beautiful green eyes. "You're right, she is."

A faint blush colored Lillian's cheeks. Timothy hoped she knew he was talking about her. If she did, she gave no sign of it. Was he mistaken in thinking she returned his affection?

Was friendship all she wanted from him?

The first student came bursting in the door. It was Carl Mast. "Teacher, look what I made for you."

He proudly handed Lillian a drawing of stick figures gathered around a campfire. One of the figures had smoke circling around his head. "This is my family. That's Davey because he smokes now and *Daed* doesn't like it. *Daed* won't talk to him, but Davey says it's okay if I do. Is it okay, Teacher?"

Lillian knelt to be on Carl's level. "It is fine for you to talk to Davey. You are not yet baptized and the rules on shunning don't apply to you. I'm sorry your father won't speak to him. He wants Davey to come back to the church. We all pray for that, but each man must find his own way to God. Maybe that's what Davey is doing."

She glanced at Timothy and caught his nod. He agreed with her attempt to comfort the child and explain a difficult subject. Religion was not part of their school curriculum. That was the sacred duty of parents and church ministers. She looked at the picture and then at Carl. "I want you to go hang this with the other art work. You did a fine job."

"Danki." He smiled a gap-toothed grin, went to the corkboard behind her desk and pinned it up.

She looked at Timothy. "Would you erase the board and put up the new arithmetic assignment? I've written them out in the red notebook on my desk."

"Of course. Carl, would you like to help me?"

"Sure." The boy scampered to his side and began making big sweeps with the eraser as high as he could reach.

As the day went on, Lillian knew the board had made a wise decision when they hired Timothy. He moved among the children offering help, encouragement and praise. Twice he stepped behind Abe and stopped the boy from passing a note. He whispered something in the boy's ear that she didn't hear, but it was effective. Abe was as good as gold the rest of the day.

At recess, he joined the older children in a ball game and earned huge marks for his ability to hit the ball over the outfield fence. As the last student went out the door at the end of the day, Timothy sank into his chair and looked at her. "This isn't the job for me."

"Are you going to quit?" Lillian's stunned expression told Timothy she had taken him seriously.

"I have said I would teach for one term. I'm not going to break my word, but I feel sorry for the *kinder* that will have to put up with me until summer."

"You didn't do so badly." She sat in the student desk next to him.

"I didn't do that well. There has to be someone better out there."

"They did not step forward when the position was opened. You're going to do fine. Give yourself a chance."

"All of your students can conjugate verbs better than

I can. I felt foolish trying to explain something I don't understand."

"Now you know how I feel about teaching science. I am woefully inadequate in that field, but I can conjugate with the best of them. Present tense. I see. You see. He sees. We see. You see. They see."

"Right. So explain to me why everyone can see, but he/she/it sees."

"English is a complicated language."

"It is. It was. It will be."

She smiled at him. "Very good."

"Only because Susan Yoder did it for me."

"She'll make a fine teacher someday, and so will you."

"Can we go over the lesson plans for tomorrow? I don't want to feel so flat-footed in front of the children again."

"Of course. Pull your chair over here." She scooted her chair to the end of her desk to make room for him.

"How long did it take you to learn all this?" he asked.

"I haven't learned it all. I'm still discovering better ways to teach. I think the most frustrating thing about English is that so many words don't sound like they look. I think I am teaching the right way to say a word only to find out later that I have been mispronouncing something for ages."

"High German is much more straightforward," he said.

"I agree."

"Have you noticed how much trouble Hannah has reading aloud?" he asked.

"I've been working with her, but I can't seem to find the key that will boost her confidence."

"I've read that some children do better at reading to their pets than reading to other people. Have you heard of that?"

"I have. Do you think we should let Bella come to school?"

"It's worth a try, isn't it?"

"Sure."

She flipped open a ledger and found tomorrow's date. "Your upper grades will study cell structure and write an essay on the subject at the end of the week."

"At least that's something I can handle."

"I'm glad, because that is something that completely escapes my understanding. Why don't we leak away if we are 90 percent water? What makes all our cells stick together in the same fashion every day?"

"We don't leak because of cell membranes. They keep the fluids inside."

She started chuckling. "What's so funny?" he demanded.

"Do you realize how well suited to this job we would be if we could somehow combine us into one new and improved teacher?"

"I prefer to think we complement each other. Where I lack, you excel and vice versa."

"It does seem that way." Her voice was little more than a whisper.

"We make a good team," he said softly. He fought down the urge to reach out and touch her face.

"Yes, we do." She sounded almost breathless now.

If he leaned in a little more, he could kiss her. Would she let him?

She pulled back and looked away. "That's why you can't quit. I need your help."

"I won't quit. Not until the school board can find someone to replace me."

She stood and gathered her books into her arms, holding them close to her chest. "I hope that takes a very long time. I knew I would enjoy working with you, but I must get home. Do you need a textbook to read up on your subjects for tomorrow?"

"That would be great."

She moved across the room to the shelves that held the school's library books. After scanning the contents, she selected a volume and held it toward him. "I have found this book to be the most helpful with science. It has some wonderful illustrations."

Timothy tipped his head to the side at a new sound. "Do I hear a siren?"

Lillian listened. "I hear it, too. Not again."

They went outside and turned in every direction. He couldn't see any sign of smoke.

"Maybe it's a medical call," Timothy said.

Somehow he knew in his heart it wasn't. As they stood in front of the school, the siren grew louder until the fire engine rounded the curve, heading toward the ridge. Luke leaned out the passenger's side and shouted, "Weaver's farm. Get on the next truck."

Lillian clutched Timothy's arm. "Amanda is spending the day with Granny Weaver. She lives in the *daadi* house at the Weaver place."

"We'll take care of her. Don't worry." He hoped it wasn't an empty promise. The second, smaller fire truck came around the bend. It stopped to let him get on and then roared away.

Looking back, he saw Lillian running toward home.

Chapter Sixteen

Everyone in the Amish school was subdued the next morning, including the teachers. Lillian knew all the children had heard about the fire. Everyone was thankful there had been no loss of life. All fifty pigs had been saved, but the new hog house under construction had been a total loss. Lillian could see the unease on the young faces of those looking to her for comfort and guidance, and she wasn't sure how to help them.

Amanda had refused to go to Granny Weaver's home that morning. She sat at a small student desk beside Lillian's large one. She was quietly coloring in one of her books, but Lillian noticed every page had been scribbled over with red.

Lillian sent Timothy a silent plea for help. She had already opened the morning with a Bible verse, the twenty-third Psalm, and the children had recited the Lord's Prayer. Normally, she would have the children come up to sing, but today did not seem normal.

Timothy moved his chair from his desk and parked it at the top of the aisle between the rows of children. "Many of you know that I serve as a volunteer fireman. I helped put out the fire last night. I was wondering if any of you have questions that I might be able to answer."

Susan Yoder tentatively raised her hand. He motioned to her. She rose to her feet. "My *daed* says the fire was started on purpose by an *Englisch* fellow riding a four-wheeler. Is that who did it?"

"No one saw who started the fire. Granny Weaver did see a fellow on a four-wheeler about twenty minutes before she noticed the smoke. It could've been that man. But maybe he was just out having a good time and had nothing to do with the fire."

Hannah stood up. Bella, her yellow Lab, lay quietly beside her chair. "I wish you and my *daed* wouldn't go to the fires anymore. I heard my *mamm* say it's getting too dangerous."

"A fire is a dangerous thing. But your *daed* and I and all the other firemen are very careful. We don't want anyone to get hurt."

"Why do the *Englisch* hate us?" Abe asked.

"The *Englisch* do not hate us," Lillian replied.

"Then why are they starting all these fires?" Gabriel demanded.

"My *mamm* says she isn't going to sell any more quilts to them," little Marietta Yoder said with a fierce scowl on her face. Her older sister, Susan, hushed her.

Timothy laced his fingers together and leaned forward with his elbows on his knees. "We must not hold a grudge or blame everyone for the acts of one or two people."

"He is right." Lillian moved to stand beside him. "We must forgive those that trespass against us. Isn't that what we say when we repeat the Lord's Prayer? Forgive us our trespasses as we forgive those who trespass against us. We do not punish or condemn. That is not our way."

"What should we do?" Susan asked.

"We must do as we have always done. Take care of one another and trust the Lord to guide and protect us. We must be kind. We must be gentle in the way we live and humble before God. Our Lord has a greater purpose for each one of us. If we are quiet in our hearts, we can hear His will and obey."

Timothy stood up. "All right, fourth-grade class, I need you to take out your spelling workbooks. We are having a pop quiz."

Lillian heard a small groan from the class but decided to ignore it. She beckoned to Susan Yoder. "For reading today, I want each of the second graders to go to the chair I have set up in the back corner, and each of them is to spend fifteen minutes reading to Bella."

"To the dog?" Susan looked as if she hadn't heard correctly.

"To the dog. The students are to raise their hand if they don't know a word. Otherwise, they are simply to read aloud. They may choose any book they would like."

"Why?"

"It's an experiment."

"It's kind of silly, but okay. Is the dog going to be tested over what she has heard?"

Lillian cupped a hand over her chin as if she were considering the idea. After a few seconds, she smiled and shook her head.

Timothy winked at Lillian before he turned to Susan. "I'm afraid the dog would score higher than the rest of us, and that wouldn't look good on our year-end report."

Lillian burst out laughing, and Timothy joined in. Susan walked away shaking her head at their foolishness.

Over the next two weeks, Timothy found his footing in his new job and began to enjoy it. Each hurdle that one of his students overcame filled him with joy. Abe had stopped pestering the younger children. Once Timothy realized Abe was bored with schoolwork that was too easy for him, he started bringing him harder and harder assignments. He looked forward to the spring when he and the upper-grade boys would be doing real-life problem-solving for Brandon's project.

Often during the day, Timothy would catch Lillian watching him with a tiny smile on her face that told him she was pleased with his progress. Although he once thought he would be able to spend a lot of time with her, forty-two students turned out to be incredibly efficient chaperones. At best, he and Lillian had a few minutes before the students arrived and a few minutes after they left to enjoy each other's company. Even that time was often spent discussing new lesson plans and potential curriculum changes for the coming year. She had to hurry home to take care of Amanda and run her home, while he had to put in several hours in his father's workshop.

His younger cousins Mark and Paul Bowman had arrived the previous weekend. While they didn't have a great deal of skill as woodworkers, they had a lot of enthusiasm.

Like everyone else, Timothy and his family were on edge wondering when and who the arsonist would target next. Distrust of their *Englisch* neighbors was growing within the community. The Hansons had been the only non-Amish family targeted. The investigation by the fire marshal was ongoing, but he divulged little or no information, further frustrating the Amish.

On the last Friday of the month, Timothy and Lillian walked outside after the children had been dismissed. The air held a decided chill. Winter was tapping at the door.

The playground was empty. The students had gone. Timothy breathed in the clean, crisp air and smiled. It had been a wonderful week. Wonderful because he had been able to share it with Lillian.

She pulled her shawl tight across her chest. "Don't you love how quiet it is when they aren't here?"

"Actually, I kind of miss the noise."

Looking over the schoolyard, he noticed a doll that had been forgotten beside the swing set. Walking over, he picked it up and brushed the dirt from the little black apron. "I see one of our scholars couldn't bear to leave school."

Lillian took it from him. "This belongs to Marietta. She'll be missing it soon. She rarely goes anywhere without it. I'll drop it by her house on my way home."

Lillian would do anything for her students. "I see why you do it. I see why you say you love this job. You are so good at it."

She poked him in the chest. "So are you. Hannah has been struggling to read for ages. She was embarrassed to read aloud in front of the other students. Having her read to Bella was the perfect answer."

"It was only something I read. I wasn't sure it would work."

"Bella makes a wonderful teacher's helper. Devoted, uncritical of Hannah's slow and painful progress. She simply wants to have Hannah and the others beside her. It is the dog's acceptance of their less than perfect attempts that give them the courage to try more."

"We should ask the school board to give Bella a salary," he said with a chuckle.

"You can give the dog the credit if you want, but you are the one who helped Hannah succeed. I saw the light in her eyes when she finished her first book. She was so excited."

"I saw it, too," he admitted.

Lillian took a seat on the swing, pushed back and began to swing to and fro. "That is exactly why I love this profession. Every child has such bright potential. To see them uncover that potential is a gift."

Timothy stepped behind her and gave her a gentle push. "I wonder if you know how much your eyes light up when you talk about these children."

Lillian smiled. "I know pride is a sin, but I am proud of the children and all they accomplish."

"It is not a sin to take pride in what others have accomplished. Only to take pride in what we believe we have achieved, when God is the giver of every gift. I'm amazed at what you and the children have taught me. The Lord has blessed me with many gifts, Lillian, but chief among them is the friendship of an honorable woman."

She felt the heat rise in her cheeks. "*Danki.* Your friendship is a gift to me, too. What interesting thing do you have planned for your seventh and eighth graders next week?" she asked to steer the conversation away from personal things.

"For my history class, I thought we would build several Native American structures, since we're studying the tribes of the Eastern states first. By the end of the week, we will be studying the Plains Indians and the tribes of the desert Southwest. Since we don't have any cliffs that we can carve into homes, I thought I would have them build a tipi and a wigwam. Then I think I'll have them write an essay on comparisons using the structures for our English lesson." He gave her a shove, sending her swinging higher.

"Killing two birds with one stone, very *goot.* Turning your history lesson into an English lesson is smart, and I'm sure the children will enjoy it."

"I expect I will have to supply the poles and saplings."

"At least you don't have to kill a buffalo for the hide."

"*Nee,* I think a large tarp will serve the same purpose."

She leaned backward in the swing so that she could see him. "This is fun, isn't it?"

"Playing on the swings?"

"*Nee*, talking about the children, about their problems and their successes. Sharing what we would like them to learn. It's fulfilling." She hadn't realized how lonely it had been being the only teacher. Now that she had Timothy to share her joys and sorrows, it made her happiness complete.

He stopped her and twisted the chains around so that she was facing him. "I do like sharing my days with you. These past two weeks, I have been happier than I've ever been in my life, and it's all because of you."

She knew that he was going to kiss her. The rational part of her mind said all she had to do was turn her face aside. The lonely womanly part of her mind made her lift her face to him and close her eyes.

The touch of his lips was oh so gentle. He pulled back. She opened her eyes. He was waiting for her protest. She didn't want to object. All she wanted was to feel the touch of his lips again. And that was foolishness.

She slipped out of the swing and stood. He let go of the chains and cupped her face in his hands. "You are so beautiful."

Before she could reply, he was kissing her again. Somehow her arms found their way to his shoulders and then around his neck as he pulled her close and deepened the kiss. Nothing had ever felt as wonderful as being held in his embrace. She leaned closer and the world slipped away leaving them the only two creatures in the universe, bound together by a newfound passion.

His lips were firm but gentle as he brushed the corner of her mouth. She tipped her head slightly offering him her silent consent. He took advantage of her willingness. His mouth moved back to hers and he deepened the kiss. It was more wonderful than she had imagined. Her heart galloped in her chest as her breath came in short bursts. She gripped his shoulders to steady herself and kissed him back.

A few long wonderful seconds later, he pulled away. She opened her eyes to stare up at him. His face mirrored her wonderment. She didn't know how to react or what to say.

Regret slowly filled his eyes. "I'm sorry, Lillian. I shouldn't have done that."

She pressed her hand to her lips. They still tingled from his touch. There was no going back to the way things were before. "Don't be sorry."

"I never meant for this to happen."

"I know, but it has. Now we have to face the fact that we are only human."

"I care for you. As a friend and as a woman."

"Then as my friend, I'm going to ask you to forget that this happened."

"I don't think I can."

She touched her fingers to his lips. "You must. There is no future for us on this path."

"How can you say that?"

She stepped away from him. "I say it because it is the truth. You're a fine man. The woman who wins your heart will be blessed above all others. My heart belongs to the children, Timothy. I won't give them up. There can't be a repeat of this. Perhaps you should go now."

She could see he wanted to say more, but in the end, he simply nodded.

"All right. I'm sorry." He turned and walked away.

Lillian watched him until he was out of sight around the bend in the road. Then she sank to her knees as silent tears marked their paths down her cheeks.

Timothy walked home with his emotions in turmoil. He didn't regret kissing Lillian, but it had been a mistake. He had asked her to choose between him and the thing she loved. She cared deeply for him, her kiss told him that, but she wasn't going to give up teaching.

He reached the bridge and started across the river using the pedestrian walkway that had been built alongside the covered bridge. Halfway across, he stopped and rested his arms on the railing as he stared down into the churning waters. He'd been a fool, but at least he didn't have to hide his feelings any longer.

"I hope you aren't planning to jump."

He looked up to see Joshua coming toward him. "I'm not. I don't see how getting cold and wet will improve my outlook."

"What's wrong?" Joshua stopped beside him.

Timothy continued staring at the water. "I kissed Lillian."

"I take it things didn't go well afterward."

"Not exactly. She likes me a lot, but she won't give up teaching."

"That's tough. What are you going to do about it? I'd sure hate to see you quit. Hannah speaks very highly of you. She says Abe Mast doesn't tease her anymore because you won't let him."

"I'm glad I made one person happy."

"Did you tell Lillian she doesn't have to make a decision right away? That you would wait for her?"

"I didn't get a chance to say much, but I don't want to wait."

"Isn't she worth it?"

"She is worth it. Do you think I've ruined my chances with her?"

"No one but Lillian can answer that."

"What do you think I should do?"

When she got home that evening, Lillian washed her face at the outside pump, scrubbing away the last traces of her tears. She didn't expect Jeremiah to notice she had been crying, but she didn't want to explain if he did. Entering the house, she hung her bonnet and shawl from a peg by the front door. She noticed that Amanda's shawl was missing.

Turning around, she saw Amanda running in from the

other room to greet her. Jeremiah came to the door of the living room. "You're kind of late getting home tonight."

"I had a lot to do at school." She looked down at Amanda. "Where have you left your cloak this time?"

Amanda scrunched up her face as she tried to remember. "I think I left it in Jeremiah's buggy. We went to see the puppies again and we had supper with the Weaver family. I might get a puppy of my own when they are old enough. Shall I go get my cloak?"

Lillian shook her head. "Go get ready for bed and say your prayers. I will find it in the morning."

Jeremiah said, "Mrs. Weaver sent some supper home with us. It's in the oven if you want it."

"*Danki*. How is the job going?" He had won the bid on their construction project.

"It's good. I might have another job lined up when I'm done with this one."

"You're working so hard. *Daed* will be pleased with you. Was there any mail?"

He gestured toward the counter. "A letter from *Mamm*. I'll let you read it. I'm going to turn in."

"Good night."

Lillian pulled her supper out of the stove, but found she wasn't hungry. She ate a few bites and put the rest away. She wasn't sleepy; far from it. She needed something to take her mind off Timothy's kisses. His wonderful, wonderful kisses. Now that she knew what she was giving up, it was even harder to think about staying friends.

She opened her mother's letter and read through the three pages quickly. *Onkel* Albert continued to improve, and her father now planned to return to Wisconsin permanently. They would be home in two weeks to pack up and arrange the move. There were two openings for teachers in the area if Lillian decided she didn't want to stay in Bowmans Crossing but wanted to return to Wisconsin with her parents and Amanda. The decision wasn't as simple as it had seemed before Timothy kissed her.

Restless, and undecided, she pulled on her shawl and opened the door, hoping a short walk would bring some peace of mind. Her brother had parked the buggy in its usual place beside the barn. Taking a flashlight from the kitchen drawer, Lillian went to get her sister's cloak.

The night air had a distinct chill to it and she wished she had taken the time to put on her heavier cloak. She hurried across the yard and opened the buggy door. She shone the light on the front seat, but it was empty. Amanda had probably left her shawl at the Weaver Farm. She just hoped it hadn't been left with the puppies.

She pulled open the back door, swept her light across the interior and caught sight of a small amount of fringe sticking out from under the seat. She reached over and pulled the garment free. As she did, a blue metal canister rolled out with it. Lillian realized she was looking at a propane tank. Picking it up, she could tell it was full by the weight. The cool metal tank was perfectly harmless by itself. It was only when it was attached to a device made especially for it, such as a lantern, a flame-spreading head or a camp stove, that the gas inside was released and could be ignited.

She turned the beam of her light under the seat and pulled out two more canisters. Why would her brother have so many of these small bottles? Jeremiah had never cared for campouts and she'd never seen him with a propane lantern. He preferred battery-operated torches like the one she held.

A cold breeze sent a sudden shiver down her spine. Were these the same kinds of canisters the arsonist had used to start his fires?

Timothy would know. Should she tell him? What if her brother had them for an innocent purpose and he was unjustly arrested because of her? It had happened to Timothy's brother. She was duty-bound to protect Jeremiah until she was absolutely sure of his guilt.

The simple thing to do was to ask Jeremiah why he had them, but she couldn't. How could she admit she suspected her own brother had committed these crimes?

Lillian bundled the canisters together in Amanda's shawl and carried them into the house. Both Amanda and Jeremiah had gone to bed. In her room, she found a box and laid the canisters in it. Glancing around, she realized it would be easy for Jeremiah to find them if he searched the house. She needed a better hiding place. Would he think to search the school? Maybe, but it was better than having them where he might easily find them.

Grabbing her heavy cloak, she went out the door and walked silently through the night until she reached the school. She placed the box in the bottom drawer of a filing cabinet and locked the drawer. On Monday, she would ask Timothy what she should do. He was the one person she knew she could trust.

Chapter Seventeen

Early on Saturday morning, Timothy hitched up his buggy and drove to the home of Bishop Beachy. He needed advice. There had to be a way to let Lillian keep teaching and for them to be together. The bishop came out of the house when Timothy arrived.

Lines of worry sat heavily on the bishop's face, but he managed a smile. "Good Morning, Brother Timothy. What brings you out this way?"

"I am in need of your counsel."

"Well, then, come in. What is troubling you?" The bishop opened the door of his house and Timothy stepped into the kitchen that smelled of dough and fresh-baked bread.

The bishop's wife looked up with a bright smile. "Hello, Timothy. I'm afraid you caught me making bread. I'm covered in flour."

"Don't mind me. *Mamm* is making bread this morning, too."

"It's all right, dear," the bishop said. "Timothy and I will be in my office."

"Shall I bring you some coffee?" she offered, dusting her hands on her apron.

"Nothing for me, *danki*," Timothy said.

"Don't interrupt your work. We'll be fine." The bishop led the way to the rear of the house and a small bedroom that now served as his cluttered workspace. He moved some books from a chair and gestured to Timothy. "Sit down. How can I help you?"

"You know that Lillian and I are both teaching at the school."

"*Ja*. How is that working out for you?"

"Fine. I love it. Never in my wildest dreams would I have considered being a teacher, but now I can't imagine doing anything else."

"I'm happy to hear that. The Lord moves in mysterious ways, does He not? So, what is the problem?"

"Lillian loves teaching, too. As much as I do, or more."

"We are blessed to have two people so dedicated to our children."

"I want to ask Lillian to marry me."

"Oh, I see. That's a big step. Are you sure this is what God wants for you?"

"I hope it is. I've prayed about it, but I know Lillian doesn't want to give up teaching. Is there a reason she can't teach after we are married?"

"Being a wife and a mother is a sacred duty that must come before any job, Timothy. I'm sure you understand that."

"I do, but couldn't she continue to teach until our first babe arrives?"

"This is an unusual request. I, too, must pray about it."

Timothy hid his disappointment. He wanted an answer today.

"Will it be awkward for the two of you to continue to work together?" the bishop asked.

Timothy shook his head. "The children take all our time during school hours. They have our full attention. I don't let my feelings for Lillian interfere with my work."

"How do you think the *kinder* would feel knowing the two of you were wed?"

"I think they would accept it. Many married couples work together. Emma and Luke will work together in her store. Rebecca helps Samuel with record-keeping and orders for the business. Every wife is a helpmate to her husband."

"What you say is true. If the school board has no objections, I can offer none."

Timothy left the bishop's home feeling more hopeful. If he could convince Lillian he was willing to have a long engagement and that she could work after their marriage until their own children came along, she might find it acceptable. There was only one flaw in his plan. Lillian hadn't said that she loved him.

Timothy returned home and stopped by the woodworking building to pick up the pager. It was his day to be on call. After that, he hitched up a team to the planter. As he drove the horses across the bridge, he saw Brandon and Debra waiting for him at the edge of the field.

"Your horses are so pretty." Debra immediately went to the head of the team. The big gray Percherons lowered their heads for some attention.

Brandon stood at his vehicle with an array of soil testing chemicals spread out on the hood. "I'm almost finished."

"Do you have the seed you wish to plant?"

"In the trunk."

Timothy pulled out the bags, cut them open and began filling his planter. "How many pounds and what depth do you want?"

He and Brandon discussed the best planting strategies and then Timothy made a single round of the field. Brandon analyzed the planting depth and seed thickness and gave Timothy the thumbs-up sign. After planting half the field, Timothy pulled the team to a stop again when Brandon walked out to meet him. "Can I ride along with you?" he asked.

"Would you like to drive them?" Timothy offered.

"I'd love to." Brandon climbed into the seat with Timothy's help. Standing behind him, Timothy showed him how to hold the reins and what commands to give the horse.

Debra rushed up with her cell phone out. "I have to have a picture of this."

Timothy held a hand in front of his face palm out. "No pictures of me, please."

She looked mortified. "I'm sorry. I forgot. I'll delete this one."

He smiled. "I appreciate that. Let me step away so you can get a good picture of your brother."

He did and she took a couple of shots before putting her phone away. After that, he made several rounds of the field with Brandon's help and then let him off. Debra declined to ride. Each time he passed by the school, Timothy's gaze was drawn to the swing set beside it. He'd never again look at it without remembering that was where he had kissed Lillian. He half hoped she would come by to visit with Debra and Brandon, but she didn't. Was he the reason? Was she avoiding him now?

A little after noon, his mother and Mary came to the field with a picnic hamper. He stopped and enjoyed a hearty ham sandwich and homemade pickles for lunch. Debra had her first whoopee pie and couldn't stop raving about it. When lunch was over, she followed the women back to the house to do some shopping in his mother's gift shop.

It was growing late by the time he finished planting the large field. He stopped the team by the car where Brandon and Debra were waiting for him. "That's it," he said.

"Now all we need is a little rain," Brandon said with a smile.

Timothy wiped the sweat from his brow with the back of his sleeve. "Did you find something at the gift shop?"

"I did. Two wonderful baby quilts, several jars of homemade jam and two cute gourd birdhouses."

"I'll tell my brother Luke that you like them."

Debra sniffed the air. "Do I smell smoke?"

Timothy scanned the area. "You may be smelling the burned-out trees by the river."

"No, she's right. I smell smoke, too," Brandon said with a frown.

A second later, Timothy's pager went off. He read the message, raised the planter out of the dirt and sent his team galloping for home.

In the early-morning hours, the only wall left standing still bore traces of faint blue lettering, but the words were illegible. Lillian knew it once read Bowmans Crossing Amish-Made Gifts and Furniture. Timothy's mother's gift shop lay in ruins. Sadly, three other fires had been set in the night. Silas Mast's dairy barn was gone and thirty head of cattle had perished in the flames. Two other Amish barns had been heavily damaged. It had taken eight fire companies from the surrounding counties to control the blazes.

Emma, Mary and Rebecca were weeping openly. Joshua put his arm around his wife. "I painted that sign when I was a kid and I painted it again after I got out of prison. I reckon I can make another."

"It was too fancy anyway," Isaac said, wiping his hand across his sweaty and smoke-stained brow.

"The bishop never objected." Dry-eyed, Ana stood beside Isaac with her hands on her hips.

Isaac nudged her with his elbow. "Because he has always had a soft spot for you."

They shared a tender smile.

Lillian saw Timothy among the firemen raking through the debris and dousing embers. She longed to comfort him, but had to wait quietly until his work was done. She noticed Debra and Brandon at the edge of a group of onlookers and went over to them. Debra saw her and came to put her arms around Lillian. "This is terrible. What kind of monster does this to such peaceful people?"

"We must forgive him." Lillian gave lip service to her belief, but letting go of the anger in her heart was harder.

Brandon patted his sister on the shoulder. "What are these people going to do now?"

"Help each other rebuild," Lillian said, wondering how that was going to be possible. Everyone in the community had already given what assistance they could afford to the earlier victims.

Debra turned pleading eyes to her brother. "Brandon, we have to do something."

"We will, sis."

The fire chief came up to Isaac. "I'm afraid it looks like arson. The burn pattern matches the others. The flames were shooting up the outside of the building. It didn't start inside. We'll send pieces of wood to the lab for analysis, but I'm sure they are going to tell us it was soaked with gasoline."

"Did you find another propane bottle?"

"No, not yet," the chief admitted. "We'll do a more thorough search when the debris cools enough to let our arson squad inside. In the meantime, it's off-limits to everyone."

He turned and spoke to the crowd of onlookers. "I want everyone to go home now."

Someone shouted from the back, "Why haven't you caught this fellow? All our business and homes are at risk."

Sheriff Bradley moved to stand beside Chief Swanson. "We are working hard to find out who is behind this, but we need everyone's help. Be aware of what is going on around you. Don't be afraid to call 9-1-1 if you see something suspicious. We will check it out. If it's nothing, good. If it helps break this case, better. Now please go home."

The group reluctantly began to disperse. Timothy along with Luke came to stand beside their parents. They looked bone-tired. Lillian resisted the urge to put her arm around Timothy and offer him support. He caught sight of her, nodded and walked over. Her heart did a funny little flip as their eyes met. She was well and truly smitten.

He wiped his brow with his shirtsleeve. "I'm off duty now. I'd like to talk to you if you have some time."

"Wouldn't you like to get some rest first?"

"*Nee*, I'll wash off the grime and meet you out back of the house in *Mamm*'s garden if you can stay awhile longer."

"Are you sure it can't wait?"

"Please, humor me."

"Okay." She wasn't sure which she wanted more. A repeat of yesterday's kisses or for him to tell her they would simply be friends again.

Timothy prayed he was doing the right thing as he left the house, his hair still wet from his shower. Lillian was seated on a lattice bench beside his mother's rosebush. He took a seat beside her and took one of her hands between his own. "I have something important to say to you."

"You look so serious. What's wrong?"

"Nothing is wrong. I hope what I have to say will make you happy. I spoke with the bishop yesterday. I wanted to speak to him before I spoke with you. I know you believe you will have to give up teaching if you marry, but that isn't the case. I didn't want to say anything until I was sure."

"No, Timothy. Don't." She turned her face away from him.

He cupped her cheek. "Don't what? Don't tell you how much you mean to me? Don't tell you how happy I am when I am near you? I can't keep these things a secret any longer. I love you, Lillian. As a friend, yes, but also as the woman who holds my heart in the palm of her hand. I want you to be my wife. I want the right to hold you in my arms. I want to grow old beside you. Tell me that you love me, too. I long to hear those words from your lips."

She closed her eyes and he knew a moment of gut-wrenching fear. What if she didn't love him? How could he go on?

She pressed her hand over his where it rested on her cheek. "You don't know how hard this is."

He steeled himself to hear her rejection. "If you don't feel as I do, I understand."

Please, God, let her love me.

"Before you answer me, Lillian, let me tell you what the bishop said. I asked him if we could go on teaching together as husband and wife. He said that it would be acceptable if the school board agrees. Do you understand what I'm saying? You don't have to give up teaching. Not for a while anyway. Not until the Lord blesses us with children of our own. I can endure a long engagement if it means you will be mine in the end. Will you marry me? I love you more than life itself."

Lillian could barely see his face through her tears. She moved her hand to cup his cheek. "I know how important having children is to you, Timothy. I know you have dreams of a big family."

"I do want a big family, but more than that, I want you to be the mother of my children."

"And for that reason, I must tell you that I can't marry you." Her voice cracked as did her heart. She hated hurting him this way.

Disbelief filled his eyes. "You care for me. I know you do. I feel it in your touch. I see it when you look at me. I hear it in your laughter. You love me. I know you do."

"I do love you, Timothy."

"Then I don't understand."

"It is because I love you that I will never marry you. This is my burden, and I must carry it alone. I'm barren, Timothy. I can never have children."

He frowned. "How can you know this?"

"Shortly after my family moved to Wisconsin, I became ill. I had developed a rare form of cancer. The surgery to remove it saved my life, but it left me unable to have children. I'm sorry, Timothy. I won't marry you or anyone."

It was a shock to him. Lillian saw it on his face and wished she could have spared him this pain. She couldn't bear his look of sorrow a moment longer. "I have to go now."

She rose to her feet, and he didn't try to stop her. She was thankful for that. She didn't want him to see her heart was breaking, too.

Timothy remained on the bench in the garden at the back of the house overlooking the river. The morning air held the scents of his mother's roses and the sweet autumn clematis that climbed the trellis against the wall. The river was a wide swath of dark water traveling endlessly along. The surface looked calm, but he knew there were eddies and currents that swirled beneath the surface much like the turbulent emotions that ran ceaselessly through his brain.

"What is troubling you, my son?"

Timothy looked up to find his father standing beside him. He hadn't heard his approach. For a second, Timothy was tempted to deny he was troubled, but the words stuck in his throat. His father sat down. "This is a good thinking spot. I have always liked watching the river, don't you?"

"I do, too."

"I often sit here when I need to pray about something. I like to think I'm talking to the good Lord as a friend when I sit here in your mother's garden. Am I interrupting your prayers?"

"*Nee*, I wasn't praying."

"Should you be?"

"I would if I knew what to pray for." He met his father's gaze. "I asked Lillian to marry me."

"Did you, now? Not much of a surprise in that. The two of you seem made for each other."

Timothy leaned forward with his elbows propped on his knees. "I thought so, too. She turned me down."

"I'm sorry to hear that. It may not be any of my business, but did she give you a reason?"

"She said it would be unfair to me."

"Because her heart lies elsewhere?"

"*Nee*, she says she loves me, but won't wed me because she can't have children. She doesn't want to bind me to a barren wife for all my life."

His father stroked his long beard. "I see. She is certain of her condition?"

"She is. The doctors she saw in Wisconsin told her she would never have a child."

His father was silent for a long time. Then he said, "Children are among God's greatest gift to us. Knowing that I have sons to carry on after me gives me great comfort. I know your mother will never be alone or in need should something happen to me."

Timothy looked at his father. "My whole life I wanted to be as good a father as you have been to me."

"That is fine praise, but being a father has not always been easy. My sons are so different from each other that I sometimes used to wonder if the midwife slipped me a cowbird egg or two. Happily, I have come to see your mother and me in all of you. You take after your mother the most. You are tenderhearted and yet sensible. You care for the land and the business I have built, but you care more for the people around you. Do you love Lillian?"

"With all my heart."

"I thought as much. Do you believe she is the woman chosen by God to be your life mate?"

"I did. I don't know what to believe now. How can I see Lillian every day and know she will never be mine? I'm not strong enough, *Daed*. I had such dreams for us. I don't know how to let those go."

"Do you wish to marry her in spite of what she has told you?"

"That's just it. I'm not sure. I love her, but I want a family."

"And what is a family?"

His father's question puzzled Timothy. "Children and a wife."

"Your children?"

"*Ja.*"

"Do you love Hannah?"

Timothy frowned at the sudden change of topic. "Of course I do."

"Joshua loves Hannah with all his heart. I love her, too, as does your mother. We all love that child, but she is no blood relation to us. Yet our family would be incomplete without her."

Hannah had been four years old when Joshua met

Mary. Joshua often said he fell in love with Hannah first and had to marry Mary in order to keep the child.

Timothy gazed out at the river again. If only the Lord would send him a sign. Something to help him know what to do. "Would you have married Mother had you known she couldn't give you sons?"

"I married your mother because God chose her to be my better half, for now and forever. There was no guarantee of children in that bargain."

"Yet you both hoped and prayed for children."

"We did pray for strong sons, and the Lord heard us. Telling a man to give up his hopes and dreams of having a family one day is a difficult thing. I cannot tell you what to do. You must decide."

The problem was, he couldn't decide. Which did he want more? Lillian or his dreams of a large and loving family?

Chapter Eighteen

On Sunday, the bishop and minister preached about Moses and the troubles he and his people endured before they reached the Promised Land. Some lost their faith, others faltered and recovered, but God was with them all along. Lillian knew it was an attempt to raise the spirits of the community, but it did nothing to raise hers.

A collection was taken for the victims of the fires, but the amount raised didn't come close to covering the losses. The bishop assured people he would make appeals to other churches and they had to be content with that. The community had been pushed into poverty in a matter of days. It would take them years to recover.

Lillian avoided seeing Timothy after the service by leaving early. Amanda was upset that she couldn't stay and play with her friends, but Lillian promised she could have a friend come for a sleepover later in the week and that mollified her.

Lillian spent the day writing a long letter to her parents explaining about the fires and the law's inability to find those responsible. She thought of the box in her desk and wondered what she should say to Jeremiah. He hadn't mentioned missing the canisters, and there had been fires set without them. He had to be innocent. She believed that in her soul.

As much as she dreaded facing Timothy on Monday, she was still happy to see his dear face when he walked into the schoolhouse before classes. He didn't mention their last meeting and neither did she. They were polite and kind to each other. It was as if a large and invisible glass wall had been erected between them. She had no idea how to break through without cutting her heart to shreds.

How long could they go on this way?

The children were all quiet and studious. Everyone had been affected by the senseless violence against them. Lillian realized that the joy she felt when she was teaching had vanished, but she owed it to the children to give her best.

On Wednesday night, she was surprised to see Silas Mast at her door. She bade him come in. He stood in her kitchen with his hat in his hands, turning it round and round as he stared at the floor. Unease crept up her spine. "What's wrong, Silas?"

He looked at her then. "You know that our community has been hard hit by these fires. Everyone has emptied their pockets to help one other, and still there are those who will bear a hard financial burden from these events."

"I know that you more than anyone have suffered a great loss," she said kindly.

"The Lord does not give us more than we can bear. However, I must think about the needs of others as well as my own needs. I have met with the school board earlier tonight. We have decided that this district can no longer afford to pay two teachers."

"I see. Have you told Timothy?"

"I came to speak with you first and offer you the job, but I know your family is moving back to Wisconsin and you may wish to go with them."

She had prayed for a sign, and the Lord was showing her a clear path, although not one she expected. But this way she wouldn't have to face Timothy every day and endure the pain of knowing he loved her and she loved him in vain.

"Timothy has proven his worth," she said. "The children adore him. Let him keep the job. You are right. I would like to return to Wisconsin with my family."

He looked relieved at her quick decision. "Will you stay out the month?"

Two more weeks of seeing Timothy every day? Could she do it?

She didn't want to give up one more minute with him, but a clean break would be easier for both of them. "My parents will be home this weekend and we'll be leaving again as soon as possible. Friday must be my last day."

"As you wish. Shall I tell Timothy?"

"I will see him tomorrow. I can do it." She pasted a smile on her face in spite of the pain in her heart.

After the end of school the following day, she shared the news with Timothy. Drawing a deep breath, she kept her gaze pinned to the floor. "I have decided to move with my family." She looked up to see his reaction.

He was clearly taken aback. "You're leaving?"

Lillian hadn't felt so miserable in ages. The bewildered look in Timothy's eyes made her long to cup her hands on either side of his face and tell him none of it was his fault. The fault lay with her alone.

She thought she had accepted God's plan for her life. To be a teacher, not a wife and mother. To that end, she had hardened her heart against loving any man, but love had crept in unnoticed in the guise of friendship. The friendship of a wonderful, kind and generous man.

"When?" His voice broke on the word.

"This is my last week."

"I see." The resignation in his tone told her more than his words that he wasn't ready to let her go.

"It's for the best. This is too hard."

"I don't know what to say." His eyes bored into hers.

"Wish me well." *Tell me you love me. Ask me not to go.*

"I wish you every good thing, Lillian, you know that. I'll miss you."

"I'll miss you, too."

She saw the glint of tears in his eyes as he left.

Standing in her empty classroom, she raised her eyes to heaven, praying for strength. Someday Timothy would fall in love, marry and, God willing, have children. If she stayed, she would one day teach them in this school. How could she bear it? Why was she being tested this way?

"Lillian, are you all right?" Debra asked softly from the doorway.

"*Nee*, I'm not."

"Can I do something to help?"

"Show me how to fall out of love. Do you have a pill for that?"

"Oh, my poor dear." Debra came and put her arms around Lillian.

Her kindness was the final straw. A raw sob broke from Lillian's throat. It opened a floodgate of tears. Pouring her sorrow out on Debra's shoulder, Lillian was only vaguely aware that Debra led her to a chair and sat down beside her.

When Lillian was done crying, she pulled away from Debra. "I'm sorry."

"Don't be. Tears are good for us."

"I know. We all need puffy eyes and red noses." She sniffed once. "What are you doing here?"

"I came bearing gifts."

"For who?"

"You because I don't know anyone else well enough to give them this." Debra took her bag off her shoulder and pulled out a slip of paper. It was a check for a huge sum of money.

Lillian looked at her in shock. "I can't take this."

"You can and you will. Give it to your bishop to divide it among the people who have lost so much."

"How can you possibly afford to give so large a sum?"

Debra laughed. "You're right. It would take a few years to earn this at my salary. Have you heard of crowd funding?"

Lillian shook her head.

"I shouldn't be surprised, since you don't use a computer. There are internet sites where you post a plea for money and people can donate to your cause if they believe in it."

"People gave this amount? Strangers?"

"Many people gave a little. A few gave a lot. One person gave a whole lot. I'm sure there will be more money coming in as word spreads about this violence against innocent and humble people."

"I don't know what to say."

"I think the word is *danki*," Debra said with a cheesy grin.

"That is the word." Lillian threw her arms around Debra and hugged her with gratitude overflowing from her heart.

"Now would you like to tell me why I found you in tears? I take it you are in love with someone who doesn't love you back?"

"He does love me, and that is the problem."

"Girl, you are going to have to explain this from the top."

Lillian was sitting at her desk when Timothy came in the next morning. He spoke quickly. "Our chief just told us they know who's been starting these fires."

She quelled the sudden panic in her gut. "Have they said who it is?"

"He wouldn't give a name until an arrest has been made, but it is a local man."

Where was Jeremiah? He hadn't come home last night. How could she help him?

Timothy sat down on the chair beside her. "People will find it hard to accept that it was one of us. You don't look surprised, Lillian."

It was no use pretending anymore. "I have suspected for some time that Jeremiah might be involved."

"What? I can't believe that. Your brother is an honest fellow. What makes you suspect him?"

Lillian unlocked the large bottom drawer of the filing cabinet and pulled out the cardboard box. She took off the lid and set the box on the top of her desk. In it were the three propane canisters she had discovered under her brother's buggy seat. "I don't know what reason Jeremiah has been keeping these. I discovered them by accident under the seat of his buggy. These are the same kind that were used to start the fire at the Hanson Farm and in Bishop Beachy's hayfield, aren't they?"

"I think so."

"What should I do, Timothy? He's my brother and I love him. Your brother made mistakes and he repented. I know Jeremiah is a good man. I don't understand why he would do such a thing. In my heart I don't believe he would, but then I see this evidence."

"You don't have to do anything, sister."

She looked up to see her brother walking toward her.

"Jeremiah, what are you doing here?"

"I came to tell you that Davey Mast has been arrested."

The relief that surged to her was short-lived. "What about these?" She gestured toward the propane canisters.

"I took them out of his car. I thought I could prevent him from starting another fire, but that failed. I have tried to convince him to stop, but he wouldn't listen to reason."

She rose and ran to her brother, throwing her arms around his neck. "I never wanted to believe it was you, but you have been acting so strangely."

He returned her embrace. "I'm sorry that I frightened you. I knew what Davey had done, and I have been trying to talk him into giving himself up."

She drew back. "Poor Silas. This will be a terrible blow."

Jeremiah nodded. "Davey was the one who told me that Hanson had fired his boss's crew for stealing tools. He said he could hire an Amish crew to harvest the field for half the price. I thought it was odd, knowing Hanson never cared for us, but I wanted to make some extra money. Davey offered to drive me to the Hanson place before anyone else found out he was looking to hire a new crew. I know I shouldn't have accepted a ride from him, but Davey and I have been friends for years. If Hanson hired us, Davey would work for me and not lose any pay."

"But Mr. Hanson wasn't looking for an Amish crew," Timothy said.

"He started yelling and ordering us off the place. He called Davey a liar and a thief and said the only thing worse than an Amish was an ex-Amish thief. Davey was furious."

Lillian cupped her brother's sad face. "I know his shunning was hard on you."

"I knew there was good in him. I thought I could get him to come back to us. He never meant to put the school and all the children in danger. He said that fire just got out of hand."

"So why did he start the fires at Bishop Beachy's hay-field and why would he burn down his father's barn?" Lillian asked, still trying to wrap her mind around the fact that someone she had known for years could do such things.

Jeremiah shook his head. "I don't know what happened to him. Maybe getting away with the Hanson Farm fire made him think he could do it again. He once told me the bishop should be punished for shunning him. I know his father's refusal to even speak to him hurt him deeply. He honestly did try to keep the fire from spreading by stopping it that day."

"We all thought he was a hero," Timothy said, shaking his head.

"All men are made up of good and evil," Lillian said.

Jeremiah stepped back and held Lillian at arm's length. "I also came here to tell you that I will be moving to Wisconsin with *Mamm* and *Daed*. There is more work for me there and fewer bad memories."

"I'm coming, too."

He looked from her to Timothy. "Are you sure you want to do that?"

Lillian raised her chin. "It's what I need to do. I have news of my own. Debra and her brother have been fundraising for us. I have a check to deliver to the bishop for many thousands of dollars. Everyone who lost things in the fire will get enough money to help them recover."

Jeremiah tipped his head to the side. "The *Englisch* are sending money to us? *Daed* will never believe it."

"It looks like God has smiled on us after we endured our trials," Timothy said.

She handed the check to her brother. "Will you deliver this to the bishop for me?"

"Gladly. This is wonderful news. All our problems are solved," Jeremiah said as he headed out the door.

Lillian felt the awkwardness return now that she and Timothy were alone. Jeremiah was wrong. Not all their problems had been solved. Could she really leave Timothy?

Chapter Nineteen

Somehow Timothy made it through the weekend, but the pain in his heart never let up. How long would it take him to get over Lillian? A year? A lifetime?

His family was busy with plans to rebuild the gift shop and help with numerous barn raisings. Like most of the community, they were saddened to know the arsonist had once been a member of their faith.

Newspaper reporters and a few television crews came to Bowmans Crossing looking for a story angle. They went away frustrated when the Amish they tried to interview avoided their questions and their cameras.

Monday morning finally arrived. For the first time in his short career, he approached the school with dragging steps. She wouldn't be there today or ever again.

He opened the door. The schoolroom was as empty as his heart without her. He walked across the plank floors, his footsteps echoing softly in the stillness. He stopped in front of her desk. She wasn't coming back. She wouldn't be here to help him learn to be a good teacher. She wouldn't be here to make him smile at her teasing or to share some wonderful new story with. How was he going to go on without her?

He stepped behind the desk and looked out over the empty rows of student desks waiting patiently for the children to arrive. He was their teacher now, and he wouldn't let them down. For such a small woman, Lillian had left him big shoes to fill. The children would miss her, too. He couldn't allow a broken heart to interfere with his most important task.

He pulled out the chair and sat down at her desk. One by one, he opened the drawers searching for some trace of her. He found it in the bottom right drawer. A blue sweater, folded and forgotten.

He pulled it out and pressed the soft wool to his face as he inhaled her fragrance. Tears stung his eyes. He couldn't let her go. He had to find a way to convince her to return.

It didn't matter that they wouldn't have children together. If that was God's plan for them, he would face it with a glad heart if only she would be his wife. How could he make her believe that?

"Timothy?"

He looked up and saw her standing in the doorway with the morning light streaming in around her. He wasn't sure he could trust his eyes. "Lillian? I prayed you would come back."

"I left my sweater here. I came to collect it before I left." She held out her hand.

"You can't have it. I love you, Lillian. Please don't go away. I can't breathe when you aren't near me."

Tears filled her eyes. "Nothing has changed."

"Yes, it has. I've changed. I'm a teacher who needs help. I wanted children, and now I have forty-two of them looking to me for guidance. How can I be all I need to be without you by my side?"

"They won't be your children. Your flesh and blood."

"They will demand blood, sweat and tears from me. From both of us. It's enough for me. Isn't it enough for you? Now that the community has been blessed with such generous donations, I'm sure the school board will hire you back. If they don't, they will have to find another teacher, for I won't stay without you."

She took a step toward him. "I don't want you to settle for something you will regret later."

He walked toward her and took her in his arms. Slowly, she wrapped her arms around his waist. He sighed and laid his cheek on the top of her *kapp*. "I will never regret loving you. How could I? You are the soul mate our Lord God fashioned for me before the earth was made. You complete me."

Her lips trembled. "I'm afraid."

He drew back to look at her face. "Afraid of what?"

"I'm afraid to be this happy."

"Ah, my sweet." He pulled her close again. "I will spend my life making you happy for every year that God gives us. Will you stay?"

Lillian couldn't believe how close she had come to giving up and leaving. One favorite sweater was all that had stood between this happiness and a lifetime of regret. If it hadn't been a misplaced sweater, she would have found another reason to see Timothy for one last time. She thanked God for giving her this wonderful accepting man.

"Okay." She managed a breathless whisper.

"Okay you'll stay?"

She nodded.

"Okay, you love me?"

She nodded again.

"Okay you will marry me?"

"Yes." It was a tiny squeak of a reply, but he heard it and pulled her close.

"Thank you, my sweet, sweet Lillian. You have just made me the happiest man on earth."

She raised her face to his and kissed him with all the passion she'd held inside for so long.

The final day of Silas's barn raising, a semitrailer turned off the highway and came slowly up Silas's lane. It was a cattle hauler. The truck stopped near the newly completed barn where Timothy and his brothers were laying down the shingles. The truck door opened. A small, wry man with a thick gray mustache and a beat-up cowboy hat got out. Lillian was amazed to see he was a little person. She and the Bowman women were setting out the food for the men working, as it was almost noon.

"Howdy, folks. Is this the farm of Silas Mast?" the cowboy asked.

Silas stepped forward and nodded. "It is."

"Would you be Silas?"

"I am."

The cowboy held out his hand and Silas shook it. "Nice to meet you. My name is Barney Mast. I don't reckon we're any kind of kin, as I'm from Oklahoma, but when I saw what you folks had gone through, I was moved to help. You may not know it, but you're the answer to an old man's prayers."

"In what way?"

"I'm a dairyman myself. Been one all my life just like my daddy and granddaddy. My wife has been harping at me to retire for the last five years. We never had any kids, so I didn't have anyone to take over my spread. Know what I mean? Dairy cows are a 24/7 operation. I raised every one of my cows and their mothers and their mother's mothers. I know them like I know the back of my hand. I can sell my land, but I couldn't sell my gals to just anyone, so I brought them here."

Timothy and his brothers had come down and now stood beside Lillian. Silas shook his head sadly. "I'm afraid you have traveled a long way for nothing. I can't afford to buy your herd."

"Oh, I don't want to sell them, but I can sure give them to a man who'll appreciate every last one of them. That you and me share the same last name is just icing on the cake for me. I'd like to get them unloaded. They're gonna need to be milked soon. We've been on the road for near eighteen hours."

"You are giving your dairy herd to me?"

"Yup. I read about the fires and your loss and how you Amish folks take care of one another and I thought that's the kind of people I want looking after my gals."

Silas pulled off his hat and ran his hand through his hair. "I don't know what to say."

"Say thanks and we're even. My wife is tickled pink that I'm finally gonna retire and do some traveling with her. She's been waiting fifty years to see the ocean. I don't understand what's so special about a lot of water, but I'm taking her to Hawaii as soon as I get back."

Lillian leaned against Timothy as tears pricked at the back of her eyes. The Lord did indeed move in strange and wonderful ways.

* * *

Lillian and Timothy's intention to marry was announced to the congregation three weeks after he proposed. The wedding would take place the first Tuesday in November. Lillian expected her friends to be surprised by her engagement, but most of them weren't. Emma said, "We all knew that you two were made for each other. Friends don't look at friends the way you and Timothy look at each other."

A whirlwind of activity began for Lillian the day after the banns were published. Invitations had to be sent as soon as possible so that far-flung relatives and friends could make travel arrangements. She sat with her mother at the kitchen and looked at the stack of envelopes waiting to be addressed.

"I'm glad we don't have a huge family," Lillian said, picking up the first envelope. There were only a few cousins and her great-uncle in Wisconsin. She didn't expect many of them to come, but she hoped they would.

Lillian tucked an invitation inside the envelope and licked it. "Do you think Uncle Arthur will come?"

"If he is well, I'm sure of it," her mother said. "He was always fond of you and I think he wants to make up for the time he lost with us. God was good to give him this second chance."

Lillian smiled. God was indeed good. He'd given her this chance at a lifetime of love with a man who was her best friend. To think she had almost thrown it all away out of pride!

After filling out the first set of invitations, her mother pointed to a group of envelopes already bundled together. "Who are those invitations for?"

"I am sending one to each of the children at school.

Timothy and I want to make sure all of them were included."

"Has Timothy given you his list?"

"He brought it over last night." Lillian concentrated on the card in her hand, hoping her mother wouldn't notice the blush heating her cheeks. She and Timothy had spent a long, happy evening exchanging kisses and talking about their plans for the future.

"Are you inviting the *Englisch* nurse and her brother?"

"Of course. Their intervention and charity made a huge difference to this community."

The pile of invitations was just the start of Lillian's duties. Her days were soon filled with sewing her wedding dress, cleaning, cooking and preparations for the big day. She was thankful she didn't have the added burden of teaching on top of it all. She chose a deep blue material for her wedding gown. She would be married in it and buried in it, as was the custom of her people.

The one thing she didn't like about all the activity was that she saw little of Timothy except at school. The board had happily given her back her job, but she and Timothy rarely found time to be alone for more than a few stolen moments.

The day before the wedding, her married friends and members of the church arrived to prepare the wedding feast and the house for the bridal party. A generous meal would be served following the wedding, but the celebration would continue until evening, when a second meal would be needed for all the guests who remained.

When the day finally arrived, Lillian was up at four thirty in the morning. Anticipation filled her stomach with butterflies. By noon, she would be Timothy's wife.

Closing her eyes, she whispered a grateful prayer thanking God for this wondrous gift.

She went to the window to see the stars shining over a winter wonderland scene. Fresh snow coated everything. Timothy would be up by now. What was he feeling? If she married Timothy, he would never have sons and daughters of his own. What if he came to regret this decision?

Timothy stood at the window of his room gazing out at the bare winter trees silhouetted against the new-fallen snow. Was Lillian up? Was she experiencing the same kind of jitters? Was he doing the right thing? Marriage was forever.

She would be his forever.

He drew a deep cleansing breath. Forever with Lillian wouldn't be enough time to show her how much he loved her.

A tap on the door made Timothy glance that way. It was Luke. "It's time. Noah has the buggy here for you, and the others are ready."

Timothy and Lillian had asked Rebecca and Samuel along with Emma and Luke to be members of the bridal party. Noah was acting as hostler, the driver for the group who would all be traveling to Lillian's house together.

Timothy took another deep breath, and his nervousness vanished. With God's help, he would be a good husband. He would provide for her and cherish her all the days of his life. What had he done to deserve such happiness?

He walked downstairs to see his brothers and his father waiting for him. Samuel gave him a lopsided grin. "Noah wanted me to give you a message."

"What is it?"

"He said he picked the fastest horse in case you change your mind and want to head in another direction."

Their mother bustled into the room. "Nonsense. Timothy is too smart to leave a woman like Lillian waiting at the altar."

"He takes after his mother," Isaac said, patting his wife's plump cheek. She batted his hand away and blushed.

Timothy turned to his oldest brother. "What do you think, Samuel?"

"My advice is to go through with it. When you have found the right woman, being married is *wunderbar*."

"Good answer," Rebecca said, coming into the room from the kitchen with their infant son in her arms. She rose on tiptoe and kissed Samuel. The light in their eyes told Timothy they were still crazy about each other after almost two years. He wanted Lillian to smile at him the way Rebecca and Samuel were smiling at each other, as if they shared some profound understanding.

"I don't know why we are all standing around. I want to get hitched." Timothy opened the door and went out into the clear, cold morning air.

Chapter Twenty

Timothy was waiting for Lillian at the foot of the stairs when she came down. He looked incredibly handsome in his new black suit and bow tie. Her husband-to-be smiled and held out his hand. "Are you ready?"

She grasped his fingers tightly. "I am. Are you? Now is the time to change your mind."

"*Nee*, you are stuck with me, woman."

Her heart turned over with joy. "*Goot*, for I am so happy I'm surprised I'm not floating on air."

He squeezed her fingers. "I will keep you grounded. I will be your anchor."

She gazed into his eyes. "We're going to be all right, aren't we?"

"*Ja*, we are going to be fine."

"We will never have children. I know having sons was important to you."

He smiled at her tenderly. "We will have thirty or forty children for nine months out of the year. That's enough. And if it isn't, we will adopt ten or twelve. There are children who need parents everywhere. God will show us our path. Whatever life brings, we can face it together."

"You are wonderful and wise." She laid a hand on his cheek.

"I don't know about the wise part, but I am wonderful."

"*Demut*, Timothy. Try to be humble for a change."

"Okay. I am a simple man grateful for God's gifts and you are wonderful."

She grinned. "Much better."

They weren't alone for long. A few minutes after seven o'clock, the guests began to arrive. The pocket doors between the rooms had been pushed open, and the benches were being set up by her brother and her father.

Together, Lillian and Timothy greeted the early guests as they came in. The ceremony wouldn't take place until nine. Timothy was happy to see Brandon, his wife and children and Debra walk through the door. These outsiders had been instrumental in getting the families of Bowmans Crossing back on their feet. The two people he hadn't expected were Mr. and Mrs. Hanson.

He shook Mr. Hanson's hand. "It's good to see you looking well."

"My wife tells me I need to be more neighborly. Reckon this is as good a place to start as any."

"We are delighted you could come," Lillian said, giving them a beaming smile.

She motioned to Susan Yoder. "Would you sit by these people and translate for them?"

"Sure. Come this way. I'll seat you in the back where we have some soft chairs."

At a quarter till, the wedding party took their places

on the benches at the front of the room where the ceremony would be held. Lillian, Rebecca and Emma sat on one side of the room, Timothy with Samuel and Luke sat on the other.

Their *forgeher*, four married couples from their church group, escorted the guests to places on one of the long wooden benches. When the bishop entered the room, he motioned for Lillian and Timothy to come with him as the congregation began singing.

It was customary for the bishop to counsel the couple before the ceremony. Lillian and Timothy listened intently to his instructions, but Lillian was too excited to take in much.

When the bishop was finished, she and Timothy returned to where the guests were seated and took their places on the front benches. The singing continued, punctuated by sermons from the ministers, including her father, for almost three hours. Lillian tried to keep her mind on what was being said, but mostly she thought about the coming days and nights when she would become a true wife to Timothy.

Standing in front of Timothy, the bishop asked, "Do you believe, brother, that God has provided this woman as a marriage partner for you?"

"I do believe it." Timothy smiled at her, and her heart beat faster.

The bishop then turned to her. "Do you believe, sister, that God has provided this man as a marriage partner for you?"

"I do."

"Timothy, do you also promise Lillian that you will care for her in sickness or bodily weakness as befits a

Christian husband? Do you promise you will love, forgive and be patient with her until God separates you by death?"

"I do so promise," Timothy answered solemnly.

The bishop asked Lillian the same questions. She focused on Timothy. He was waiting for her answer, too. Taking a deep breath, she nodded. "I promise."

The bishop took her hand, placed it in Timothy's hand and covered their fingers with his own. "The God of Abraham, of Isaac and of Jacob be with you. May He bestow His blessings richly upon you through Jesus Christ, amen."

And with that prayer, they were made husband and wife. Love and happiness spilled out of her heart and flooded her body as she gazed at Timothy. Her overwhelming love was reflected in his eyes and the wonderful smile on his face.

A final prayer ended the ceremony, and the festivities began. The women of the congregation began preparing the wedding meal in the kitchen as the men arranged the tables in a U shape around the walls of the living room. Lillian went upstairs to change out of her wedding dress.

The *eck*, the honored corner table, was quickly set up for the wedding party in the corner of the room facing the front door. When everything was ready, she and Timothy took their places.

He was married. Timothy found it hard to wrap his mind around the fact. He took his place with his groomsmen seated to his right. Lillian was ushered in and took her seat at his left-hand side. It symbolized the place she would occupy in his buggy and in his life. Her cheeks were flushed a rosy red and her eyes sparkled with happiness. There would be a long day of celebration and feasting, but tonight would come, and she would be his alone. Could he make her happy? He would try his best. He reached over and squeezed her hand. She gave him a shy smile in return.

After a very long day, the wedding guests had all gone home at last. Lillian sat at the kitchen table and waited for Timothy to join her. He had gone out to say goodbye to his brothers and see them on their way. The outside door opened and he walked in. Joy rushed through her at the sight of his handsome face.

"Wife, would you care to join me for a short walk this evening? It's a nice night out."

"A walk sounds lovely, my husband."

"Have I told you today how much I love you?" He crossed the room and took her hand, pulling her to her feet and into his arms.

She melted against him, loving the way he made her feel. "You may have mentioned it. I'm not sure."

"Lillian Bowman, I love you. Today, tomorrow, for the rest of eternity. I love you."

Would she ever tire of those words? Never. "I love you, too. What did I do to deserve such happiness?"

"I ask myself the same question. I reckon only God knows the answer."

"He has truly blessed us." She rose on her tiptoes to press a kiss to his lips.

Wrapping his arms around her, he pulled her closer and kissed her until her head was spinning and she was breathless. Pulling away, he took a deep breath. "Maybe that walk can wait."

Sliding her arms around his neck, she snuggled against him. "Yes, my husband. I've waited to be in your arms for long enough. Kiss me again."

He smiled and gave her a quick peck on the lips. "I will always do what the teacher tells me."

* * * * *

PLAIN TARGET

Dana R. Lynn

This book is dedicated to the memory
of my aunt Norma, who first introduced me
to the genre of romance, sparking a lifelong
fascination with happily-ever-afters.

Acknowledgments

Although writing is a solitary career, I couldn't do
it without the love and support of so many people.

First, to my wonderful husband, Brad,
and our kids. You alternately kept me sane
and drove me crazy during this process,
and I wouldn't have it any other way!

To my editor, Elizabeth Mazer,
who took the time to brainstorm with me to
make this story come to life. You are awesome,
and I am so grateful to be able to work with you.

A special bittersweet thanks to my late agent,
Mary Sue Seymour, who passed away before this
book was completed. She loved this project and
cheered me on from the beginning. She was a
woman of great faith, energy and kindness. I was
truly blessed to have been able to work with her.

My heartfelt gratitude to my Lord and Savior.
I pray that my words will always point to
Your love and mercy.

My God will fully supply whatever you need, in accord with His glorious riches in Christ Jesus.
—*Philippians* 4:19

Chapter One

"Fire!"

Jess McGrath tore the fire extinguisher off the wall before running back to the blaze in her brother's office. For the first time in five weeks she entered the room where she had found Cody dead from his own hand. Behind her, her hearing aids caught the eruption of sound as her visitors, Rebecca and Levi Miller, scurried to help the two daytime workers release the horses into the pasture. Gratitude surged briefly. Rebecca was her oldest friend. No one else had stuck by her when the scandal started, leading to Cody's disgrace and the near ruin of their training stables. Her Amish-raised friend didn't even consider abandoning Jess. It was fortunate that Rebecca had persuaded her indulgent older brother to give her a ride in to visit Jess today on his buggy. With staff down to the bare-bones minimum, Jess needed all the help she could get.

Pulling the pin, Jess aimed the extinguisher at the flames consuming the exterior wall. Would it be enough?

Please, Lord, let everyone and the horses be safe.
The pictures on the wall connected to the stalls vibrated

as the horses were led out. They would go directly to the pasture.

The flames died out and the extinguisher sputtered as it emptied. Jess stared at the destruction before her. Cody's desk had taken the brunt of it, along with the wall. How had it started? The electrical systems had all been updated within the past three years. And no one had been in the office for weeks.

Not since the police had taken all Cody's files when he came under suspicion for various charges of fraudulent practices. A third of the clientele to the stables and training facilities she owned with her brother had taken their business, and their horses, elsewhere. River Road Stables was facing bankruptcy if she didn't find a way to improve business.

Her eyes landed on the still smoldering heap that had been a garbage can. It was unrecognizable. Only the fact that Jess knew what it should be helped her identify it. Her stomach turned. Trembling began from her toes up. Had the fire started there?

The floor vibrated, almost a heaving feeling. Jess spun around in time to see the large bookcase rock forward. The frame was anchored to the wall, but she could see the screws being ripped out. Even as she jumped out of its way, she knew she hadn't jumped far enough. The heavy shelf toppled, knocking into her as it fell. She crashed to the ground. A sharp pain exploded in her head.

Jess struggled to open her eyes. The left side of her face ached. Her ears rang. With a groan, she lifted her head, only to drop it as nausea rolled over her.

A warm hand patted her shoulder. She risked opening her eyes again. A paramedic loomed over her, a concerned frown digging furrows in his forehead. He looked vaguely familiar. Her head ached too much to wonder where she had seen him before.

"Jessica? Jess, can you hear me?"

She blinked, incredulous. Who was this man? She had to have met him somewhere. Not only did he know her name, but he had also signed as he spoke. Of course, she was wearing her hearing aids, so it wasn't fully necessary. It was appreciated all the same.

She moved her head. Oww.

"My head hurts," she moaned.

He nodded, watching her carefully. "I think you may have a concussion. We'll know better once a doctor examines you. I did check your vitals. They look good." He continued to sign while he spoke.

"How did you know I'm deaf?"

His eyes widened, a surprised expression crossing his face. Followed immediately by a guilty one. His gaze shifted nervously before returning to rest on her face again.

"You don't recognize me?" He seemed wary of her answer.

She shook her head slowly, wincing as her aching head protested. "No, but you look really familiar."

He sighed. "High school."

It couldn't be.

Narrowing her eyes, she looked closer. It was. How had she not recognized him? But he had changed so much from the gangly sixteen-year-old boy she had known so briefly eleven years ago. His black curly hair was shorter, and his scrawny body had shot up in height and was well muscled. The nerdy glasses were gone. But the eyes…she did remember them. Deep brown eyes that she had crushed on for several months during her freshman year before realizing that the sweet boy she thought she knew didn't exist. He had been a bad boy who was only interested in flouting the rules and irritating his high-society parents.

"Seth Travis." The words felt bitter on her tongue.

He nodded, then focused his attention off himself. "Do I need to sign, or can you hear me well enough if I just talk? I can help you faster if I don't sign."

"Yeah, as long as I have my hearing aids on and it's quiet and I can see your face, I'm good."

"I remember that."

Of course he did. Seth had always been brilliant. On track to be the salutatorian. Not to mention his memory. She had been amazed at his ability to recall even the smallest of details. She didn't remember him signing in high school, though. When had he learned? And why bother?

"I'm surprised you didn't recognize me. What with my dad being the senator and all."

She shrugged. "It's been a long time since I saw you and you've changed a lot. And I don't pay attention to politics. Never have."

"So you never saw my old man on television?" His mouth curled in a slight sneer. Problems with his dad, apparently. It was none of her business, but she couldn't say she approved of his attitude. She would never have disrespected her parents that way.

"I don't own a TV." She didn't add that she had better things to do with her time than to watch the drama of the spoiled rich kid she remembered play out before her.

Rebecca entered the stables, and Jess settled her attention on her dearest friend. Rebecca's brother, Levi, followed her at a slower pace. It still looked odd to see Rebecca dressed *Englisch* when she stood next to her Amish brother. But it warmed her heart, too, knowing that Rebecca's family supported her choices. Jess knew that Rebecca's social circle was very small, due in part to her deafness. It could have been smaller. If she had left her community after she'd been baptized, she would have been shunned, even by her family. The fact that she had decided to leave her Amish community instead of being baptized had enabled her to keep her close ties to her family.

"Is everyone okay? The horses?" Jess signed to Rebecca, who was born profoundly deaf. Unlike Jess, Rebecca depended totally on American Sign Language, or ASL. People were always surprised to find out how little she could lip read. English was a difficult language to lip read well, with so many sounds looking the same on the lips. Add the fact that Rebecca's family spoke Pennsylvania Dutch at home into the mix, it was no wonder she hadn't bothered with it.

"Yes. We helped your two employees move them to the back pasture. How are you? I was scared when I found you unconscious." Rebecca's hands flew.

Jess looked at Seth. Did he need her to interpret? Her mouth fell open when he answered Rebecca in almost fluent ASL. That was a whole different skill set than putting signs to English grammar. She was impressed in spite of herself.

"My partner and I need to take her to the hospital," he signed, indicating someone behind her.

Jess hadn't even noticed the other paramedic. The

woman walked their way, pushing a stretcher. She gave Jess a professional smile.

Jess turned her attention back to Rebecca and Levi. "Did anyone call the fire department?"

They both shook their heads. "We didn't think it was necessary," Levi answered her. "The fire was out. It was *gut, jah*?"

No surprise there. Calling for outside help would not enter Levi's mind unless it was absolutely crucial.

She hesitated. Part of her was relieved not to have to handle the firefighters or police. She had dealt with so much scandal recently, she didn't have the heart to face more. But the other part of her wondered if the fire was an accident. It just seemed odd that it started in Cody's office for no apparent reason.

A stretcher halted on her left side. The female paramedic had reached their small group.

"I called the fire department a few minutes ago." The blond woman leaned over to check something on the stretcher. "It's not uncommon for a fire to restart hours after it's put out. It's pretty standard procedure to have the local fire department check it out."

So there was no longer any choice. Jess sighed. She just wanted this day to be over. Quickly, she murmured a prayer for strength. Seth gave her a startled glance, but didn't comment. Instead, he and his partner loaded her into the ambulance and whisked her off to the hospital.

Two hours later, she was receiving her release papers and, except for a lingering headache, a clean bill of health. What was unexpected was that Seth reappeared as she was getting ready to leave with Rebecca. And with him was a police officer. A very grim-faced officer.

"Jess, this is Sergeant Jackson from the LaMar Pond

Police Department. He needs to speak with you for a minute." He signed the introductions, then started to back away.

Without thought, her hand shot out and caught at his. "Stay. Please."

He raised his eyebrows, but nodded. She closed her eyes, feeling some of the tension in her chest disintegrate. As little as she trusted Seth, he was someone she knew. Being alone with a police officer was a frightening prospect for her. All she could think of were the accusations of fraud and theft, not to mention the thorough searches she'd endured, that had happened both before and after Cody's death. No matter how much she and Cody had protested that he hadn't stolen money from his foundation or rigged horse races, no one believed them. And even knowing the police were just doing their job didn't shake her feeling that they looked at her with suspicion.

Plus, she reasoned, Seth signed, which could help. As well as she read lips, she sometimes needed to see the words to be sure she understood them. And interpreters were hard to find. She could be here hours if she waited for one.

Sergeant Jackson cleared his throat. "Miss McGrath, the fire department investigated the fire at the stables. It's their inspector's opinion that the fire might have been deliberately set."

A shiver worked its way up her spine. Her day had just gotten much worse.

Gravel crunched under the tires of Seth's Ford pickup truck as he turned into the driveway of River Road Stables the next morning. Water splashed up on his tires.

The heavy scent of wet hay slipped through the inch-wide crack in his window. It had stormed the night before, and puddles were everywhere. His front tire hit a particularly deep puddle, and he was jarred by the motion as his truck bounced. Man, they really needed to fix the potholes on this driveway.

A yawn crept up on him. He had barely been able to sleep last night. The image of Jess's distraught face haunted him. A queasy sensation settled in his stomach as he realized that the only reason she wasn't being investigated for possibly causing the fire was because of her injury. Yet. He had seen the look in Gavin Jackson's eyes. And he had been around cops enough to know that often arson was committed for insurance fraud.

He expected to continue up the lane to find Jessica in her one-story ranch house where she should be resting, as per doctor's orders. His plan shifted when he spotted her brown ponytail swaying as she walked into the barn. Pressing his lips together, he parked his truck in front of the barn. Frustration and worry mingled. As hard as it was to believe, she didn't have a concussion from her accident yesterday. Still, he was sure she probably was feeling some aches and pains. Enough to convince most people to take it easy and rest. A sigh escaped. Not that he was surprised that she refused to slow down. She always had pushed herself harder than others around her. In his mind, he had always wondered if she felt that being deaf, she had to overachieve in order to prove herself.

To be fair, she had probably been right. He could remember the one class they had together—biology. The teacher had tried to convince her to drop the class, telling her in front of her peers that he didn't have time to waste trying to keep her caught up.

But she had been stubborn. And the guidance counselor had asked Seth to tutor her, to ensure her success. He'd agreed, reluctantly, knowing it would look good to the teachers and guidance counselors who would eventually write him college recommendation letters. And soon found that they had all underestimated her. Had started to admire her, to like her—and that was where the trouble had begun.

He winced. Those were memories he didn't want to relive.

Parking the truck, he grabbed the wallet he had found on his floorboard that morning. If she had noticed it missing, she might be panicking about now. It gave him the excuse he needed to pay her a visit, although he refused to think about why he was so anxious to see her again. He was a paramedic—it was his job to worry about people, particularly people who had just been injured. He had been skeptical when she had agreed to follow the doctor's directives. Something told him that she wouldn't be able to sit still. He had seen the stubborn look in her eyes.

Obviously he had been right.

Didn't she know she needed to rest? He admitted to himself that he was concerned. Working alone in the barn was not safe for her. And she had said the day before that no one would be coming in until after lunch. It hadn't struck him until he had dropped her off that someone—meaning her—would have to come out to take care of the horses in the morning. All alone like that, she would be an easy target if the person who'd attacked her stables came back. He shook off the thought.

For all he knew, the fire was a random act by a group of kids. Yeah, right.

The stable door was standing open. He headed that way, pausing just inside it. Jessica stood outside the office door, her arms closed tight against her belly, her eyes squeezed shut. He started, ready to rush in and...what? Comfort her? He wasn't sure, but he knew he didn't like seeing her so vulnerable. Never had, even though their association had been so brief. Which made what had happened even more contemptible. When he had betrayed her trust, he had left her open to the cruelty of others. It didn't matter that he hadn't been a part of the actions they had taken against her. He knew what a soft heart she had. And that she had a crush on him. But instead of protecting her, he'd stepped back and allowed her to be hurt in a disaster which ended with her being pulled from the school.

He drew himself away from his painful memories. Then he noticed her lips were moving. She was praying. Okay, now he felt really uncomfortable. He wasn't big on prayer. Not that he minded other people praying. He just hadn't had much experience with it personally. And to be honest, he rather doubted it did any good.

A few seconds later she opened her eyes. They widened as she saw him poised in the doorway.

"Seth! What are you doing here?" Her voice was low and pleasant. Although her inflections were slightly irregular, most people probably wouldn't even pick up on that.

"You left this in my truck." He waved the bright pink wallet at her.

Jess's hazel eyes widened. "Oh, no! I hadn't even noticed it was missing."

"No worries. It was safe. And I'm even a little glad 'cuz it gave me an excuse to check up on you. Make sure you were taking it easy." He gave her a pointed look.

She bit her lip. Dropping her gaze to the floor, she scuffed the toe of her boot in the dirt. When she flicked her glance back up to his face, he was momentarily distracted by her wide hazel eyes. He hadn't let himself feel attracted to a woman for a long time. His behavior in high school, and his poor judgment six years ago with his former fiancée, had taught him that he was not husband material. As bitter as it made him feel, he had been forced to acknowledge that he was too much like his father. Selfish and prone to hurt those close to him. Shaking himself out of it, he asked, "What's wrong?"

He held his breath while he waited to see if she would answer. He wouldn't blame her if she brushed him off. She had no reason to trust him. Past events would tell her not to. But he really hoped she would.

Finally, she sucked in a deep breath. Let it out slowly.

"You know that the police are toying with the idea that I started the fire?" She waited for him to nod before she continued. "What I couldn't tell the officer last night was the fire wasn't the first accident."

"What?" He hadn't meant to shout, but her words terrified him. He wanted to sweep her into his truck and drive her to a safe place. The feeling surprised him. And made him uncomfortable.

Jess squirmed. Then she lifted her chin and seemed to collect herself. "I didn't realize at first that they were anything more than accidents. I put it down to carelessness. Until last week. A new ladder broke when I took it out to paint. That's when I started to wonder if someone was behind the accidents. Then this happened."

"How long has this been going on?" He kept his voice calm with an effort.

"About three weeks."

"You should have mentioned it to Sergeant Jackson last night," Seth admonished her.

Hazel eyes blazed up at him. "And you think he would believe me? Just when my barn suffers extensive fire damage and I'm a person of interest?"

She had a point. It would have looked like she was lying to cover her tracks.

"I think it started because I was asking too many questions."

He wasn't going to like this. "Asking questions about what?"

Those soft lips started to tremble. She squished them together. "I know that people think my brother was guilty of something, what with him dying the way he did and all. But I can't believe that of him. He was the most gentle, sincere person I have ever known. I have been trying to find evidence to take to the police to clear his name."

He knew something dicey had happened, although he was foggy on all the details.

"What is it that they think he'd done, exactly?"

For a long moment, she stood, jaw clenched. Clearly it wasn't a topic she enjoyed discussing, and he felt a twinge of guilt for even bringing it up. But he needed to know what they were dealing with if he was going to help her.

"My brother had started a rescue foundation for abused racehorses. Several months ago, one of his volunteers noticed that money was being stolen. The police suspected Cody. The fact that he spent so much time at

the race track was suspicious. I guess there was suspicion that he was using funds to support a gambling
habit. They questioned him, and there was an investigation. It was never closed. Cody was never even officially
charged—they didn't have enough evidence against him.
But when he took his own life, everyone seemed to take
that as an admission of guilt. People who had contrib-
uted to the foundation felt hurt, betrayed. I can understand that," she admitted, "but that doesn't mean I'm all
right with people continuing to say such horrible things
about him when no one has been able to provide a scrap
of evidence proving that he did anything wrong."

"So you spoke up in his defense," Seth concluded,
"both when he was first questioned, and then later after
his death. And that's turned people against you?"

She nodded.

"Including the police?" he asked.

"Especially the police. Not only was I unable to convince them he was innocent, they made it clear that I was
also on their radar, since I worked for the foundation in
a minor role. They wouldn't listen to me."

Frustrated, he shoved a hand through his hair. "You
have to let the police know about the other accidents,
Jess. This is no joke."

She started to shake head. "Don't you understand?
There is no way they will believe me! And the stables
are already losing clients. If these things keep happening, then I will have to sell the horses and the stable."
Tears shimmered in her eyes. "Seth, owning a training
stable has been my dream for as long as I can remember. I have already lost my brother. I can't lose this, too."

A constriction formed in his throat. It was necessary

to swallow several times to ease the tightness. A sudden thought popped into his head.

"Wait a minute! Jess, my brother-in-law is a lieutenant in the LaMar Pond Police Department. You can talk to him." Why hadn't he thought of that earlier? Dan was pretty easygoing. And he was head-over-heels ridiculously in love with Seth's half sister Maggie, which meant he'd do just about anything Seth asked—including hearing Jess out, and giving her the benefit of the doubt.

"I didn't know you had siblings." There was that suspicious look on her face again. He was going to have to work hard to earn her trust.

"It's a long story. But Maggie is my half sister. I met her almost a year ago for the first time, but we've gotten close. And her husband, Dan, is a good guy."

A humorless laugh left her mouth. "I can't believe I'm considering listening to you. Seth, we knew each other in high school, but that was eleven years ago. And you betrayed my trust back then. Why should I give it to you now?"

Why, indeed.

Chapter Two

Seth's teeth snapped together with a loud click. He knew his jaw would ache later. Turning away from Jess, he began to pace as he battled to keep the anger and fear simmering beneath the surface from exploding out of him. The temper he had learned to keep under wraps for so long threatened to overwhelm him. It wouldn't do anyone any good to lose it now.

When he had himself under control, he faced Jess again. She eyed him warily.

"Are you okay?" she asked.

Unbelievable. He rolled his eyes.

"Am *I* okay? I'm not the one whose stable was set on fire and I haven't been the victim of any strange accidents. I'm amazed you're not a basket case right now."

Jess shrugged. Her attempt at nonchalance didn't fool him. She was scared. He had to admire her determination to tough it out on her own.

But enough was enough.

"Jess." He took a step closer. Close enough to smell her perfume. Her eyes widened. He needed to make sure he was completely understood. "Come with me to my sister's house. My brother-in-law is off today so we should be able to talk with him in private."

He braced himself to argue with her. Turned out, he didn't need to. She met his eyes, and slowly nodded her head. Reluctant surrender was written all over her face.

"Will you stay? Just in case I need an interpreter?"

Why did he think she actually wanted him there for moral support? She didn't say it, but the plea was in her shadow-filled eyes.

"I won't leave your side," he promised.

Some of the tension drained from her shoulders, and the corners of her lips tilted in a slight smile. The urge to comfort her with a hug crept up, but he resisted. The last thing she would want would be to be touched by him. He was well aware of the fact that he had a long way to go to make up for the jerk he'd been eleven years ago.

Leading her out to his truck, he held the door while she pulled herself up into the cab. Good thing he hadn't parked next to a puddle. As he shut the door behind her and jogged around to his side, he ignored the anticipation dancing through him at the thought of spending more time in her presence. It wasn't as if they were going on a picnic. It started to rain again once they were under-way. The overcast sky and the loud patter of raindrops on the roofs made the space inside the cab seem close. The fragrance of her light perfume added to the impression. Perfume? Since when did he pay attention to perfume unless it was too strong? Weird. Just weird.

He glanced into the rearview window, frowning at a car riding right on his tail. "Back up, buddy," he muttered. Seth slowed the car, then made a right turn. The dark green sedan continued to keep pace with him. The

tinted glass made it difficult to see who was driving the vehicle. Someone was in a hurry.

"What?"

He shot a reassuring grin at Jess. "Sorry. Talking to myself. We have a tailgater."

Jess looked back over her shoulder, and froze. Seth stopped grinning as he saw the look of fear on her face. Her hands were fisted on her lap, the knuckles white.

"Jess? Jessica! What's wrong?"

"I have seen that car almost everywhere I have gone in the past couple of weeks. I can never tell who's driving it."

The thought of someone shadowing her, stalking her, set his teeth on edge. "Are you sure it's the same car?" He used one hand to sign the question so there would be no mistake.

Jess shook her head. "Sure? No, I have never gotten close enough to see a license plate. And there are hundreds of cars that look like that one. Except for the dark windows."

Without considering his actions, Seth spun the wheel and started to pull off onto the berm. The green car slowed down. Then it suddenly shot forward. Its tires hit a large puddle, and water splashed Seth's windshield. His left hand shot out to activate the wipers, hoping to clear his view in time to get a glimpse of the license plate, but it was too late. The car whipped around the corner. And another car was coming far too fast for Seth to get back on the road and follow him.

Frustrated, he waited for the other car to pass and then resumed driving toward Maggie and Dan's house. His mind was full of questions. And doubts. Was it possible Jess was being stalked, or was she letting her anxiety rule her thoughts? After all, even she had admitted the car wasn't an uncommon model. Except for the windows. He rejected the idea that she was imagining things almost as soon as it entered his mind. She had always been very down to earth, never one to exaggerate or jump to conclusions. "Okay, we need to remember to tell Dan about the car."

Out of the corner of his eye, he saw her nodding, but her expression remained troubled. It was time to see if they could make some sense of the current situation, while they were alone. And the quiet of the truck meant she would be able to hear him. And if she couldn't, it was light enough that she could see him sign, or read his lips if necessary.

"Why don't we try and get our ducks in a row before talking to Dan. He's going to want to know about the people you work with at the barn. Because chances are good that one of them might be the person responsible for the fire."

A shake of her head denied any such possibility, but shadows crept into her expression. As much as she might want to believe none of her coworkers would hurt her, the doubt had taken root in her mind.

"So who worked for you yesterday?" Man, he hated doing this to her. But it was necessary for her protection, he argued with himself.

For a moment, he wasn't sure if she would answer. Finally she sighed. "Kim and Eric. They're both fairly young. Kim just started working for us about seven months ago, but Eric has been coming for years, first as a student, and later as a worker and part-time trainer. I would trust him without hesitation."

"And Kim?"

He knew the answer the moment she bit her lower lip. As painful as it was, Kim was a possible suspect.

"Okay, how about Rebecca—"

The words weren't even out of his mouth before she interrupted him.

"Don't even go there. I would trust her and Levi with my life. We went to the same deaf and hard-of-hearing program for years. In fact, we rode the same bus. She was two years behind me, but we stayed friends even after I returned to my home district for high school."

He nodded. "Okay. And she was Amish?"

"Yeah. Until she was seventeen. She made the choice to leave instead of being baptized, which means she can still visit her family."

"But still, there would have been years when you didn't see her because you left…" His voice petered out as he realized what he was saying. The last thing he wanted to do was bring up why she had left high school, and his role in all of it, but it was too late now. If he could, he would have swallowed those words back. But he couldn't. Maybe she would let it go. He glanced at her. Her lips tightened, her shoulders grew stiff. Nope.

"Yeah, I left to go back to my district's school so I could be closer to home and take advantage of the clubs and sports programs. Things most high school students take for granted. I just didn't expect that to include you telling your bully friends that the weird deaf girl you tutored had an annoying crush on you. And I definitely didn't expect them to decide to teach me a lesson to show me how unworthy I was."

"I never meant—"

"They ganged up on me, drew the word *IDIOT* on my forehead with a permanent marker and shoved me into a dark janitor's closet. It was small, no lights and no windows, and I missed my bus. I was stuck in that small, smelly place for five hours until my parents and the principal found me. I was terrified to go back there. And Rebecca had left the deaf program. Amish students only go to school through eighth grade. I convinced my parents to send me to the Western PA School for the Deaf so I wouldn't have to face any of my attackers again."

So that's where she had gone.

He could hear her ragged breathing. Remorse choked him. What a moron he had been.

"I would do anything to take that back. I only said something to get my girlfriend, Trish, off my back. She was jealous of the time we spent together."

She grimaced. "She was cruel. All your friends were. Except that dark haired girl you sat with in bio."

Melanie. His best friend. He'd messed that up, too.

He sighed, wishing he could go back in time and shake some sense into the stupid, arrogant kid he used to be. "I couldn't believe Trish would do something like that. We had a huge fight over it and finally broke up. I wanted to track you down and apologize…but no one knew where you'd gone."

"How hard did you look?" she asked, her voice cold and accusatory.

"Not very," he admitted. "I figured you wanted to leave me and everything I'd done in the past. It didn't seem right to force you to have to sit through my sad excuses if you'd moved on with your life."

"And yet here you are."

"To help," he insisted. "I know it doesn't change the past, but you're in trouble now and you shouldn't be

forced to deal with it alone. I'd like to help you, the way I should have back then."

Silence settled between them, tense and awkward. After a few minutes, he felt her hand touch his arm. Brow rising in surprise, he turned to face her.

"Can I ask you a question?" Jess's voice was hesitant. It was an olive branch, and he knew it and gladly seized it.

"Yeah, sure." His voice was thick. He cleared his throat. He spared her a glance to be sure she heard him. Her face was turned toward him, eyes intent.

"I don't remember ever seeing you sign before. But yesterday you were signing like you'd been doing it for years. How did you learn? Why?"

He shrugged. "I had a roommate in college who was deaf. Ernie. He taught me some sign. And I went home with him several times. His whole family was deaf, so it was sink or swim. After I decided that I had zero interest in following my dad into law and politics, I took other classes to find what interested me. Including ASL."

"Ernie Mitchell?"

His eyebrows rose. "You know him?"

"He attends Deaf church with me."

The mention of church was unsettling. He and Ernie had stayed in touch since college but they didn't talk religion much. Seth blew out a relieved breath as his sister's house came in view. Soon, he would be able to tell Dan everything. Then the police could take control of the situation. Jess would be safe and would no longer need him. That last thought made him frown. The idea of walking away from her now when she was in danger didn't sit well with him at all. But sticking around held the risk of his becoming attached to her. He realized that he liked and admired her. The last thing he wanted was to see her hurt again. And he would hurt her. How could he not? He was his father's son, after all.

Pulling into his sister's driveway, he frowned, feeling uneasy. Dan's truck was there, but the minivan was nowhere in sight. And the blinds were closed. Maggie always opened the blinds. Getting out of his truck, he walked over to the garage and peered in. The motorcycle was there, but no van.

Whipping out his cell, he sent his sister a text. Hey sis. Where r u?

A minute later he received an answer. And groaned. Pittsburgh. Visiting Ty. Back 2morrow. Everything OK?

Ty was Dan's foster brother. What now? He would just have to keep an eye on Jess until Dan returned. He sent back a text to tell his sister he needed to see Dan as soon as they returned. Then he climbed back in his truck. Jess was watching him, those gorgeous hazel eyes wide and curious. How would she react to the news that she'd have to wait to talk with Dan? Would she give up on speaking to the police altogether?

"Okay. Change of plans. Maggie and Dan are in Pittsburgh for the day."

A soft sigh came from the woman beside him. Relief or resignation? Hmm. Not sure he knew.

"Do you want to go back to your place?" he offered. Man, he hated the thought of bringing her back to that ranch house alone. The stables were far too secluded. Her face paled.

Taking a deep breath, Jess squared her shoulders and lifted her jaw. Probably trying to look brave. To his sympathetic eye, she looked vulnerable. And scared. As she glanced up, her posture shifted. Eyes narrowing, she

looked closer at the fancy invitation trapped behind the sun visor. Her slender fingers reached out and touched the fine paper, hesitant, almost awed.

"May I?" she asked. Unsure what she was thinking, he nodded.

Jess plucked the card from its spot and brushed her hands across the return address on the engraved invitation. A stallion was prominently embossed on the front.

"Ted Taylor," she breathed. "You know Ted Taylor."

Huh? Her voice was almost reverent.

"Yeah, that's my uncle." Seth gently pulled the invite from her fingers to glance at it. "I had forgotten this. He's throwing a big blowout tonight."

"You could help me!"

Seth found himself on the receiving end of a stunning smile. Jess leaned toward him, and he could practically smell her eagerness. For some reason his stomach tightened. He had the feeling he wasn't going to like what she suggested.

"I can't believe I let you talk me into this."

Jess grinned and rolled her eyes. That was the third time Seth had complained. He was smiling and shaking his head as he said it, though, so she decided he wasn't too upset with her. Plus, he was driving toward his uncle's house.

She couldn't get over the fact that she had never connected him with Ted Taylor. Ted Taylor owned the most renowned stable for breeding racehorses in this part of the country. He was an influential man who sat on various committees dealing with equine care and treatment. His passion was abused horses. Just as Cody's had been. His endorsement could sway public opinion in her favor.

She shivered. On the other hand, a cold shoulder from him would convince many she and her brother were guilty. But she had to try.

And he was also well known for throwing lavish parties. Like this one. Parties where everyone brought an overnight bag because one day wasn't long enough to celebrate. Not to mention the fact that he lived almost an hour away from LaMar Pond on the outskirts of Spartansburg. Ted always opened the spring season up with a bang. Anyone who was anyone in the equestrian circle in northwestern Pennsylvania would be there. Breeders, coaches, trainers. All people who she and her brother had met in one capacity or another. It was possible that someone there might be able to provide some answers about what had really happened in the last few months of Cody's life.

"Are you sure you can spare this much time away from the stables?"

Seth was precious when he was concerned. *No way. Not going there.* Even if it was true, it would do no good for her to become attached. The butterflies currently fluttering in her stomach would go away if she ignored them. She cut a quick glance toward him and met melting brown eyes. Instead of going away the butterflies intensified.

What was the question? Oh, yeah.

"The stables will be fine. I texted my staff so they'll know to come in and take care of the morning chores. Even if I don't show up for a few days, the workers keep things moving. We keep charts on which animals need what to be done, so someone will be able to pick up the slack."

As the truck sloshed through the back roads toward

Ted Taylor's party, she watched as the puddles on the road became progressively deeper. Rain continued to pound on the truck. The rhythmic swipe of the wipers could barely keep up. Her teeth tugged at her lower lip. Maybe convincing Seth to bring her to the party with him as his "plus one" hadn't been a great idea. With weather like this, they wouldn't be able to leave the party quickly or easily if she was treated badly by the other guests—which was a definite possibility. Many of them had treated her as if she had leprosy since Cody's death. Or as if she were a criminal. Which certainly accounted for the fact that she had not received an invite to this weekend's event for the first time in two years. Willa Taylor was a social snob.

Of course, it was also possible that one of them was responsible for the accidents. She shuddered and promised herself that if she saw a dark green sedan parked outside the ranch house, she'd have Seth take her home again. She cautioned herself against relying on him too heavily. She had struggled hard to prove herself to be a strong, independent woman. It wouldn't do to allow her former crush to gain too much leverage over her.

"This water is getting really deep," Seth stated, a frown pulling down the corners of his mouth. Outside, everything was gray. Gray clouds, gray sky, gray pools of liquid surrounding them as they drove. They went over the bridge. Jess looked down and felt a niggle of dread. The water was higher than she had ever seen it.

"There it is." Seth raised one hand to indicate the sprawling ranch ahead of them. His blinker flashed as he steered the truck into the long winding lane that served as the Taylor residence's driveway. The driveway was like the rest of Pennsylvania. It rose and dipped. It wasn't the smoothest ride, but Jess still released a sigh of relief that they'd finally arrived. It was followed by a shriek as Seth's tires hydroplaned. The back end of the pickup swerved to the right. Seth managed to get the vehicle back on track just in time to drive it through the next puddle. Only the puddle was more like a small pond. The motor sputtered and stalled. Stopped.

They were stuck at the ranch.

Seth tossed her a reassuring grin. "Don't worry. I'm sure we can find someone to help us get the truck started again. Or a lift back to town. It'll be fine."

She wasn't fooled. His grin was strained, and his jaw was tight.

Seth opened the door and splashed over to Jess's side to help her down. Grabbing her overnight bag with her fancy dress and toiletries safely tucked inside, she let Seth take her empty hand and jumped out. She landed with a muddy splash and grimaced. She was almost knee-deep in freezing water. Her cowboy boots would be trashed. Good thing she hadn't decided to wear the dress and heels in the truck. Seth shrugged out of his jacket and slung it over her shoulders. And shushed her when she started to protest. Giving in gracefully, she allowed Seth to grab her hand again and pull her up to the lane to the house. Standing beside Seth, she tensed as he raised his hand and jabbed the doorbell with his finger. Within seconds, the door swung open and their host came out to grab Seth in a bear hug.

Ted Taylor was an impressive-looking man in his mid-fifties. Now that she saw him and Seth side by side, she could see the resemblance in the shape of their faces and in the way they held themselves.

"Seth! So glad you could make it, son!" His booming

voice made the voices inside the house grow silent. "So many people canceled because of the weather. You and your girlfriend will make an even dozen."

Jess forced herself to stand still and smile as he turned kind eyes to her. "It's good to see you again, Jess. I was very sorry to hear about your brother. Cody was a fine young man, and I for one have never doubted his integrity."

Blinking to clear her suddenly blurred vision, Jess cleared her throat. Even so, she knew her voice sounded more like a croak when she spoke. "Thank you, sir. It means a lot to hear that."

She stiffened her knees to cease their sudden trembling. If Ted believed in Cody's innocence, and hers, there was hope.

"What's she doing here?" an angry voice said.

Heat crawled up her face as Jess found herself the target of hostile stares. Apparently, Ted's faith in her wasn't universal. Well, she hadn't expected it would be. Yet. Resigned, she turned to face Ted's snobbish, socially conscious wife.

"Aunt Willa, this is my friend, Jess. My good friend." Her bruised heart warmed when Seth squeezed her hand.

Hardly a good friend. But she appreciated the show of support when those gathered glared.

"I'm surprised you would bring the likes of her into your family's house," his aunt said with a scornful sniff. "Or perhaps you saw a pretty face and didn't realize what kind of girl she was."

What kind of girl she was? Seriously?

"Actually, Jess and I go way back. Since high school."

Jess could just barely make out the sound of voices tumbling over each other. Yet even without hearing the words, she could tell by the frowns on their faces that the other guests were not pleased to have her in their midst. But none of that seemed to affect Seth. She read his lips and saw that he was basically telling his family that he believed in her and trusted her. Suspicion was nudged out of the way by shame and gratitude. Gratitude that God hadn't completely abandoned her. And shame that she was still harboring a grudge against Seth. Mortified, she remembered her bitter words in the truck. Was that really just a couple of hours ago?

"Seth, that girl's brother was…"

Ted shook his head at his wife. Sullenly, she quieted, but the baleful glint of her eyes let Jess know she was far from appeased. With false joviality, Ted pulled them into the house and began introducing them around. Jess found herself the recipient of several slights and sneers. It didn't help that her hearing aids amplified all the noise of music and voices to the same level. The harsh jumble of sound made separating individual voices out from the background ruckus impossible. She was forced to rely totally on lip reading. Soon her eyes grew strained and she felt a tension headache coming on. She understood enough to realize that the majority of the guests had felt in some way cheated or betrayed by her brother, and they were quite willing to transfer that anger to her, even though she wasn't deeply involved in the foundation. She should have been more invested. And maybe if she had been, she'd be more aware of what had occurred.

At one point, she looked over in the corner and saw a familiar face. Her brother's fiancée, Deborah, gave her a nod, but made no move to come over. She understood. Deborah had suffered enough. She had told Jess quite clearly after the funeral that she needed to put it all behind her. The man standing beside Deborah was familiar, too. Russ Breen, one of Ted's star trainers. She had heard that Deborah had attached herself to a new man. It seemed a little quick, and Jess's throat tightened seeing how rapidly Cody had been replaced in the other woman's life. It had only been a few months. She couldn't understand how someone could move on that easily.

She sure hadn't.

Seth tapped on her shoulder. Glancing over, she was surprised to see anger tightening the skin around his eyes. What had she done? Her own eyes widened when she realized that he was angry with the others, on her behalf. He lifted his hands and signed to her.

"We can't stay here. Let's get some help with the truck and go. I will help you find answers another way."

Glancing around, she swallowed. He was right. She wouldn't be able to get any answers here. She nodded at him.

Seth asked around to find out who could lend a hand with the truck. Soon they had a group of four men who agreed to help. She followed them outside and down the driveway. And gasped.

The truck was where they had left it. Water was up to the top of the wheels.

The bridge was gone.

Further investigation confirmed what she already suspected. All the roads were under water as a flash flood washed in. The ranch itself was safe on raised ground. But every path out of it was blocked.

Walking back into the house beside Seth, she folded her arms in front of her, rubbing her hands up and down them to bring some warmth back into her chilled body. The lights flickered, but thankfully stayed on. When she had suggested coming to the party with Seth, it had sounded like a good idea. She would have a chance to meet with people from the horse community and gauge their reactions. Maybe even be able to get some clue as to what had really happened. She had been so naive.

Ted walked back over to where she stood with Seth. He said something in a low voice that she wasn't able to catch. And he didn't move his lips much, so she couldn't read what he'd said. Seth angled his body and signed discreetly to her.

"Uncle Ted says our rooms are ready if we want to go up and rest or clean up a bit."

Translation: the other guests were not happy with her presence. And she understood that he felt it was better if they were moved away from the party. She wouldn't complain. The sooner she was away from the angry and disapproving stares, the easier she would feel. She walked up the stairs to her room ten minutes later, Seth behind her like he was guarding her back. Which, in a way, he was.

In the hallway, a man with a cowboy hat approached from the other side. There was something familiar about him. She had probably seen him at some horse event, but had never been introduced. Odd, because she knew most of the equestrian crowd in the area.

He never even glanced at her as he was passing. But instead, with a quick side step, he knocked her into the wall with his shoulder. Pain lanced through her as she hit the wall. He dashed down the steps.

"Hey!" Seth turned, clearly intending to give chase.

"No, please, Seth, I don't want to be up here by myself."

He hesitated, but nodded, a grim look around his

mouth. She was fairly certain that he wasn't going give up. He'd be watching for that cowboy. And given his fantastic ability to recall details, he would be able to spot the man in an instant.

Outside her door, there was a copy of today's newspaper. On the front page was a picture of her barn, with a police car in the parking lot. The article was circled in red. Had the cowboy left it here? Was he the person responsible for the fire?

Her breath caught in her throat. She was trapped with a house full of hostile people. And one of them was out to get her.

Chapter Three

Seth pushed open the door to the guest room assigned to Jess and stalked inside. The anger simmering inside him demanded action, but he had no outlet for it at the moment, other than making sure she was safe. Leaving no corner unchecked, he searched her room for any dangers, hidden or otherwise. It really burned him that someone had decided to play games with her. She was an innocent, no matter what her brother may have done. Or not done. Because right now, he was feeling like there was something other than revenge behind these attacks. Not that he could make that call. He wasn't a cop.

Speaking of calls, he pulled out his cell and glanced at it. Still no bars. He had tried to contact the police department on Ted's landline, but couldn't get through. He'd lived through enough flash floods and tornado warnings to know that the lines could get overwhelmed. Or that power lines in town could get knocked out easily enough. So now they were sitting ducks. Which meant that it was up to him to see that Jess was safe.

He needed to have a talk with his uncle about the dude in the hallway. His gut said the man wasn't the same person who had been following them earlier. Why act out in the open after being so secretive? But he was definitely a threat.

"Okay, Jess. I don't see anything," he declared after ten minutes. "I think you can go ahead and clean up. I'm going to go downstairs and grab us something to eat. Lock the door behind me. I think we should stay up here tonight, and then tomorrow see if we can find a way out of this mess."

She nodded, but didn't look comforted. Her mouth opened, then shut again. He waited.

"Do you think someone is just trying to scare me? Or am I really in danger?" Her hazel eyes glistened, but she didn't cry. He wouldn't have blamed her if she had. The urge to comfort her and tell her everything would be fine was strong. But even stronger was his need to be honest. His father had taught him how to deceive, and he resisted any semblance of similarity to that man.

"Jess, as much as I want to tell you no, I really think you're in trouble. Whoever this jerk is, we have to assume he's dangerous. He didn't hesitate to start a fire at the stables, did he?"

The last expression he expected to see cross her face was a smile. It was no more than a slight upward curling of her lips, but it was there. "What?"

She glanced down, heat staining her pale cheeks. "It's been a long time since I felt like someone was on my side, other than Rebecca and her family. Even the other workers at my stable aren't really people I feel I know. Cody hired them, not me."

That surprised him. "What about your parents?"

"You didn't know?"

"Know what?"

"My parents were killed in a car accident the summer I graduated from high school. My brother became my guardian."

Seth groaned. "He was all you had." Reaching out, he snagged her into a hug. She resisted for a second, then accepted the embrace, leaning against him. But only for an instant. When she started to pull away, he let her go.

"I wasn't alone, Seth. I had the Lord to lean on. And Rebecca's family was great. They have been checking on me constantly."

"What about the people at your church?" he asked. "Surely, you feel some sort of connection with them?"

Even her ponytail seemed to droop as she shook her head.

"No, not really." Furrows appeared on her forehead. She brought one hand up and rubbed at them, as if she could massage them away. "To be honest, I didn't give them much of a chance. At the funeral, I could see people staring at me, and couldn't deal with their pity. So I changed churches. I drive to Erie each Sunday and attend there where no one knows me. Well, except for Ernie. But he doesn't pry."

He blinked, but didn't ask any questions. He was anxious to move the conversation away from the topic of God. He had an itchy feeling whenever she mentioned her faith. There was even a brief moment when they arrived when he had been tempted to say a prayer. Just to see if it worked. Tempted. He didn't succumb. That didn't stop the feeling that he was on a slippery slope. There would be no point to it, he knew. His mother had trusted in God all her life. And she ended up cheated on and betrayed by her own husband. Not just once, but over and over. No, he was just fine as he was. God was okay for others, but he didn't see the need for himself.

But he was saddened to see Jess abandon her church community. His mother had found support in hers.

Jess tilted her head. Probably wondering where he had gone mentally.

The flickering lights reminded them both of their situation.

"I will be back." Seth retreated to the hall and pulled the door shut behind him. He waited until he heard the door lock click. Then he made his way down to the kitchen, hoping he wouldn't run into anyone along the way. Answering questions or fending snide comments about Jess was not high on his list of things he wanted to do. For the first time in his life, he found himself grateful that his uncle had inherited his family's taste for ostentation. The house he had built in the middle of nowhere, in addition to having enough bedrooms to rival a modest hotel, had two staircases leading down to the main level. Seth took the back stairs, which ended in a short hallway right outside the kitchen. Which was empty. His uncle had gone all out and had the event catered, so all the food and beverages were displayed in a fancy buffet line in the dining room. Music and laughter pounded in the air.

Efficiently, Seth put together some sandwiches and grabbed some bottles of water. He nabbed a couple pieces of fruit from a basket on the counter. Where did his aunt keep plastic bags? Opening the cupboard under the sink, he found one and stuffed the food inside.

Turning back to exit, he was dismayed to find he was no longer the sole occupant of the kitchen. The man standing in the doorway was watching him with cold eyes, a distinct sneer on his face. Great. First the man on the stairs, and now this guy. As far as Seth could recall, he had never seen him before. He was a bulky man, his beefy arms crossed over his barrel chest as he scowled at Seth.

Seth moved forward. He had done nothing wrong, and he was in his uncle's house. This man wasn't going to keep him from Jess.

"Where's your girlfriend, boy?" the man growled, an ugly edge to his rough voice.

"Excuse me." Seth made to move past the man. But the guy just wouldn't let him pass. Instead, he planted himself firmly in Seth's path.

"How dare you bring that little crook here? She and her brother cost me thousands of dollars. And a prize horse. Spreading tales about honest folk." Fury oozed from him. Quivering, he took a step toward Seth, nostrils flaring. Seth had no idea what the man was talking about. "I'll bet she's here to spread her brother's lies, isn't she? Thinks good ole Ted Taylor will be on her side? Well, I won't let her get the best of me again. She'd better watch who she messes with."

He probably expected Seth to back up. Seth wasn't about to give in. Instead, he took a step closer to him.

"You need to let me pass," Seth stated, keeping his voice low. "Whatever happened, it had nothing to do with Jess. And from what I know, you don't even have solid proof that it had anything to do with her brother, either." He took another step forward. And another. Satisfaction filled him when the man's eyes widened, confusion on his face. Seth managed to keep his expression and voice clear of all emotion. Years of dealing with his father had taught him that the best way to get a reaction was to show no emotion. "You don't want to do this. Not in my family's home."

The sneer returned to his opponent's face, although Seth noted he did step aside to allow Seth to move past. Still, he managed to get out one last taunt before Seth could walk away.

"I would be careful who I hung out with. She's going down." He swung around and stormed back toward the other guests. Seth watched him, filing away in his mind details about the man's appearance and what he said. That was definitely someone to keep a close eye on.

Carrying his cache of food, he returned back upstairs the same way he had come. He breathed easier when he arrived at Jess's room without further incident. He rapped sharply on the door, then grimaced. Deaf girl. Could she hear the knock? Maybe he should slide something under the door...

The door swung open, causing him to jump. Color flooded his face as she observed him, her eyebrows lifted, an amused expression on her face.

"Didn't you expect me to answer the door?" she queried.

"I wasn't sure if you could hear me knock."

Jess nodded, making her brown ponytail bounce. "It depends on how low the sound is."

A thought occurred to him. "We should have found a way to signal you, so you would know it was me."

When she shrugged and reached for the food, he recalled the meeting in the kitchen. Casually, trying not to seem too concerned so she wouldn't worry, he mentioned the confrontation and described the man.

A disturbed look came into her eyes. Lowering her chin, she sighed. He wished he could have waited before telling her something that so clearly upset her, but she needed to know. For her own protection.

"It sounds like Bob Harvey. He and his wife Lisa are very involved in breeding racehorses. They have been the loudest voices against us."

A sharp, sizzling sound made Seth jerk his head up. It was followed by a pop. A transformer had been blown. The room was pitched into darkness.

Jess froze. Her entire body grew tense.

She'd never told anyone, but she was afraid of the dark. And closed-in places. Had been ever since the incident in high school. A cold sweat covered her body as she remembered the feeling of cobwebs brushing against her skin. The musty smell of a wet mop sitting in a bucket of dirty water. The smell was so pungent, she could taste it on her tongue. Clenching her fists, she folded her arms across her chest and shoved her fists under them. She could still feel them shaking. The trembling spread to her legs.

Breathe, Jess. Breathe. Spiders are NOT crawling over you. You are not locked in a room. And you are not alone. Stranded for hours and hours. Getting colder...

No! She wouldn't think about that! She was a grown woman now. Surely she could get past this irrational fear. The fear that even now was holding her paralyzed. After a few deep breaths, she baby-stepped her way in the direction of the window, grunting as her shin knocked into something. At the window, she felt around until she located the cord to the blinds. Tugging on it, she sighed in relief as light drifted into the room. It pooled in the center of the room, leaving the edges in shadow. She shivered. Creepy.

Light? Where on Earth was light coming from? It was pouring outside. Glancing out the window, she saw a row of solar lights. The kind that only come on when it is dark outside. Ah. She hadn't noticed them before, probably because there had been other sources of light.

Seth stepped into the light, and she shivered again. For a very different reason.

"Jess, are you okay?"

She nodded. "Fine."

He folded his arms. Clearly she wasn't convincing enough.

"What do we do now?" she asked him. *Focus, Jess.* Yes, he's handsome and being kind. And yes, she was enjoying his company. But there was a maniac in this house waiting to get her and this power outage—whether accidental or deliberate—might give her attacker an opportunity. She needed to deal with that possibility. Attraction to Seth was a complication she couldn't afford.

"I'm not leaving you alone to deal with this tonight."

She shook her head, frowning. "You can't stay in my room. It wouldn't be right."

Did he just roll his eyes? Was he mocking her convictions? Drawing herself up to defend her beliefs, she paused when he raised his hands.

"I'm not suggesting that I stay in your room. But I do intend to camp outside your door."

Something soft and melty nudged her heart.

"But you need to rest, too," she argued. "Your room is just down the hall. You'd be close by if I needed you." It was a token protest at best. The idea of him going so far away in this hostile environment made her feel vulnerable.

Seth scoffed. "Like I'd rest in my own room? Sorry,

Jess, but I'd be coming out to check on you every five minutes. There's no way I'd be able to sleep not knowing if you were safe."

The tension which had locked onto her neck loosened and rolled off her shoulders. He wasn't leaving her.

Jess squinted and looked at him. Really looked at him. His jaw was clenched and he was glaring at her. Like he was daring her to argue. A smile tugged at her mouth. He had no idea how unappealing the idea of staying here alone was. Deciding to let him think he'd won, she nodded. He nodded back. And although he didn't smile back at her, she sensed that her response had eased his belligerence.

"Good. Now that that issue is settled, I suggest we eat."

Gingerly, she lowered herself to sit cross-legged on the floor. Seth followed her example, then handed her a sandwich and a bottle of water. The darkness surrounding them made the room feel oddly intimate. Her cheeks grew warm, and she became aware of the subtle scent of his aftershave.

In complete silence they ate. The moment they were done, Seth excused himself to clean up. He made quick work of it, she was relieved to note. Then she scolded herself for being anxious just because he had left her side.

"I will be right outside the door," he promised. He used the flashlight app on his phone and pointed it so he could look around the room. What was he looking for? He strode to the desk and grabbed the plain wooden chair. Dragging it out into the hall, he placed it firmly in front of her door. She retreated back into the room. Even in the dim light, she could make out the bed. And if she remembered correctly…yes. There was an extra blanket on the end of it. Silently, she handed it to Seth. He smiled his thanks.

"Lock the door."

"Seth…"

She stopped when he shook his head. The weariness on his face tore at her, but she knew he wouldn't give in. One thing that she remembered clearly about Seth was that he had always been stubborn. It was no use trying to get him to change his mind. And frankly she was too tired to bother. Closing the door, she left him in the hall—locking the door, as he'd ordered. Grabbing her bag, she changed into sweats and a T-shirt. With a prayer for their continued safety she moved into the room and lay down on the bed.

Turning on her side, she tried to get comfortable, but her hearing aid was pressed into the side of her head. It wasn't painful, but the sensation bothered her. Should she take the hearing aids off for the night? She always did when she went to sleep. It drained the batteries to wear them constantly. But she was almost completely deaf without them. At least with them, she could hear voices and environmental noises, even if she couldn't make out what was being said. When had she last changed the batteries? Was it really only this morning? Calculating, she figured even if she left them in tonight, she had another three days. And she had spare batteries in her overnight bag.

That settled it. They were staying in.

Flopping over onto her back, she sighed.

She didn't expect to fall asleep, but soon found herself drifting off.

She woke suddenly and bolted upright, heart pounding.

Grabbing her phone, she checked the time. She had been asleep for two hours. What had wakened her? Sliding her legs over the side of her bed, she stood up and glanced around the room for some clue. Thunder rumbled and shook the house. The storm was directly overhead. That must have been what had startled her from sleep.

While she was relieved to have an explanation, she still felt anxious and unsettled. Rushing to the door, she opened it and peered out. Darkness enveloped everything. She knew the shadow in front of her was Seth, but dread filled her. She needed to see his face, to make sure he was safe.

"Seth?" she whispered. Her hand reached out and touched his face.

His phone light flashed on. He brought it closer to his face, probably so she could see his lips better. Standing, he stepped just inside her doorway.

"What's wrong?" he said, signing at the same time.

"I don't know. I just suddenly felt something was wrong."

He started to answer her, then abruptly stopped. His head swung around to the left, and he used his phone to peer into the darkness.

"What?"

He made a shushing motion. Bringing the phone close enough so she could see his hands again he signed, "I think someone might have just walked out of my room."

"Why didn't you notice them going into it?" she signed back.

"I fell asleep. The storm just woke me."

He stood up, every movement careful, and motioned that he was going to check his room. She grabbed his arm. Was he crazy, going after some maniac by himself? Using his phone for light again, he signed. "We are trapped. We'll be safer once we know. Wait for me in your room."

She wasn't so confident that confronting her attacker would make them any safer, but it did make sense to figure out who they were dealing with. But as for waiting for him in her room… She looked back into the dark cavern beyond her doorway. Uh-uh.

Decision made, she stepped out into the hallway and started to follow him. A frown crossed his face. But he didn't argue.

They crept to his room, but didn't enter. He pointed toward the stairs and signed. She nodded to show she understood. Someone was arguing downstairs. Possibly whoever had left his room. She needed to keep close. He began to creep down the stairs, his steps exaggerated. For a second, she hesitated. She could make out the sounds of muffled voices below. The voices were too low and garbled for her to decipher much more than that. There were at least two voices, but she couldn't even tell what gender they were.

Seth was getting ahead of her. She watched his shadow creep down another step. She went after him, using her hands to guide her along the wall. Fortunately, there was enough light coming in from the windows on the outside wall that she could make out the outline of the steps. She took care to step as gently as she could, fighting panic, knowing she wouldn't hear it if the stairs creaked. But whoever was at the bottom of the stairs would.

The hair on the back of her neck stood on end. Without knowing why, Jess knew something was wrong.

A hand grabbed her shoulder. Jess jumped, starting to turn. For a brief instant, she was aware of a slight aroma that she could not quite place. A second hand touched her back. A single hard shove propelled her toward the edge of the stairs. A scream ripped from her throat as she crashed downward into the darkness.

Chapter Four

Air whooshed past her ears as she fell, tumbling into the darkness. She pitched forward, flailing her arms, desperate to catch the railing, or anything that might break her fall. Her fist clipped something.

Seth's chin.

He must have turned toward her. She landed against him.

Unfortunately, instead of stopping her fall, he was knocked off balance, as well. His arms closed around her, and even in her terror she realized he was trying to shield her as they continued crashing down the stairs.

But the crashing thankfully only lasted for another second.

Their downward spiral came to an abrupt halt. Seth's whole body shuddered as his back slammed against the wall on the landing. Inertia had her thudding hard against his chest.

"Oof!" Seth's breath puffed against her ear. His arms tightened around her. Lying so close to him, she could feel both their hearts racing. Briefly, she dipped her head and pressed her forehead to his chest.

They were alive. Someone had deliberately pushed her down the stairs, but they had survived. But for how long? It wasn't likely that whoever had pushed her was going to give up. On the contrary, the attacks were escalating.

Why had the person chosen to show their hand, here? Did they think the hostile environment would leave her so vulnerable that no one would notice, would assist her?

Gratitude welled in her heart. Because she wasn't alone. God had sent her Seth. An unlikely hero, given their past, but who was she to question the ways of the Almighty?

Carefully, she pushed away from Seth. He stood, then gave her a hand to help her up. The arguing they had heard moments before was gone. She could hear doors around them slamming, felt the vibrations on the landing of someone moving up the stairs toward them. She tensed. Seth's arms moved again, this time to shove her behind him.

A wide beam of light cut through the dark, moving in a back and forth pattern as someone approached. It came to land on them and Jess could see that it came from a heavy-duty LED flashlight.

"Seth? Jess? What's going on?" Ted exclaimed, his loud voice echoing in the stairway. "I thought I heard someone screaming."

"It's okay, Ted. Jess—"

"I just tripped on the stairs," she interrupted Seth. He had no clue that she had been pushed, and she didn't want to get into it now, not when everyone else was closing in. For now, she just wanted to hurry and move to a new location. Already the top of the staircase and the landing below were filling with other guests, their flashlights aimed straight at them. And although she couldn't see their faces clearly, she imagined many of them were filled with anger at being awakened. Or maybe even malicious joy that she had suffered a mishap.

"Probably stumbling under the weight of all that guilt," a familiar voice called out. Bob Harvey. Jess kept herself from reacting, although she could do nothing about the anxiety crawling like ants over her skin.

Seth put a hand on her shoulder, then leaned over and whispered something in his uncle's ear. Ted started. She literally saw the beam of light from his flashlight jump.

"It's okay, folks," their host called back in an overly jovial voice. Was she the only one who could tell how forced his tone was? "Go on back to bed. I'm sure all will be set to rights in the morning."

Meaning the electricity would be back on and the flood waters would recede, she supposed. One could only hope.

Seth, keeping her at his back, moved slightly away from her. She shivered. It had gotten colder. Or at least that's how it felt without his warmth nearby.

She kept her eyes focused on Ted and Seth as the other guests meandered back to their rooms, taking their flashlights with them. Amazing how long it took people to walk a few feet. After the last door had closed, Ted nodded and jerked his head, indicating they were to follow him.

Jess was startled when a hand closed over hers. Seth had reached back to take her hand. Tears stung the back of her eyes at his silent care. Rapidly, she blinked them away, chastising herself for giving in to irrational emotions. Of course he took her hand. He was just being a gentleman, making sure she didn't fall again.

Whatever. She was still touched by his actions.

Ted led them into a room on the other side of the house. Even with the high-powered flashlight, she still managed to bang her shins on objects twice. Tomorrow she was sure to have bruises to remember this fun evening by. Upon entering the room, she was pleased to note a fireplace with a roaring blaze. There were three candles flickering on tables. It was a relief to be in a room that was warm and reasonably well lit.

Ted turned off his light, then swiveled to shut and lock the door. When he faced them again, his normally cheerful face was more serious than she could ever recall seeing it before. The direness of their situation stabbed at her.

"Okay, son, want to tell me what this is about?"

Seth glanced over and met her eyes. She understood what he was asking. Slowly, she nodded, hoping she was making the right decision. Her instincts said to trust Ted; that he was on her side. But she knew it was very possible he was only being a good host. Or worse. Yet either way, what choice did she have, really? She was stuck in his house until they could find a way out of this mess.

"Do you need me to sign?" Seth asked her.

Again, she was surprised by his thoughtfulness. The longer she was around him, the more she felt sure he had truly changed.

"No. It's quiet, so I can hear you pretty well. And there's enough light for me to read lips, if necessary. Thanks for checking."

He nodded, then got down to business.

"Someone is after Jess, Uncle Ted," Seth began. "Even before we arrived here, we had the feeling someone was trying to hurt her, but since yesterday, things have escalated." Seth explained about the cowboy in the hallway, and the intruder in his room. He even mentioned his confrontation in the kitchen with Bob Harvey. At that, anger crossed Ted's affable face. Even in the less than perfect light, she could see the angry tide of red rolling up his neck.

"I should have known that hothead would cause trouble. But to confront my own nephew in my house? Why, I have half a mind to—"

"There's something else you should know." Jess hated to butt in, but she knew she needed to say something before her courage deserted her. Or before he got off on a tangent, which Ted was well-known for doing.

Both men turned to face her. Seth's eyebrows rose in surprise.

"I didn't fall down those steps. I was pushed."

Complete.

Silence.

Jess swallowed, the reality of her situation crashing down on her as she said the words out loud. Her shoulder and back tingled where her attacker had touched her. "Someone pushed me." Just saying the words made the fear and shock rise again, even worse than before. "I'm going to be sick!"

Her stomach rebelled, and she had to focus all her attention on keeping the contents of their late supper down. She retched, but thankfully nothing came up. Still, she had a nasty taste in her mouth.

An arm came around her shoulders. Seth.

"Easy, Jess. It's the shock. You're safe. I'm here. If you need to be sick, that's okay. I'll take care of you."

"I'm good," she whispered, suddenly drained. "Just want to sit down."

Seth led her over to the recliner positioned next to the fireplace. Ignoring her protests, he helped her to sit down, than covered her with the afghan from the couch. She felt like such a baby, being fussed over.

"Jessica, are you sure someone pushed you? You couldn't have fallen?" Looking into Ted's anxious face, she wished with all her heart she could tell him that she could have been mistaken. But she knew what she had felt.

"I'm sorry, Ted. I felt someone shove me. There was no way I fell."

Seth knelt down beside the chair, his face pinched and concerned.

"Did you happen to get a look at who it was? If it was a man or a woman?"

"No, I'm sorry. It happened so quickly."

Ted paced for a moment. Then he came to stand in front of them, his large hands fisted on his hips. "We need to call the police!"

Seth sighed, scrubbing his hands over his face. He dropped them, and shook his head. "I agree, but how? The cell service here is nonexistent. Is your landline functional?"

Crossing the room with long strides, Ted picked up the wireless phone sitting on the end table. He pushed a button and listened for a moment. Shoulders drooping, he set it back down. "No dial tone. Don't know if it's the lines or if the battery is drained. This phone has been spotty for the past few weeks."

"So we're stuck." Jess stated the obvious.

"We're stuck," Seth repeated, pounding his fist on

his thigh. "The question is who here could be out to get you?"

Jess snorted. Seth looked at her, eyebrows raised.

"Sorry, but I mean, who isn't?" she said. "You saw that crowd. Honestly, Seth, even your aunt treated me like so much garbage."

Oops. That was probably not the right thing to say. Both Seth and Ted stiffened. Then Ted relaxed and rubbed the back of his neck. A tired chuckle rumbled from his mouth. Surprised, Jess looked at him.

"Yeah, my Willa can come on strong. But she has a heart of gold. You'll have to trust me on this one."

She wasn't so sure, but decided now was not the time to anger their one ally.

Turning the conversation in a different direction, she asked, "What about the car?"

Ted shook his head. "Car? What car?"

"I've been followed by a green sedan."

Even before she finished, he was shaking his head again. "Little lady, in case you haven't noticed, this is pickup country. No self-respecting person in this house would dare to drive any vehicle that wasn't fit to tow a horse trailer."

Well, there was that. Now what?

Ted turned to his silent nephew. Silent, but those deep eyes were alert. If she could read his mind, she was pretty sure he was storing up every nuance, every word being said to dissect later.

"I don't think y'all should go back to your rooms tonight, Seth."

Ted's pronouncement had both their heads turning to face him in surprise. And if Jess was being honest, she was relieved, too. Down here near the fire seemed a whole lot safer than upstairs in her quiet room, nestled so near those who wished her miles away. Or dead.

"Where should we stay?" Seth asked, his air cautious.

"Right here. The door is locked. There's a fire. And you and I can take turns keeping watch. Then in the morning we can come up with a plan. Things always look brighter when the sun's up."

"What about Aunt Willa?"

Ted snorted. "Your aunt is sound asleep. She won't even notice that I'm not there until morning. And I'm always up by five to take care of the horses, anyway. She never stirs before eight."

Jess felt her clenched muscles relax bit by bit as he spoke.

Morning. She just had to hang on until morning.

Could they hang tight until morning?

She claimed someone had pushed her. If he hadn't been in front of her to protect her from the worst of the fall, or if the stairwell had been a straight drop without that landing... Anger flooded his once logical mind. Here, in his uncle's house, she was being stalked and attacked. He had let her down so long ago. This time, he was resolved to redeem himself. He would keep her safe, no matter what. Seth was no cop, but he was a grown man, and he was fit.

He would stand between her and any dangers.

Maybe a prayer wouldn't hurt?

He shook his head, ridding himself of the thought. God had stopped listening to him years ago.

Ted moved with his lumbering gait toward the door, his flashlight once again in his large hand. "I'm going to go get some extra bedding from the linen closet. Lock the door behind me. I'll call out to you when I come back so you'll know it's me. If anyone else knocks, well, just let 'em stew. Don't even acknowledge it."

As if. Seth merely nodded. Rising, he followed Ted to the door, locking it securely behind his uncle. He listened to the familiar heavy footsteps fading. What now? Peeking over at Jess, he frowned. With the poor lighting, it was hard to tell, but he was sure she looked pale. And why not? The poor woman had already had enough hurled at her to wear anyone down. She needed to rest.

He moved in front of her, squatting so they were eye to eye. Her gaze was steady. Good, even if she was scared, which he knew she had to be, she wasn't allowing it to control her. His respect for her rose a notch.

"Jess, why don't you try to get some rest?" he suggested. "Tomorrow's gonna be a hard day, and you'll need to be able to keep on your toes."

Her head tilted, causing her hair to tumble over her shoulder. When had she removed her ponytail? He had the sudden urge to brush the caramel-colored strands back, just to see if they were as soft as they looked.

Yeah. Like that was an appropriate thought to be having right now. *Use your head, Seth. Even if you weren't in a dangerous situation, there's no way someone like her would want to be with someone like you.* That thought brought him up short. He wasn't a man who could do relationships. There was too much of a risk that he would harm the woman he was seeing, unthinkingly.

"What about you?" her soft voice, slightly slurred with exhaustion, reminded him of his question.

"You heard my uncle. He and I will take turns. And I will sleep while he has the watch." Something occurred to him. "You did hear him, right?"

The barest hint of a smile teased him. "Yes. I heard him. Although, if you and he are both here with me, maybe I can take out my hearing aids? Save the batteries? I don't want to have to use the spares I brought until I have to. Who knows how long we'll be out here."

Hopefully not long.

"Go ahead."

Reassured, she reached up and removed her hearing aids. He watched as she opened the battery doors to turn them off, and set them on the end table beside the chair. Hearing Ted's voice outside the door, he hurried over and let his uncle in. Ted passed out blankets, then sat down in the rocking chair near the door.

"Jess. Jess?" No answer. She couldn't hear him, and her eyes were closed. Was she asleep already? Unbelievable. He could never fall asleep that quickly.

"I'll take first watch, Seth."

He nodded at his uncle, then looked at the couch. It went against the grain for him to lie down while she was in the chair. But Jess was curled up on the only other possible spot in the room—and if she was already asleep then he certainly wasn't going to wake her up to move her. Reluctantly, he lay down.

"Wake me in a couple of hours?" he asked his uncle.

"Yep. You just get some sleep, son. Mornin' will be here before you know it."

Seth came awake slowly. He stretched, frowning. Man, he had the worst crick in his neck. Suddenly, the memories of what had happened before he fell asleep flooded his mind. He shot up on the couch, knocking the fluffy little pillow he had been using on the floor. His eyes flew to the clock. It was almost five in the morning.

His uncle was sitting in his chair, rocking slightly as he watched his nephew.

"Why didn't you wake me?"

"Seemed a shame...you were both sleeping so soundly. And I figured you would need to stay on your toes later. We both will."

"Electric still off?"

"Yep. Got some emergency generators that kicked on, but that's about it. Landline's still down. I'm getting one bar on my cell phone—doubt it's enough for a call to go through, though." The older man stood with a groan, putting his hand on his back. "You're awake now. I'm going to go take care of the horses."

The older man left. When he returned forty-five minutes later, he had a couple more flashlights. Seth excused himself to go to his room. While he had the opportunity, and before the other guests stirred, he wanted to go through his things and see if he could find what last night's intruder was after.

The house was still dark. He tightened his grip on the flashlight he had borrowed. Arriving at his room, he cautiously pushed the door open. Whoever had been in there hadn't shut it the whole way. Probably didn't want the noise to awaken Seth from his perch outside Jess's room. The hair prickled on his neck as he entered the room. What could they have been searching for? Nothing seemed to be out of place. His duffel bag was still sitting on the chair next to the bed. But wait...was it unzipped? Yeah, it was—and he was sure he hadn't left it that way. He quickly emptied the contents on the bed, holding the light between his chin and chest. He couldn't see that anything was missing.

Shoving everything back in his bag, he scowled. So what were they looking for?

Unless…

Unless they weren't sure which room was his. The thought curdled his blood. If they had been searching for Jess's room, what were they planning to do if they'd found her?

Seth shuddered, and forced his mind back to the present. He couldn't afford to let the "what ifs" get control.

Head full of questions, Seth left the room and headed back down to join Jess. As soon as it was light out, they'd start looking for a way out of here.

Passing her room, he paused. Listened. Someone was in there. And from the sound of it, they were searching for something with a vengeance. Holding his breath, he stepped closer to the door and gently turned the knob.

Paused.

Waiting.

The sound of things being moved around inside continued. Whoever was inside hadn't heard him.

I should go get Ted, he thought to himself. That was clearly the intelligent thing to do. Except that any movement away from the door might alert whomever was inside. And what if the intruder was finished and left the room before he returned? They might miss the chance to find out who Jess's attacker was. He couldn't let the opportunity to stop this nut case pass him by.

The blood was roaring in his ears as he carefully opened the door and stepped inside the room.

The first strains of morning coming in the window highlighted the contents of Jess's overnight bag strewn all over the floor, her toiletries everywhere. A large hulking figure stood over her bag, systematically pulling items out one at a time.

That was it. Seeing the man's hands on Jess's personal items was the last straw.

At Seth's entrance, the man dropped the bag and charged at Seth. Seth backed up against the door for more room, and swung the flashlight. Thwack! With a grunt, the man stopped. But only for a second. Before Seth could call for help, the man was upon him, trying to get his hands at Seth's throat.

Falling back on the moves he'd learned during his days on the high school wrestling team, Seth twisted away and dove for his attacker's knees. Using his weight, he pushed the man off balance. Where his attacker had breadth and pounds on Seth, Seth had agility and years of weight training behind him.

The larger man managed to get an elbow into Seth's windpipe, but it gave Seth the opening he needed to hook the man's arm with his, forcing it back. Using his legs as leverage, he forced the man over, the one arm twisted at an impossible angle. The man's breath started to come out in wheezing gasps.

Suddenly, a bright light shone upon the two on the floor.

"Seth! What are you doing? Bob? Is that you?"

Ted moved into the room.

Seth let Bob Harvey go and stood next to his uncle, keeping his glare fixed on Bob.

"He was going through Jess's things. I'm guessing he's her attacker."

Bob's head jolted up. The sneer melted off his face. "Hey! I never attacked your girl."

Seth clenched his fists. It would feel so good to slug

the dude. But it would solve nothing. "Then what were you doing? This—" he swept his arm out, indicating the mess Bob had made "—doesn't exactly look like innocent behavior."

An angry flush stole up the man's thick neck. Any second, steam would pour from his ears. "I told you, her brother was spinning stories about me before he killed himself. I'm aiming to see if she's planning on messing with my rep."

As far as excuses went, it was pretty weak.

Seth started to scoff, then realized something. If Ted was here, then Jess was...

"Ted! What are you doing up here? Where's Jess?"

"I got a text from you that you had the intruder and needed my help."

Alarm bells went off in his head. "I never sent any texts."

Reaching into his back pocket, he found just what he was expecting to find. Nothing. His cell phone was gone. The last time he had had it was last night on the stairs.

"My phone's gone! I dropped it last night when I tried to catch Jess. Someone must have picked it up."

Ted cast a threatening look at Bob.

Heart sinking, Seth knew they had a problem. "It wasn't him, Ted. He was in here searching her room when that text must have been sent. And he had no idea I was with him until I burst in on him."

The uncle and nephew looked at each other, horror dawning on both their expressions.

"Jess!"

Chapter Five

Where was Seth?

Jess put her hearing aids in and glanced at the clock on the wall. Ted had only been gone for a few minutes. She thought back to the text Ted had received. Why had Seth specifically said he needed her to stay where she was? Why wasn't it safe for her to accompany the older man?

Her phone vibrated in her back pocket. Finally! Grabbing the phone, she swiftly swiped her finger across the screen to unlock it and access the text.

The number was unfamiliar.

This is Seth. Situation under control. I need you to meet me by the back door.

Did she ever give Seth her number? She couldn't recall, although maybe he got it from Ted. His uncle was listed under her business contacts. But it would have made more sense for Ted to have sent the text. Unless Ted was busy with whatever they were doing?

She shrugged, trying to rid herself of the prickly unease dancing over her skin. Every instinct was screaming for her to stay where she was. She pulled her bottom lip in between her teeth and gnawed at it gently while she juggled her choices. She could, of course, remain in the room near the warm fire. That seemed the sensible thing to do. But what if Seth honestly did need her? She hated to think of him waiting for her. Especially if he had found something important. But why couldn't he have just said so? Maybe he was afraid someone else would see the text.

Whatever. How much could it hurt just to go to the door and look out? Maybe if someone friendly, like Ted or even Deborah, came by, she could ask them to go with her.

Replacing her phone, she got to her feet and strode to the door with the intention of just sticking her head out and peeking down the hallway. Instead, she opened the door and came face to face with Willa Taylor. So much for Ted's declaration that Willa wouldn't awaken before eight. Seeing the frozen sneer on the lady of the house's face silenced any hesitation ringing in her head. She couldn't remain in the same room as Willa.

Not giving the lady the time to say anything snide, Jess ducked past her and into the hall. She couldn't resist turning her head to look over her shoulder. And grimaced. Willa had marched straight into the room and was dramatically spraying disinfectant over the slept-on furniture.

Ouch.

Jess hurried on to the kitchen. She slowed her pace as she heard voices coming from the living room. She definitely didn't want to run into anyone else. Not in this hostile environment. Tucking herself in against the wall, she peeked around the corner. The cowboy she had met on the stairs was in the room, talking to Lisa Harvey.

Whipping her head back before they saw her, Jess struggled to control her breathing. Again, she doubted her wisdom in coming to find Seth. She should have just sent a text back telling him to come and get her. Now she was stuck. She couldn't go back to the parlor where she'd spent the night, not with Willa prowling around in there. And she couldn't stay here, out in the open.

Sucking in a deep breath to calm her nerves, she muttered a prayer under her breath. Then, she gathered up her courage and peered around the corner again. A sigh of relief slipped from her. Cowboy and Lisa Harvey were heading out the front door. A few moments later, she spotted Lisa out the window, heading away from the house.

Now was her chance.

Staying close to the walls, Jess continued on to the large kitchen.

To her dismay, she found the room empty.

Seth was nowhere in sight.

Doubt whispered to her again. Maybe it hadn't been Seth sending the text. She should have followed her gut and stayed locked in the parlor, safe and out of sight. Too late now. Most likely, one of the other guests was holding him up. Maybe even trying to question him about her.

She shuddered.

Surely he would understand if she sent him a text telling him to meet her somewhere else. Somewhere more secure, where she wouldn't feel so vulnerable and out in the open. Decision made, Jess started to turn. The aroma she'd smelled on the stairs tickled her nose right before an arm wrapped tight around her neck. She couldn't breathe!

Clawing at the arm, she kicked her legs and fought to pry the arm off her windpipe. Spots danced in front of her eyes.

A burning sensation bit into the tender skin on the side of her neck. Her vision blurred.

Even as she struggled, a heavy, weighted feeling slid through her.

She was going down.

It was freezing.

Why was she on the floor? Pressing her palms against the smooth surface—concrete?—Jess pushed herself to her hands and knees. A rush of dizziness threatened to send her toppling. She bowed her head and waited for the wave to pass.

Steady now, she slowly gained her feet. Wherever she was, it was pitch dark.

A whimper crawled up her throat. She bit her lips to keep it inside. She shuddered, and knew only a fraction of it was from the cold.

Had she slept through the day? That hardly seemed likely. Something had happened…

The memory of her struggle with her attacker slammed into her, robbing her breath. She could still feel that arm around her throat. And the burning sensation in her neck. Reaching up, she touched one cold finger to her neck, wincing at the tender spot covered in something crusty. Blood. She must have bled when the person jabbed her with whatever it was they used. She slipped her left hand to her back pocket, reaching for her phone. Her jeans were icy and stiff. For the first time she realized that her back was wet. And apparently covered with mud. She pushed her frozen fingers under the mud, and was unsurprised to discover her pocket was empty. Her phone was gone. She really hadn't expected her attacker to leave it on her.

The dark pressed in on her. The silence surrounded her like thick cotton. One hearing aid was missing, the other was weak.

Okay, Jess. Okay. Think. Don't panic. Seth is going to be looking for you.

But what if he wasn't? What if he was trapped, too?

This line of thought was helping no one. *Please, Lord, help me. And please let Seth be okay.*

She needed to figure out where she was. She held her arms out to start feeling her way around the space, shivering at the cold air swirling around her. Her jaw was starting to ache. Her teeth had never chattered so hard in her life.

Taking a small step forward, her left hand bumped into something. Something cold. Hard. It was large, and swung slightly.

Horror dripped down her spine as a suspicion began to grow in her mind. She blocked it. She had to be mistaken. Until her right hand bumped a second one.

She was in the slaughterhouse freezer.

She knew Ted ran a slaughterhouse on his property as a second business. Many of the Amish in the area used his services since he was so close.

What she couldn't figure out was why she was in it.

There was a high probability that she wouldn't be found until the flood waters receded. Which could be days. No one was going to coming to pick up their meat or drop off new orders before then.

Every instinct in her urged her to scream. She was stuck in a cold, dark, small enclosed area. Images of dying here popped into her head. She squeezed her eyes shut and focused on breathing normally. Forcing panic aside, she turned her body and felt for the door. Her fingers were tingling. Was she getting frostbite?

Ignoring her physical distress, she bumped around the cold freezer, her movements growing clumsier as the cold started to take its toll. She no longer noticed her aching jaw.

Finally, after what seemed like an eternity, she bumped into the door. It wouldn't budge. Locked. Or blocked. It didn't matter which.

Banging her fists against the door, she screamed. Pain shot through her hands. Her wrists. Up her arms and into her shoulders. She kept banging as the air became thin. The walls…she couldn't see them, but they were closing in on her. Something crawled across her skull. A spider? Panic gained control.

"Help! Help me! I'm stuck in the freezer!"

She yelled until her throat became raw. She leaned her head against the door. It was no use. Who was going to hear her out here? Everyone else was safe inside the warm house. Weariness melted into her bones. Wait… when had her eyes closed?

Dragging them open, she blinked. It was so hard to keep them open, but she continued to struggle to do just that. After a while, she forgot why it was so important. She was so tired. All she wanted was to rest. Leaning against the freezer door she gave in and let her eyes close. Just for a minute. All she needed was a short nap.

Her legs seemed to lose strength. Weariness weighed her down. The door was smooth against her cheek as she allowed herself to slide down. Down, down, down until she was sitting on the floor.

Dropping her hands to her lap, she let her head fall forward. Her chin touched her chest.

There was something she needed to do, but whatever it was eluded her.

Something about Seth?

She'd worry about it later. She was so sleepy. Needed…nap…

Seth dashed down the stairs, his uncle hot on his heels. Tearing through the house, he ignored the few guests who dove out of his way, muttering in displeasure. He arrived in the parlor to find his aunt inside. Jess was nowhere to be seen.

Where was she? Every fiber of his body screamed at him that she was in danger.

One thought darted across his brain, standing out.

I should pray. Jess would want me to pray.

The impulse was an uncomfortable one, and his inclination was to ignore it. But he couldn't shake the feeling that Jess would want him to pray. And if he was the one missing, she would no doubt pray for him.

Lord, protect her.

Was that enough? He hoped so.

"Aunt Willa, where's Jess?"

His aunt faced him, her lips pinched and eyes narrowed. He winced. He hadn't meant to raise his voice to her.

"Please, it's really important."

She sniffed. "I came in just after she snuck out of here. No telling what she was up to."

Calm. Stay calm. "Any idea where she was headed?"

"Well, I didn't actually stop to talk with her. She could have tried to swim home for all I care… Hey! Seth Travis! Come back here!"

Seth ignored her voice, shrieking after him. He dashed out the door, nearly colliding with his uncle.

"She's not here. We have to find her."

To his credit, Ted didn't stop to ask time-wasting questions. Although Seth did note that he tossed an angry glare toward his wife. The two men began to search the house inch by inch. Unsurprisingly, no one was willing to admit that they had seen Jess. Over an hour later, he met his uncle again in the kitchen.

He stopped in the doorway. Jess wasn't in the room. He hadn't really expected to find her there, he admitted to himself. His eyes scanned the room. And stopped. He crouched down. There, a couple of feet away from the door, lay a Behind-the-Ear, or BTE hearing aid. He had missed it the first time through. It was half hidden by the welcome mat. He reached out one hand and picked it up, bringing it close to inspect it.

"What is it, son?"

Seth looked into Ted's concerned face. Flicking his eyes behind the older man, he could see a group of the other guests gathered there. His mouth tightened when he saw Bob Harvey amongst them.

"It's Jess's hearing aid," he answered his uncle. His uncle's face paled. "It's broken. I'd say someone stepped on it."

Willa entered the room. The haughty expression she normally wore had been replaced by confusion. "She left her hearing aid in the kitchen?"

Shaking his head, Seth stood and walked to the back

door. "No. She would never go without her aid. She's completely deaf without them. Something happened to her."

Why had he left her alone? Noticing that his fingers were trembling slightly, he closed them around the fractured hearing aid. The shattered plastic scratched his palm. He felt it all the way to his heart.

Ignoring the burst of chatter that broke out, he walked outside. And sucked in a breath.

Amidst the rain-soaked muck that was out the back door, a clear path had been left by something being dragged. Something that was big enough to be a human body. All the moisture in his mouth instantaneously dried up. The path was narrow and straight enough that he doubted the person being dragged had been conscious enough to struggle. And, knowing that person was Jess, he rushed outside, regardless of the rain pelting his head, molding his hair to his scalp and running mercilessly into his eyes.

None of that mattered. Neither did the clomping feet behind him.

Except...

"First-aid kit!" he barked at his uncle.

Ted nodded once before pivoting mid-step and rushing back toward the house.

The path wound around the side of the house. Seth quickened his pace, gritting his teeth in frustration when he was forced to slow down or risk slipping and falling flat on his face.

The path led to the front of his uncle's slaughterhouse. Ripping open the front door, he saw immediately that the path continued. The scant light from the cloudy skies was enough for him to see inside the building. His uncle reappeared just as he entered.

"Open the blinds!" Ted yelled. He and another guest went from window to window, pulling up the blinds to let the morning light filter inside.

Seth stopped in front of a large metal door, horrified. He knew from memory that the door in front of him was to the walk-in freezer. Granted, there was no electricity right now, but there was enough frozen food in that freezer to keep it arctic for days.

Shoving the latch aside with fingers that shook, he pulled the huge door open.

And caught Jess as she toppled out.

Her face was white, tinged with blue. The back of her head and body was covered with a thick coat of crusty, frozen mud.

Gently, he picked her up and carried her into the main room. As he held her close, he glanced down, and nearly lost his composure at the sight of the blood dried on the side of her throat. Swallowing the rage that vibrated in his gut, he laid her down on the floor as if she was made of porcelain.

And then he set about doing what he did best. For the first time in his life, he wondered if God had put the desire to be a paramedic in his heart for this moment. Ridiculous. He drew upon his training to focus all his thoughts, all his energies, on his patient. Now was not the time for philosophizing. Or for letting worry for the lovely, deathly pale woman at his feet distract him. *Box up your emotions and ship 'em out, Seth.*

The well-known mantra calmed him.

First thing first, check her vitals.

She was breathing, and had a steady pulse. Check.

Now, to get her warm.

Someone shuffled too close to him, hampering his movements.

"Get back!" he ordered, barely recognizing the harsh voice as his own.

"Seth," his aunt quavered, wringing her hands. Her normally haughty expression was edging on frantic, her voice whiny. "I'm sure this was an accident. No one here would…"

"Get. Out. Of. My. Way." He bit off each word, all but snarling at the woman beside him.

Willa jumped away, her expression an odd combination of dismay and affront. He'd worry about smoothing her feathers later. Maybe. Right now, Jess was all that mattered.

Efficiently, he called for blankets and clean clothes. Within minutes, Jess was in dry clothes and bundled in blankets, her feet elevated.

He monitored her closely, relieved to note her color was returning. She was beginning to stir.

"Jess? Jess? Can you hear me?" He raised his voice. A thought occurred to him. Gently, he reached over and removed her other hearing aid. Cupping his hand over the small microphone, he lifted it close to his ear, listening for feedback. But there was no whistling. The tiny battery was dead, drained by the frigid temperature. Or possibly the device itself had been damaged by being slogged through the wet, muddy terrain.

But Jess was alive.

"Why isn't she answering?"

He sighed as his aunt's anxious voice reached his ears. Now that the immediate danger was past, he'd have to deal with her.

"She's still unconscious. And without her aids, she can't hear me calling."

Hearing the sharpness in his tone, he sucked in a deep breath of cold, Pennsylvania air to calm himself. None of this was his aunt's fault. But really, the woman needed to take it down a notch. She was family, but he was this close to publicly disowning her.

Okay, not really.

Whispers distracted him. Glancing behind her, he grimaced. At least six other people were standing behind the Taylors. Great. He had an audience to witness the drama unfolding.

Before he could say anything to the nosy, judgmental crowd, Jess moaned. Immediately the conversation ceased. Seth switched back into paramedic mode and began taking stock of her condition, watching her for any signs of injury or disorientation.

With a flutter, her eyes opened. His breath left him with a whoosh as he saw the confused, but alert, expression in the hazel depths.

"Seth?" As she said his name, her eyes widened. "I can't hear."

A panicked expression crossed her face as she moved under the blankets. He understood. She wanted to free her hands to check on her hearing aids. He reached out and touched her shoulder. She stilled, her eyes seeking his.

"Your left aid was on the kitchen floor, smashed," he told her grimly, signing and speaking at the same time. "The right one isn't working, either. I suspect that the battery is dead, but it could have water damage."

"Water damage?"

"You were dragged outside through the rain." Fury

rose up in him. For a second, he couldn't breathe through the anger choking him. He had never understood the phrase "seeing red." Now he did. When he could talk again, he continued. "They left you in the freezer."

The color that had so recently filled her pretty face drained out again.

"Someone attacked me in the kitchen. I was looking for you. You sent me a text…"

Her voice dwindled as he shook his head slowly. Someone was going to pay for this.

"I never sent a text. My phone is gone." He cast a fierce glance at the crowd behind him. "Someone took it."

"Seth, look what I found in the freezer."

Ted knelt down on the other side of Jess. His face seemed to have aged ten years since last night. Just one more reason for Seth to feel guilty about his ill-advised decision to bring Jess here. He heaved a sigh, then glanced down at the object in his uncle's hand. And did a double take.

"I've seen that hat before!"

"So have I!" Willa exclaimed, stepping forward. "That's Lisa Harvey's!"

The onlookers began murmuring behind him. Seth looked around, catching sight of Lisa's pale face as she held up both hands and backed away from the mob.

"Wait a minute!" she gasped. "I had nothing to do with this!"

"It wasn't her."

All voices stilled as Jess's voice, hoarse and raw, remarked from her place on the floor.

"I saw her out the window just moments before I was

attacked. She couldn't have come back in so fast without me knowing it."

Seth wasn't convinced. If Lisa, or Bob for that matter, had someone working with them, it would have been easy enough for them to make the attack happen without getting their hands dirty.

"Why attack her here? There are so many people around." Seth tilted his head at his aunt. Her face was stiff with disapproval. At Jess or at the fact that someone could behave so poorly at her house, he wasn't sure. Seth had a theory about the attack, but it wasn't something he intended to discuss in front of a crowd. One of whom might be the person responsible.

One thing was sure. He didn't plan on giving the attacker another opportunity to harm Jess.

"Seth." Jess reached out a hand, slowly, her reflexes still sluggish, and touched his face. "You've been hurt."

He wanted to close his eyes and enjoy the feel of the hand on his face. For so many years, he'd pushed away women. Now this girl from his past was getting under his skin. Gently, he removed her hand from his face. It was too intimate. But he couldn't bring himself to let go of her hand completely. It might have been the selfishness he inherited from his arrogant father, but he craved the comfort she brought.

"I'll tell you about it when we're alone. Don't worry about it. I'm more concerned about the fact that someone in my uncle's house tried to kill you."

Chapter Six

An hour later, once Jess had recovered enough to move, Seth and Jess retreated back to her room. Seth had warned Jess about the mess Bob had made of her things, but she still blanched when the door swung open. It looked a whole lot worse in the morning light than he had imagined. The fancy dress she had brought was crumpled in a heap on the floor. Those big hazel eyes puddled and blinked. Seth prepared himself for tears.

She surprised him, though. Her hands clenched into fists and her jaw tightened. "I thank You, Father, that Seth and I are alive."

What? Her room had been trashed and she was thankful? He tried to wrap his brain around that.

Turning his attention back to Jess, he saw that she had stiffened her resolve and was moving toward the pile of her belongings, which were still dumped on the bed where Bob had left them. Methodically, she sorted the items, her eyes fierce. With a glad cry, she located her batteries. Her hands shook so hard she dropped the tiny, round battery while trying to insert it into the hearing aid. Thankfully, it landed on the bed and didn't roll off.

"It works!" she sighed a minute later.

Seth dug out the other one. "Sorry, Jess. This one's toast. Fixing hearing aids wasn't taught in paramedic school."

To his astonishment, she gave a dry chuckle and shook her head. Why had he never noticed that dimple on her right cheek? It was adorable. The sudden urge to run his finger down her cheek shook him. He reminded himself that he was not here to romance her.

Pulling his mind back to the matter at hand, he tried to work out the best course of action. It was imperative that he keep Jess safe. That much was clear. Also clear was the fact that it wasn't going to be easy in this house.

An idea began to form in his mind. But would it work?

"We can't stay here."

Nice. Just blurt it out, Travis.

Her wide eyes spoke of her surprise. But she said nothing. He switched to sign, just in case there were ears at the door.

"I'm serious, Jess. We have to leave. I think our being here has scared whoever is after you past the point of caution. If that fall down the stairs had killed you—" she winced, but he kept going "—that would have looked like an accident. But it didn't, and you were able to tell someone you were pushed. Someone who believed you. And obviously, Uncle Ted believes you, and his opinion carries a lot of weight in the horse community. I don't know. But knocking you out and locking you in the freezer wasn't subtle at all, so apparently they're done making any attempts a secret. We're sitting ducks here."

"And how are we supposed to leave? And, even if we do leave, where would we go? The power is still down and the creek's still flooded," she countered, following his lead and signing.

She had a point. The situation wasn't ideal, but he wasn't an Eagle Scout for nothing. He was always prepared.

"We're just going to have to rough it," he announced. Now she was looking worried. "I have my camping pack in the bed of my truck. It has my rock-climbing equipment, camping gear, and stuff like that. I will get it and we will leave quietly at the first opportunity."

"Rock climbing?" Her eyebrows disappeared under her bangs. Again, he fought the urge to brush the soft fringe aside. What was the matter with him?

"Yeah. Rock climbing. I'm an assistant scout master with the local troop. I teach the rock climbing and rappelling merit badges. Just did it last weekend, in fact. Which is why I have the pack in my truck."

Okay, so he was trying to impress her. Just a little.

Her brows lowered. Her teeth gnawed at her full lower lip. Determined to avoid her brand of distraction, he turned his gaze out the window. Still raining. Although, it seemed to have let up some. Maybe things would look up soon.

"Seth."

Her voice made him turn around. "Yeah?"

She reverted back to sign for her next words. "We're about five miles out from where Rebecca's parents live."

"Do you trust her family?" He was pretty sure he already knew the answer, but needed to make sure.

"Yeah. I'm sure her family would help us if we could just get to their house."

He considered it. "Where do they live?"

She told him. "Most of the houses on their street are

owned by the Amish. And the lumber mill Levi works at is close by. We could probably get over there and use the business phone to call the police."

"Tomorrow—"

She interrupted him. "Tomorrow is Sunday. The family is very strict about no work on Sunday. We will have to wait to call until Monday."

Another day lost. Except at least they would be away from Jess's attacker.

"Better there than here. If we can sneak into the woods without being seen, we have a chance."

He waited for her slow nod.

"Let's do it."

Decision made, they made their way quietly downstairs, careful to keep away from the parts of the house where the rest of the guests were congregated. Ted had decreed that he wanted the others to stick together in the main part of the house. No one alone, just in case someone else were to become a target. Not that anyone believed for a second that anyone was in danger except for Jess.

Ted had told Seth privately that he wanted to keep an eye on the Harveys. And on Vic Horn, the cowboy who had accosted Jess in the hall and the one who was seen talking with Lisa Harvey just minutes before the attack. Ted had recognized him by Jess's description. Trouble was, no one seemed to be able to find said cowboy. Vic Horn was nowhere to be found.

Which, in Seth's mind, put him at the top of the list of suspects. Just above the Harveys.

Muted voices drifted from the main part of the house. Even from a distance, it was clear the day's events had put a damper on everyone's spirits. Lifting his hand, he signed to Jess that the others were in the front room area. She nodded, hazel eyes shadowed, but made no reply. What was going through her mind?

Footsteps were headed toward them. He could hear the heels of cowboy boots on the wooden floor. Uncle Ted. He was the only one who dared wear shoes on Aunt Willa's pristine floors. He smirked, and glanced back at Jess. Then did a double take. She grabbed his hand, eyes wide.

"Someone's coming, I can feel the vibrations," she signed with her other hand, her movements jerky.

"It's okay," he reassured her, "it's Ted."

"Oh."

Her cheeks warmed and she dropped her eyes, obviously embarrassed by her reactions. When her eyes landed on their hands, still joined, her flush deepened and she tugged her hand away from his. Reluctantly, he let her go.

Ted rounded the corner, his face one dark thundercloud. The expression was so different from the normal jovial uncle he was used to, it gave Seth pause.

The warmth at his back increased. Jess had moved in closer, tucking herself neatly into his protection. Seth almost smiled. He liked the thought of her turning to him as her knight in shining armor. Except his armor was tarnished.

The thought wiped any smile off his face. He was no one's hero. He had learned long ago that he had too much in common with his father, no matter how hard he tried to be different. If he said he'd do something, it was as good as done. He never broke his word. Nor was he scared of hard work. But he'd hurt Jess. He'd let down his former fiancée when she'd needed him years before. When it came to women, he knew he couldn't be trusted.

Ted stomped to a halt in front of him.

Seth waited.

"Those people in there are driving me nuts," his uncle finally said.

This time, Seth cracked an amused grin. "Those people always drive me nuts. But what's getting to you?"

Ted gave him a glare for his trouble. "Well, Vic Horn still hasn't shown up. And the Harveys are apparently everyone's scapegoat for what happened. Not that they don't look the guiltiest, especially with Bob's antics. What was he looking for in her room, anyway?"

Seth shook his head. He wasn't in the mood to go over it right now. "Later."

Ted shrugged. "Fine. Anyway, Bob is trying to divert blame from his wife by insisting that your girl there locked herself in the freezer to make us feel sorry for her."

Jess gasped. "I did not!"

Holding up his hands and wagging his head, Ted shushed her. "Honey, I know you didn't. It's not physically possible to lock the door from the inside."

"I need to get her outta here," Seth declared, keeping his voice low. "Can I borrow your hip-waders? I need to get stuff from my truck and it's still surrounded by water."

"Yep."

Wearing the hip-high boots and suspenders, Seth stole from the house and splashed his way over to the truck. Twice he started to slip as his boots squished on the drenched grass beneath his feet. He couldn't afford to walk down the meandering driveway...too out in the open for anyone looking out the windows. Arriving at the passenger side of the truck, he reached in behind the seat for his backpack. In his mind, he debated whether or not he should go through the pack, just to lighten the load, getting rid of anything unnecessary. No time, he decided. Mind made up, he hauled it out and strapped it around himself. Done. He glanced up. And frowned.

Jess was standing outside of the house, her back pressed against the bricks.

Why hadn't she stayed inside?

Every nerve was on high alert as she watched Seth grabbing his pack. He was staying low, but she could still see him over the window.

A gasp left her when he suddenly motioned for her to hide, then ducked behind the truck himself.

Hide? Where could she go? And what was coming?

That's when she picked up the indistinct murmur of voices. For her to be able to hear them with only one hearing aid in place meant that they were closer than was safe. She wasn't able to isolate individual voices, but the group was heading her way.

Keeping her back against the wall, she pushed herself into the bushes lined up parallel to the house, wincing as branches scraped her face. She was small, but the space between the shrubs and the building was practically non-existent. She found herself literally between branches. She had no idea how she'd escape without being flayed or getting her hair pulled out.

If she escaped.

The voices came closer. She edged farther into her hiding place. Three figures rounded the corner. Bob and Lisa Harvey, and…Willa Taylor? Leaning in, she tried to catch part of their conversation. But between having just one aid, the loud roar of the rushing creek, the rain and the pounding of her own heart, she was only able to catch a random word here and there. And she couldn't lip read from this distance.

They seemed to be arguing. Willa's long face was pinched, her lips pursed. Lisa was stomping along beside her, mouth screwed up in an angry scowl. Both women appeared to be unhappy with whatever Bob was telling them. His loud voice boomed out, and Jess was able to hear part of what he said.

"…thief. Only way… Not going to jail for murder."

Jess shuddered. Had the trio tried to murder her? Were they responsible for the attacks and accidents?

Another thought hit her hard. Willa was Seth's aunt. What if he had led her into an ambush deliberately? Sure, she had asked him to bring her to the party, but he hadn't protested that hard. Not really.

But he'd wanted her to go to the police. Yeah, but he'd picked his brother-in-law, who conveniently wasn't home.

And he had admitted his father used people to forward his own agenda. It was possible that Seth was like his father in that way.

No, it wasn't.

He could have let her die in the freezer, she argued with herself. Could have let her fall to her death down the stairs. But both times, he had saved her. And he had protected her all night. Back and forth, she went over the incidents in her mind. Her heart said to trust him, that he had changed since high school, and was now a man of his word. Her mind, though, urged caution. She couldn't allow herself to be blinded by her emotions.

Thinking of Seth, she worried that the trio walking past would see him and catch on to their plans to get away. Craning her neck, she peered toward the truck, only to become frustrated when the prickly branches blocked her view. She had no idea if he had been found or not. Nor, she realized, did she have any way of knowing when it was safe for her to rise from her hiding place.

Tentatively, she pulled her head back. Ouch! Her hair was caught, tangled up in the shrubbery in at least four places. Her fingers trembled and her eyes watered as she worked to free each strand. Twice, she gasped as thorns pricked her tender flesh. Her efforts finally paid off, and she was able to stand back. Her throat was dry as she poked her head up to get a cautious look around her.

No one was there.

Willa and the Harveys had disappeared.

But what about Seth? A breath she hadn't realized she was holding exploded from her as she watched his curly hair rise up from behind the truck so he could assess the area. His eyes were sharp as he glanced away. Almost remote. But they seemed to warm with relief when they landed on her.

Without a word, he motioned for her to meet him near the back of the house. She nodded to show her understanding, then painfully began to inch her way out of the bushes. Heart pounding, she forced herself to move past the large picture window, thankful that the curtains were still drawn. Although there was a tiny gap in the center where someone could see her if they had been looking that direction at just the right moment.

Shaking her head to forcibly stop that thought from gaining hold of her imagination, she continued on, step by terrifying step. She had never felt as vulnerable as she did now. Even in high school, she feared only bullies who would harass and humiliate her but had no interest in physically harming her. Now, she was afraid someone would leap out and kill her.

When she finally arrived to meet Seth, he still didn't say a word. Instead, he grabbed hold of her cold hand and started walking toward the woods behind his uncle's house.

Unable to resist, Jess looked back over her shoulder. The rain had stopped, and the house and grounds looked peaceful. The flooded creek was still swollen, angrily rushing and churning. The bridge…well, the bridge wasn't. Not anymore. It was buried under the water.

They had no choice.

Setting her jaw, she turned back and followed Seth. Whether or not he had an agenda, he was her only hope right now.

Not her only hope. She sent up a swift prayer. *Protect us, Lord. Keep us safe. And please let Seth be someone I can trust.*

It didn't take long before walking quietly through the mud and the muck grew old. Her boots frequently met resistance when she set her feet down in a particularly squishy spot, forcing her to slow down to jerk her foot loose.

Five miles. They had to move five miles to reach the Miller house, most of it through Amish country. If they were on the main road, there would even be a sign that announced to tourists Welcome to Amish Country.

Lots of hills. Lots of dirt roads. There would be businesses and traffic on the main street, but most of the traffic around the Millers would be buggies and the occasional truck. It would either be the best place to hide from a killer or the easiest place to be found.

She shuddered. Not a thought she wanted in her head at the moment, thank you very much. She'd had enough of being chased by a maniac to last her several lifetimes. Her mind filled with the memory of being shoved down the stairs.

How far had they gone? Was it safe enough to talk? She had to say something or she'd go out of her mind from her own imagination.

"Seth!"

Seth whirled, his eyes jerking back and forth. Uh-oh. He thought there was trouble. She flinched. She hadn't meant to say his name that loud.

"Sorry. Just wondered if we could talk now? I'm going crazy with my own thoughts."

After a moment of hesitation, he nodded slowly, but his expression was wary. "We can talk," he said, signing as he spoke. It was a good thing—he was talking so softly she could barely make out what he was saying. "What do you want to discuss?"

Now was the time to lay her cards out on the table. See his reaction when his aunt's name was brought up. Caution kept her tongue still even as every instinct told her he wasn't involved in anything.

When she didn't say anything, he shrugged and started to move again. She had no choice but to follow. Guess they weren't going to talk, after all. Swallowing a disappointed sigh, she trudged along, irritation brewing.

A moment later, he slowed down so they could walk side by side.

"Tell me about Cody," he said, breaking the silence

and jarring her composure with the quick intrusion into her personal life. "But only if you want to?"

Huh? Oh, she hadn't replied. Did she want to tell him about Cody? Yes, she was shocked to say she did.

"Sorry. Didn't mean to shut down on you there. You startled me that's all." What to say? "Cody was a really good guy. And a great brother. He was the only one in my family who really got me, you know?" She took his quick half smile as acknowledgment and plunged ahead. "When we were growing up, my parents were so busy working, often it was just the two of us. He didn't care that I needed him to face me when he talked. Or that I sometimes needed him to sign. His friends told him I was faking to get attention, using my deafness like a game."

"I have noticed that sometimes you seem to do better at reading lips than others."

She nodded. There hadn't been any censure in his expression, she was relieved to note. Only acceptance. "Yeah. English is a tricky thing. So many words look the same. And then some voices I can hear better than others. Mostly male voices."

"I noticed that."

She tossed him a smirk. "And then there are some people who cover their mouths with their hands while they talk. Or barely move their mouths…"

"Or have beards," he interrupted with an air of revelation. "Ernie once said if he were president he would ban full beards and mustaches."

She choked back a laugh, not wanting to be too loud. "Yeah, beards can be really bad."

Sobering, she let her mind drift over memories of growing up with Cody. "What I really loved about Cody was his gentleness. He was truly hurt by cruelty toward horses. The foundation was his passion. He was driven to protect and rescue the horses. There's no way he would have stolen money. Or done anything to injure the horses. And he was very devout. I refuse to believe he would or could go against God that way."

Seth shuffled a bit, head down.

"Sorry, I didn't mean to make you uncomfortable."

A hint of a smile flickered on his face and was gone.

"No. That's okay. Growing up in my house, I learned skepticism at a young age."

What did you say to that? Except, "You want to talk about it?"

He shook his head. Then seemed to change his mind. "My mom was sick for as long as I could remember. I learned early on that my dad wasn't faithful to her. They went to church every week, and still he cheated on her. Joe Travis, such a great family man."

Bitterness twisted his mouth. "It really hit home one day when I was in high school. I think it was just after you left. I came home and my mom was unconscious on the floor. I called 911. And I tried to call my dad but his office staff had no idea where he was. The paramedics showed up just as my mom started having a seizure. I know they saved her life. My dad arrived after she was already at the hospital. He looked worried, said all the right things, but when I got close to him, I saw that he had the proverbial lipstick on his collar. I used to think that was such a cliché. Until I saw it on my old man."

He stalked away a few feet, leaned with one hand against a tree. Her heart broke for him. She went to him and placed a hand on his shoulder. Her hand trembled. So did his shoulder.

He moved away, and her hand dropped back to her side. When he turned back to her, his face had been wiped clean of all emotion.

Beckoning with his head, he indicated that they should continue moving.

Desperate for a positive direction to take the conversation, she focused on the rest of what he'd said—the way the paramedics had saved his mother.

"Is that why you became a paramedic?" she asked.

"Yes. And it's also why I haven't set foot in a church, outside of a few weddings and funerals here and there, since high school. I figure God kinda turned His back on me. So I just returned the favor."

Chapter Seven

They wound their way through the woods until Jess no longer had any sense of which direction they were traveling in. The rain-scented mist filled her nostrils. Her boots sank into the wet earth with each step. Gradually, her socks became wet. She must have a crack somewhere in her supposedly waterproof boots. Great. Just what she needed.

Still, she said nothing. Just followed where Seth led. Every now and then, he glanced down at the compass he had pulled from his pack. But he never slowed, never appeared unsure of where they were going.

She had to admit, she was pretty impressed with him so far. He was showing a side of himself she never would have imagined. It was no longer a stretch to picture him teaching survival skills to a group of eager boys.

He slowed, and turned to face her. It never failed to amaze her how aware of her need to see his face he was. It wasn't that he rarely forgot. He *never* forgot. Ever.

"How are you doing?"

"Fine." She didn't want to admit her feet were getting wet and sore. What good would it do? He raised his brows, tilting his head to give her a searching glance. Obviously, he wasn't convinced.

"Are you sure?" he asked. "We've probably only gone about a mile and a half. I can still hear the creek, so we're going in the right direction."

That surprised her. "The creek?"

He nodded. "Yeah, we have to follow it for about three miles, then head west for the last two."

"Okay." Restraining the sigh that wanted to break free, she gave him what she hoped was a willing smile.

And received a concerned look from his brown eyes in return.

She really needed to work on her acting skills.

"Look, Jess, I wish we could rest, but my gut says we need to keep going. Sooner or later someone will notice we are gone. And I want to be far away when that happens."

"I'm not complaining. Let's keep going."

He sighed, straightened his pack, and they started off again.

Five minutes later, they spotted the creek. It looked less frightening, now that they were above it. She could still see that it was higher than normal, but from this height, it was hard to determine how much higher.

Jess opened her mouth to comment. The comment was never made, however, as Seth whirled and threw a sharp glance behind them.

"I hear voices," he signed.

She felt the blood draining from her face. There was nothing to hold anyone back from openly attacking her out here. And it was quite possible if they were killed, no one would ever find the bodies.

Seth grabbed hold of her hand and pulled her off the

path. They moved at an angle, forward and closer to the creek, taking care to stay in the grass. *No tracks*, she thought.

"There's an old path a little below us," he signed. "If we're quiet, we can use it, and hopefully no one will even know we're there."

Trepidation filled her as they walked closer to the edge of the shallow cliff. Looking down, she could clearly see a narrow path…about fifty feet below. Wildly, she whipped her gaze in Seth's direction. He was kidding, right?

Nope. He was digging through his pack, bringing out ropes and a harness.

Her stomach lurched, but she swallowed hard to force it under control. If she got sick right here, that would leave a real clue as to where they were.

In spite of her trepidation, there was no way she could argue with Seth's plan. They needed to leave this area. Every second they were closer to being found.

With sure and swift hands, Seth harnessed her and attached the rope.

"I'm going to lower you down. When you get to the path, move to the side, and keep your back against the cliff until I join you."

She nodded, then allowed him to start lowering her. He had wrapped the rope around a tree, using it as a sort of pulley. His biceps bulged as he held the rope with both hands, using a foot against the tree to assist him in controlling the speed of her descent. She would have appreciated the sight a whole lot more if it weren't for the terror racing through her system.

Her mind blank with panic, all she could think was, *Please, Lord. Please, Lord.* All the way down, she repeated her litany until her feet touched the path. The relief was so great, her knees started to buckle. Stiffening her legs, she remembered Seth's directions and backed up against the wall over to the side, waiting for Seth. It seemed to take forever. What if he was having a problem? The sudden thump of his pack landing beside her made her start.

She looked up, and thought her heart had stopped.

Seth was on his way down, but he was climbing, rock by rock. Once he missed the rock with his foot, and in her mind, she could she him tumbling backward and over the edge to the creek below. Shoving her knuckles in her mouth to stifle any cries that might distract him, she watched, spellbound, as he made his way to her.

When he was a couple of feet above the path, he allowed himself to drop the rest of the way. Jess didn't stop to think. She pushed herself away from the cliff and threw both arms around his waist, burying her head in his neck. She couldn't stop shaking.

For about two seconds, Seth was still. Then his arms gently closed around her, and his hands rubbed her back. She felt his lips touch her hair.

Calmer, she backed out of his arms, slightly ashamed of her outburst. He didn't seem bothered by it. His kind eyes searched her face. Then, apparently satisfied, he backed away, letting his own arms drop. With a rapidity that could only come from hours of practice, he had his gear repacked and his pack back on his shoulders.

"It's okay," he signed. "Let's move along this path." He bent his knees and brought his face level with hers. Trying to see directly into her eyes, she realized. Feeling self-conscious, she ducked her head. After a second, she glanced up under her lashes at him to find he was still focused on her face, a concerned twist to his mouth.

"I'm fine," she signed.

She tried to still her trembling as he ran his eyes over her again. She was beginning to recognize that gaze as his paramedic one. It was focused and detached. But she thought she detected warmth in it.

His sudden grin distracted her. Cocky. Yeah, she remembered that grin. She felt herself grinning back without knowing why. His smile had always had that effect.

"It's a good thing I didn't lighten my pack." He signed. "I debated on it, and decided not to."

She held in her snort. Barely.

"It wasn't just chance, you know. It was the inspiration of the Holy Spirit. God knew we would need that stuff. He's always watching over us, trying to guide us. But He won't force His will on us. The choice is ours."

The discomfort that covered his face made her roll her eyes. Somehow she'd get through to him.

Or maybe not. *Lord, use me to bring Seth back to You. And if not me, then bring him in contact with someone who will.*

God could handle it from here. They had wasted enough time. She dropped the subject.

"Let's just keep moving."

The tension melted from his expression. He nodded and readjusted his pack. Then with a confidence she could only envy, he moved down the narrow path. Swallowing, she made the mistake of glancing down at the creek. Whoa. For a moment, she battled nausea. Sucking in deep breaths of cool air helped. There was something soothing about the smell of the forest.

"We are in Your hands, Lord. I trust You."

It helped to keep one hand on the wall of dirt and rock beside her as she walked. It also made her feel safer when she noticed that Seth kept checking on her. Despite her earlier fears about him, she now felt sure that he would do everything he could to keep her safe.

She had no concept of how long they traveled on that narrow path. The wind had kicked up, stinging her cheeks and making her eyes water as she trudged along. She had to frequently blink to clear her blurred vision.

What really made her anxious was that she had no idea what was happening up above. Her neck tingled with the feeling that there were eyes watching her. Her one good hearing aid was picking up the sound of the creek and amplifying it to the point that she was incapable of hearing anything else. Even if there were voices directly overhead, she would never hear them. Just one more way she was completely dependent on Seth.

No sooner had the thought popped into her mind than he abruptly stopped walking and half whirled toward her, eyes shooting her a desperate warning. Jess stopped dead in her tracks. What was she supposed to do?

Seth took care of that for her. Hurrying back to where she stood, he grabbed on to her and pulled her back with him up against the rocks. They stood silently together, hidden by a small overhang. If she moved forward three inches, she would be out of its protection. Her body started to tremble as she realized what was happening.

Someone was above them. She still couldn't hear anyone, but she saw the rocks and debris that tumbled down past them from someone standing on the edge over their heads. Jess buried her face against Seth and squeezed her eyes shut. Beneath her cheek she felt the solid thud of his heart.

She focused on keeping her breathing calm. All she could do was stand still until Seth gave her a sign that it was clear.

They were trapped.

There were at least two people above him. Seth could hear the feet shuffling as one walked north and the other south. Then they moved together again. His body tensed as he heard the footsteps coming closer to the edge. Instinct had him holding Jess tighter, pressing their bodies closer to the rocks. She was trembling, and the hand gripping his was like ice.

Probably a mixture of cold and fear. When they escaped from this situation, he'd have to see what he could do about making her warmer.

For a second, he allowed himself to cast his eyes down at her face. Then he looked longer. What he had expected to see was fear and anxiety. Maybe some tears. Instead, her forehead was pressed against his shoulder, but her face was calm. Her lips were moving soundlessly.

She was praying. He should have figured.

The thought bothered him, but not as much as it would have a week ago. He remembered praying briefly while searching for her earlier that morning. Looking back, he realized that brief prayer had refocused him, given him a small measure of peace. Peace that he'd been too busy working to save her life to analyze. Yet now, here in the forest, he realized that he had sensed something.

Maybe God hadn't completely abandoned him.

Tentatively, he said a quick prayer for help. Not that he was sure how much good it would do, but it wouldn't hurt. Surely, they were sitting ducks until the people on the ledge moved.

Or found them.

He drew Jess closer, rubbing his chin against her soft hair. He had failed too many people in the past. Jess. His mom. Melanie. He had let his fear of becoming like his father cripple him emotionally. Now was his chance to set things to right. If that meant putting himself at risk to protect the woman in his arms, so be it. If need be, he was certain he could distract those after her so she could run to safety.

He frowned, feeling uneasy. That would only work if she would run. He had already learned that she had a core of loyalty. Chances of her leaving him to deal with the bad guys weren't good.

"They ain't here!" a voice boomed out above, rich with belligerence. The voice was so loud, it echoed several times. It was a voice he was unfamiliar with.

Jess jerked her head up, eyes wide. So she had heard the man, too.

The man's partner must have answered, even though he couldn't hear it, because the man continued speaking.

"Disguise my voice? What for? I tell you, there ain't no one here but us and the squirrels.

"You know what? I think you're just paranoid. No one's going to connect her getting stuck in a freezer to me. I didn't leave that many footprints. Besides, all those other idiots trampled on my footprints."

Silence. He was probably listening to whatever the other person was saying.

"And I'm sick an' tired of you giving me orders!" Now the man sounded angry. There was a definite sneer in his voice. "I'm not getting paid enough to take that from you. It ain't my fault she didn't die. If you had done your part—"

The other person must have said or done something to cut him off because he was silent for a moment before releasing an ugly laugh. Seth had never heard a laugh so cold and vicious. What kind of monsters were they dealing with?

"I'll tell you what," his voice came again, silky and dangerous. "Let's just renegotiate our deal. I think my price has just increased. Doubled. The kind of things you want done aren't easy. Or cheap. And don't think I'm messing around, here, either. It would be no skin off my back to let you take the rap for everything."

A laugh—but not the same one from before. Seth's head shot up, shock making his mouth drop open. Was that a woman's laugh? It was so muffled, it was hard to tell. He looked at Jess. She didn't look like she had heard it. Either it was too soft, or too high pitched for her to catch it.

Who did it sound like? It was so brief, how could he say for sure?

Was it Aunt Willa? No, he couldn't believe that. It would devastate Ted. And his aunt wasn't that cruel, was she? But he remembered the coldness of her eyes as she had looked at Jess when they had first arrived. His stomach tightened.

What about Lisa Harvey? Her hat had been found in the freezer. Maybe this guy had left it there as some sort of insurance.

Even in the cold, he was starting to sweat.

"Wait! What are you doing?" the man said, sudden

panic in his voice. "Put that down! There's no reason we can't talk about this calm—"

A shot rang out. The woods filled with clatter as dozens of startled birds squawked and flew from their branches.

Jess flinched back against the rock, gasping. Seth covered her mouth with his hand, his heart beating wildly in his chest.

Seth heard a shuffling noise above. Like something large being pushed...or dragged...

Jess looked up, her eyes widening. Noting the color draining from her face, Seth followed her gaze...just in time to see a body start to tip over the edge. Pressing them both against the rocks, he covered Jess with his body as much as he could to protect her. The man's hand brushed against his boot as he tumbled past them and disappeared into the angry waters below. Seth could see his lifeless face pop out of the water once before it was pulled under again.

Vic Horn.

So now they knew who had locked Jess up in the freezer. But on whose orders?

Hunched down, they waited for Vic's partner to finish searching. From the sound of things, the shooter was cleaning up. Possibly getting rid of evidence. A flurry of leaves and debris fluttered past them. Maybe Vic's blood had spilled on the leaves. He wished he could be certain it was a woman who was responsible—it would cut the list of suspects in half. If only he could hear the shooter's voice.

And how was he supposed to do that? Yell up and say, "Hey, you who just shot this guy and tossed him over the edge...are you male or female?" He almost snorted at the thought.

Then his glance fell on the creek where mere seconds before Vic Horn's lifeless body had fallen.

He shuddered. He was trained to save lives. Sure, he'd had his share of patients die. But not before he had done his best to save them. The casual way Vic's partner had shot him and tossed him away like so much garbage was not something he could easily understand. Even more incredible was the fact that it was likely someone he knew who had done it. Incomprehensible.

But what he did understand was that the person mere feet above them would eliminate him and Jess in the same manner without blinking an eye.

Not if he could help it.

He wasn't a cop or former soldier like his brother-in-law, but he did know how to survive.

Maybe half an hour went by before he felt they could safely move. It had been twenty minutes since any noise had drifted down to them.

Moving slowly, he pushed himself away from the rocks and away from Jess. No one shot him. Letting out a breath, he ran an assessing glance over Jess. She looked tired. And she was shivering. But otherwise seemed to be holding up. Ignoring her protests, he shrugged out of his jacket. He was warm enough in his layers of clothing. And her jacket wasn't doing the job.

"You need to stay warm," he signed. "We still have at least an hour or two ahead of us."

Seth bit back a smile at the disgruntled frown she sent him before she reluctantly agreed and put his coat on. A surge of affection welled up inside him. She was adorable in the oversize coat. Her hazel eyes and ponytail made her look almost fragile. But he knew she had strength. And determination.

He was relying on that determination now.

Chapter Eight

Jess tugged Seth's collar up closer to her nose and inhaled. She had noticed how good he smelled before. Now she was overwhelmed by the scent.

Of course, being warm was rather nice, too. For a while, she had wondered if she would ever feel warm again. Now, everything was toasty, except her feet. And she knew they wouldn't be warm until she could get out of these old boots. Which meant not until they reached the Millers' house.

She wished she could talk to Seth. It would take her mind off the sight of Vic Horn slamming into the current and being carried away. A shiver worked its way up her spine. She rubbed the spot on her neck that had burned before she'd blacked out and woken up in the freezer. It had to have been a needle of some kind. Knowing that he had so callously drugged her and dragged her into the freezer to die was horrible. Knowing someone else was also in on it was unspeakable.

According to Seth, who had given her a quick recap of what he'd heard before they'd started walking again, the other voice might have been female. Unless that was a disguise.

Seth had a disturbed look around his eyes, and his mouth was tight as he looked over his shoulder at her. It made her ache inside. It didn't take much to understand he was worried that his aunt might be involved in all this. She wished she could take that pain away from him, but knew it was impossible.

Still, the need to offer him some sort of comfort wouldn't let her go. Half an hour later, they left the narrow path beside the creek and headed west toward the Millers' house. They were forced to slog through the mud and leaves between the trees, but there was one benefit. There was room to move side by side.

Without giving herself a chance to talk herself out of it, Jess quickened her step and moved up beside Seth. He gave her a startled glance when she took his hand. Embarrassed, and afraid he might take offense, she started to move away. But found he wouldn't release her hand. Instead, he gripped it, squeezing slightly while giving her a sad smile. Well, not really a smile. Just the corners of his lips curling up. But he seemed to understand her intent.

"Thanks," he mouthed.

She nodded.

The sky was growing dark when they left the woods and found themselves on a dirt road. The houses were spaced far apart, but they had definitely reached the Amish community. The first house they passed was a large farmhouse with a woman in a plain blue dress and a white prayer *kapp* sweeping the front porch. She gave them a smile and bobbed her head as they passed. Two little girls splashed through the puddles in the front yard.

"How far is it?" Seth asked, still signing while he talked.

"Near the end of this road," she replied. She didn't bother to sign. He could understand her just fine. She pointed to her left. "We're about a mile from the middle of town, that way. There isn't a lot of car traffic on this road. Although if we were to go to the end of this road, there's another paved road. It's a main road, so it's pretty busy."

After what seemed like forever, they arrived at the Miller house. No one was outside, and Jess started to feel panicky. What if no one was home? She knew they had family in Ohio. Sometimes the family traveled there to visit. What if…?

The door opened as they walked up to the wide, wrap-around porch. They came face to face with Levi, whose eyes were wide and troubled.

"Jess? What are you doing here? Rebecca is not here."

She had to work to understand him. Between his accent and his habit of barely moving his lips while he talked, he had always been a challenge to understand. Thankfully, he was the best signer in the Miller family, so she could always ask him to sign if necessary. Although she would save that for a last resort. She knew that Levi wasn't comfortable switching to sign.

"I know, Levi. Do you remember Seth, the paramedic?" Impatience made her talk quicker than usual. Any moment she expected someone to burst from the woods brandishing a gun.

"*Jah*. I remember. It is *gut* to see you again."

Yeah, it might have been good, but he still looked troubled.

"Levi, I'm sorry to intrude, but can we come in? We're in serious trouble."

Silently, the serious young man swung his kind eyes between them. Finally, he nodded.

"*Jah.* You are always welcome, Jess. Mam and Dat will be pleased to see you."

Swinging the door wide, he motioned for them to enter the house.

Jess needed no further invitation. She entered the house, being careful to remove her muddy boots just inside the door. Seth did the same. She hurried into the large, warm kitchen area, aware of Seth at her heels. Rebecca's mother, Martha, turned from where she stood cooking at the large stove. Jess sniffed in appreciation, her stomach rumbling as the smell of homemade stew hit her nostrils.

"Jessica!" Martha said in her strongly accented English. "We did not expect you to visit. Is the flooding gone?"

Martha's keen blue eyes swept over Jess and Seth. Jess flushed, realizing the picture they made. A quick glance at Seth showed that he was dirty and looked ready to collapse. It wasn't hard to imagine that she probably looked about the same, maybe even a little worse after trekking through the woods and going over a cliff. And she was still wearing Seth's jacket, which hung on her smaller frame.

She cleared her throat, but Seth beat her at answering.

"No, ma'am. I'm Jess's friend Seth. We were stranded on this side of the creek when it flooded, and haven't been able to get home yet."

Alarm filled Martha's round face. "Have you been out in this weather all this time?"

"No, we were at my uncle's house when it started."

Jess could see the confusion cross Martha's face. She had a fairly good idea of what the woman was thinking. Why would they leave the comfort of his relatives' house and travel here? A sudden dread struck her. What if the Millers felt they were too high risk to let them stay? She had never known them to turn anyone away, but what if her situation was just too much for them to take on?

Her nerves and the cold caught up with her all at once. Her body began to tremble with a vengeance. Even tugging Seth's jacket around her did nothing to lessen the chill sweeping over her slender frame. The chattering of her teeth caused her jaw to ache.

An arm around her shoulder startled her. Seth. Looking up at him, she noted vaguely that he looked blurry.

"She's half frozen. And ready to collapse," she heard him say close to her good ear.

Martha swiftly crossed the room to her, and hustled her to a chair near the wood burning stove. She gave Levi a firm command. Jess couldn't understand it, but she recognized the sounds of Pennsylvania Dutch. Levi answered in the same language, then stoked up the fire inside.

Soon, she found herself seated, her soggy socks replaced with a clean pair of thick, warm ones. It took another fifteen minutes for her to feel truly warm. When Martha brought her a bowl of hearty stew and a thick slab of homemade bread, she accepted gratefully, thanking her hostess with feeling.

Between the food and the warmth of the fire, she began to nod off. Only through sheer will did she manage to remain awake. She focused her attention on where Seth was seated with Martha and Levi. It took some effort, but she managed to catch most of the conversation flowing between them as Seth explained their situation.

Martha and Levi seemed genuinely shocked and concerned about the predicament they found themselves in. Although not, she was glad to note, in any apparent hurry to shoo them out the door. If anything, Martha's face started to resemble that of a mother bear as she heard about someone literally gunning for her daughter's oldest friend.

Warmth tugged at Jess's heart. It had been so long since she had felt so protected. The feeling was followed by an ache at the realization that such moments were going to be rare for her, and not permanent. After all, she had no family anymore, and her prospects were low.

But she wasn't going to sit here and have a pity party. Straightening in her chair, she narrowed her gaze on Seth's solemn face. The sudden longing in her soul took her by surprise. She remembered her doubts about him earlier. Was that really only several hours ago? Now, looking at his honest face, she couldn't believe she had wondered if she could trust him. He had put himself in harm's way for her more than once, and never once had he hesitated. He had more than proven himself worthy of her trust.

Shame grew in her as she realized that in doubting him, she was also, to some extent, doubting God. For she could clearly see God's hand in giving her the perfect protector. Who else would have known how to ensure they'd survive? Or how to save her when she was injured? Even his ability to sign proved that he was the perfect person to help her.

No more doubting, she decided. *From now on, Lord, I will trust You and Your providence without fail.*

Which didn't mean she would be so foolish as to allow herself to make the huge mistake of falling for him. It would be so easy, she mused as she watched him shove his thick curls back from his forehead. She knew how devastating his charm could be. But even though she believed she could trust him, she also was aware of his determination to avoid any sort of emotional commitment. No, friendship was all she could ever share with him. She had to be satisfied with that.

But she wasn't satisfied. Her heart had already started to latch on to him.

Well, no more. She would just have to stay on her guard around him.

That resolution firm in her mind, she returned to the conversation in front of her, battling to keep her eyes open. At last, she gave in and let her weary eyelids drift shut, secure in the knowledge that she was safe.

At least for the moment.

Jess was snoring. Soft little purring sounds that made him think of a kitten.

Seth ducked his head, hiding his grin behind the mug of black coffee Martha had just set before him. His grin faded as he continued to watch her. She was exhausted and scuffed up. There were several scratches on her face and neck.

All at once, impatience swamped him. He wanted action. The need to move, to be doing something, to fix things, crawled over his skin.

Only when Levi gave him a pointed look did he realize his leg was furiously bouncing up and down, his heel making a staccato tapping sound on the hardwood floor. Abashed, he forced his leg to still.

"Sorry," he muttered.

Levi nodded, his eyes understanding. "You want to be active, *jah*?"

Seth blew out a breath and ran his hands over his face. "Yeah. I can't be easy until I know that whoever wants to hurt Jess is out of the way."

Martha stood and began to clear the table. "You must leave it in Gott's hands."

Sure. Easier said than done.

"There is nothing to be done this evening," Levi said. "Tomorrow, we can think more about it."

"Levi," Martha reproved her son. "Tomorrow is the Lord's day."

"*Jah*, I know, Mam. We will talk, not work. That will wait for Monday."

"Don't you have some kind of community phone?" He took a long slurp of coffee. Caffeine might not be healthy, but maybe it would jolt his system enough to keep him alert.

"*Jah*. We have one. It is not working now. It was hit by a tractor."

Seth winced. The small wooden phone booths used to house a single emergency phone would not be able to withstand the force of a large tractor crashing into it.

I now know what would make someone want to bang their head against a wall, Seth mused, twisting his mouth. Still, maybe a day of quiet would be a good thing. Jess obviously needed the rest. And the water level wouldn't be down enough for them to cross the creek and return to LaMar Pond until Monday, at the earliest. Although, he suspected the electricity would be back by tomorrow. It might even be back now, but not where he was at.

A new thought occurred to him. Was their sudden appearance throwing a wrench in the family's plans? Funny, he hadn't thought of it before, but now he shifted in his seat. He wasn't religious. Hadn't been inside a church since Maggie and Dan married. And even though he had prayed a couple of times in the past day or so, faith was still a bit of an alien concept to him. But for the Miller family, he suspected it was a way of life. And now he and Jess had disrupted this family's life without warning just before the Sabbath day.

"Um, I never thought… I mean, Jess and I, we don't want to get in the way of your plans. So, um, if you need to, you know, go to church or something tomorrow?" He let the unfinished question hang there, feeling his ears grow warm as both Levi and his mother smiled at him.

"We attend church every two weeks, and this is our at home week," Levi reassured him. "After you and Jessica rest tonight, I will help you plan your next move. Tomorrow."

And with that, he had to be satisfied.

If they could get to a phone, he could call Dan and bring him up to date on the facts. He knew his brother-in-law. Dan would take the situation seriously. Especially now that a body was involved. He and the rest of the police would want to drag the creek and search for Horn's body so they could process it for evidence, like the ballistics from the bullet that killed him.

The sawmill Levi worked at wasn't that far from here. Three miles? Four? If Levi would agree to bring them there to use the phone, a whole lot of problems could be solved. He mentioned his line of thought to Levi.

"Would the bullet help them find the person who killed the man who went over the cliff?"

Seth smiled. It was kind of refreshing to talk with someone who wasn't hooked on crime shows. He had gotten used to family members of patients questioning his decisions based on things they had seen on TV. Like that didn't get old fast.

"I can't be sure. I'm not a cop, but I think that sometimes bullets can be traced to a specific type of gun. Maybe even a single gun, if it's registered." He rolled his eyes at that.

"You don't think this will happen?"

A wry chuckle slipped out. "I find it highly unlikely that anyone would shoot someone with a gun registered in their own name. Unless it was an accident. And I doubt very much that this shooting was an accident. It's more likely that whoever shot Horn intended to kill him all along. Horn threatened her, but I don't think that made a difference."

"Her?" Levi's eyes sharpened. Martha gasped as she walked into the room and heard the last comment.

Seth colored. What a time to forget himself. That was not information he had planned on sharing. The Millers would be safer the less they knew.

"I can't be sure. But I thought I heard a laugh. It might have been a woman's. Or it might have just sounded that way because I was so far away."

"What was the name of the man who was killed?" Levi took a gulp of hot coffee, nodding his thanks to his mother, who continued to unobtrusively fuss over the men and straighten up the large, cozy room. Sitting so near the warmth of the fire as the scents of coffee and pine mingled in the air was making him feel a little drowsy himself. It was no wonder Jess had fallen asleep.

What had Levi asked? Oh, yeah. The name.

"Vic Horn. I assume that's short for Victor. I had never seen him before this weekend, and I thought I was pretty well acquainted with the horse crowd."

Levi rubbed his chin between his thumb and his forefinger, deep furrows creasing his forehead. "I have heard that name before."

Seth sat up, the sleepy fog that had started to envelop him disappearing.

"You have? Where?" In his excitement, he unintentionally raised his voice. Both Levi and Martha looked at him, startled. Flushing, he realized he had come half up out of his chair, his hands clenched on the wooden arms. "Sorry," he muttered, lowering himself back down into his seat.

Martha returned to her chores. Levi flashed an unexpected half smile at him. It transformed his solemn face, making him look youthful.

"I understand. You are anxious to find the person who would hurt Jessica. I do not remember where I have heard the name. I will try to remember so I can help you."

Disappointed, Seth nodded. How he wished he could do more.

Right now, though, he was too tired to do anything.

Martha had anticipated his needs. A bed in the small guest room had been made up with fresh sheets.

"Jessica can sleep in Rebecca's old room," the motherly woman announced.

Gently, Seth shook Jess's shoulder. She jerked awake, eyes wide with fear.

"Easy, Jess," he signed to her. "You'll be more comfortable in a bed. Mrs. Miller said you can sleep in Rebecca's room."

She reminded him of a little girl as she yawned and used her knuckles to rub the sleep out of her eyes.

"Where will you be?" She caught her lower lip in her teeth. Seth had seen that expression so often, yet now, seeing her tug at her lip made him wonder what it would be like to lean down and kiss her…

Whoa, boy! This is no time to be thinking of romance. And you are certainly not the man to be considering any long-term relationship. The old argument felt false now. He wished he could make a different choice. The decision to remain single and unattached had seemed so logical, but now it seemed like a cold future.

"I'll be down here, Jess. Don't worry. I will still be here in the morning."

He gave her what he hoped was an encouraging smile. Her smile back at him was somewhat confused, so he probably hadn't completely succeeded. But she let Martha lead her up the stairs without comment. He was strangely heartened when she looked back over her shoulder at him before she entered the room.

Then guilt struck. If she was starting to develop feelings for him, it would not end well for her. The last thing he wanted was to hurt her, again. Deep down, where he kept his feelings locked up, a round ball of fear festered. That fear that said he could never make any woman truly, lastingly happy. That he would never be worthy of a woman's love.

Jess's words in the woods wove through his brain, making his heart ache with longing for what he had always believed was out of reach. Could she be right? Was God watching over them, prompting them softly like a father? Was God just waiting for him to make the next move?

A wave of exhaustion crashed over him, and he felt himself swaying where he stood. Well, he was of no use to anyone like this.

A hand on his shoulder jerked him alert.

"Come," Levi said, "I will show you where you will sleep." Levi led him down a hall to a small bedroom near the back of the house. The room was big enough for a bed and a dresser, and not much else. Fine with him. Looking closer, gratitude seized him. A pair of plain blue pajamas had been set on the bed. He hadn't expected more than a place to rest for the night. Overwhelmed by the hospitality shown to him by these strangers, he thanked Levi in a choked voice.

Wishing Levi a good night, he entered the room and prepared for bed. Changed and comfortable, he took a closer look at his clothes, shaking his head. It was a wonder these people let him into their house! They were covered in mud, and he counted no less than five rips in his shirt. Probably from rock climbing without protective gear. Well, he couldn't regret that. Leaving a rope tied around a tree while he climbed down would have been like leaving a neon sign pointing directly to where he and Jess had been hiding. No. He would gladly accept a ripped up shirt if it meant that Jess was safe.

As tired as he was, he should have fallen asleep immediately. Instead, he tossed and turned, the events of the past couple days rumbling around in his head, like equations that he needed to solve. But he didn't have all the variables. Piece by piece, his mind sorted through the facts. Finally, he fell into a troubled sleep, dreaming of people falling off cliffs, bullet holes in their chests.

He was jerked from his restless slumber several hours later, heart pounding. Faint light was streaming in through the window. It had to be closing in on five in the morning.

Several dogs barked and growled ferociously right outside his window. A moment later, he heard something crashing. Running to the window, he was in time to see a shadowy figure limp away and disappear behind the barn. The dogs lurched forward on their chains, enraged, before they were jerked back by their collars. It couldn't be a coincidence that an intruder would come to the house mere hours after they had arrived. And that meant just one thing.

They had been found.

Chapter Nine

Seth rushed from his room, intent on stopping who-ever was outside.

Levi beat him to the back door. Without wasting time, the Amish man handed Seth a lantern and headed out-side. Even though the sun was coming up, it was still dark in the woods and in the barn. Soon they were joined by an older man. Mr. Miller, Seth assumed. It was hard to make out the man's features in the morning light. But what he could make out was the shape of a shotgun grasped in the older man's large hands.

Seth was shocked. He thought the Amish didn't be-lieve in violence. He said as much to Levi.

"We will not shoot at a person, it is true," Levi ex-plained in his slow, deep voice. "We have had trouble with foxes getting to our chickens."

Mr. Miller nodded. "I am certain that is what has upset the dogs."

The three men carefully circled the house.

"I don't know. I have a bad feeling that whoever is after Jess might have found us." Seth's eyes scanned the horizon. Shadows danced near the woods, playing tricks on his imagination.

Mr. Miller clucked his tongue. Seth knew disapproval when he heard it. "You must trust *Gott*. He will protect us."

Doubtful. Seth bit back a stinging retort, partially because he didn't want to be disrespectful toward the man who was allowing Seth and Jess to stay in his home. But also because, in spite of himself, a small sliver of doubt had managed to wedge itself into his soul. He could no longer ignore the questions that had started to plague him about faith. Questions, he realized, that he had locked deep inside for years, but which had never really gone away. Somewhere in his heart, he had always wanted to believe.

"I thought I saw someone limping away through there." Seth pointed in the direction of the barn. Levi inclined his head. Seth understood. Lead the way. A sigh of relief burst from him. They might not believe in violence, but they would stand by his side as he tracked whatever he had seen from inside the house. He set out at a quick walk, almost a jog, carefully scanning the area around them as he moved. He was aware of Levi and Mr. Miller silently jogging at his elbows.

Half an hour later, the men returned to the house, no closer to figuring out who or what the dogs had seen.

Mr. Miller didn't seem concerned. He mumbled something about trespassers as he shrugged out of his jacket. Then he replaced his gun and returned to his room.

Seth stared after him, unsure what to do. "Levi, what if the trespasser was whoever's after Jess? I can't shake the feeling that we've been found."

"How?" Levi said in his calm, reasonable voice.

Frustration bit at Seth. How on earth was he supposed to protect Jess when he couldn't even tell where the danger was coming from?

Why not ask God?

No longer shocked by such thoughts, he paused.

Fine. God, please help me protect Jessie.

It was amazing, the sense of release that came with the thought. Huh. Maybe there was something to all this praying stuff, after all.

"Seth, we can do nothing at the moment. Get some more sleep, and after we take care of the chores and eat breakfast, I will help you look again."

Sighing, Seth gave in. What else could he do?

"I think even if you have been found, you are safe here, *jah*? The dogs will keep strangers away from the house. Jess is on the second floor. I do not believe anyone can get into her room without us knowing about it."

And with that, he had to be satisfied. Reluctantly, he went back into his room, knowing going back to sleep was impossible. Dragging a chair to the window, he sat, keeping watch.

Seth left his room, tucking the clean shirt that had been left for him into his trousers. Levi's, he assumed. Good thing the Amish fellow was about his size. He followed the soft voices speaking in Pennsylvania Dutch to the kitchen.

He braked as he entered the large room. There were a whole lot more people than he had been expecting. Mr. Miller came in the door, stomping his boots as he crossed to the table. He was followed by two younger men. Seth guessed their ages to be mid-to-late teens. A girl of around ten was near the counter with her mother. An older girl stood directly behind her. She didn't spare Seth a glance as he entered, intent on fixing her sister's hair. Neither girl wore a prayer *kapp*, although they were fully dressed in every other way.

The rest of the room's occupants waved greetings at him as he came to a clumsy halt. None of them showed any surprise at the sight of him, so they had probably all been made aware of their guests.

Speaking of the guests... Seth felt someone at his shoulder, and knew without turning that it was Jess. He cast his eyes over his shoulder. His breath caught as he met her clear hazel eyes. The night's sleep seemed to have done her good. Her eyes were bright, and there was color in her cheeks.

She doesn't know. The sheer cheekiness of the smile she tossed at him told him that she was completely unaware that her attacker might have found them. Now was not the time to let her know. Too many people around. He would wait until they had more privacy.

Brushing past him, her fingers bumped into his hand. Electricity jolted through him. Her startled eyes met his. So she felt it, too. His fingers twitched.

Not. Going. To. Happen.

Distance, dude. Distance.

Giving her what he hoped was a nonchalant smile, he returned his focus to the Millers.

The door opened and Levi stomped in, his movements nearly identical to those of his father. He gave a small shake of his head at Seth. The pit of his stomach dropped. The message was clear. Levi had found no more trace of their early morning visitor.

"The mare is lame this morning, Dat. Her left front leg seems to be paining her," Levi announced.

"Would you like me to look at her for you?"

Seth blinked. He was a bit cowed surrounded by the large family. But Jess? She looked completely at ease, even though she was back in her dirty clothes from the day before. Maybe no one here was her size.

Levi ducked his head at Jess. "*Jah.* I did not see you. But I would like you to look at her."

Mr. Miller opened his mouth. He's going to object, Seth thought. But Levi cut him off.

"She knows more about horses than either of us, Dat."

Seth held his breath. If he went with her, then maybe that would be the opportunity to tell Jess about the trespasser. If she became emotional, there would be fewer eyes to see. He knew her well enough that she would hate others to see her in a weak moment.

"It is time to eat." Martha smoothly moved between the two men. Perfect timing. Seth wiped his mouth on his sleeve, hiding the smile that threatened to erupt at Martha's obvious intervention. Out of the corner of his eye, Jess mimicked his movement.

"Will you join us for breakfast?" Levi waved an arm toward the wooden table. Still off-balance, Seth waited until Jess sat, before placing himself at her side. Only when he was beside her did he remember his decision to distance himself. It didn't matter that he had meant emotional distance. Sitting so close to her was like putting a cookie jar in front of a child with a sweet tooth.

"Jessica, you are feeling better this morning, *jah*?" Martha asked.

Silence.

Frowning, Seth turned to Jess. It wasn't like Jess to be

rude and ignore her hostess. Jess met his gaze, a puzzled wrinkle creasing her brow. Adorable. Mentally shaking his head, Seth repeated the question, signing.

Rich color flooded her cheeks.

"Oh! I'm so sorry, Mrs. Miller! I didn't hear you," her mortified face whipped around to meet the older woman's understanding gaze.

"I understand. I forgot to get your attention before I spoke. You are *gut*?"

"Yes, ma'am. I am feeling well today."

Martha brought a heaping plate of pancakes to the table. Seth's mouth watered as the aroma hit his nose. Closing his eyes, he inhaled deeply. Then his eyes popped open again as his stomach growled. Loud.

The children covered their mouths, but he still heard the snickers. Grinning, he shrugged. Well, now everyone knew he was hungry.

He was scooping a large bite of pancake dripping with warm maple syrup in his mouth when Jess raised her arm suddenly, knocking his food off his fork. It landed with a sticky slurp on his clean shirt. Grabbing the cloth napkin, he removed the mess, scrubbing at the spot, aware that he was making it worse. Finally giving up, he placed his napkin back on the table.

Jess was most likely wanting to crawl under the table with embarrassment, he mused. He turned to face her, prepared to make a joke of the accident. The joke died on his lips. Jess was rocking in her seat, her eyes darting from person to person. Actually, she was looking from face to face, zeroing in on their mouths as they talked.

Her panicked eyes caught his. He knew what she was going to say even before she signed it.

"My battery died. I can't hear."

Perfect. That was just great.

Because they needed one more challenge in their bid to survive.

Jess tried to remember when she had changed her battery last. Yesterday morning. Her batteries always lasted longer than that. What a time to get a bum battery!

She was trying to read lips so fast her vision was strained. If this continued, she would have a headache before lunch.

When Levi stood to go to the barn and look at the lame horse, she shoved her chair back and stood with more alacrity than grace. Belatedly, she remembered her manners. Heat seared her cheeks as she paused to thank her hostess.

"Thank you, Mrs. Miller. Breakfast was delicious."

"You're welcome, Jess. We are glad you decided to come to us."

Frustrated, Jess watched her hostess's mouth move, unable to decipher the rest of the words. A wave caught her attention. Discreetly, Seth signed, keeping his hands low. "She said you are like family."

A lump clogged her throat. Jess had felt bereft of family since her brother died. Just knowing that Rebecca's family accepted her touched her more than she could say. Again, the Lord blessed her when she needed it. Unable to reply without tearing up, she smiled and nodded before following Levi, aware that Seth had risen and joined them. Tension knotted her neck muscles as they walked to the barn. The way the men kept constant surveillance made her feel squirrely. By the time they reached the barn, she half expected someone to jump out at them. Men!

Jess fell in love with the mare Levi led her to the second she saw her. She was a chestnut thoroughbred, and stood about sixteen hands. The mare's legs weren't swollen, so that was good. She leaned down to feel the legs. No extra heat. Also good. The mare stood quietly while she examined her, not even protesting when Jess lifted her leg to look at the hoof. When she moved the horse to look at her gaits, the animal moved without pampering one limb over another.

"What a sweet girl," she crooned. The horse nudged her with her nose. "I can't see any problems. My guess is that she stepped on a rock or something, and it bothered her for a few steps. Nothing permanent. Keep an eye on her for the next day or so, just in case."

That done, she figured they would head back to the house. As it was Sunday, the family might have plans to visit family or neighbors. Now that the animals had been tended to, there was no more work that they would do.

So she was somewhat startled when Seth laid a gentle hand on her shoulder, holding her back.

"Jess, there's a situation you should know about before we go," Seth signed.

"What situation?" Her stomach started to hurt, the way it always did when she was scared.

"Early this morning, the dogs woke the two of us," he indicated Levi and himself, "and I saw someone running behind the barn. I don't know who it was. It might have nothing to do with us, but I thought you should know."

"You think we've been found." It wasn't a question. And if Seth believed it, she believed it, too. He was observant, and had seen enough to know how serious their situation was.

Nor did Seth try to sugarcoat things. All her life, people had tried to shield her from bad news. It was something of a relief to meet someone who didn't try to keep information from her. Even if it was unpleasant information.

"So what you're saying is someone could be watching us right now?"

Seth nodded. Levi merely shrugged, a skeptical expression on his face. He apparently didn't feel they were in danger here. But as long as Seth did, she would assume the same.

"What do we do?" *Calm. We need to stay calm.* She repeated the words in her mind over and over.

Levi spoke. She was relieved when Seth signed, interpreting for her. It was exhausting to try and read Levi's lips.

"Mam and Dat will go visiting today. My brothers were out courting last night, so they will remain at home today. I had planned on visiting my girl today. If you need me, I could stay here."

"Oh, no! I don't want to interrupt your plans," she replied. Then curiosity got the better of her. "You have a girl?"

Seth sent her a glare, which she ignored. Yes, she was being nosy. But she had never known Levi to go courting before.

She almost relented when he shifted uncomfortably. "Yes, I have a girl. We are getting to know each other."

"Then you must go and see her. Seth and I can stay here out of the way. We have plenty of information we need to sort through. And plenty of suspects to consider.

I'm going back and forth about whether or not I think Lisa and Bob Harvey could be guilty."

"Lisa and Bob Harvey? My girl cleans house for several *Englisch* families. The Harveys are one of them."

Jess's mouth dropped open. So did Seth's. Any plans to stay quietly tucked safe and sound at the Miller house fled. A golden opportunity had just been handed to them. She for one didn't want to waste it.

Seth apparently agreed. "We would very much like to talk with your girlfriend. Do you think she would agree?"

There was a brief hesitation. It might have been her imagination, but she knew it wasn't. It was one thing to allow them to enter his family's home. Quite another to introduce them to his girlfriend. If she remembered what Rebecca had told her correctly, dating couples didn't officially tell their families until a marriage proposal had been made. Although everyone knew.

Slowly, Levi nodded.

"*Jah.* I do not know if she will talk with you. She's shy. But you are my sister's oldest friend. I don't believe you are in danger here. But if someone is after you, it would be right to help." Levi's stern expression softened. "But you should not go dressed like you are now."

"I don't have anything else with me."

"*Jah*, but Rebecca left most of her clothes when she left. You could wear those."

She blinked. Wasn't there some kind of rule against what he was suggesting?

"You want us to dress Plain?"

Confirmation never hurt.

"*Jah.* I think it the best way. I think it would be safer for Laura if your enemy didn't recognize you."

Her heart softened. "Levi, I don't know how to thank you."

A casual shrug lifted his shoulders. "We will leave when you are ready. And when we come home tonight…"

"No," Seth interrupted.

"No?" Maybe she had read the single word that fell from Seth's lips wrong. No was such a small word. And there were other English words that looked the same. Like *toe*. Or *lo*. Both were quite a stretch.

He flicked his gaze toward her. It was filled with tenderness. And regret. Her breath got stuck in her lungs. This was either going to be very good, or very bad. Riveted, she gulped as he started to speak, signing for her benefit.

"I'm sorry, Jess. I know that you are among friends here. And Levi, we appreciate all that your family has done for us. Is still doing for us. But I know I saw someone this morning and I firmly believe that they were here for Jess and me. I doubt the person will go after your family, because they have nothing to do with this. And anyone who lives in the area knows the Amish community wouldn't go to the police to solve their problems. But if he or she recognizes Jess at your house, someone else might get hurt. So I think the best plan would be to let us talk with Laura, then help us find shelter for the night. You can pick us up tomorrow on your way to work so we can use the phone."

Her heart heavy, Jess agreed.

Levi did not. He started to argue. Before he could get too far, though, his mother called him in to the house to assist her.

"This isn't finished." Seth waited for her to walk out of the stall, then he relatched it.

Jess held her tongue. Hopefully, their discussion with Levi's girlfriend would provide answers. They were out of options.

Chapter Ten

Jess was ready to crawl out of her own skin. She just knew someone was watching them. Her shoulder blades twitched under the plain blue dress, feeling a stare boring holes in her back. Her hand trembled, itching to reach up and adjust the white prayer *kapp* she had placed on her head. Resisting the urge was difficult.

With each step she took she braced herself for the bullet she expected to pierce her skin. It was a toss-up whether her inability to hear was a pro or a con at the moment. Did she want to hear a gunshot and know that death was coming if there was no escape?

Think of how Rebecca walks, she reminded herself. Concentrating on taking quick, gentle steps like her friend helped take her mind off the eminent danger. After all, she was wearing Rebecca's old dress and shoes. Might as well pretend to be her for the next fifty feet or so.

Closer. Closer.

Almost there.

The last few steps she had to force herself not to run. The questionable safety of the buggy beckoned to her.

Seth stepped up beside her to offer her a hand into the buggy. She avoided his eyes. Not because she was upset with him. She wasn't. Both he and Levi were doing their best to keep her safe. Levi had even gone as far as raiding the family's clothes to locate an appropriate disguise for her and Seth. Her fear was that if she risked raising her head, her attacker would get a look at her face.

Jess didn't know much about the attacker. One thing she was absolutely certain of, however, was that it was someone she knew. Or at least someone who knew her. How else could they have known where she'd go to take shelter on this side of the flooded creek? That's why it had been so crucial to mimic Rebecca's mannerisms. To become someone else for even a few minutes.

Without needing to be told she moved to the back of the buggy, sliding into one corner on the dark gray bench inside. Levi had cautioned her not to let her head be seen out of the side windows. It meant she had to sit at an awkward angle, but she didn't care. If staying alive meant she had to twist herself up like a pretzel, then that's what she would do.

The buggy shook as Seth took a seat in the back with her. She had to smile. He looked very uncomfortable in Levi's old hat and plain clothes. The buggy moved forward with a lurch, and they were both pitched against the back wall.

"I will never complain about how small my car is," she signed to Seth.

Only the tiniest twitch at the corners of his mouth told her he was amused. She was getting good at reading his eyes, though. They were warm and full of caring. But guarded.

"I'm sorry that I put you in such danger," he said.

He thought he'd put her in danger?

"I think you have that backward. I'm the one who convinced you to bring me to that party in the first place, even though I knew someone was out to get me. So technically, I put you in danger." She rested her hands in her lap, waiting.

He tilted his head back against the wall, but kept his eyes slanted toward her.

"I wasn't really that hard to convince," he signed. "I thought you would be safer at my uncle's house than in your house all by yourself."

For some odd reason, that statement struck her as funny. She started to snicker, covering her mouth with her hand, trying to hold the gasps and giggles in. How much she succeeded, she had no way of knowing. Not much, she guessed, as his shoulders shook.

"It's not your job to protect me, you know," she signed after she had finally managed to control herself.

Uh, oh. She would know that stubborn look anywhere. And if she wasn't mistaken, her words had offended him. Well, that certainly hadn't been her intent. How was she to know he was so sensitive?

"I'm not helping you because it's my job," he told her, his signs quick, jerky. Definitely irritated. "I'm helping you because you're my friend. And friends are supposed to look out for each other."

Wow. Friends with Seth Travis. She had known they were growing closer, but to be let into the circle of his friends was humbling.

Uh, oh. His face tightened. She hadn't responded. Bad move.

Okay, then. She needed to make this right. How?

"I'm sorry I offended you. I am glad you consider me

your friend. I was afraid that you considered me an obligation. You know, as if you had to atone for high school, or something stupid like that."

A stillness came over him. Something she had said had struck a chord. Good or bad, she wasn't sure. The expression on his face changed. He looked...vulnerable?

"Whether you know it or not, I do need to make amends. And not just to you. I allowed my arrogance and my bad relationship with my father turn me into someone I'm not proud of."

He shifted, turning his face away. Jess held her breath, waiting. She could sense the struggle inside him. *Please, Lord, help him.*

Shifting again, she saw his chest rise and fall with a sigh. "I don't know if you remember my friend, Melanie?"

She nodded. In her mind, she could picture the pretty brunette.

"After I broke up with Trish, Mel and I started dating. After a few years, we even got engaged. But then I let my father turn me against her. I abandoned her when she needed me most. She ended up spending four years of her life in jail. And she was innocent. How do I reconcile that?" He signed, meeting her gaze, his own anguished. "I mean, we're friends again, but I don't understand it. How she could forgive me. How her husband could let me be a part of their lives. And even my sister, she doesn't hold a grudge toward my father. Even though he was a jerk to her mom."

He may not understand, but she was pretty sure that she did.

"They're Christians, aren't they? Melanie and your sister?"

Caution entered his face, but he nodded.

"They forgave you because it's what their faith, their love for God, tells them to do. Just like He forgives us, when we ask Him." She sighed at his closed expression. "Seth, no matter what you have done, He wants to forgive you. No one loves you more than God. And He is waiting for you to trust Him."

"How do you know?" His hands were clumsy. He was getting emotional, even though his face didn't show it. "I have done so many things I'm not proud of. What if I fail again?"

She couldn't help it. She rolled her eyes. "Please. Like you have a monopoly on failing those around you? It's called being human. We all fail. And you may be your father's son, but you have been very brave and heroic since we met again."

He sneered, apparently thinking she was being sarcastic.

"Seriously, Seth. You have saved my life half a dozen times. And you have not abandoned me. That means a lot to me."

She had shocked him. She could tell by the way he kept raising his hands, then setting them down again. He didn't quite know how to respond to that.

"I guess." Pause. "You know what the saddest thing about my father is?"

She shook her head, not really knowing if he wanted a response. "He's had so many affairs that he has several children. Not just me and Maggie. One is in jail. One is dead. And I have another sister, although I have no idea where she is. Yet for all those kids, not one of them is close to him. Maggie tolerates him, but she doesn't trust him."

"What about the child who is...lost?" Should she have asked?

"Her name is Carrie. She's a teenager being raised by her older half sister. I have never even met her, though I want to. It hurts knowing I may never meet her."

"Maybe you will. Someday."

He shrugged. "Yeah, maybe. Maggie and I have tried to find her. But she moves around a lot. Anyway, I figure if I don't get involved with anyone, then I can't hurt them, either."

And there it was. The warning to keep her distance. But she knew it was too late. She swallowed, wanting to cry. But would she be crying for Seth, who was choosing to shut life out and live in solitude? Or would her tears be for herself, knowing the man she was falling for was placing himself out of her reach?

He couldn't believe he had gone on like that. He never talked about his relationship with his father. Or about Carrie. She was like some deep dark secret in his family. The only person he had ever mentioned her to was Maggie.

Until now.

What was it about Jess? She was way too easy to talk to. Getting him to go all emo like that. Not cool.

Except he didn't feel like a dork. Instead, it was like a little bit of the pressure that had been building inside of him had been released and now there was more room to breathe.

Unfortunately, there was also more to think about. Her words about God swirled around in his brain, so fast he could barely keep track of them.

God loved him. Did He?

God would forgive him—how did she know?

The buggy lurched again, breaking into his thoughts. Seth pushed his hand down on the seat to brace himself. The clop, clop sound made by the hooves or the horse changed. Sharpened.

"Are we on the paved road now?" he called up to Levi.

"*Jah*. We will be on the paved road for the next mile until we reach the Hostetlers' road."

Paved road. That meant more traffic. Was that good or bad? They were more out in the open, true. Also true was the fact that there was more of a chance that there would be witnesses if anyone came after them. And it would be made even more difficult if the person coming after them was on foot still.

Route 89 twisted like a thick, lazy snake through the outer edges of Spartansburg. Seth could hear the hum of an engine behind them. Even knowing that their hunter was most likely on foot didn't eliminate the urge to peek through the small window in the back of the buggy. If he stretched upward just an inch or two he could get a look at what was happening behind them. Not that he had any intention of doing that. But the temptation tickled his mind again and again.

The engine revved again, and moved to the side. The buggy swayed. The vehicle was rushing past. Good.

Jess reached across the space dividing them and grabbed his hand. Her face was white.

She couldn't hear what was happening, although he had no doubt she had felt the buggy move.

"A car is passing," he signed with his free hand.

She nodded, but her hand remained in his. The warmth of her slim hand seeped into his skin. When was the last time someone had truly touched him so intimately, with so much trust? His protective shell cracked. His gaze was pulled down to their joined hands. They looked right together.

No.

Tightening his resolve, he pulled his hand from hers and used it to scratch his opposite shoulder so as not to hurt her feelings. Dipping his head so he could see her expression, he sighed. *Jerk. You hurt her anyway.*

Jess folded her hands together in her lap and leaned her head against the side of the buggy, closing her eyes with a sigh. Yeah, he got that message loud and clear. Conversation was done. He'd been shut out as definitely as if she had slammed a door in his face. And locked it.

Fair enough—it was what he deserved.

Discomfort shrouded the remainder of the journey.

Bumps and creaks announced their return to a gravel road. The sharp clop of hooves hitting pavement softened.

Beside him, Jess sat straight up.

"Do I smell sawdust? That means we're close to the sawmill! We're almost there!" She reached out and shook Seth's arm. Then just as quickly pulled her hand back.

Way to go, Travis. She's really offended.

But she gave no other sign of being offended. Instead, she bounced on the seat like a small child. A chuckle slipped past his lips. He didn't even try to hold it in, knowing she wouldn't hear it. *Man, there's that dimple again.*

"We are at the Hostetlers' house now. I'm going to take the buggy back to the garage. Laura's *dat* will not approve of you wearing Plain clothes. You can change in the barn."

With a quick flick of his wrists, Levi steered the horse

into the driveway. Seth angled his head so he could view the large white house as they drove past it. The drive veered to the right, and they moved into the barn. The smell of hay and animal waste assaulted his nostrils.

Ugh. He liked horses and enjoyed riding, but could do without the odor that accompanied them. He would never make a good farmer. Not that he had any interest in giving up his job as a paramedic. The sudden image of Jess out cold on the freezer floor filled his mind. A single, sharp shake banished the image.

Levi halted the buggy and jumped down. "I will go find Laura now before the family becomes curious. There is a room in the back you can take turns and change in."

Without a backward look he hurried from the barn. It was up to Seth to jump down and lend Jess a hand. He grinned at the annoyed frown creasing her brow. She was such an independent woman; it probably galled her to need help from the buggy. Wearing Rebecca's dress, though, she didn't have much of a choice. Which was probably why she didn't complain. As she settled her hand on his shoulder, he found he had no wish to complain, either. What would it be like to be the recipient of such simple intimacies with her on a daily basis?

"What's going on?" Jess asked. He couldn't believe he had forgotten to sign what was happening to her. Just one more example of how he was the wrong man for her. A worthy man would have remembered to include her in the conversation.

"Stop that!"

Jess's voice slashed like a whip, startling him out of his maudlin thoughts. Planting her fists on her slim hips, she faced him. The demure, modest Amish dress and *kapp* contrasted with the tense, stubborn line of her jaw and the fire flashing from her eyes.

"Huh? Stop what?"

"You're blaming yourself for something. I didn't realize at first what that expression on your face meant. But now I recognize it. It's the same look you wear right before you apologize for some imagined wrong you've done."

Oh, yeah? This was good.

"You can't seriously be telling me that I haven't done anything I need to apologize for."

He got an exaggerated eye roll for his trouble.

"Not since high school. And I forgave that one."

His mouth went dry, making him need to swallow before he could speak. And then he found that he couldn't think of anything to say. Because her forgiveness left him feeling…what? Free? Light? Both, he decided.

Remembering her question, and the fact that Levi would be returning soon with Laura, he repeated the plan. Jess nodded, leaning back inside the buggy to grab her rolled up bundle of clothes.

"Catch!" she called out, hefting his own bundle toward him. Winking, she sashayed back to the room to change.

Seth watched her go, suddenly aware that he was grinning like a loon.

But as she closed the door, the smile slipped from his face. He hadn't yet told her that they would have to remain here overnight. Nor had he convinced Levi yet. But if they returned back to the Millers' house, he couldn't shake the feeling that they would be putting the Miller family in danger. It was hard to believe that anyone could have followed them to the Hostetler house.

In spite of that, a chill swept up his spine. He wished more than anything that he could take this danger away from her, make himself the target instead. He'd be happy to stand in the killer's sights if it meant that Jess was safe.

"Your turn."

Pivoting to face Jess, he filled his lungs with barn air, stunned as the truth slapped him in the face. This woman, this brave, fierce woman, challenged and inspired him. And he was falling in love with her.

But that didn't mean he was free to pursue her. He couldn't take the chance. He had too many memories of his father failing his family. Memories of the tears his mother had tried to hide from him. Of the forced smiles she would hold on her face for him.

Of his mother fighting for her life while his father wined and dined some woman across town.

All his adult life he had struggled to be different from his father. And he believed he had succeeded. But Jess was too precious to take the chance.

He would protect her. He would risk his life for her, wouldn't even hesitate. And then, he would walk away.

Even if it killed him.

Chapter Eleven

Seth paced back and forth in front of the barn door, his hands knotted together behind his back. How long did it take to run up to the house and back? He and Jess had been waiting for Levi's return for nearly an hour.

"What if something happened to him?"

Jess's question echoed his own fears.

"He's fine," he asserted.

A slapping noise alerted him to people approaching. Levi? Maybe...or maybe not. Waving Jess to get back into the shadows, he grabbed a shovel and slunk low against the barn wall. Wincing as a splinter wedged itself into his arm, he concentrated on the door. If anyone other than Levi or his friends entered, he wanted to be ready. His stomach clenched. Even if it was his aunt. Willa might look like a harmless flake, but he knew that she was a dead shot. He had accompanied the Taylors to the shooting range twice a month for the last five years. The question wasn't whether or not Willa had the skill. She did. No, the question was whether she was cold blooded enough to pull the trigger on a human being.

And if she'd pulled the trigger on Vic Horn.

The barn door shuddered. Someone on the other side had grasped the handle and was sliding it open. Light sliced through the crevice in a narrow beam, increasing as the opening widened. It pierced the shadows, leaving Jess and Seth vulnerable.

He gripped the shovel, hefting it to his shoulder.

Then let it drop as Levi sauntered through the opening. The Amish gentleman reared back, mouth dropping open. After a startled second, he flashed a grin at Seth. A petite woman stepped through the door after him. Seeing Seth, she dropped her eyes.

Feeling foolish, Seth leaned the offending tool against the wall before shoving his hands in his pockets.

"This is my Laura," Levi introduced his girlfriend, pride ringing in his voice.

A sharp twinge of envy pricked Seth. How he wished he could say, "This is my Jess!"

Don't go there. It didn't do any good to dwell on what he could never have.

"Levi wanted me to talk to you about my work," Laura murmured.

But she didn't want to. That was clear. The Amish were deeply committed to not interfering in the affairs of others, particularly those outside of their community. Sharing information about her employers—information that might lead to them facing criminal charges—must be incredibly difficult for her. Seth wondered how long Levi had needed to talk to her, to persuade her to come out and talk with a couple of strange *Englisch-ers.* His gratitude to the man increased. That must have been awkward, especially considering how he felt about Laura.

Seth repeated her comment in sign to Jess.

"Hi, Laura," Jess greeted the woman, her voice low and calm. Almost as if she were approaching a skittish animal. So he wasn't the only one who sensed her concern. "We're very grateful that you consented to help us. It means a lot."

Laura flicked her narrowed gaze between them. Suspicion poured off her, but she nodded her head cautiously. "Levi says you are in danger. And that you are his sister's oldest friend. Also, I know that the people I work for are *Englisch*, so they are still under your law."

"That's right," Seth responded, making sure to use his voice and sign simultaneously.

He was unsure how to begin the discussion. Turned out, he didn't need to. Jess took the bull by the horns and dove in.

"Okay, here's the situation. We were stranded at Ted and Willa Taylor's house Friday night. Someone there was trying to harm us, and we believe whoever it was has followed us. This is all connected to my brother, who died in suspicious circumstances after being accused of stealing money."

She stopped and drew in a deep breath.

Laura tilted her head, pursing her mouth into a tight little bow.

"I am sorry that your brother died. I am confused, though. I do not understand how my employers are connected with your problems."

Seth broke in. "The Harveys were at my uncle's house, and they were seen talking with someone who ended up dead." He went on to explain about the run-ins they'd had since arriving at the Taylors' house.

"I'm not sure how they are connected with Cody's organization. What was the name of it, Jess?"

"Racing to the Rescue," Jess replied.

"Oh!" Laura's hand flashed up to cover her mouth. "I know of this organization!"

He had never actually seen anyone do a double take, but Levi sure did one now. His normally calm face was comical as his mouth dropped open and his eyes bugged in his face.

"You have heard of it? I know of it because I am familiar with Jessica and her brother. How did you hear of it?"

Laura cast her gaze down, then flicked it up again. "About six months ago, I was cleaning the Harveys' house. I was in the living room, dusting. Mr. Harvey arrived home, unexpectedly." She licked her lips and shifted her weight. "I was surprised. I leave before suppertime, so he never comes home while I am there. Mr. and Mrs. Harvey went into another room, the den, and I could hear them arguing. I can't recall the whole conversation, but I do remember that it had something to do with a racehorse they owned. Someone had accused them of abusing the horse. Mr. Harvey was afraid they would lose the horse and the money it had cost them. Or that they would go to prison. Mrs. Harvey was crying and carrying on something awful. She was afraid they would lose everything. I had never heard a grown woman take on so. I remember them talking about someone from Racing to the Rescue. They were scared. Real scared."

"Did you hear anything more? See anything?" Seth leaned toward her.

She backed up.

Whoa. Hold on, man. Coming on a little too intense.

"Sorry. Didn't mean to startle you. Jess and I need something we can take to the police."

Moving closer to Laura, Levi glared at Seth.

"She will tell you what she knows. Give her time."

Time. The one thing they were running out of. Because even if they got back to LaMar Pond tomorrow, which he desperately hoped they would, there was still the small matter of some psychopath gunning for his girl. How was he supposed to keep her safe if they couldn't narrow down the field of suspects?

He had spent enough time with Dan and with Jace—Melanie's husband, who was also on the police force—to know that they needed solid evidence to go on if they were going to reopen the case of Cody's death. And if they reopened the case, who was to say that the killer wouldn't take her attacks on Jess up a notch? Just to get Jess out of the way.

Laura and Levi were holding a private conversation. Jess quirked one eyebrow at him, asking a question. He shrugged back. "They're talking Amish," he signed to her.

That sweet mouth curved in amusement, drawing his eyes to it. He wrenched them away, slipping two fingers beneath his suddenly too-tight collar to loosen it.

"It's called Pennsylvania Dutch," she signed, obviously unaware of the level of attraction he was fighting.

Another clue that they weren't meant for each other. Sometimes he was so sure she felt something for him, but other times, she didn't seem affected by his presence at all.

"There was something more," Laura stated.

Seth whipped his head around, even as his hands signed her response.

He waited. Tapped his foot.

Laura pressed her lips together and twisted her hands. Still Seth waited. Something brushed his arm. Jess moved forward, leaning in as her eyes bore into Laura's face. Probably trying to read Laura's lips instead of relying on Seth to relay the information. Poor Laura squirmed. He understood. Jess could be quite intense when she wanted something.

"A few minutes after they argued, Mr. Harvey left the den and ran into the living room with his arms full of papers. He threw them into the fireplace. When he looked around and saw me, he got real red and yelled at me to go work in another room. Mrs. Harvey apologized after he left. But I noticed something…he had dropped a couple of papers. Mrs. Harvey picked them up, and I saw her shove them into the top drawer of the china cabinet."

"Tell them the rest," Levi urged her.

"Mrs. Harvey has been taking shooting lessons this past year." The Amish girl raised her head and aimed a level glance at them. "She has shown me awards she has won at shooting contests."

"Seth," Jess breathed, her hand clutching at his arm.

"This might be what we need, Jess." Throwing his arm around her shoulders, he squeezed tightly, laughing softly when she squealed. The laughter died in his throat when he caught her eyes. The air between them hummed with electricity. He was sure that if he looked down at his arms, he would see the hairs standing on end. He removed his arm from her shoulders, but it didn't help. It took all his effort to pull his gaze from her. Facing Levi and Laura, he found them watching with curiosity. Levi's expression was sympathetic.

He knows, Seth thought. He knows how I feel about her.

So much for stopping himself from falling for her.

Too late.

He had fallen too deeply to extricate himself without pain. The most he could hope for was leaving without hurting her, as well.

She was breathless, light-headed. But wasn't sure why. Was it because they finally had something real to bring to the police? Or was it because of the tension flowing between her and Seth like a wave, connecting them?

A little of both, most likely.

She could tell that Seth didn't want to feel the connection. His face was tight, drawn. He had removed his arm so fast, it was as if lightning had struck it. Now he was clenching and unclenching his fists. Fine. Just fine. She should have learned her lesson by the way he reacted to a simple touch in the back of the buggy.

How long had Levi been gone? At their insistence, he had gone inside the house to visit with Laura. Leaving Jess and Seth alone.

Shifting back a step, she put distance between them, mentally and physically. By sheer force of will she kept her face blank. It was a true challenge. Inside, she fumed. *Give it to God*, she reminded herself, hating the way bitterness churned her emotions and thoughts. *Give Seth to God. Only He can help him.* Dragging in a deep breath, she sent a prayer up to God. Only then was she able to let go of the angst gnawing away at her mind.

It was time to get back to figuring out what had happened to Cody. Time to stop whoever was out to get her. And time to go back to her life. Alone.

When it was time for Levi to return home a couple of hours later, Seth stopped him.

"Levi…look, I appreciate all you are doing for us. I really do. But Jess and I, well, I don't think we should stay at your place tonight. It doesn't feel right, putting your family in danger."

Crossing his arms over his chest, Levi shook his head. "I do not agree. We saw no sign of anyone following us this morning. You need to trust *Gott*. He will protect you."

Seth set his feet apart and matched the Amish man, stare for stare.

Uh, oh. This could become ugly. Men. Why were they always so stubborn?

"Levi," Jess broke in. "I have to go with Seth on this one. I would feel guilty forever if something happened to anyone in your family because of me. I have already dragged Seth into my troubles."

She ignored Seth when he moved impatiently. If Seth was irritated, that was just too bad.

"Jessica, what is your other choice?" Levi asked slowly. Her heart softened. He was trying to make sure she could lip read him. She knew that even though his sister was deaf, Levi was uncomfortable signing. Felt it drew too much attention to himself. But he tried to find other ways to accommodate her and Rebecca. He was a good brother. Just like Cody had been. "You cannot go off on your own and spend a night in this man's company. Even if you are in danger. It would not be right."

A few more minutes were spent arguing. Levi and Seth were both unmovable in their stance.

"You have to go," Laura interrupted. "My *dat* will not like it if you stay in his barn alone tonight. You go with Levi. You cannot stay here."

And it was settled.

Not that Jess was satisfied with the outcome. Neither was Seth. She could see worry etching deep lines in his forehead. Her fingers tingled with the desire to reach out and smooth the wrinkles away.

She slammed her hands into her pockets instead.

The short walk to the buggy was tense. By unspoken agreement, Seth and Levi sandwiched her between them. The blue sky had darkened to a heavy gray. She sniffed the air. More rain? Her heart sank at the thought. The clouds moving in had banished the sunlight, creating the perfect background for a horror story. Unfortunately, the horror story was her life. Again, her shoulder blades twitched, as she imagined someone watching them. Without her hearing aids to give her some clue about what was going on around her she was relying on her vision, eyes in constant motion, side to side. Was that a movement? Was someone in the trees? Good grief. She was going to drive herself crazy.

Her neck soon started to ache from the way she'd been holding herself so stiffly. The urge to lengthen her strides was strong.

That wouldn't do. She forced herself to slow down. *Calm. Have to appear calm.*

Seth moved his head to gaze at her. He slowed, motioning her into the buggy ahead of him. As she moved past him, his hand snaked out and grabbed hers. Startled, she glanced up at him.

"Jessie, I won't let anything happen to you."

Jessie? Maybe she had read it wrong, but she didn't think so. Blinking, she pushed back the moisture gathering in her eyes. It had been so long since anyone called her Jessie. Only her father ever had. But he was gone now. Everyone was gone. And the one man to make her feel alive didn't want her.

Straightening her shoulders, she pulled away from Seth. "I'm good."

He tilted his head and narrowed his eyes. Clearly, the man didn't believe her. Well, that was his problem. Ignoring him, she reached up and pulled herself into the buggy. Warmth crept up her cheeks as he grasped her elbow to assist her. Tingles swept up her arm from where he touched her.

"Thanks," she muttered.

If only she could hear her voice right now. Did it sound normal? She often read in the Christian romance novels she enjoyed that the heroine's voice sounded breathless when she was affected by the hero's presence. Did she sound breathless? She certainly felt that way. And was none too happy about it. The last thing she wanted was to give Seth the idea that she was attracted to him. Even if she was. Maybe she should stick to sign only until she had her aids back.

When they pulled up outside the Miller house, it was still quiet. The family hadn't returned from visiting for the day. Levi hopped down from his seat and went to unharness the horse. "I will put the horse in the back field for the night. Make yourself at home." Leading the horse, he disappeared around the corner.

"We might as well go in," Jess murmured. She made to jump out, but Seth pulled her back.

"Let me go first."

She rolled her eyes, but let her macho companion lead the way. Suddenly, she remembered what he had said before about failing those he cared about and realized that his attitude wasn't macho. It was the sign of a brave man putting others' safety ahead of his own. She couldn't mock him for that. Her insides trembled as he stood clear outside, like a target. On purpose. She was about to call him back when he nodded and climbed back inside.

"I don't see anyone, but I'm not sure I trust that. I was sure I saw someone this morning, even if Levi and his dad disagree. How fast can you move into the house?"

"I can move very fast in these...oh, no!" Her hands covered her mouth. Seth raised his eyebrows, waiting. "Seth, we left our Amish clothes back at Laura's barn. Anyone watching us will know who we are."

He shrugged. "Yeah, I thought of that a few minutes ago, but there was no way we could go back. I had the feeling we had all but worn out our welcome there. Not to mention the fact that anyone noticing us signing to each other will figure it out. You ready?"

No.

"Yes."

Clambering down, they started running to the house. Seth grabbed her hand and dragged her to match his quicker pace.

A chunk of driveway blew up in front of her. Someone was shooting at them. A second shot hit the front post of the porch. A golf ball–sized hole appeared, the smooth white paint and wood beneath it disappearing in a puff of smoke.

Racing together they ran up the steps. Two steps before the door, Seth lurched forward, slamming against the wall next to the door.

A dark red stain spread out, covering the top of his left arm.

Seth had been shot.

Chapter Twelve

Jess yanked the door open, using her body as a wedge. She reached out and tugged at Seth, intent on bringing him into the house for safety. He staggered toward her, his face pale, but seeming otherwise alert and coherent. Once they were both inside, she slammed the door behind them.

Oh, no. Levi. Just as she was wondering how to get to him, the floor beneath her feet vibrated from the pounding of approaching footsteps. Whirling in terror, she braced herself to face a monster with a gun. Instead she saw her friend charging inside, his straw hat flying off his head in his haste.

"Are you well?" Levi shouted.

"Seth has been shot. I don't know what to do."

Seth tugged at her hand. She turned to see him sinking into one of the wooden chairs from the kitchen table. A chair far from the kitchen window, she noted. Which meant that he couldn't be seen from a distance. Not unless someone walked right up to the house. She shuddered.

"Easy, Jess," he said, closing his eyes briefly. "It's

just my arm. Nothing serious. I need your help though. I can't do this alone."

"Anything," she declared. And it was true. She would do anything to help this man.

"Help me get this shirt off."

He had already unbuttoned the flannel shirt, revealing a dark black-and-gold football T-shirt underneath. She stepped over to maneuver the shirt inch by inch down his injured arm. He tensed beneath her fingertips when she moved the material over the wound. She bit her lip hard, and blinked back the tears that sprouted, clouding her vision. Using her own sleeve, she wiped her face, then continued working.

After what felt like a lifetime, the shirt was off. Rolling up his T-shirt sleeve, she saw the wound for the first time. The sight of the blood coating his muscled arm made her dizzy. She refused to give in to her weakness. Not when he needed her.

Seth reached over and chucked her under the chin with his good hand. "It's not that bad. Honest." He smiled, but it was weak.

"Really?"

"Really. It looks bad because it bled a lot, but look. It's just a graze. If we went outside, I think there's a good chance we'd find the bullet lodged in the side of the house. When we get to a phone, we'll have to remember to tell the police to search for it."

Moving her head closer, she inspected the wound. Sure enough, there was no hole. The bullet wasn't inside him. And the bleeding seemed to have slowed down significantly already. She sighed. And for some odd reason, wanted to cry again.

She held off until she had finished bandaging Seth's arms using the cloths that Levi had brought them.

As she stood back to inspect her handiwork, the horror of the situation sank into her soul. Someone had shot Seth. Aiming for her, no doubt, and missed. Unable to help herself, she glanced down at the flannel shirt lying on the kitchen floor. The sight of the jagged hole in the material, surrounded by a bloody stain, was the final straw. She began to shake. Her mind urged her to flee the room, to hide her tears, but her legs wouldn't obey. Instead, all she could do was bring her shaking hands up to cover her face.

Warm arms embraced her, cradling her close. She felt Seth's breath in her hair, and knew he was probably talking to her. Whether he was whispering words of comfort or telling her to stop being a baby, she neither knew nor cared. Both hands grasped at his shirt as she buried her face in the soft fabric and sobbed. Sobbed so hard her chest hurt, for what felt like hours.

Finally, the tears trickled to a halt. She grew aware of her surroundings again. Mortified, she realized that she had lost total control in front of Seth. All she wanted to do now was go and hide.

Releasing her death grip, she backed out of the comforting circle of the strong arms holding her. Her movement met with slight resistance as he tightened his hold, just for a second, before letting her go.

As she moved away, she couldn't help but see the humongous wet spot on the front of his shirt. Mortification raced back in a warm rush up her neck and cheeks.

A gentle hand moved to her chin. Her breath stilled. Seth tilted her face up and studied her. His expression was torn. Almost tortured. She saw compassion, yearning and regret all mixed. The yearning won out as Seth's mouth moved. Her name. That's all he said before his head descended. His lips met hers and her lids fluttered shut.

Everything else faded. As he lifted his head, she could feel his breath stir across her lips before he kissed her again. Deeper and longer.

A quaking started deep in her soul. Now was not the time to explore her feelings. And yet she couldn't bring herself to pull away. Not when this kiss felt like it was mending every bruised and battered strand of her heart.

The kiss ended as gently as it had begun. Seth placed his forehead against hers.

Jess had no idea how long they had stayed like that. Vibrations under her feet indicated Levi was coming back into the room. Was he walking that heavily on purpose, giving them warning before he entered? The thought that he might have seen them kissing should have embarrassed her, but it didn't. No. A single kiss may not alter the fact that both Jess and Seth had issues to work out. And the odds were not in favor of a lasting relationship between them.

But she had no regrets.

That kiss had been a beautiful gift in a time of ugliness and fear. No matter what happened, she would always treasure it.

Seth wouldn't, though. She could already read the self-recriminations lurking in his face.

He had kissed her. Not once, but twice. And if he hadn't heard Levi's voice calling his name, he would have kissed her again!

To say he regretted giving in to the urge was a gross

understatement. The kiss just made him want what he couldn't have. Walking away from her when all of this was over just became ten times harder.

Yeah, because it would have been so easy before.

Levi waved a note at them. "My *mam* and *dat* and the others decided to go visiting today. They will be staying overnight."

"Oh, I'm so glad!" Jess folded her hands beneath her chin, shooting a smile at Levi. Her lips trembled. "I would hate it if they came home while some maniac is out there shooting anything that moves."

Hardly anything, Seth mused, pressing his lips together. *Just you*. Of course, he would never point that out. No reason to scare her. But he had no doubt she would come to that conclusion on her own.

"I do not think anyone will shoot at Mam and Dat if you are not with them."

Thanks a lot, Mr. Sensitive. Seth released a sigh. Loudly.

Before Jess could start blaming herself, Seth tapped her shoulder.

"Come on," he said, nudging her, deliberately overlooking her stricken expression. "We've been still too long. We need to make sure the doors and windows are locked or barricaded. I don't think we can rely on only the dogs to keep us safe."

A sense of urgency pushed them into action. The lock on the back door was so worn, it was more for show. It would never withstand the pressure of someone trying to break in. Levi grabbed nails and two hammers. Seth took one and together they nailed the door shut to secure it. Seth shoved the hammer in his pocket and stepped back to inspect their work. Only a temporary fix, but hopefully it would be enough to keep them safe until they could figure out what else to do.

The window over the kitchen sink proved to be the most problematic. Not only was the locking mechanism pathetic, the window itself had no covering. Not even a decorative valance. Anyone could look in.

"Okay, Jess, Levi. I think we need to somehow cover this window. Maybe a towel. It will cut down on the light in the house, but we could use candles if we get desperate." His arm was aching. He knew he should be resting, but the safety of the others had to come first. Always.

Levi left the room to search for the items they needed. He returned a minute later and laid the towel and some candles on the table. Seth pulled the hammer they had used on the back door out of his pocket.

"Jess, you need to get back." They couldn't risk the shooter seeing her through the window and taking another shot. Her nod was unenthusiastic, to say the least, but at least she didn't object.

Light flashed briefly out the window. Then it was gone. Foreboding washed over him, sending trickles of unease into his mind. Leaning closer to the window, he narrowed his eyes. There it was again. Something in the trees was reflecting the sunlight.

"Get down!"

Even as he shouted at Levi, he caught Jess in his arms and dove to the ground with her, instinctively angling so he took the brunt of the impact as they hit the floor. He grunted in pain as she landed squarely on his injured arm.

CRASH.

The window shattered inward, spewing glass over them. A chunk of the kitchen wall splintered.

Jess screamed as the bullet made its home in the wall. Using his hands to indicate that she needed to keep low, Seth pushed himself to kneel.

Dogs barked outside the house, the bloodthirsty howls raising the hair on the back of his neck.

A second shot rang out. It lodged in the wall next to the first one. Kneeling on the ground between Jess and Levi, Seth's mouth went dry as he stared at the two bullets. If he hadn't looked out the window when he did, those bullets would have been lodged inside Jess and himself. It wasn't a coincidence that had caused the killer to miss them. God had protected them.

"Thank You, Jesus."

The prayer was sincere.

"Amen," Levi responded.

He shot a glance toward Jess. Her eyes were wide. She had read the prayer on his lips. Right now, all he saw was the trickle of blood on her cheek. The glass had struck her. It was a small cut, but to his mind it was still too much.

They knew exactly where the shooter was. Adrenalin spiked his heart rate. This could be their chance.

Maybe, if he drew the killer's attention, Jess could escape into town. But how?

How, indeed.

No cars. The buggy was out in the open and unhitched.

The horses, though…

"The horses. You can ride bareback, right?"

Okay, she might deny it later, but that was definitely a snort of disgust at the ridiculousness of the question. Jess's nose wrinkled and her lip curled in disdain. "Please."

"I'll take that as a yes. Levi?"

"*Jah*. But where will we go?"

"And," Jess drew the word out, her eyes narrowed on him, "how will we get out of here without drawing more fire?"

"We won't. You and Levi will." As she opened her mouth to protest, he continued quickly, signing to make sure he was understood. "We know that the shooter is out front. I will go out the front door, and make a run for it. Hopefully, the shooter will aim for me. I'm fast, so I have a good chance. You and Levi will slip out a window in the back. Head for the horses in the field, and try to ride to town. Find a phone and call the police. And if there are no phones, at least find someone who can help us."

Levi shook his head. "I should go out the front door. This is my house."

"No. You'll want to make for Spartansburg, and I don't know that area well. Or the people. You can find help quicker."

That, and he didn't know if Levi was a quick runner. There was a chance that he'd be shot before he stepped three feet out the door.

"Most people won't be out on a Sunday. Only in emergencies."

"I would think this qualifies as an emergency," Seth muttered.

"*Jah*," Levi frowned. "This morning Dat and I thought you had imagined the person in the woods. There didn't seem to be a reason to rush out and use a phone on a Sunday. Tomorrow seemed soon enough."

Seth read what the other man didn't say. If they had believed him, maybe none of this would have happened.

"No use second-guessing. It is what it is."

Jess. Always practical.

A dog growled right outside the door. It was joined by a second one. The barking resumed. One of the dogs yelped in pain. And it was too close to the house.

A new aroma wafted in the window.

Smoke. Something was on fire.

"Seth!"

He nodded. "I smell it. Something's burning. Stay low."

The smoke started to drift in the air. It formed a hazy cloud.

"It's coming from the back door," Levi stated. His voice was calm, in contrast to the ashen cast on his face.

On hands and knees, Seth crawled to the sink. There were several damp clothes hanging on it. He handed them to Jess and Levi. He grabbed a third. It wasn't as damp as he would have liked, but would have to do. Indicating that they needed to hold it over their mouths and noses, he began crawling toward the next room. His injured arm throbbed. Gritting his teeth, he kept crawling. He'd rather deal with a little pain than be dead. Entering the living room, he saw immediately that the smoke was thicker. It hung in the air like a wet blanket. Heavy.

He stopped.

Because he had no idea where to go. The shooter was out there, and there was smoke coming in by the back door. Was the killer trying to force them out the front door?

A few seconds later, he grimly dismissed that idea. Smoke had started to pour in under the front door. The idea evidently wasn't to smoke them out. No. The killer had no interest in luring them out into the open.

The sadistic person waiting outside the house had decided to burn them to a crisp. And the fact that there were innocent bystanders inside with him and Jess didn't seem to bother him, or her, overmuch.

"Seth. Now what?"

Seth winced at Jess's hoarse voice.

He was out of ideas.

They were trapped.

Chapter Thirteen

Her lungs were burning. She blinked to clear her vision. It did no good. Water continued to pool in her eyes. A blurry shape was coming her way, wriggling like a large caterpillar. Seth. He army-crawled to her.

She blinked again as he put his face a couple of inches from hers.

"Are you okay?" he mouthed. How she wished she could hear his voice!

She nodded, but it was a lie. No, she wasn't okay. She was terrified. And in pain. But he didn't need to know that. Why place that burden on him when he couldn't change the circumstances? He yelled something at Levi.

Squinting, she was just able to see her old friend pointing. When Levi started crawling toward the other side of the house, Seth gestured for her to follow.

A spark of hope lit inside her soul. Could there be another way out? With renewed vigor, she crawled after Levi, praying as she struggled along. Every few feet, she glanced back over her shoulders, heartened to see Seth coming along behind her. He could have moved faster if he was ahead of her. But he wouldn't do that.

The man she had come to know and trust in the past few days would never take the chance that she would be left behind.

Immediately upon entering the room, she noticed a decrease of smoke. Seth came in behind her and closed the door. That would buy them a few extra minutes.

Levi waved Seth forward, and together the two men pushed an oval area rug out of the way. A wooden trap-door was revealed. It had a single slide latch lock near the bottom corner.

The cellar.

Jess hadn't seen it in so many years, she had entirely forgotten it existed.

The two men cleared the rug the rest of the way off the door and Levi wrestled with the latch. *Come on, come on*, she urged silently. The lock was stuck. It would open. It had to. She refused to believe they had come this far, only to die now. Frantically throwing her glance around the room, she spied a large tool near the wood basket. A maul. For splitting wood. A weird place to find such a tool. But she didn't have time to wonder about it now.

"Seth!"

His head whipped toward her and she pointed at the maul. His face cracked into a relieved grin. Grabbing the maul, he marched to where Levi was. Levi backed off to allow him to swing at the latch. It was lifted clear off the door with the first blow. Levi opened the door, wrinkling his nose.

A second later, so did Jess. The rank odor of mold and stale water rose out of the cellar and assaulted her nostrils. The rain had flooded the cellar.

Jess shuddered, a horrible realization slamming into

her. The open door yawned before her, leading into a dark, swampy pit. She was going to have to wade through the dark again. Her life depended on it. Fear held her legs paralyzed.

The two men hadn't noticed her predicament yet. Instead, they were rounding up candles and matches. Levi lit his candle. The flame danced, flickering like it was laughing at her cowardice.

Seth lit a second candle. He turned to her, an expectant smile curling the corners of his mouth. The smile faded as he took in her frozen posture. Concern etched itself on his handsome features.

"Jess?" He signed as he spoke. No wonder. Smoke was starting to come in under the door. The air was beginning to get hazy. "Jess, we have to go, honey. This is our only chance."

"It's dark." She knew she was whispering, even though she couldn't hear her own voice. But she knew Seth heard it when his brows rose. Then his frown deepened.

"It's dark, yes. But we have candles. And we'll be together."

She nodded. Forcing her legs into motion, she gripped the hand he held out to her.

"Afraid of the dark?"

"And small places."

His eyes softened in tender understanding. The cellar was both. "Let's pray."

Astonishment flashed through her as he said a simple prayer. "Lord, protect us. Help Jess through her fear. Amen."

If he could surrender enough to pray, she could walk through the dark at his side.

They descended the stairs one at a time. Sandwiched between the men, Jess alternated between feeling safe and wanting to scream as claustrophobia skittered down her nerves. She arrived at the last step and put her foot down into six inches of water. She was so sick of being wet. It sure beat being dead, though, so she held in her sigh of disgust.

The light from the candles danced, casting eerie shadows on the stone walls. She shuddered and tried to ignore them.

As he stepped down behind her, Seth placed his empty hand on her shoulder. She reached up and held on to his hand. The warmth of his palm sank into her skin, bringing comfort. She wasn't alone.

Sloshing through the ice-cold water, the weary trio made their way to the wall on the opposite side. If memory served, there should be a door leading to the outside there. If things went their way, it would be unlocked and easy to open.

Once at the wall, they followed the light slipping through the cracks in the door. Jess ignored the icy water which slapped against her legs and slipped over the top of her boots to soak her feet.

In less than a minute, they arrived at the door.

Apprehension settled in. What if the shooter saw them? Granted, the door was on the opposite side of the house. It was more likely that the shooter was watching the main entrances and the windows on the ground floor.

They were about to find out.

Seth joined Levi at the double doors and the two men shoved them open. Fresh air rushed inside, soothing her lungs.

Seth helped her exit the cellar. Jess was tempted to

tell him that she was fine, but allowed herself the comfort of his assistance rather than sticking to her pride.

As they emerged, a commotion near the front of the house drew their attention. Several Amish buggies were in the driveway, the horses placidly grazing on the grass while their drivers were working together to put out the blaze. Or what was left of it. A young woman wearing capris pants and a frilly top was talking a mile a minute on a neon-pink cell phone, waving her bangled arms as she talked.

Her mouth was moving too quickly to read everything she was saying. Her bright pink lipstick helped, though. Jess was able to make out enough to know the woman was talking to a 911 operator.

Reluctantly, Jess forced herself to survey the damage herself. She turned. And grimaced.

The front porch seemed to have taken the brunt of the damage. Black scorch marks clawed from the porch up the door. The doorknob had fallen clear off. She had no idea how the back door fared, but suspected it was heavily damaged, as well.

"Levi, I'm sorry—" she started, but he wasn't there.

Seth touched her arm. "You know he doesn't care about the house," he signed. "He cares that you are safe, and that his family wasn't home."

"But if I hadn't been here, none of this would have happened."

"Maybe."

The word pierced her. So she was to blame.

"Or maybe not. But aren't you the one always telling me God provides? He provided for us today, and no one was seriously injured. That's the important thing."

Jess opened her mouth, then snapped it shut when

she realized she didn't know what to say to that. God had provided for them. More importantly, at least in her mind, Seth was acknowledging His care. Blessings came out of tragedy. She had read that several times in the past. Now she was seeing it in action.

The amazement and wonder on Jess's face made him squirm. And when she smiled at him, man, that dimple just about did him in. He felt like a hero. Saving people had become commonplace given his job. He never thought of himself as a hero before. But Jess was focusing those big hazel eyes on him and smiling softly and now he felt he could do anything.

A siren rent the air. A fire truck swerved into the driveway, and a crew of firefighters spilled out. A couple of minutes later, an ambulance pulled up. Seth closed his eyes. His chin sank to his chest as emotions engulfed him. For a moment, he couldn't trust himself to speak.

"Seth?"

Opening his eyes, he grinned at Jess. "Sorry. Just momentarily overcome. That ambulance is from across the creek. Which means the water has gone down. We can go home."

He wasn't prepared for her reaction. Those hazel eyes filled with tears and she flung her arms around him, squeezing him tight. Smiling, he gently closed his arms around her and hugged back.

"Anyone inside?"

The fireman's question, spoken to Levi who had approached the scene, broke the spell. Slowly, he backed away from Jess. Reluctant to break the contact completely, he slid an arm around her waist. She leaned against him.

"No. We were inside, but we got out," Levi explained.

Seth nudged Jess, motioning with his head that they should move closer. Levi explained what had happened inside the house and how they had escaped. The neighbors gasped and exclaimed as they listened in.

A second siren shrieked in the distance.

"Police are coming," Seth signed to Jess.

She tightened her jaw and visibly stiffened her back. *She still expects to be blamed*, he realized. Without consciously deciding to do so, he caught her hand in his.

"Hey," he said softly, knowing they were close enough for her to read his lips in the waning daylight. "They can't accuse you of anything. You have an alibi and witnesses to everything. Do you understand me?"

She bit her lip and nodded. He relaxed.

"I know that. It's just that I haven't had the best track record with the police."

Leaning forward, he planted a soft kiss on the top of her head. "I'm here. I won't leave you to fend for yourself. Promise."

And he didn't. Even as the paramedics came and checked the three of them out, he stood beside her, insisting they look them both over at the same time. His arm was cleaned and bandaged. It was determined that the injury was fine, and wouldn't need stitches.

What was a problem was that both he and Jess had started to cough. Rough, harsh gasping coughs. It sometimes happened after being exposed to smoke. The police had finished collecting reports from the neighbors and Levi, since he was the only one of the three who wasn't coughing.

"We need to take you folks to the hospital."

Levi declined treatment, claiming he was fine.

Soon they were bundled into the ambulance and en route to the hospital.

Once there, they were separated while they were checked out.

Seth was relieved to see his brother-in-law, Dan, there, along with Gavin Jackson. Jackson was skeptical when Seth started telling about everything that had happened over the past two days. Dan, however, knew him well enough to know that Seth was not prone to exaggeration.

"Jackson, I want you to be in charge of making sure there is an officer looking out for Miss McGrath while she's here."

Jackson wasn't a fan of the idea. "Dan, do we really have the manpower for—"

"I'm not asking for your opinion. Do it!" Dan barked.

Jackson straightened his shoulders, he nodded, face blank. Pivoting on his heel, he strode away, speaking into the radio hooked onto his shoulder as he went. Seth watched him, uneasy.

"Will he cause trouble?" Seth queried. They already had their share of that and didn't need more.

Dan waved his hand, dismissing the idea. "Jackson's a good guy. A little hot headed sometimes, but he never stays mad. And he doesn't hold grudges. In fact, he's probably one of the most honest and hardworking men I know in the department."

"He doesn't seem to like Jess." He should let it go, but he couldn't. If Jackson's attitude put her in danger, he wanted to know.

"It's nothing to do with her. He has had some personal tragedies in the past two years. They have made him cynical. But he'll be fine."

Seth raised his eyebrows questioningly. Dan shook his head. "No, I'm not telling you. You may be my brother-in-law, but you know I don't tell tales."

He did know that. It was one of the things he liked about Maggie's husband.

A brisk footstep in the hall heralded the entrance of the doctor. He examined Seth quickly. Seth bore with it the best he could, tempering his impatience. He was fine, he knew it. All he wanted was to go and find Jess, make sure she was all right.

"Well, Travis, you seem to be fit, except for some irritation from the smoke. I think you should consider taking the next day or so off to let yourself recover, but then you should be fine." Dr. Adams typed something into his tablet before glancing up at his patient. Shoving his reading glasses up on his thin nose, he stared at Seth over the top of them. Patent disbelief was stamped all over his narrow face. "What, no objection?"

Although the tone was mocking, Seth didn't take offense. Any other time, he would have objected, or at the very least, let his displeasure be known. He hated taking time off. Too many people in this town thought he had it easy. As if growing up rich had made him soft. To compensate, he worked extra hard to prove himself. But now he had a more important goal than proving himself to those who didn't matter to him anyway.

"No, sir."

The doctor waited, but he didn't expand on his answer. Finally the doctor sighed. "Okay, Travis, you're free to go." The doctor made to leave.

"Wait, Doc!" he blurted.

"Yes?"

"My friend, Jessica McGrath, how is she?"

"Oh, she'll live, too. You can both go home. Remember, I don't want to see you until Wednesday."

He was good with that.

Hopping off the low bed, he made to go find Jess.

"Hey, Seth, you still haven't answered all my questions."

"Aw, Dan. Can't we answer them at Jess's house? You are going to give us a ride, aren't you?"

He swallowed a grin as Dan sighed hugely. "Yeah, sure. Let's go collect your friend. Than I can brief you and get home to my family before Maggie puts the twins to bed."

Dan radioed Jackson to bring Jess down to meet them in the lobby.

When she arrived, Seth couldn't resist the impulse to go to her. It was too strong. Ignoring the narrowed eyes of the sergeant standing next to her, he ran a tender hand down her cheek.

"You okay?"

"Peachy keen." He got an impudent wink for his trouble. "But I'm so ready to go home."

"I scored us a ride." Hitching a thumb over his shoulder, he indicated Dan.

"Hey! Is that all I am? A ride?" Dan's voice was insulted, but he knew better.

Jackson stepped up to him. With his back to Jess, he murmured softly to Seth. "Are you sure you know what you're getting yourself into, Travis? You might want to think twice about getting too friendly with her."

"Step back, Gavin. She's been through enough. And frankly, so have I."

"Whatever. It's your funeral." Jackson shrugged, but his mouth turned down.

So he wasn't happy with Seth's decision. That was just too bad.

Fortunately, they didn't have to ride in the car with him back to River Road Stables. Sitting next to Jess in the backseat, Seth heard her happy sigh as they pulled into the driveway. In the fading light, her eyes shimmered.

"Wait, Dan. Her front door is open. It wasn't open when we left."

"Are you sure it latched completely?" Dan asked. Putting the car in park, he slipped his hand into his jacket. Getting his gun.

"Yeah, I'm sure. I watched her turn the bolt. You know I wouldn't forget."

Dan nodded. Seth didn't brag about it, but he knew that his recall ability had frequently impressed those who knew him.

"You two stay here."

Dan didn't wait around for their response. He stepped out of the car and went to meet with Jackson. Together, the two men went to check out the situation.

Looping his arms around Jess, Seth felt her tremble. Lowering his head, he placed his cheek on her hair.

"When will this end?" she moaned into his shoulder.

He had no answer. All he could do was hold her.

Chapter Fourteen

An hour later, she was able to enter her house. Lieutenant Willis—Dan, as he'd told her to call him—met her at the door. The compassion in his gaze almost did her in. Without thought, she stepped back so she was touching Seth, her arm to his. Just the warmth of him through her shirt steadied her. Gulping in a deep breath, she let it out slowly.

"Miss McGrath, I'm afraid your home was invaded while you were gone. It's difficult to say when it happened. There's been some damage. I will need you to take inventory of anything that might be missing."

Some damage? She walked through her house like a zombie, paying the cops no mind as she surveyed her ransacked home. Icy fingers played up and down her spine. Her legs trembled. She had stopped even trying to control the tears of anger and pain that slipped down her face and dribbled onto her shirt.

Every nerve ending was frayed.

Seth kept near her side, silent. For that she was grateful. She didn't think she could handle conversation at the moment. One thing she was really beginning to treasure about having Seth as a friend…he seemed to have a second sense about her, telling him what she needed at any particular moment. Not in a weird way. Just that he always seemed sensitive to her thoughts and feelings. No other man in her life had ever understood her so well. Not her father. Not Cody. No one.

"I don't see anything missing," she concluded after an hour. Slowly, she rotated in the center of her home office. The room that had taken the worst damage. Seth, Jackson and Dan all stood near the wall, watching her. They stayed silent. "Of course, there's so much chaos in here, it's a bit difficult to say, you know?"

Something niggled at the back of her mind. "Look, can I go put a battery in my hearing aid? While I think?"

As soon as Dan nodded, she darted into her room. Momentarily, she choked at the sight of her open dresser drawers, feeling violated. It was difficult, but she managed to put that aside as she fumbled for her spare batteries. Pulling her good hearing aid from her pocket, she inserted a battery and pushed it into her ear, nudging the rubber mold into place. And was rewarded with the low hum of masculine voices in the next room. Smiling for the first time in hours, she picked up the empty battery package and moved to throw it into the trash can beside her dresser.

Her smile froze on her face as her gaze fell on the empty cat bed.

"My cats!" She dashed from the room, crashing into Seth. Her fist, still clutching the battery package, slammed into his hard stomach.

"Oof!" His face reddened as he doubled over slightly. Oh, no.

Manfully straightening up, Seth gave her what was

probably meant to be a nonchalant grin. What he actually managed was a pained grimace. "You have cats? How many? Who was taking care of them?"

How she had missed that beautiful, deep voice of his!

"I have two cats. Parsley and Sage. They are house cats, and very independent. I have an automatic feeding system, so they had enough food and water, and their litter was changed right before we left. I didn't ask anyone to come and watch them."

"Did anyone have keys to your house?" Dan asked, his face serious.

"Not that I am aware of." Panic scratched at her throat. She tugged at her collar in agitation.

An arm wrapped around her shoulder, pulling her close to a muscular side. Seth. She bent her head into his shoulder.

"Is there any room we haven't checked yet?"

Jackson. For the first time since she had met him, he wasn't sporting a challenging attitude. Was he finally starting to believe her? Or maybe he was just more sympathetic to cats than to people.

"Um, I don't think so. I went through every... Oh!" A hand slapped her forehead. "The basement. I never even thought of the basement. That was Cody's office. I keep it locked."

All three men straightened to attention.

"His office," Jackson said. "We went through that pretty thoroughly a few months ago. Let's check it out and see if you notice anything missing."

The whole group moved down the stairs to the office. When they were two feet from the door, Seth put a hand on Jess's arm.

"I hear meowing."

Joy filled her. Then it faded. If the cats were in there that meant someone else had been, too. There was no pet flap in the door—for the cats to have gotten in, someone had opened it for them.

Tension filled the air as the policemen waved them back. Jess found herself with her back against the cold cement walls, Seth blocking her. Her hero. He was determined to keep her from harm, willingly placing himself in harm's way, again and again.

Jackson held his gun at the ready while Willis flung the door wide.

And two short-haired tabby kittens pounced on his feet.

"Gah!"

Seth hooted in laughter. A giggle welled up, both from humor and from the rush of relief as the bubble of tension around them burst. She couldn't help it.

"But...but, I don't understand," she managed finally. A stray giggle threatened, but she squelched it firmly. "Wouldn't the person after me risk blowing his cover by going through my house like this?"

Sober now, Dan and Jackson both nodded. "The killer doesn't care now," Seth stated, glancing back and forth between the cops. "Am I right? Enough has happened that whoever it is figures there's no use hiding."

He had said something similar at the house. She had so hoped he was wrong. But one look at Dan's face said his brother-in-law was in complete agreement.

Her fear was affirmed when he nodded.

"Yes. I hate to be the one to tell you this, but right now, the person or persons after you seem to feel you are a risk that must be eliminated, no matter what. Maybe they thought there was incriminating evidence here in the house. Get rid of the evidence, get rid of you, and our chances of catching them shrink."

She swayed slightly. Her breath caught, as if hot irons had pierced her lungs.

Yanking his cell phone out of his pocket, Dan started dialing. "I'm getting someone to watch over you for the night. Until we catch this guy, Miss McGrath, you need to be with someone at all times."

She heard what he didn't say, even as her freedom was again taken away.

If she didn't have protection, she would be dead. Just like her brother.

Seth followed Dan outside. Jess was in the kitchen, making coffee and something to eat. More to keep herself busy than out of any real hunger, he thought. He could read the claustrophobia looming in her eyes.

He grimaced. Claustrophobia. He remembered the fear that had paralyzed her earlier. Funny, he didn't remember her being claustrophobic. In fact, he remembered a field trip to some caves in high school. She hadn't been exactly social, but if his memory served, and it always did, she hadn't been scared, either. Just the opposite. She'd been fascinated by the damp, dark caves.

Something had happened to change that.

I was stuck in that small, smelly place for five hours until my parents and the principal found me.

It was his fault. Her fearless curiosity had been killed by his own careless stupidity. He had failed her, even worse than he had realized.

No. I can't dwell on that now, he thought fiercely. *Lord, if I could undo the damage I did to that sweet woman I would. Just help me to keep her safe. Please.*

Quickening his pace, he was striding next to his brother-in-law in two steps.

"I need to talk to you," he muttered, cutting his eyes toward Dan, while keeping his face forward.

"Okay."

"Not here," he hissed as Dan started to slow down. "I don't want Jess to read my lips."

Avid curiosity and doubt mingled on Dan's face. But he followed Seth behind the car, much to Seth's relief.

"This is far enough."

"All right, Seth. What's this about?"

Seth proceeded to tell Dan all his fears about the killer possibly being a woman. The alert look that came to Dan's face let him know the other man was taking him seriously. He sucked in a deep breath. Now to tell the rest. "We learned from the girl who cleans house for the Harveys that they are skilled shooters. What I didn't tell Jess is that so is my aunt. Their house was broken into years ago and she freaked. Bought a gun and learned how to shoot."

Dan nodded. "When Miles gets here, I will let him know all this. Why don't you hang out until then? I can give you a ride back to your place after that."

"No."

Not much surprised a reaction out of Dan, but apparently Seth had managed it this time. The cop's blond eyebrows rose high over his gray eyes.

"No? Wanna explain that, Seth?"

No, he didn't, as a matter of fact. But he knew he didn't have an option. He needed to be straight with the man if he had a hope of convincing him.

"I need to stay. Jess trusts me. She doesn't trust

Miles." When his chest hurt, he realized he was holding his breath.

Dan smirked. "Yeah? Well, if I remember correctly, last time I left you to play hero, you ended up with your head bashed in."

He sobered as soon as he said it. Both men were silent, remembering the attacks that had focused on Maggie, putting her life in danger over and over again. On that particular day when Seth had volunteered to help, Tony Martello, one of LaMar Pond's finest, had died in the line of duty, leaving a widow and two young sons behind.

He sighed dramatically, trying to lighten the somber mood. "You ever gonna let me forget about it?"

"Nah. That's what brothers do. Anyway, there's no real reason for you to stay. She'll be fine." He raised his brows. Seth knew that look. Dan wasn't fooled, and was waiting for the real reason to come out.

So he used his trump card. "What if she needs someone to interpret for her? I should stay 'cause I know how to sign."

He smiled, sure he had made his point.

"That a fact? Well, so can Miles."

"Since when?"

Dan smirked.

"Since always. Almost his entire family on his father's side is deaf. Grandparents, uncle. You name it. He grew up signing."

Deflated, Seth stared at him.

"You need to rest up, Seth. Take time off." Dan shifted his weight, getting ready to walk away.

"I can't." Dan tilted his head, listening. "Dan, a man should be allowed to protect the woman he loves."

There was, he reflected, some satisfaction in catching his brother-in-law off guard. Which was probably an understatement, seeing how Dan's jaw had dropped open more than he had thought possible.

"Love? You love her? Does she know?"

Seth shook his head even while he was speaking.

"No, she doesn't know. And I don't plan on telling her."

Dan frowned. "Why on earth not?"

"Really? Dan, you know how badly I messed up with Melanie. And my dad is a complete womanizer. You know how your own wife suffered because of his selfishness. My family has a history of disastrous relationships. Why would I put someone I loved through that? I can't take the chance of hurting her."

"Seth, you have more than made up for any past errors. As for your dad, you can't be held accountable for that. You are not him." Dan held up a hand, forestalling any protests that Seth might make. "Listen, buddy, I know how it feels to think you're unworthy of a woman. I felt that way for years. I was wrong. And so are you."

Guilt swamped him. He knew that Dan had almost let Maggie get away. He suffered from PTSD, and had some terrible issues to work through. But he had manned up and gotten the job done. Seth didn't know of another man who could bring such joy to Maggie's life.

Dan's hand on his shoulder brought his head up.

"I know you don't go to church, but I will pray for you."

"Actually, I would appreciate that. I think I may have gotten the God thing wrong."

A grin creased Dan's face. "See? You're learning already. Seriously, though. You were kind of a cocky jerk when I met you," Seth rolled his eyes, but Dan continued, "but you're one of the best men I know. I know that you mean the world to Mags. And the twins adore you."

"Yeah, they're great kids." Just thinking of Siobhan and Rory warmed his heart.

"Don't give up on love, Seth. You are worthy."

Dan ambled away.

"I'm not leaving!" he called after him.

"Yeah, yeah," came the response.

He stood outside for a few minutes after Dan left, just thinking. Could he possibly consider a future with Jess?

He wandered inside, deep in thought.

Miles arrived and parked outside, ready to stand watch to keep Jess safe. He could hear Dan briefing him.

The floor creaked behind him. Jess. She was drying her hands on a dish towel, anxiety emanating from her.

"What's going on?"

He walked over to her, taking the towel from her so he could hold her hand. He watched her face. If he needed to switch to sign he would.

"The cop who is keeping watch is here. Dan is telling him what's happening."

"Oh." It was amazing how much disappointment one little monosyllable could contain. "So, what now? Are you leaving?"

He hesitated. But only for a moment. He knew he was committing himself over and beyond what he should do in order to keep his distance, but it was like he had told Dan. He couldn't walk away while the love of his life was in danger. It just wasn't in him. So he opened his mouth and made the commitment. "No, I'm not leaving. If it's okay with you, I'm going to camp out on your couch."

The relieved sigh that burst from her went a long way to ease his heart. "I'll get you some blankets."

Instead of walking away, though, she threw her arms around him.

"Thanks. I know he's a policeman and that he's here to protect me, but I just wouldn't feel comfortable with him."

"He signs," he threw out, just to be sure.

Jess stubbornly set her jaw. "Nope. Doesn't matter. I don't know him. I know you. And I trust you."

And there it was. That one little statement was the best gift he had ever received in his entire life.

Chapter Fifteen

The following morning, Seth woke up at seven, an hour past the time he usually did. Several things clicked immediately. His body was one mass of aches and pains. His back was hurting from being crunched up on a couch too short for his frame. His arm was throbbing where the bullet had grazed him. Even his neck twinged as he sat up.

The second thing to come to his attention was the absolute stillness in the house. It set his teeth on edge. Rising to his feet, he found that the cats were both curled up, watching him with suspicion.

"Is your mistress up yet?" he asked, then winced. Talking to the cats? What next?

Working his way toward the kitchen, he noticed that Jess's bedroom door was open.

Worry shot through him. Despite his aches, he pulled his boots on and marched to the front door. Miles was gone, too. But his car was still there.

Seth felt his breathing and heartbeat speed up. *Slow down, keep your cool.* Forcing himself to remain calm, he observed his surroundings, keeping his mind alert.

Movement. Down by the barn.

Without hesitation, he started down the winding driveway that led to the barn. Pulling the door open, he saw Officer Miles Olsen standing in the aisle. The young cop appeared at home in the barn. It was easy to picture him working on a farm, mucking out stalls. Maybe he had, before he became a cop.

"Where is she?"

Miles jerked his head toward the tack room. "In there."

"Thanks."

Moving past the young officer, he entered the tack room.

Jess glanced up with a smile, and the sun came out for him.

"Hey. You weren't there when I woke up." *Brilliant, Travis. Like she didn't already know that.*

"Uh-huh." She shrugged and flashed him that dimple that drove him crazy. "I didn't want to wake you. I know you've been run pretty ragged. And I knew you were there, if I needed you."

Something loosened inside him. Only once the feeling was gone did he realize that he had been jealous. Jealous that she had replaced him with Miles. Which was ridiculous.

"Whatcha up to?"

"I missed the horses. So I came down to check on them. And it's a good thing I did. Kim never showed up today." A frown carved into her brow. "I can't understand it. Kim always leaves a message if she can't come in. I have a text answering machine. But she didn't leave any messages. I hope she's okay."

A cell phone rang. In the aisle, he heard Miles answer it. Although he couldn't make out the words, he could hear the tension and excitement in the voice. He continued listening, and wasn't surprised when he heard footsteps running toward them. A second later, Miles burst into the room.

"I just got a call from the lieutenant," Miles stated. "A green car like you described was found this morning."

Jess gasped. Seth was in full agreement with the sentiment. He felt a little like gasping himself. Except it wouldn't be manly. Finding the car, though. That could be a huge break in the case. If it were the right car.

"Are the two of you up to coming to take a look, see if you can ID it?"

Neither of them needed their arms to be twisted. Within minutes, they were tucked into the backseat of Miles's cruiser. Seth sat beside Jess, aware of her hands clenched so tight in her lap, the knuckles were bone white. Her left leg bounced up and down in constant motion.

Reaching out, he pried her hands apart and intertwined their fingers. She gripped onto his hand like it was a lifeline.

Flashing lights in the distance warned them that they were approaching the scene. Seth and Jess both sat up as Miles slowed the cruiser, veering expertly onto the shoulder behind the small green car with dark tinted windows. Sergeant Jackson was waiting for them.

Beside him, Jess's breathing grew harsh, shallow. The hand in his grasp trembled. The need to comfort her in some way tugged at him. But he had nothing. Instead, he offered a prayer for her strength and endurance as she faced this new fear.

Sliding across the seat to the door Miles held open,

they emerged from the cruiser and shuffled toward the car. Jess shivered. He tucked her closer to his side.

"No driver?" he murmured to Miles.

"We haven't found one yet. But the car is registered to a Keith Barnes."

"Keith!" Jess's voice was strangled. "That's Kim's older brother. But there's no way he was driving that car. He's in the service. Deployed overseas. He won't be home for months."

Seth's mind made a connection he didn't want it to make. But it was the logical explanation. "Jess, you said Kim never showed up for work. Is it possible she was driving the car, and that she was behind some of this?"

Jess started backing away, shaking her head. She stumbled over a branch. He grabbed hold of her before she could fall. He was surprised she didn't fight his hold, but seemed to melt into it.

"I don't want to believe it. But, Seth, she knew that I was going to be at your uncle's house. When I went to my house to pack, I left her detailed instructions, including where she could reach me in case of an emergency. I never thought I'd be in danger. Not in a house full of people."

"Reasonable assumption."

Poor Jess. She looked shattered at the possible betrayal by one of her staff.

"It's just a hunch," Miles called to Jackson. "But let's check the trunk."

In horrified fascination, Seth and Jess watched as the trunk was opened. A large black sheet was draped over the contents. His pulse thudded in his chest as Miles reached his gloved hand out and gently pulled back the sheet.

Black hair covering a pale oval face. A gunshot wound in the temple.

It didn't take a paramedic to know the young woman was dead.

Kim Barnes had been found.

The shock went too deep for tears. One of her employees, dead. In the car that had been following her for weeks. It made no sense. Kim hadn't even been in Pennsylvania when Cody had died. Her whole family was seeing her brother off in Texas.

It made no sense. None at all.

But then again, some of it did fit. Kim might not have killed Cody, but she did have access to Jess's schedule. And to some of their client information. Suddenly, her employee appeared more like a snake that had been deliberately dropped into her life. Why?

She didn't know how much more she could take. Thankfully, she wasn't alone. She had God. Her faith was being tested fiercely, but she wasn't letting go. And she also had Seth with her, a tangible person to hold on to when she felt the need.

But he was more than that, her mind whispered. She blocked out the murmurs. Her emotions were in too much turmoil to deal with her growing affection for the dark haired man sitting at her side.

She had positively identified the car as the one that had been following her. And she had identified the body in the trunk as her employee. Former employee. Now she just wanted to go home. What was the hold up? What else could she do?

"Here is your coffee, Miss McGrath." Lieutenant Willis and Officer Olsen sat down across from her.

"What are we waiting for? When can I go home?"

"Ma'am, we need to wait for the certified interpreter to arrive. She's traveling from Erie, and should be here within the next ten minutes."

"Where's Seth?" Oh, she hated showing weakness, but she really wanted Seth with her. Part of her was tempted to tell them that she didn't need an interpreter, but that was foolish. Of course she needed the interpreter. Lip reading could only work so far. And she only had one working ear, so to speak. This was too important not to understand everything to her fullest capability.

For a tough man, Lieutenant Dan Willis had an amazingly gentle smile. "Don't worry about Seth. He's still here. But we can't have him in the room while we talk to you."

A chill settled in her chest. Her heart stuttered.

"Am I in trouble?"

"No, ma'am. But we are looking at reopening your brother's case. I need all the information you can provide."

She was ready to scream by the time the door opened and a tall woman with sleek blond hair entered. She introduced herself as the certified interpreter and the questioning began in earnest. At one point, she was surprised when Lieutenant Willis let on that they had found large deposits in Kim's checking account. She was apparently being paid to spy on Jess. Hopefully spying was all she did. It would feel so much worse to know that the girl she had worked with and trusted had had a hand in the evil happenings.

"We haven't figured out Victor Horn's part in all this yet," the lieutenant explained. "He was fairly new to the area. He does have a record. Assault. Petty theft. We'll keep looking."

"Right now, we are working on a list of all the women at the Taylors' party this weekend," Officer Olsen interjected. "There are a few who stand out."

She reared back. "All the women? Why? Bob Harvey was the one going through my room. I would have thought he and his wife would have been among the first people looked at."

"And we *are* looking at him. He, his wife and Willa Taylor are all suspects." He slanted a frown toward his younger colleague. A frown that Olsen either ignored or didn't see.

"Besides," Olsen piped in, "Seth was pretty sure that the person talking to Mr. Horn before he was shot was a woman."

Right. They had talked about that before.

"And then there's the fact that Mrs. Taylor and Mrs. Harvey are both reputed to be the best shots of the whole party."

She couldn't breathe. All the air had been sucked out of the room, leaving her gasping. Lights swirled before her eyes for an instant.

Seth's aunt knew how to shoot a gun. Was skilled, in fact.

And he had never told her.

So much for trusting her, for being honest with her.

Lost in her feelings of betrayal, she barely heard the next sentence. Dimly, as if through a tunnel, she heard Lieutenant Willis offer to drive her home.

Nodding, she grabbed her jacket and walked beside him, feeling like a sleepwalker. Seth's face lit up with relief when he spotted her. Was it only an hour ago she was wishing for him by her side? What a joke. His smile faded to a puzzled frown as she stepped past him without acknowledging his presence. If she had opened her mouth, all the vitriol rising up inside her like a flood would spew out. Ignoring the hurt that slipped behind his eyes, she allowed Officer Olsen to hold the cruiser door open for her and slipped inside. She ignored Seth when he climbed in the backseat. Willis would follow in a second cruiser.

The car ride back to her house was awkward. She didn't care. She had nothing to say to Seth. Nothing.

Of course she couldn't keep silent forever. When the cruiser pulled up to her house, Seth started to climb out. Like he was going to stay with her.

As if. She wasn't having that.

"You don't have to stay with me. I'm not a baby." Ice dripped from her voice. It wasn't surprising. Her heart felt like it had been replaced with a chunk of ice. That was fine. It was when the ice began to thaw that she'd be in trouble.

"It's still not safe for you to be alone," he protested.

A shrug. "Officer Olsen can drop you off before returning."

Silence.

"Jessie? Honey, why are you acting this way?"

That did it. She advanced on him, fury pulsing through her veins like fire.

"Honey? How dare you call me honey!" She could just spit, she was so mad. "When were you going to tell me about your aunt's penchant for shooting guns, Seth? According to Officer Olsen, she shoots better than most of the men we know. Even while we were in danger, you were keeping vital information from me. And I can guess I know why. Because even as I thought we were becoming closer, that we might have found something special, you were choosing your aunt over me. Your vicious aunt who might have tried to kill me. Just like you picked your friends over me all those years ago. Every time I start to think I can trust you, you remind me just how little I mean to you, compared to the other people in your life."

His face lost every drop of blood.

"Jess, baby, let me explain. That wasn't it. I wasn't choosing anyone over you!"

She held up an imperious hand.

"Whatever. I don't want to hear it. Because I can't fall in love with someone who can't be honest with me. Someone who won't put me first. I just can't do it."

Whirling, she ran up the steps and into the house, slamming the door.

The tears were spilling out of her eyes, blinding her, as she fumbled with the deadbolt.

She had lied to him when she told him she couldn't fall in love with him.

She already had.

Chapter Sixteen

Jess opened her eyes the next morning with a groan. Her lids felt like sandpaper over her sensitive irises. It had taken her hours to fall asleep. She had soaked her pillowcase with tears before sheer exhaustion had won out. And when she did finally fall asleep, her sleep was restless, tormented by unsettling, disjointed dreams.

Which was why, even though she was tired enough to sleep on, she dragged herself out of bed. No telling what kind of dreams would chase her if she went back to sleep.

Wonder if Seth's awake yet?

No, no, no!

She and Seth were done. She was not going to waste any more of her valuable time worrying about that man. His sad eyes had haunted her last night. No more. Needing to keep busy, she made a pot of strong black coffee and filled a travel mug with the bitter stuff, pouring in an ample amount of mocha creamer to soften the punch. Then she poured a second mug and carried it to a very sleepy Olsen. The man was almost pathetically grateful as he took a deep sip.

Chores. Time to do chores.

She hurried to feed and water the horses. As she did so, she had time to think. Maybe she should have given Seth a chance to explain? Her mind drifted back to the times he had thrown himself in harm's way for her. And the way he had of holding her hand when she was frightened. She remembered his strength as he had climbed down the rocks without a rope. And his gradual acceptance of prayer.

The more she thought about it, the more she felt ashamed of herself. For all her hurt over being judged and treated poorly, she had turned around and done the same to him.

Maybe she could call him up later, and beg his forgiveness. She squirmed just thinking about it. What if he refused to talk with her? It would serve her right, but the idea of having egg on her face didn't appeal to her. Neither did the idea of letting him go without a fight.

If she had her cell phone, she could call him.

A shadow fell across her, startling her. Someone had entered through the side door.

Whirling, she found a familiar face. One she hadn't expected to see.

"Deborah! How did you get here? I didn't hear you pull up."

"Hello, Jess. I rode my horse over through the back trails." The other woman nodded stiffly. "I wanted to apologize."

Puzzled, she tilted her head and surveyed the blond. "What are you apologizing for?"

Deborah raised a slim hand and pushed her hair behind her ear. "Oh, well, for starters, I wasn't very nice to you at the Taylor house. I knew you had had a rough time. Everyone did. But I was worried about how everyone would talk if we were too chummy. It's been hard, dealing with the scandal of my fiancé's suicide and all."

Tightening her lips to keep the sarcastic words at bay, Jess merely nodded.

"I need to talk with you, Jess. Can we go somewhere and talk? Please? It's a great day for a trail ride. That would give us some privacy."

For some reason, Jess was reluctant to go. But that was ridiculous. She had known Deborah for years. Surely, it couldn't hurt to spend half an hour with her. Maybe when all this was over. She wasn't stupid enough to go anywhere with her while there was real danger lurking.

A car horn honked.

"Hold on, Deborah. I'll be right back."

Wiping her dusty hands on her jeans, she strolled to the doorway. Officer Olsen had driven his cruiser down. His door was open, and he was standing behind it. When he saw her he waved. And began to sign to her across the distance. Wow, his ASL was flawless.

"Bob and Lisa Harvey have just been arrested. The information you provided was enough for a warrant, and their house was searched this morning. They found evidence implicating them. I can't say what. Only that it looks like you are out of danger."

"So soon? That's great!" Doubt lingered in her mind. Even though he said she was safe, it felt too sudden.

"I'm also supposed to tell you that they are being charged with your brother's murder."

Stunned, she stared at the officer. Realizing her mouth was hanging open, she closed it with a snap.

"Murder." The word dropped from her lips like a rock. She had known it, deep inside. But to hear that

Cody had been murdered, the feeling was indescribable. She felt joy knowing the black cloud hanging over the stables was being lifted…and yet the joy was tainted. Cody hadn't killed himself, but he had been taken from her, just the same. And if what she knew of the Harveys was true, it was to protect themselves. What a senseless waste of a good man's life.

"What about the money that was stolen from the foundation? Did they take it?"

Miles shook his head. "Sorry. We don't know where the money is yet. But we'll keep looking."

"So, I don't need you to protect me, huh?"

Officer Olsen sent her a boyish grin. "Nope. It's been a pleasure, ma'am, but I need to grab a shower before I head to the station."

"I understand." She sighed. "Well, that frees me up."

"Excuse me?"

"Sorry," she apologized. "Deborah—my brother's fiancée—is inside. She wants to go for a trail ride. I hadn't thought it was safe, but I guess it is."

Feeling pinned in, she returned to Deborah and accepted her offer. The last thing she wanted to do was go for a trail ride. But she supposed she owed it to Deborah to hear out what she had to say, for Cody's sake if for no other reason. And anyway, riding her horse might lift her spirits. Maybe clear her head. If she stayed home, she'd probably dwell on Cody.

That, and the mess she'd made out of whatever was developing between Seth and herself. Correction. Had been developing. Why would he want anything to do with her now after the way she'd rejected him?

Saddling Misty, she pulled herself up on the horse and followed Deborah onto the familiar trails.

"Let's go this way," Deborah said, pointing to the trails on the right. "It's prettier. The lookout point is amazing this time of year."

Since she agreed, Jess nodded. Clicking her tongue, she asked her horse to take the path.

Something niggled at her. Something she couldn't place.

Then she knew.

"That's it!"

Deborah pulled up beside her. "That's what?"

"Officer Olsen just told me that they have arrested someone for the attacks against me and for my brother's murder."

"That's fantastic!"

"Yeah."

"You don't sound convinced," Deborah's smile seemed forced.

"I was at a conference the weekend he was murdered. So were the people the cops have arrested. So either they were working with someone else, or the evidence is wrong."

"Jessica, you should never try to play detective. It's dangerous."

For the first time that morning, she really looked at Deborah. She still had the pretty girl-next-door face Jess had always known, but it seemed harder than she remembered. A horrible suspicion bloomed in her mind. Deborah was acting a little off. And she hadn't seemed surprised to hear that Cody had been murdered even though everyone believed he'd committed suicide. When she, his sister, had only heard less than an hour ago.

Just what was Deborah's real purpose?

Deborah edged her horse closer to Jess's. Too close. Panicked, Misty backed up, tossing her head.

That's when Jess noticed two things. First, they were on a high ledge. Second, Deborah had pulled a gun from her boot. And pointed it at her.

"Get off your horse."

Silently, Jess did as she asked. Keeping vigilant, she waited for a chance to make a move.

"You are such a nuisance, Jess." Keeping the gun steady, Deborah slid off her own horse. "All you had to do was accept your brother's death was a suicide. Cry a few tears. Then move on. I never would have tried to hurt you if you had. But, no, you had to go and start asking questions."

"How did you know I—"

Deborah scoffed. "Of course I knew. I convinced that girl to apply for a job at your stables, keep tabs on you and your brother. She owed me money, so it was easy to do. But she let herself get caught. I heard y'all were looking for her car. And I knew she was thinking of coming clean to the police. I couldn't have that. Now she's no longer an issue. Which is more than I can say about you."

Seth pulled his truck into Jess's driveway. He and Dan had gone to retrieve it from his uncle's house that morning. Thankfully, it hadn't suffered extensive damage.

Willa had been painfully humble after being hauled in to the police station for questioning. When it became clear that the police had reason to believe that Cody had been framed, her arrogant facade had crumbled.

None of that was important. As soon as he had his truck back, Seth had hightailed it back to River Run Stables to plead his case with Jess. Ironically, it had taken her trying to toss him out of her life for him to realize that he didn't want to walk away. She had been right about one thing…they had started something special. Something he planned on keeping.

Shutting off the truck, he threw open the door and jumped out. The crunch of the gravel beneath his feet seemed eerily loud. There didn't seem to be anyone about. Picking up the pace, he jogged to her front door and pushed the doorbell.

Waited ten seconds. Pushed it again. He could see the blinking lights through the window. Lights that went off whenever the doorbell rang. So he knew it was working.

Where was she? And where was Miles?

He had a bad feeling about this. Really bad.

A police cruiser hummed up the driveway and came to a halt beside his truck. Miles stepped out.

"Hey, Seth!"

"Miles."

The officer raised his eyebrows, flushing slightly at Seth's cold voice.

"I thought you were going to be here watching over Jess. Why did you leave? Do you know where she is?"

Miles held up both hands as if to ward off blows. "Easy, man. It's all good. The Harveys were arrested this morning. We have evidence that implicates them."

Relief nearly swamped him. His Jess was safe.

"So why are you here, then?"

Miles smiled. "Just a formality. I have some questions to ask her to tie up some loose ends. Nothing earth-shattering."

"She's not here." Seth frowned.

"I had hoped she'd be back by now. She went on a trail ride with her friend, Deborah."

She was friends with Deborah? That was strange. They hadn't seemed all that friendly at the house party. In fact, he couldn't remember them even talking to each other. It had seemed more like Deborah was avoiding Jess.

Both men whipped around as a car roared up the driveway, screeching to a halt. Rebecca was at the wheel, and a white-faced Levi was in the passenger seat. Seth remembered Jess saying Rebecca could drive, but didn't like to. So whatever she had to say, it must have been urgent. His pulse spiked.

Throwing the door open, she hopped out, leaving the car running. Levi reached over and turned off the ignition before jumping out to join them.

"Where's Jess?" She signed, without stopping to greet them.

"Out with Deborah," Seth signed back.

Rebecca's fine features paled. "No! She's in danger," she insisted.

Danger? Seth clenched his fists. The hair on his arms bristled.

"What danger?" Miles signed.

"Levi told me the Harveys had been arrested. But they were out of town when Cody died at a conference. I know it, because Jess was there, too. I remember her telling me how awkward it was because they were so hostile. Levi remembered Laura telling him about an angry girl who had come to see them around the same time. It was Deborah. She had a man with her. Laura didn't know who. And she mentioned she had taken care of what they had been too weak to do."

"That's when I remembered where I had seen Vic Horn," Levi broke in. "I saw him with Deborah once, in town. She didn't look pleased to see him. I think she was afraid of being seen together, but he wasn't worried. I knew who she was—that she was Cody's fiancée—and I heard her call him by name. I don't think they knew I was there."

Miles didn't hesitate. He ran back to his car and dove in. Seth was at his heels. The blond officer gave him a speaking glance when Seth slammed into the passenger seat, but he was smart enough not to argue.

Rebecca jumped into the backseat, scooching over to make room for her brother. Miles rammed the car into reverse and roared out of the drive.

"Where do the trails lead?" Seth yelled, knowing Levi would sign for his sister.

Seth drummed his fingers on his thigh while he waited for the response.

"She says the left path loops out a mile and then comes back. Mostly fields. The right path goes up and around, and it looks out on the lower paths. It can be dangerous."

"That's the one!"

Miles nodded, face grim. His voice was stern as he radioed in for backup.

It didn't take more than ten minutes to find the place where the path started and park the car. But it felt like forever.

"We'll have to walk from here," Miles stated.

Walk? Not a chance. Seth took off down the path at a dead run, knowing the others would follow. He had been a runner in high school, and still ran almost daily. It wasn't long before the others fell behind.

Part of him thought about waiting for Miles to catch up. He was the one with law enforcement training and experience. He had the authority to place Deborah under arrest. Waiting for him was probably the legal thing to do. It wasn't going to happen, though. Jess could die in the time it took the others to arrive.

Leaning forward, he broke into a sprint, ducking branches and leaves. A thorn tore into his arm. He didn't slow down. What was a thorn when Jess was in danger?

He didn't ease his pace until he arrived at the fence along the road leading to the lookout point. Down below, he could see two people standing near the ledge. Too close to the ledge. Two horses grazed nearby. When the blonde waved her hand, the sun glinted off the barrel of a gun. A gun aimed straight at the heart of the woman who held his heart in her hands.

Miles arrived. He heard other feet. Expecting to find the Amish brother and sister, he was more than relieved to see Dan and Jace and Jackson.

Deborah shrieked below. Seth's blood froze. Jess was backed up as far as she could go.

They were out of time. He leapt over the fence.

Chapter Seventeen

"Deborah, I don't understand."

She had always thought Deborah was a pretty woman. But there was nothing pretty about the woman standing three feet away from her, her arms held straight out, the gun unwavering. Her lips were curled in a sneer. Tossing her head back, she shifted her stance, realigning the gun and staring down the barrel.

Hunter's eyes. How could she have missed the feral gleam? They glinted with unrelenting purpose.

She's going to kill me! If I don't do something, this will be the end of my life.

Seth. More than ever, now when it was too late, she regretted the way they had left things last night. She would never be able to tell him she loved him.

Stop it. Think, Jess. The situation was grim, but that didn't mean she had to give up.

"I've known you for years, Deb. You were going to marry my brother."

Deborah made a disgusted face. "Cody. What a pathetic excuse for a man he was. Always going on about God. And his obsession with those horses! He was a fool not to see the possibilities. All he cared about was that the horses weren't being treated properly. But what about me?"

The shriek she uttered was picked up and amplified by her hearing aid. The harsh sound reverberated inside her skull. Jess winced.

Maybe she could reason with Deborah. She doubted it, but at the moment, she was out of other options.

"Deborah, Cody loved you," she began, forcing her voice to remain level. "He—"

"Enough!" The other woman waved the gun. "What do you know? He broke up with me and was going to turn me in to the police."

What? Disbelieving, she shook her head.

Deborah nodded, smirking. "You never even guessed. He was always protecting you. But me?" She shook her head. "No. I tried to explain it to him. I promised I would return the money. As soon as my debts were paid, I would make good. But that wasn't enough for him. No, Cody McGrath was ashamed of me. How dare I gamble? How dare I steal from the foundation? Like he had never had problems. He was supposed to stand by me."

She stepped closer to Jess. Jess moved back, but found herself pressed up against the wall. In seconds, the gun was in front of her face. Swallowing, Jess tried to pray. Her mind was blank, her mouth dry. All she could do was repeat *Help me, Lord*, again and again.

"Did you kill Cody?"

It wasn't until the words blurted from her that she realized she was going to ask.

Ice crawled up her skin as the woman she had once thought would be her sister-in-law tipped her head back and laughed—a bitter, angry sound.

"I had no choice. He was going to go to the police. Expose me. What was I supposed to do? He would have ruined my life." She smiled, an unpleasant slash across her face. "I had Vic Horn help me. He would have done anything I asked. Plus, he enjoyed gambling himself. It wasn't hard for the two of us to stage the suicide. Unfortunately, Vic became cocky. When I lured you to the kitchen at the Taylor house, he was supposed to kill you and dispose of your body. Not drag you into a freezer. I would never have been so clumsy. But what can you expect from a man?" A dainty shrug and a sniff accompanied the words.

This was not the woman she'd thought she knew. Not a trace of the woman her brother had once loved was evident in the cold-blooded killer facing her.

The cold way she related the facts chilled Jess.

Deborah took a step nearer. Another foot and Jess could make a grab for the gun. She'd lose, no doubt, but if she was going to die, she'd do it fighting.

"And the Harveys?"

Deborah shrugged one slim shoulder. Careless. Almost casual. As if the lives of the ornery couple didn't matter at all.

"Oh, they're pathetic. So afraid of their own shadows. They were cheating the foundation, that much is true, but they'd never have the guts to kill anyone. The fact that your brother had turned them in for abusing their racehorses didn't hurt. And the fact that there was evidence that they had used steroids on their racehorses. They were easy scapegoats." Her painted mouth tightened. "But you had to stir the pot, didn't you? You could give them an alibi, so the police would have to keep looking. I had toyed with the idea of letting you live. Even this morning, I thought if I could just get you to let it go. But I couldn't take the chance that you would conveniently remember something that would send suspicion my way. And I knew you were too much of a Goody Two-shoes to take money to look the other way."

Heat rose in her belly.

"You wanted me to take money to forget that you killed my brother? And Kim? Even your partner? Three people, dead, and I was supposed to be okay with that?"

"If you valued your life, you would have. But it's just as well. I couldn't have relaxed knowing you might decide to let your conscience win at any given moment. So I guess it's goodbye, little Jess. It's been fun."

The deadly calm with which Deborah shifted the gun made Jess's blood curdle. She knew that if the gun fired, it would be fatal. No more time. She tensed to dive for Deborah.

"No!"

Seth!

Deborah jerked back as the shout broke through the stillness. The gun wavered, moving off Jess for a moment.

Hope flared briefly in her soul. It died and panic took its place as Deborah whirled back, determined in her fury.

CRACK!

An agonized shriek was ripped from Deborah as the gun was shot out of her hand. Jess was vaguely aware of the cops swarming over the fence and running their way.

"No! I can't go to jail. I won't!"

Blood streamed from her hand and left a trail on the rocks and grass as Deborah charged the few feet toward Jess. The force of her motion pushed Jess off balance. Wrapping her surprisingly strong arms around Jess, Deborah teetered on the edge of the cliff.

With a feeling of déjà vu, Jess remembered watching Vic Horn topple off a cliff into the river. Was she to suffer the same fate?

Seth was so close. With renewed vigor she fought. And for a second, she thought she was making progress. But then Deborah stuck her leg out and swept Jess's feet from beneath her. They both tumbled over the edge.

"Jess!"

Seth ran to the ledge. Terror grabbed hold of him. She was lying on the ground below. There was no movement. Was she dead?

Using every ounce of skill he possessed, he climbed over the edge and started a slow, painstaking descent. Rocks cut into his hands, reminding him that he wasn't wearing any protective gloves. Someone shouted after him. He tuned it out. He needed to get to his girl.

Shoving all fear, all his agony out of his mind, he focused on the task at hand. In his mind, a litany of prayer streamed out without his conscious decision. Every step down, every move, took him closer to his goal. It was probably the fastest descent of his life, but it felt like it took hours to reach her.

Finally, he reached the bottom. Dropping to the ground, he rushed over to Jess. She was just beginning to stir. Her eyes were flickering open. She was battered. Bruised. Looked like she had been through an earthquake. He thought she had never looked more beautiful.

"Jessie, are you okay? Honey, can you hear me?" he called urgently. At the same time, he was examining her for injuries. His hands shook wildly as he touched her. Never before had they trembled so while examining a patient. But then, he'd never been in love like this before. When he could ascertain no external injuries, he heaved a sigh but reminded himself that she wasn't out of danger yet. There could still be internal injuries.

"Seth." Just his name in her breathy voice. But it brought him to his knees. Her eyes focused on his face.

"Baby, I thought I had lost you." Blinking back tears, he grabbed a hand and kissed it.

"Seth. I was wrong. I didn't mean what I said."

"It's okay, baby. It's okay. Look, they are going to get you to the hospital. Check you out. But I'll be there. The whole time."

A smile flashed across her face. It was faint, followed by a grimace. "'Kay," she murmured. "Love you."

What? Had he heard her right? He couldn't ask, because she had fainted.

The next hour was filled with anxiety. Deborah had not survived the drop. Her head had hit the rocks when they fell. As awful as her actions were, Seth was sorry that she had died. He knew it would grieve Jess.

It took some maneuvering to get Jess out of her precarious position so that she could be loaded onto a stretcher. Every groan of pain that escaped her lips was a knife in Seth's heart. If he could have traded places for her, he would have. In an instant. All he could do was murmur encouragement to her. And pray. At the hospital, she was poked, prodded and x-rayed.

He was forced to wait in the hall while they examined her, as if they didn't all know him. He could feel a scowl etching itself on his face, but he didn't care. He had promised her he would stay with her.

Dan and Maggie had come to the hospital, too. Right

now they were in the cafeteria getting coffee and something to eat. Maggie said he needed fortification. The best he could do was pace as he waited.

And waited.

An hour into the wait, he heard familiar footsteps in the hall. His dad. What was he doing here?

Senator Joe Travis walked to Seth and put a hand on his shoulder.

"You okay, son?" Seth was shocked at how softly his dad spoke. Joe Travis was always boisterous, confident. Now he seemed unsure of himself. "Maggie called me. Explained about your friend. I was worried."

His dad was worried for him. Would wonders never cease? He didn't blame Maggie for calling their dad. Her relationship with him was even more strained than Seth's, but family was important to her.

"I'm okay." His voice was little more than a husky whisper. Clearing the emotion from his throat, he tried again. "I appreciate you coming."

Sorrow filled his father's face. "I'm ashamed that you felt you couldn't ask me yourself. I know I've made mistakes, Seth. Bad ones. Mistakes that have hurt you. Hurt your mother, and so many others. But I'm still your father, and I care about you."

Seth's eyes widened in shock. His father never talked about emotions. Or admitted wrongdoing.

"I love Jess." Hadn't planned on saying that. But it felt right. "I want to ask her to marry me, but—"

Joe Travis sighed, and seemed to age before his eyes. "You're afraid you'll turn out like me, aren't you? Son, you are nothing like me. I'm both proud of you and ashamed of myself. You will never betray the woman you love."

"What about you, Dad?"

His dad didn't even pretend to misunderstand. "I know you won't believe this, son, but I have regretted my behavior deeply. I can't change what I've done, but I'm trying to be a better person. I have grandkids now. And hopefully, soon a daughter-in-law."

Seth smiled, feeling more at peace than he had in a long time.

"Wait with me? I promised Jess I'd be here for her."

Soon after, they let him go in and see her. She was asleep. He settled back in a chair and continued his vigil. He was there when she opened her eyes.

"Hi," he signed at her. Man, his poor Jess had taken a beating. As long as she was alive. She had a broken rib. And a number of cuts and bruises. The doctors were all amazed at how few injuries she had sustained from her plunge. He wasn't though. He was learning that God was bigger than their circumstances.

"Hey."

How exactly did he ask her if she meant what she said?

Then it hit him. He couldn't just sit back and expect her to say it again. He had to give, too. His throat constricted. Rejection was not a good feeling, and he still had the fear that his affections would be rejected. But he owed it to her to at least try.

"I'm so sorry for not telling you everything. You mean everything to me. I will always choose you over everyone from now on." He swallowed, holding her wide eyes captive with his own. Then he raised his hand in a single sign. His thumb, index finger and little finger extended while his middle finger and ring finger folded over across his palm. "I love you."

He braced himself for rejection. Or the infamous "let's be friends" speech.

Her eyes brightened with tears. But they didn't overflow. Her lips trembled as she smiled at him, showing that dimple that absolutely slayed him. Then, almost shyly, she raised her hand and returned the gesture. "I love you, too."

Leaning forward, he kissed her gently, taking his time. After all, they had all the time in the world now.

Epilogue

Seth held hands with Jess as they meandered through the small crowd of family and friends who had come to celebrate with them. Jess laughed at something his sister said to her, and he smiled in response to the joyful sound.

He couldn't remember half of what the guests had said. His mind was completely occupied by watching the lovely woman glowing at his side. His bride. Pride swelled in his chest. As of three hours ago, she was now his wife.

How on earth had he gotten so blessed?

He said a quick prayer of thanksgiving and marveled. So much had changed in the past six months. He was in love, had returned to church and was even making some progress in healing the breach between himself and his father. Not that the last one was easy. Joe Travis wasn't an easy man to have as a father. But knowing he had a Heavenly Father helped him to deal with the one he was given here on Earth.

"It was a beautiful wedding, Seth," a soft feminine voice said to his right.

He turned. He hadn't heard Willa and Ted approach.

"Thanks." He shook hands with his uncle, and allowed his aunt to kiss the air by his cheek. Then he smiled again when Ted grabbed Jess in a warm hug and smacked a fatherly kiss on her cheek. Willa smiled stiffly. She was trying, Seth admitted, but it might take a bit more time before the women felt easy in each other's presence.

"Thanks, Uncle Ted, for letting us have the reception here at your house."

"No problem. What else could I do for my favorite nephew?"

Yeah, yeah. Only nephew. But that didn't matter.

Satisfied, he glanced around. Maggie and Dan were there with their kids, Rory and Siobhan. No one looking at Dan with the kids would know that he was their adopted father. And the twins adored him. Maggie glowed as she stood next to her husband. Neither she nor Dan could stop smiling. Their smiles were contagious. Seth felt his own lips stretching into a grin. He knew why they were so happy. Maggie had confided to him that they were expecting a baby in seven months. The thought of being an uncle again filled him with joy.

As he watched, Siobhan left Dan's side and ran across the yard. Guests parted, smiling as the toddler rushed to where her grandfather was sitting with some out of town relatives and scampered up into his lap. Joe smiled at her, his eyes creasing as he gave her a hug. Then he slyly handed her a cookie from his plate. Had Maggie seen?

He switched to look at Maggie. Yep. She rolled her eyes, and laughed.

Unbelievably, Joe Travis was becoming a doting grandfather.

His gaze moved to the couple standing next to Dan

and Maggie. Seth's former fiancée, Melanie, was there with her husband, Jace, and their infant daughter, Ellie. She was named after Jace's sister who had died tragically as a teenager. Even Irene, Jace's widowed sister, was there with her two boys.

"Chief Paul!" Matthew, the younger of her boys called, grinning, as he spotted LaMar Pond's chief of police, Paul Kennedy, coming their way. Both boys eagerly moved forward to hug their dad's longtime friend. Irene hung back, but she watched her boys, a sad smile on her lips.

Paul rustled the hair of AJ, her oldest son, and chucked Matthew under the chin before he moved past them to go stand with Dan. Soon, Jace wandered over and the three were deep in conversation. Football was probably the topic, judging by the intensity of the discussion. That and the commiserating eye rolls of their wives.

Rebecca sidled up to Jess, looking very pretty in her blue maid-of-honor dress. His eyes narrowed at the excitement and nervousness that filled his wife's face.

"Are they here?" she signed to Rebecca.

Flicking her eyes toward him, Rebecca nodded slightly.

"Who?" Seth asked.

"You'll see," Jess said in a sing-song voice. His eyes narrowed. His woman was planning something. His wife, he corrected, grinning. His wife.

He was sure of it when she motioned him to stay there and rushed out behind Rebecca. What was going on? Dan and Jace joined him, eyebrows raised. He shrugged to say he had no idea.

His surprise increased as Rebecca returned and nod-

ded to Miles. The officer left the place where he had
been talking to Jackson and moved to the side of the temporary stage. Directly in front of the table where Ernie
and a group of Jess's deaf and hard-of-hearing friends
sat. Rebecca sat down with them, her eyes on Miles.
It was clear he had been asked to interpret something.

A minute later, Jess reappeared and hurried to the
DJ's stage. After a brief whispered conversation, the
man grinned and handed her the microphone with a
small bow.

What?

"Ladies and gentlemen…may I please have your attention?" Jess's voice carried across the yard, and the
guests slowly quieted, turning to watch the stage. "I
have a special surprise for Seth. I am so grateful that
God has blessed me with such a wonderful husband.
And I know that there is one thing that Seth has wanted
for several years now."

Puzzled, he tilted his eyes. What did he want? Besides her, of course. And now that he had her, his life
was perfect. Except…his eyes widened, heart pounding. He had a sudden idea, a crazy idea, of who her surprise guest was.

"With the help of my father-in-law, I was able to hire
a private detective. It has taken almost six months, but
I am pleased to say he was successful. I would now like
to introduce Seth to his little sister, Carrie Jones, and
her guardian and half sister, Audrey."

His blood roared in his ears as Seth moved in a trance
toward the stage. He barely even looked at the lovely
woman with strawberry blond hair who entered the
room. His attention was focused on the teenager beside

her. Carrie. His half sister. Her blue eyes were wide and scared.

"She looks just like Sylvie," a tearful voice said at his side. Maggie. She had wanted to meet their half sister, too. Looking at Carrie, he agreed. She did resemble their murdered sister.

He reached the girl, and silently folded her in a hug. Maggie joined in, and the siblings stood for a few minutes just embracing. When they parted, he realized there were tears on all three of their faces. And on the faces of many of the guests as well.

There was a moment of awkwardness as Joe approached the group. Conversation stilled as he paused several feet away from his youngest child.

"Carrie," he started, then stopped to clear his throat. "Carrie, I know I have no right to expect you to be happy to meet me, but I'm your father."

The young girl stared at her wayward father. A minute ticked by. Then a slow smiled curled her lips. "I asked Mama about you many times, but she would never tell me much."

It was a start.

Jess arrived and planted herself at Seth's side. Sweeping her up in his embrace, he whirled her around, hearing her breathless laughter in his ear. He set her down, but took her sweet face in his hands and captured her lips with his. They were both breathless by the time he released her. The crowd around them applauded.

"I am so in love with you, Jessica Travis," he signed to her. "No one on earth knows me like you."

Jess, his sweet Jess, stretched up on her toes to kiss his lips softly. "I adore you, Seth. And I can't wait to show you each and every day just how much you mean to me."

Hugging her close to him, he shut his eyes, blocking out everything except the warm woman in his arms. Her scent teased his nostrils, soothing his soul.

He had come home.

* * * * *

WE HOPE YOU ENJOYED THESE **LOVE INSPIRED**® AND **LOVE INSPIRED**® **SUSPENSE** BOOKS.

Whether you prefer heartwarming contemporary romance or heart-pounding suspense, Love Inspired® books has it all!

Look for 6 new titles available every month from both Love Inspired® and Love Inspired® Suspense.

Love Inspired®

www.LoveInspired.com

Love Inspired ®

Save $1.00

on the purchase of any
Love Inspired®,
Love Inspired® Suspense or
Love Inspired® Historical book.

Available wherever books are sold,
including most bookstores, supermarkets,
drugstores and discount stores.

Save $1.00

on the purchase of any Love Inspired®, Love Inspired® Suspense
or Love Inspired® Historical book.

Coupon valid until June 30, 2018. Redeemable at participating retail outlets in the
U.S. and Canada only. Limit one coupon per customer.

52615636

5 65373 00076 2   (8100)0 12353

SPECIAL EXCERPT FROM

Love Inspired®

*Ten years ago, Jeremiah Weaver left his Amish
community to become a navy SEAL. Now that he's back,
can he convince the woman he left behind—widow and
mother of two Ava Jane Graber—that he's here to stay?*

*Read on for a sneak preview of
THEIR AMISH REUNION,
by Lenora Worth,
available April 2018 from Love Inspired!*

"What are you doing here, Jeremiah?"

"I didn't want you to see me yet," he tried to explain.

"Too late." She adjusted her *kapp* with shaking hands. "I need to go."

"Please, don't," he said. "I'm not going to bother you. I…I saw you and I didn't have time to—"

"To leave again?" she asked, her tone full of more venom than he could ever imagine coming from such a sweet soul.

"I'm not leaving," he said. "I've come back to Campton Creek to help my family. But I had planned on coming to pay you and Jacob a visit, to let you know that…I understand how things are. You're married—"

"I'm a widow now," she blurted, two bright spots forming on her cheeks. "I have to get my children home."

Kneeling, she tried to pick up her groceries, but his hand on her arm stopped her. Jeremiah took the torn bag and placed the thread, spices and canned goods inside the bottom, the feel of sticky honey on his fingers merging with the memory of her dainty arm. But the shock of her words

LIEXP0318

made him numb with regret.

I'm a widow now.

"I'm sorry," Jeremiah said in a whisper. "Beth never told me."

"You couldn't be reached."

Ah, so Beth had tried but he'd been on a mission.

"I wish I'd known. I'm so sorry."

Ava Jane kept her eyes downcast while she tried to gather the rest of her groceries and toss them into the torn bag.

"Here you go," he said, while her news echoed through his mind. "I'll go inside and get something to clean the honey."

Their eyes met as his hand brushed over hers.

A rush of deep longing shot through her eyes, jagged and fractured, and hit Jeremiah straight in his heart.

Ava Jane recoiled and stood. *"Denke."*

Then she turned and hurried toward the buggy. Just before she got inside, she pivoted back to give him one last glaring appraisal. "I wonder why you came back at all."

He watched as she got into the buggy and sat for a moment. Without a backward glance, Ava Jane held her head high. Then Jeremiah asked for a wet mop to clean the stains from the sidewalk. He only wished he could clean away the stains inside of his heart.

And just like her, he wondered why he'd returned to Campton Creek.

Don't miss
THEIR AMISH REUNION by Lenora Worth,
available April 2018 wherever
Love Inspired® books and ebooks are sold.

www.LoveInspired.com

Love Inspired®

Inspirational Romance to Warm Your Heart and Soul

Join our social communities to connect with other readers who share your love!

Sign up for the Love Inspired newsletter at **www.LoveInspired.com** to be the first to find out about upcoming titles, special promotions and exclusive content.

CONNECT WITH US AT:

Harlequin.com/Community

 Facebook.com/LoveInspiredBooks

 Twitter.com/LoveInspiredBks

LISOCIAL2017